THE HOUSE IN GROSVENOR SQUARE

LINORE ROSE BURKARD

All Scripture quotations are taken from the King James Version of the Bible.

Cover by Dugan Design Group, Bloomington, Minnesota

Cover photos © Edward White / Fotolia; Dugan Design Group

This is a work of fiction. Names, characters, places, and incidents are products of the author's imagination or are used fictitiously. Any resemblance to actual persons, living or dead, or to events or locales, is entirely coincidental.

THE HOUSE IN GROSVENOR SQUARE

Published by Harvest House Publishers
Eugene, Oregon 97402
www.harvesthousepublishers.com

Library of Congress Cataloging-in-Publication Data
Burkard, Linore Rose
The house in Grosvenor Square / Linore Rose Burkard.
p. cm.
ISBN 978-0-7369-2565-5 (pbk.)
1. Betrothal—Fiction. 2. London (England)—Fiction. I. Title.
PS3602.U754H68 2009
813'.6—dc22

2008041576

Printed in the United States of America

09 10 11 12 13 14 15 16 17 / RDM-SK / 10 9 8 7 6 5 4 3 2 1

"A really nice surprise! This is definitely an original Regency romance."

ANNE WOODLEY, Amazon.com Top 500 reviewer
patroness of the *Almack's List, Byron List,* Janeites, and the *Austen List*

"Beautifully written story, fast paced, and exciting from cover to cover, and one of the best stories I have read!"

KELLI GLESIGE, book reviewer for www.ReaderViews.com

"Well-written, interesting, **captivating, romantic, inspirational, and addictive.** I highly recommend this book."

ARMCHAIRINTERVIEWS.COM (Top 1000 reviewer)

"I laughed out loud and was also brought to tears while reading this beautifully written book."

ALICE TJIONG, Amazon.com reader

"Beautifully written, touches your heart AND keeps you entertained!"

DEBBIE HANNA, Amazon.com reader

"A must-read, a story that will lift you up and stay in your thoughts long after you've finished the last chapter."

LISA G. SMITH, Amazon.com reader

"A great, entertaining book! It had me caught from the first few pages and continued to reel me in page after page."

DONNA CRUGER, business owner, Amazon.com reader

Wonderful and beautiful book!

LILLIAN J. WONG-SUHU, Amazon.com reader

"So good that I couldn't put it down! It made me laugh out loud, and it made me cry."

LAURA LOFASO, Amazon.com reader

"Fun and inspirational. I enjoyed it from cover to cover and heartily recommend it to anyone who likes historical fiction!"

DIANE GRAZIANO, accountant, Amazon.com reader

Advance praise for *The House in Grosvenor Square...*

"*The House in Grosvenor Square* by Linore Rose Burkard is a delightful mixture of flowing narrative, clever dialogue, period adventure, and Regency descriptions that will make you want to read every book she ever writes!"

MOLLY NOBLE BULL, author of *Sanctuary*

"Linore is a writer whose love of God and the Regency period shines throughout her work. She has an impressive ear for period dialect and detail, and her heroine is unabashedly Christian. Linore will likely win many fans with *The House in Grosvenor Square.*"

JULIE KLASSEN, author of *Lady of Milkweed Manor* and *The Apothecary's Daughter*

"I'm rapidly becoming a fan of Regency romantic fiction, especially when it's written by Linore Rose Burkard! With a rich and authentic voice, eye for detail, and a wit that fits my personality style, the sequel to her successful novel *Before the Season Ends* is just as wonderful."

DEENA, reviewer at deenasbooks.blogspot.com

And reviews of Linore's first book *Before the Season Ends* continue to pour in...

"I am an avid Georgette Heyer fan. What a delight to read a book about a Christian young woman caught up in the Regency marriage mart. What an unusual twist! I loved how she threaded the gospel throughout the narrative. Well done!"

CYNTHIA, reader review

"I just finished this book this afternoon and...blissful sigh...loved it. It did my Jane Austen soul good! I devoured it. Loved it, loved it, loved it!"

ROSEANNA, reviewer at www.ChristianReviewofBooks.com

"I am proud to say I read this book in one day! I have been passing it to my circle of friends, and everyone has raved about it so far! More books, please!"

LEAH, teen reader review

"The author's command of period detail is impressive, evident in material details but also in dialogue. The theology is also period authentic. The novel even contains a glossary to help non-Regencyphiles get up to speed about the difference between ladies' pelisses and spencers. On the whole it's a tasty confection."

PUBLISHERS WEEKLY

To LCF Church,

for its love and faithfulness.

Special thanks to Nick Harrison,
Shane White, Barb Sherrill,
and all those at Harvest House Publishers
who have been so wonderfully supportive
of me and my work.
Thank you!

One

Mayfair, London
1813

Inexplicable. There was no other word for Mr. Mornay's behaviour to her that morning, and Ariana Forsythe could think of naught else unless it changed. *Soon.*

She looked at him challengingly, as she sat across from him in his expensive, plush black coach. Faultlessly handsome, Phillip Mornay was dressed stylishly in a twin-tailed frock coat, buff pantaloons, and polished black boots. His beautifully tied cravat puffed lightly out from an embroidered white waistcoat, and his dark hair and famously handsome features were framed by a top hat. Everything he wore looked new. His clothing always did, and yet he might have worn it a dozen times, so comfortable did he appear in his attire.

But he had barely looked at Ariana for more than a fleeting second since he had come for her this morning, and it was beginning to grate on her nerves. She had to think of something to say.

"Tomorrow is the day I shall see the full of your house, is it not?" She had been in Mr. Mornay's house in Grosvenor Square before, but this time she and Aunt Bentley were to get a tour, top to bottom, so she would feel more at home after the wedding in just two weeks.

The dark eyes flicked at her, and she felt a fleeting twinge of satisfaction.

"It is."

She wanted to hold his attention and began a smile, but he looked away abruptly. *What could be wrong?* Mr. Mornay often studied her when they were together. She was so used to finding the dark-eyed warm gaze upon her, in fact, that she felt somewhat abandoned to be deprived of it now. *Have I done something to displease him? He usually attends to me so deeply, as though he could read my soul.*

They were on their way to the London Orphan Society, in Mr. Mornay's upholstered coach-and-four, with its fashionable high-steppers and liveried footmen on back, to attend a special service at the society's chapel. A lady was giving a dramatic reading from Scripture; a most celebrated dramatic reading. Ariana and Mr. Mornay had received invitations for the event, with encouragement to invite anyone of their acquaintance. Thus there were also four other occupants in the carriage this morning, and seating was snug.

On either side of Ariana was a relation. Her younger sister Beatrice, just turned twelve, was to her left, and her aunt and chaperone for the season, Mrs. Agatha Bentley, sat on her right. The ladies faced the gentlemen, sitting across from them; first Mr. Peter O'Brien, a future cleric, at Beatrice's particular request, then Ariana's future husband, Mr. Mornay, silent and unapproachable, and finally the agreeable Mr. Pellham, her aunt's betrothed. (She and her aunt were betrothed at the same time—a most fortuitous turn of events; Ariana ought to have been in raptures of joy.) Unless Mr. Mornay's demeanour changed, Ariana could not enjoy herself. His inattentiveness was such a contrast to his usual behaviour that it was impossible for her to ignore it or shrug it off as mere ill humour.

It seemed ironic now that when all had been uncertain about the wedding (when Ariana had held out against her desire to marry Mr. Mornay because she would only marry a man who could share her Christian faith), that up to then, his love and affection were painfully clear. And now, after Mr. Mornay had undergone a stark change in his religion—that is, when he came to believe in a personal, loving God—and the betrothal was settled, suddenly he was behaving as though he wished it were not.

Sitting across from her, he should have been engaging her with his usual intent gaze, smiling slightly at her remarks when she amused him or spoke to others. Instead he sat staring out the window (a thing he *never* did) and appeared to be morosely preoccupied with his own thoughts. It pricked against her nerves. She *would* bring him out of this brown study if it took all her ingenuity!

And then he suddenly turned and spoke. "Did I mention I shall be occupied for the rest of the day? After leaving you at your house, following the morning's service?"

Her large, tan eyes sparkled into bluish-green, as they tended to do whenever her feelings were stirred. "No, sir, you mentioned *nothing* to me," she said, giving him a look laden with perplexity.

He responded with a brief, "Haven't I? Well, I've done so now."

Oh, dear. He is utterly not himself! Or has he taken a disgust of me?

The carriage fell silent. Mr. Mornay had thick, dark hair that tapered to the tip of his collar, short, dark sideburns, and handsome, strong-boned features. His eyes were deep, dark, and expressive, and his manner of dress, the height of manly perfection. Though he would not deign to discuss good style, he had a faultless sense of it, and many an aspiring buck or beau modeled their choice of attire after his. Like Ariana, his neatness appeared effortless. And he was universally approved of in the best houses (save for those of the staunchest Whigs, who had still not forgiven Prinny or his pals, of which Mr. Mornay was one, for abandoning them for the Tories).

Even Ariana, who had little patience for matters of dress, found herself in awe of his presence at times. All told, he was an imposing character, a man one did not ignore or take lightly. Ariana was not happy with his present tone of address nor that she would not be seeing him after the morning service. But while she decided whether to make an answer to him, Beatrice broke the silence instead. "*Achoo!*" The twelve-year-old folded her handkerchief and looked about apologetically.

Beatrice had only recently joined Ariana in London, and both girls were staying at Mrs. Bentley's town house in Hanover Square.

Mrs. Bentley gave her younger niece a severe look, which Ariana did not fail to notice. Their aunt was a wealthy widow with a good soul at heart, but the lady was too prepared to make the worst of anything or anyone who posed a threat to her plans, her schedule, or her expectations.

Alarmed at the hint of an ague in her niece, Mrs. Bentley's delicately lined face wrinkled in disapproval, while she pulled her gloves more tightly onto her hands. "How long have you had that nasty sneeze?" she asked. "Do you have an ague?"

"No, no, I assure you!" And yet the young girl had to stop even now, quickly covering her mouth and nose with her handkerchief to allow a second "*achoo!*" to escape.

"Bless you," said Mr. O'Brien, which brought a blinking smile to Beatrice's young face.

"Humph!" murmured Mrs. Bentley, deciding immediately to send the girl at the soonest convenience back to Chesterton and her family. She would not allow Ariana to contract a cold. Not with the wedding this close. Goodness knew Mrs. Bentley had seen enough threats to this marriage—a *coup d'etat* to be sure—and desired that *nothing* further imperil the event. With the ceremony so near, she was finally beginning to relax. The marriage was certain to take place. But she couldn't help remembering it hadn't always been that way. No, indeed! Why, since the day Mr. Mornay had asked for her niece, there had been one vexation after another, each more threatening than the last, each liable to ruin the man's hopes—and her own, for she wanted nothing more than to see the couple wed.

Her own niece, after all, fresh from the country, had unwittingly captured the heart of London's most famous bachelor—Mr. Phillip Mornay, known in town as the *Paragon*. So called because he possessed three of the highest virtues of the English upper class: sartorial elegance, figure, and (most importantly) a fabulous fortune. Besides the family seat in Middlesex, with a large tenantry, and the house in Grosvenor Square, he owned small holdings and properties throughout the British Empire, all of which added to his income. His unexpected match to the debutante Miss Forsythe was famous. Miss Ariana Forsythe was a beauty in her own right and rumoured to be an heiress, (a status Mrs. Bentley had fostered by putting up enough blunt for Ariana's season so that no one thought to credit her for doing so). Not since the Regent himself wed Caroline of Brunswick had there been such a general anticipation of a marriage (though one might rightly call the prince's an *infamous* match!).

It was too wonderful a happenstance to let a mere ague put a damper on the plans. If Ariana were to fall ill, the marriage would still take place, of course, but why imperil the older girl? Why give her the least excuse to raise an objection? (Ariana was far too liable to raise objections—that had been the trouble from the beginning!) What if she were to wish for a postponement? Mrs. Bentley's nerves couldn't stand for it.

No. With the assurance that Ariana was finally settled upon her fiancé, there was nought to hinder the event, and she, Mrs. Bentley, would do everything in her power to see that it remained that way. Casting her eyes upon her niece, she had to acknowledge a twinge of satisfaction (for not the first time) at how like a queen the girl wore the expensive clothing she herself had bought her. Ariana was dressed in the same modish style as her aunt, not because she could afford it or had the slightest interest in cutting a wave, but for the reasons that Mrs. Bentley could and did.

She was decidedly happy to have been so generous with the girl, for it had helped, she was certain, to catch the eye of Mornay and, indeed, of the *ton*. Was not her niece toasted at every evening supper she attended? Had not the Regent himself approved of her? True, Ariana did have to endure the occasional jest from Mornay's circle of aristocratic wags on account of her well-known piety, but even these men were gentler to her than was their usual habit concerning women.

And now she, Mrs. Bentley, had been enjoying her most successful season since her own coming-out decades earlier. Routs, card parties, soirees—the sort of things she adored—were crowding her calendar as the chaperone of Miss Forsythe. And she herself was going to marry Randolph. It was indeed an *annus mirabilis!* Just then a sudden nasty odour pulled her from her thoughts.

"Oh, dear," she murmured, turning to the Paragon. "Where is this orphan society? We are getting into neighbourhoods that I cannot like." The dignified streets of Mayfair were behind them, and now they were on roads that were muddy and crowded with carts and working-class people. Child vagabonds could be seen huddling in doorways. Pedestrians stopped what they were doing to watch the shiny black coach with its high-steppers and try to get a glimpse of the dignitaries who must be inside such a vehicle.

Ariana sat back. She had seen enough of the poor and indigent in London to know that compassion alone was worthless as far as helping anyone went. Further, she had no wish to seem pitying or condescending. The poor were entitled to dignity like anyone else. She had welcomed today's invitation precisely because of her wish to help London's less fortunate citizens. This had been a desire of her heart since coming to London earlier in the year. Her world had become a disheartening juxtaposition of unbelievable wealth against a backdrop of the ever-present poor.

Looking across at her suitor, she suddenly wondered if it would jar with his disposition to become a philanthropist? Certainly it was expected of the wealthy, wasn't it? Even in her little town of Chesterton, it was the wealthiest families, those with the huge estates, who held the annual balls, the Harvest Home, and the Christmas hall festivities. Mr. Mornay was part of this wealthy class. She hoped it would fall to her as his wife to organize charitable events.

"Ariana!" She was torn from her thoughts by her aunt's strident tone. "Did you say which street the orphanage is on?"

Before Ariana could reply, Mr. Mornay spoke in her stead, "The society is on Folgate Street, Spitalfields. Just north of Spitalfields Market." He met Ariana's eyes and added, "I own a property on the street, you know."

"Do you?" She was greatly surprised. It was not a fashionable part of the city. "A house?" she asked, trying to prolong the conversation. Finally he was at least giving her his attention.

"A tenement."

Mrs. Bentley's curiosity got the best of her. "*You* own property *there*?"

He gave a rueful smile. "Won it in a wager, I'm afraid. My man of business sees to letting it and so forth. I've never laid eyes on it, actually, though I've been meaning to give it a look."

Mrs. Bentley fished an expensive, lace-edged handkerchief from her reticule and held it now over her mouth and nose, as if the mere fact of passing through the neighbourhood might result in being exposed to noxious vapours.

Mr. Pellham took her other hand and patted it soothingly.

Beatrice, all eyes, extended her own hand out toward Mr. O'Brien. "Would you like to take my hand, Mr. O'Brien?" she asked.

His eyes opened rather wide, but before he could say anything, Mrs. Bentley chided, "Hush!" and, reaching across Ariana, landed a harmless slap with her handkerchief to the girl's outstretched hand. *Why do youngsters have to do the most foolish things imaginable? Isn't it enough that I have had to steer Ariana clear of the future cleric? Will I now have to do the same for my younger niece when she comes of age?*

Mr. O'Brien, meanwhile, smiled briefly at the girl to be kind, but he was much more concerned, despite his best efforts, with her elder sister. He was quite ill at ease in the presence of the striking Miss Forsythe, and so he smoothed his coat lapels and adjusted his cravat to cover his discomfort. He'd been taking as many glances at Ariana as he could safely take, all the while trying to conceal his admiration of her. He had lost her to Mornay, there was no way around it, but it was a difficult pill to swallow, indeed.

Mr. O'Brien had entertained hopes of forming a betrothal with Ariana. He was not wealthy, and he was Irish—both of which were not in his favour, particularly with the standards that Miss Forsythe's aunt seemed to demand from any of her niece's would-be suitors. He was mildly uncomfortable, therefore, despite his being included on Beatrice's account. (The girl had taken an instant partiality to him and insisted on his company as often as possible.) He could not rid himself of his still-strong admiration for her elder sister. Couple that with a touch of pique—he'd had such hopes of her—and he was moved to join her company whenever possible. Miss Forsythe had been too friendly for him to think she felt nothing more than mere friendship for him!

But it wasn't becoming in a man of faith to nurse a grudge. His calling was in the church, which even if he had not been a third son, he would have chosen because he had strong religious leanings. But he could not resist the chance to be in her company. So he tried to avoid looking at her, having no wish to make a jackanape of himself, but it was difficult indeed, with such proximity to her beauty.

Furthermore, it was decidedly unusual for him to be welcomed into the presence of the Paragon, a man he felt more than a little antipathy toward. To be seated beside him now seemed extraordinary, and he was mute with a mixture of caution, jealousy, and surprise. He had always scoffed at the man's reputation for excellent taste, but in his presence, he could not deny a feeling of reluctant admiration. Mr. Mornay's clothing made a stark contrast to his own less costly attire. The man's dark double-breasted tailcoat with tapered sleeves made his frock coat, though sturdy, appear plain, indeed.

At that moment Beatrice unhelpfully exclaimed, "Your coach is ever so pretty, Mr. Mornay! It is far more comfortable than my father's." She fingered the dark burgundy velvet of her seat. "I wish my mother and father could see it."

"Hush!" Ariana said, not without affection.

"Do you not fancy the coach? I could ride in it for days!" she exclaimed, wide-eyed.

"Of course I fancy it, but it doesn't signify."

"Is your carriage as agreeable as this one, Mr. O'Brien?" the girl asked.

Her question made him shudder inwardly, as he thought of the single family equipage he used when taking his mama and sisters about town. Compared to Mornay's gleaming, springed, and upholstered vehicle, his was unmistakably shabby. "No," he answered, trying to smile with the word.

Just then everyone's attention was diverted as they pulled up outside a large Palladian-style building that was fenced in by black iron gates. The London Orphan Society was a stately institution. Mr. Pellham exclaimed, "Undoubtedly the work of Mr. Nash, wouldn't you say, Mornay?"

Mr. Mornay, observing the building as best he could from the interior of the coach, nodded his head. "Very likely." All was quiet and neat on the outside. A gateman opened the way for them, and the coach moved forward and into a circular drive, which brought them round to the front entrance.

As the group stepped into the building, Mrs.Bentley raised her ankle-length pelisse as though it might drag on the tiled floor. Ariana straightened her dark blue, French-style canezou, which had a deep flounce along the shoulders, neckline, and empire waist. Beneath her bonnet, which sported two round puffs of pale, gathered fabric at the top, a few little ringlets of blonde hair framed her face—evidence of enduring a night with curling papers beneath her cap. She was bright with youthful beauty this morning, as most days. Ariana happily accepted Mr. Mornay's arm and continued to search his countenance for a clue to his feelings, but he maintained a stony disregard of her. If not for his past effusive reassurances of love, she might have been exceedingly disconcerted. She refused to believe anything of import was behind his distant manner, as she tucked one arm through his and placed her other hand upon his coat sleeve with feeling.

The little group followed the headmistress, Mrs. Gullweather, who had, curtseying, given her name; and two female servants down a long, wide stone hall that ended at the chapel. A manservant led them to seats in a front row. Ariana was impressed with the massive interior, the circular ceiling, and long, stained-glass windows, beautiful against the morning light outside. The benches around and behind them were full of children of all ages, who emitted only a low murmur from their ranks.

Ariana sat down, cognizant of the pleasure of being next to Mr. Mornay. She glanced at him now, but he continued to study the area ahead, where Mrs. Gullweather was preparing to speak. Ariana felt as though Phillip was somewhere else today, far distant from the proceedings, far distant from *her*. But she turned her attention to the front of the room just as he had. She would think no more on it for now.

"Before we begin," Mrs. Gullweather said to the assembled guests, who, in addition to Ariana and her party, took up the first two rows of seats across the chapel, "we have arranged for the children to entertain you. We do endeavour to educate them profitably. Most of our graduates, when they leave us, go on to lead productive lives in society. We have had dozens of young people go off to be missionaries in foreign lands, and we have also furnished a good many governesses, cooks, and housemaids for people of quality. Many of our young gentlemen, it must be added, who do not choose the mission field, go on to find apprenticeships or serve as footmen or grooms in the best households."

With a wave of her hand, she added, "These are the same children who are brought to us destitute, with nothing but poverty, death, or a life of crime facing them. It is only by the generous help of our patrons," she smiled benignly toward them, "that we are able to effect such changes for society." After a brief pause for effect, she then said, "And now—the children."

The sight of the needy young orphans erased all other concerns from Ariana's heart. How glad she was to have come today. She so wanted to somehow make a difference for children like these! God knew each by name and loved every one of them.

The children stood in file and on cue began to sing an old hymn, "Ye Holy Angels, Bright." By the end of the song, Ariana was thoroughly satisfied that the London Orphan Society was a worthy cause, indeed.

When the dramatic actress, Mrs. Tiernan, finally stood before them, silent, even grave of countenance, a hush fell over the audience, including its youngest members. Her gown was of the classical Roman style, more like those that had been in vogue a decade ago. Expecting the actress to begin, the audience waited. But the woman kept her eyes fixed on a spot overhead, toward a window.

When she continued to stare at that fixed point against the opposite wall, people began to look at it too. Was it supposed to mean something?

Then just when everyone despaired of her ever doing anything other than staring at the window, she turned and faced the assembly. This time she stared down the main aisle, as though she were in a trance. Then suddenly, with a dramatic flourish of her arm, she cried, "*Hear the Word of the Lord!*" Her voice rang out loud and piercing as it cut into the silence.

Then in a quieter tone, "*A dramatic reading from the book of Revelation, chapter one, verses ten through twenty.*" She slowly moved her gaze to take in the onlookers. Her eyes were calm and yet seemed to blaze from within, settling to flicker momentarily upon Ariana and her companions.

Again the hush grew deep with anticipation. Mrs. Tiernan dropped suddenly to her knees, her arms raised high, and then turned her head as if listening. In a clear tone, which carried an authoritative quality, she began in earnest.

"*I was in the Spirit on the Lord's day, and I heard behind me a great voice, as a trumpet.*" She added measured movements of her arms and even her body, so that she made a captivating sight.

"*I turned to see the voice that spake with me. And being I turned, I saw seven golden candlesticks.*"

"*His feet like unto fine brass, as if they burned in a furnace; and his voice,*" she said, lifting her head to listen, "*as the sound of many waters...in his right hand seven stars: and out of his mouth went a sharp two-edged sword.*" She made a motion as if taking a sword from its sheath, and then, magically, a small leather book was in her hand! How had she done it? Ariana didn't know. But there it was, a concrete allusion to the "two-edged sword" being the Word of God.

And then the book was gone. Vanished as if it had never been there. The audience gasped, and she continued, "*His countenance was as the sun shineth in his strength.*"

When the reading ended, Mrs. Tiernan froze, statue-like except that her head was bowed. In a minute people began to applaud, led by Mr. O'Brien, which would have been rather amazing except that he had the impetus of knowing the presentation had ended for he alone had been following along in his little leather Bible. Mrs. Tiernan remained with her head bowed as the clapping slowly grew stronger. Finally when the applause ceased, the lady bowed low, so that everyone had to clap again. She then said, "Thank you! Thank you!" and swept out of sight, leaving from a hidden exit behind the pulpit.

Soon the guests were led to a small breakfast room, where a light repast was waiting. While they ate, they shared thoughts on what they'd seen.

"I daresay she cast a spell on us," chuckled Mr. Pellham, tugging on his moustache thoughtfully.

Mrs. Bentley added, "Rather a bit of a trickster, I should think. Making that little book appear and disappear as if by magic. And in a chapel!"

Mr. O'Brien cleared his throat. He hated to disagree with anyone who was socially superior to him, but he had to correct what he saw as near-blasphemous thinking.

"But, ma'am," he managed to say, "it was only for effect. To heighten the power of her presentation, which, I thought in all honesty, to be quite... quite *good.*"

"I thought it was wonderful!" put in Beatrice, loyally—and loudly. "Did you not think so, Ariana?"

Ariana smiled. "I was impressed." She glanced at Mr. Mornay and felt a fresh concern. Instead of finding the warm eyes and gentle smile she loved, she saw his blank expression. It was an expression she recognized as being his "tolerant" look—he was merely enduring the proceedings, nothing more.

Mr. Mornay turned to the faces around the table. "It was interesting, and," he paused and chose his word carefully and continued, "worthwhile."

While they continued eating, Mrs. Gullweather approached with a little bald man, who wore spectacles and carried a small, bound leather book in which he was jotting information.

"I hope you have enjoyed our little entertainment," she began. "And now we must rely upon your patience and goodness a little longer, while we beg you to consider making our orphanage a grateful recipient of the generosity that so distinguishes your class among men." Ariana wished devoutly that she had the means to be as generous as possible but knew that within her reticule lay a single crown. It was the last of her money.

Mr. Mornay, meanwhile, had no wish to listen to any flummery and spoke to the man with the book. "Are you recording donations?" The man looked up, startled to be addressed, but quickly replied, "I am, sir."

He rounded the table to where Ariana and Mr. Mornay were sitting, across from one another. He waited, pencil poised and ready to enter an amount in his account book. Meanwhile Mrs. Bentley offered the woman a few guineas, which she accepted gratefully. Mr. Pellham followed with a bank note of an unknown sum. Beatrice solemnly gave sixpence, and Mr. O'Brien just a little above that, as this unfortunate time of the month always found him in low water.

Mr. Mornay, meanwhile, had turned to Ariana. "I should like you to propose the amount." It was an embarrassing moment, as the topic of money was considered ungenteel. One did not discuss it, as important as it was. She blushed.

"I dare not think of it."

With surprise, he asked, leaning in toward her for privacy, "Do you not wish to support the place?"

"Oh, I do, of course. I mean to give my last crown…"

"I've no doubt. But tell me the amount you should like to give if you had the means. Only name it, and it is done."

She eyed him uncertainly. Suddenly his distance keeping seemed to have fled, and he was himself again. And he loved her. He was asking her to make a financial decision for the two of them! Many a woman would have been astounded at it. Perhaps Ariana was astounded, for she could only reply, "I think perhaps that *you* ought to—"

"No, it must be you. I wouldn't be here if it weren't for you, and I am certain you will be more generous than I."

"But that is what I fear!" she hissed in a whisper. "What if I name a sum that is too high?"

He smiled and simply said, "Name it."

"Oh, dear! Very well," she said and smiled back, bringing her two hands together in thought. But she was enormously pleased to have received that smile. It was the first she'd seen him wear all morning. "Would…twenty-five pounds per annum be appropriate?"

He said nothing to her but then turned to the recorder. "Send the bill to my house," he commanded and went on to give the information necessary, while the appreciative clerk scribbled in his book.

Ariana watched, with a spurt of elation. A heady delight. A feeling of unexpected *power*. She found herself staring at Mr. Mornay as if realizing his great wealth for the first time.

"Stop looking at me like that," he said with amusement. "'Tis only money."

Only money! She knew of widows who lived on little more than what she had just been able to procure for the orphanage. With a few words, she had made a difference for the children. It was a marvelous new feeling, exhilarating and intoxicating. Of course it was Phillip's money, not her own, but had not her aunt told her numerous times that all he had would soon be hers? That Mr. Mornay had offered her everything that was his? Any amount of pin money she wanted? She had never paid the least attention to the thought of sharing in Phillip's wealth, but suddenly it presented a world of possibilities to her.

She barely noticed the rest of the proceedings, the thank-yous and good-byes. Only the parade of orphans, waiting to wave and cheer them off, brought her fully alert to her surroundings. As they pulled away in the coach, she looked at each child in a new way. What if she could afford to give them all a new article of clothing every year? Or new shoes? What if she and Phillip were to—to start their own society? There were still hundreds and hundreds of hungry, cold children on the streets. More orphans than this one asylum could house. As the carriage exited the iron gates of the grounds, Ariana was lost in a world of new thoughts and ideas. It seemed as if she'd been waiting all her life to have such thoughts—thoughts she'd never had the means to have before.

As Mrs. Phillip Mornay she *would* have the means.

As Mrs. Phillip Mornay she could do much good.

Her eyes wandered to her silent, handsome future husband. Studying him, she felt a strong wave of love. She recalled wrapping her arms around his neck and the wonderful feel of his arms firmly about her. The night of their betrothal, he had taken her into his coach and put her upon his lap and they'd kissed.

He was listening to Beatrice's absent chatter, or she would have bestowed upon him a most adoring smile. As she studied the appealing face, strong nose and chin, and the rich, neat attire, her heart swelled with love and pride—but also a slight discomposure. She was appreciating his circumstances in a way she had never done. Was it wrong? Was it selfish? To be happy that she would be married to a rich man? But she thought of all the charities she could support, the good works she could do, and her qualms dissipated. Mr. Mornay had been only too happy to let her name the sum for the orphanage. Surely he would always be that way, wouldn't he?

During the drive home, she dreamed of the future benefactress to the poor she would become. The usually deflating scenes of needy children on the streets did not affect her as usual.

Soon, soon, my dear children, she thought, *Mrs. Mornay will come to your aide!* At that moment her beloved turned his gaze upon her, and her inner musings came to an abrupt halt.

Once again there was nothing of warmth in his eyes, nothing of the affection she usually found in them. *Would* the future Mrs. Mornay be a benefactress to the poor?

Or was he having a sudden change of heart? Did he wish to—to *cry off from the wedding?* Had he allowed her to name the sum for the orphanage to lessen the blow of his change of heart? Her thoughts of helping the poor paled in light of this disturbing notion. *Is he regretting our wedding plans? Why else the coldness of his manner, the absence of meaning in his looks to me? I will need to find a way to speak with him privately. Perhaps his distracted behaviour has nothing to do with me at all.* She frowned. *If it does not, there was something else on his mind that was troublesome. In either case, I must seek to help.*

Somehow she had to speak to him alone and soon. Something was most certainly wrong.

Two

Ariana was in her bedchamber, looking at the clothing which constituted her trousseau, strewn for the moment across the bed and furniture. Silk, cotton, taffeta, bombazine, ostrich feathers, ribbons and bonnets—my, it was a colourful lot! Stockings, slippers, chemises, stays, gowns, shawls, turbans, handkerchiefs, and gloves—more things than she had ever owned in her life. Delighted with the glorious mess, she picked up a shoe or boot here, a new glove, brooch, or fan there. The sight of the parasol, shawl, even the laced drawers (if Princess Charlotte wore them, Ariana could too, Mrs. Bentley had said) filled Ariana with anticipation.

Her future husband had paid for the lot of it, a fact which would have sent more than one haughty brow to its pinnacle, and which might have eroded Ariana's standing in society, were it known. But only she and her family and, of course, Mr. Mornay were aware of the fact. Mrs. Bentley had done her usual part in taking Ariana shopping and bespoke all the items on the list from her betrothed with rare satisfaction.

To Ariana the rounds of fittings and measurings all over town seemed to go on and on. From Bond Street to Threadneedle, from Ludgate Hill to Pall Mall to Jermyn, Ariana felt they'd been everywhere. She wheedled her aunt into allowing her a quick browse at Hatchard's on the condition that she would choose a perfume from Floris's. Although Ariana did not care to wear scent, she had agreed to purchase a mild vial of the stuff in exchange for the chance to snatch up the second edition of *Sense and Sensibility.*

Except for one trunk's worth of clothes and a few hat boxes, Ariana's aunt had arranged to have everything in front of her moved to Mr. Mornay's house in Grosvenor Square, only a few streets from Hanover Square. Despite the fact that she had not managed to speak with her betrothed alone yet, his keeping to the schedule Mrs. Bentley had written was encouraging. Mr. Mornay had even sent a fine coach for the occasion. Although most of the trousseau would be transported in the splendid carriage, some items would be hand-carried by servants on foot and accompanied by Mrs. Bentley, Ariana, and Beatrice. Surely if Mr. Mornay was entertaining thoughts of calling off the wedding, he would not have encouraged such an elaborate transfer.

Nor would he have given his approbation to the proposed tour she was to take of the house. Ariana was looking forward to seeing it—Phillip's house! She would be surrounded by his things, his tastes, his life. Perchance somehow the house would even open secret doors to his character. She might know him better by seeing it.

Because he had made it clear that he would be away for the day, she wracked her brain for a way to leave a reminder of her presence there. Something he would see when he returned home later, perhaps. But she got so busy being hurried along by Mrs. Bentley that she forgot to choose such a remembrance.

As Harrietta and another maid began folding and packing the articles—specimens of the finest textiles and accessories available in England—Beatrice entered the room without knocking.

"May I watch, 'Ana? I long to look at your beautiful things!" The younger girl gave a sigh of bliss as she looked around. Ariana wore costly apparel as though she was born for it but in truth would have been content with less. Beatrice, however, thought her elder sister had cause for joy that only entering the gates of heaven might equal.

"You may watch *if* you have finished packing your own things," Mrs. Bentley interjected, as she came into the room behind the girl. Mrs. Bentley's plans to send Beatrice home were all for naught because upon hearing of the intended banishment, the O'Briens took pity on the girl. After Beatrice had given Mr. O'Brien a long rant on the evils of agues and how providence had ceased to smile upon her (a saying she had once heard her father use), the gentleman regaled his family with the story. They were greatly amused, and soon after Miss Beatrice was issued an invitation directly, entreating the young lady to stay with them on Blandford Street.

Mrs. O'Brien considered it providential because her youngest daughter, Miss Alice, was Beatrice's age exactly. Now the girl would have a companion to share her days with. They sent a message to Hanover Square so that Mrs. Bentley would not remove the child from town. "Let her visit us and see if she and Alice do not suit first," Mrs. O'Brien's note had said. But at home Mrs. O'Brien used words of a much different tone. "Certainly Mrs. Bentley is acting in a hasty manner to send the girl packing! A mere cold is no cause to ruin the happiness of not only Miss Beatrice but of her sister, who must want her in London for the wedding. Even a younger sister is some small comfort, I daresay."

Mr. Mornay had indeed made certain that he would not be in residence when Ariana was to come. Rather, he was endeavouring to keep himself occupied—and away from her. He had no intention of being home when she would be in the house. It was the necessary measure he had to take, finding it difficult to be near her without feeling a powerful unrest—a sensation he hadn't struggled with since he was in his teens—all the more potent, it seemed, for having so long been denied. Thinking on it now, he realized that somehow he had trained his mind not to contemplate the delights of women. But that was before Ariana, before falling in love.

He was discovering a new man within himself. A man with whom he was not familiar—a man who longed to be a woman's lover. More, her husband. The father of her children. It was much, much easier to wait calmly for the wedding when he was not in the company of his beguiling bride-to-be.

Indeed, the idea of his future bride in his house was almost too happy a thought. He wouldn't dare remain on the premises with her. The little blonde minx addled his brain and upset his customarily detached attitude! He wanted nothing more than to be married to her—yesterday! He wished to be done with waiting. However, society and good manners demanded he wait for the wedding date set forth by Mr. and Mrs. Forsythe, and so he had no choice but to comply.

He'd searched his brain and faintly remembered how other men had been struck with the anguish of loving a woman, heart, soul and body, to such a degree that waiting was torturous. He'd thought them idiotic, besotted fools. And now (it was no use denying) he was one of them. No reason why all of London had to know it, and so he was being careful—very careful—to keep his head, maintain his usual style of detachment, and force himself to wait. Especially as there was nothing else for it.

He had arranged to watch a fencing match, followed by lunch with some friends at his favourite club, White's. Then having received notice by messenger that a new coat—the one he would wear for the wedding ceremony—was ready for a fitting, he'd make his way to Weston's and give the tailor as good a fitting as he ever had. From there he intended to inspect a few horses, which were soon to be up for auction, to see if one might suit Ariana. It would be a wedding gift. The dapple-gray Arabian he wanted was only available because its owner lost a formidable fortune—ten thousand pounds—at cards and hoped to make up his losses by selling his renowned race stock.

Ariana did not need a racing horse, but this mare had seen a good amount of action and was due to be retired. With years of racing behind it, the mare was spent and would be safe for his new wife. He would never bid on a horse without first inspecting it himself and procuring the opinion of his head groom, Quibb. Ariana was, therefore, to have the house to herself all afternoon. He tried not to think about her in his house and set about the day. He was not ready to concede that he was in the pitiable condition of being a lovesick fool!

He recognized the irony of his behavior; that he had often avoided women in the past because they dared to set their cap at him. Now he was avoiding the one woman he loved for quite a different reason. Let Ariana keep herself occupied with whatever things women did before their marriage, and he would do the same. It was a simple, sensible solution. Thirteen days was really a short period of time, and he did not anticipate any problems.

Ariana did not question his busy schedule. He was about to become a married man after having been a bachelor for near three decades. Surely that was reason enough for a man to desire some time to do whatever it was men did. (What did they do? Shoot? Play cricket? Fence? She had no clear idea what he would be up to, but no matter, she had enough to occupy her mind.) She *was* looking forward to seeing the house. Number 25 Grosvenor Square was a masterpiece of Georgian architecture. It was sure to be a delightful afternoon.

When the servants finished packing the clothing, Ariana and Beatrice joined Aunt Bentley in the hall, preparing to leave the house. Ariana, wearing a tunic over her gown and a turban, moved out to the pavement in a strange state of mind. It felt like a dream. Could she really be preparing to move into a town mansion? There was a fluttering in her stomach at the thought. She longed to be Mrs. Mornay, to have Phillip as her very own. Being mistress of a large establishment had never been her aim, however, and she was startled to find herself unnerved at the thought of it.

The hustle and bustle of the servants and Mrs. Bentley's shrill voice giving orders only added to her detached feeling. It was all happening around her, to her, and she had nothing to do with it. Nothing at all. How odd. How exceedingly odd.

A coach came rumbling to a stop directly behind the one containing a load of hatboxes and bandboxes. When Ariana saw the curious faces of Mrs. Herley and Lavinia peering from the window, her friends' warm smiles restored Ariana's presence of mind. Mr. Mornay's coach started moving, being led into a turnaround to head back to Grosvenor Square. A small parade of servants waited on the pavement for their mistress to lead the way.

From the window of their coach, Mrs. Herley begged to know what was all the to-do. When she understood what was afoot, she asked if she and her daughter could be included. Mrs. Bentley's face broke into a disapproving frown, but Ariana was delighted to have her friend along and welcomed them heartily. The ladies sent their carriage ahead and joined the threesome on the pavement.

"I am so glad we thought to call upon you just now," gushed Lavinia, as they fell into step together. "To think I shall see the whole of the Paragon's establishment! And that it is to be your house! Can you quite conceive of it, my dear Ariana?"

This was the very thing she was actually having trouble conceiving. "In truth I cannot."

"You'll soon be living there as mistress! Is it not exciting?" Lavinia giggled.

Suddenly Beatrice exclaimed, "Oh, 'tis Mr. O'Brien and his mama! I mustn't go to their house yet! Please say they may come with us, Ariana, so that I shan't miss your new house! May they come? Please say they may!"

"They have been so kind to open their home to you. Of course they may," the elder sister responded. "But who is to say they desire to come?"

"We cannot invite the whole town, Miss Beatrice!" Mrs. Bentley's words were sharp and not without a hint of disapproval, but when the twosome reached the group, Beatrice burst out, "Hullo! What do you think? We are going to Mr. Mornay's establishment to deliver Ariana's trousseau and look over the whole house! And you may come, if you like!" She was smiling from ear to ear.

Mrs. O'Brien, responding with a little smile of her own, curtseyed hastily for Mrs. Bentley, Ariana, and the Herleys and looked thoughtfully at the young girl.

Mr. O'Brien's countenance was less promising. He had no way of knowing that the Paragon would not be at home and no wish to see him if he was.

Beatrice registered Mr. O'Brien's response, refocused on Mrs. O'Brien, and said with precocious intuition, "You will see the Paragon's house! It will be enormous fun! Everything expensive and agreeable!"

Ariana's lips tightened.

"Oh, do let us go," said Mrs. O'Brien to her son, looking at him plaintively.

He hesitated. Then as his gaze took in Ariana, dressed in a lovely walking-out gown of light, jaconet muslin and an over-tunic trimmed with satin ribbon applique and lace, he felt his repulsion of Mr. Mornay melt in the face of the prospect of spending time with her. Her head was framed in a gauze turban with a single egret plume. Just at that moment, while he watched, she looked over and smiled a gentle greeting at him.

And that settled it. He agreed—if Miss Forsythe had no objection.

"I have already asked her," put in Beatrice, "so 'tis settled!"

When they had reached the corner of Brook and David Street, Mr. Pellham appeared, as he had been sent for by Mrs. Bentley via messenger. Ariana greeted him happily, and he bowed his head at her and the other ladies before offering his arm to Mrs. Bentley, who was already smiling at him fondly.

Mr. Pellham was glad to be included and hoped to see Mr. Mornay. Mornay's intervention, sending his own surgeon to look after Mr. Pellham's ankle injury earlier in the season, was responsible for its healing so prettily. He would always use a cane, but then he had favored the use of one even before he had taken that nasty fall leading to the painfully prolonged injury.

This meeting of friends on the street resulted in quite a large entourage, including the parade of servants, moving along in a merry swarm of caps, bonnets, feathers, and top hats and descending upon the house in Grosvenor Square that morning at half past twelve. As they approached the Paragon's dwelling, they cheerfully admired other stately homes, for Grosvenor Square was circled by famous dwellings. Although the Georgian townhouses they passed were near palatial, the company was never more admiring than when they reached number 25—Ariana's future home.

They stopped to survey the stately building of Portland Stone. Such architectural details! Such carvings and moulded stonework! Intricate plasterwork. Wonderful portico and pillared frontage. All was elegant, neat, and classical. Ariana smiled and nodded, giggling now and then at the sheer exuberance of the company and how they were all so eager to be pleased. She enjoyed the beauty of Mr. Mornay's house herself—indeed marveled at it—but she felt rather like a mother hen in a barnyard full of cheeping, trailing chicks. She would have to lead these chicks through the entire three-storey structure, as well as the garret and basement kitchens and service area. To the rear of the house were stables and coach and mews houses—were they also to be toured? She hoped she had the energy.

So intent was the little group on admiring the stately mansion that no one noticed an old black coach parked at the curb of the square. It was a little farther down and across the street from house number 25, with a pair of sorry-looking nags harnessed in front. Behind the equipage, the equestrian statue of George I stood high and dignified—and ignored.

Generally such equipages were not seen in the vicinity of Grosvenor Square, and on another day, it might have elicited curiosity. But the jolly group admiring the Paragon's house paid it no mind whatsoever. From inside the coach, the two faces peeking covertly out at the company were very much on the alert. They were intensely scrutinizing the arrivals on the sidewalk, mindful to see but not be seen.

"I knew this vigil would pay off," said the elder of the two.

The other suddenly cried, "I say 'tis Miss Herley!"

"To the devil with Miss Herley!" came the caustic response. "She's done with you. Which is the one we want?" There was a pause, while the first speaker swallowed his pride and no small distress. Was Miss Herley indeed done with him? But of course she was. That's what this was all about! He looked glumly at the merry-looking company, with Miss Forsythe clearly visible near the head of the party.

"She's there, wearing the white and yellow, next to Miss Herley."

Ariana and Lavinia were engrossed in an animated dialogue, and Ariana laughed at a small joke her friend told. Her face shone prettily with youth and happiness.

The other gave a low whistle. "A prime article, indeed."

"I told you she was top o' the trees. Only I wish there was another way!"

"Don't get pasty-faced. You're stronger when you're in your cups. We've agreed on this, haven't we?"

The younger one nodded reluctantly.

"There's nothing left for us, in any case. We've nothing to lose, and I daresay we shall exact a pretty penny for that piece of work."

"Nothing to lose?" said the first. "Only our heads, I suppose."

"Don't be such a gull!" came the disgusted response. "Who's that young chit? Just a girl."

The younger man reluctantly tore his eyes from Miss Lavinia Herley, whom he had not seen for some few weeks now and studied the youngest member of the promenade.

"Must be a sister. She's not a Herley."

"As I thought. Hmmm, if the elder one is trouble, we can always take the younger. Her absence might provoke stronger feelings altogether, in fact."

But the younger man was paying little heed to his brother. His eyes were once again on the object of his affection—Lavinia Herley. The entourage was moving into the house now. The house where their enemy, Phillip Mornay—he would never call him the Paragon—dwelt.

As the party entered the house, they walked past the whole of Mr. Mornay's staff, who had been summoned by Frederick to line up and greet their soon-to-be mistress. While the guests exclaimed at the loveliness and expense of the delicate hand-painted Chinese wallpaper, Frederick gave Ariana the name and station of each servant. Beatrice walked aside her sister, her eyes large as if she too were soon to relocate to the square. She was fascinated, she would later say to the O'Briens—utterly fascinated—by the number of servants her sister should command!

Each servant dropped a respectful curtsey or bow, some smiling shyly. Ariana recognized a few of the footmen and a handful of the maids, including gaunt Lettie and the rosy-cheeked, plump cook. When she came to the new scullery maid, the lowliest of the staff, she smiled and said, "Why, 'tis Molly!" The little girl almost smiled, curtseyed shyly, but kept her eyes lowered. "Are you happy here, my gel?"

The servant nodded.

"Excellent!" said Ariana, and then she moved on.

Meanwhile the upper staff were roiling with the wonder of how their future mistress could know the least important member of the servants, stopping to speak to her! It was rather shocking. She had stopped to merely smile and nod a greeting at the rest of them. It was felt as a snub.

Mrs. Hamilton, the housekeeper, felt a distinct chill as she watched her future mistress. Mr. Mornay hired her less than a year ago to replace Mrs. Addison, who had passed away unexpectedly while visiting her sister in Brighton ten months prior. Mrs. Hamilton had never set eyes on Miss Forsythe prior to this day and indeed had been dreading doing so. A young mistress, to her mind, spelled trouble. Had not her own mother twice been dismissed by a new young mistress? Her mother, who had been an excellent housekeeper in her day, twice had lost her situation due to the capricious whims of spoilt young women. Miss Forsythe, she just knew in her bones, would be no different!

She would undoubtedly bring her own favourite servants, and if she, Mrs. Hamilton, did not get on with them, she'd be out on the street before the honeymoon ended. Ladies were loyal only to their own maids—it was a fact of life.

The hardest part of it was that Grosvenor Square had been Mrs. Hamilton's best station to date. And now she was convinced the fate which had twice befallen her mother, was about to occur to her. With a sudden strong fear, she thought of Margate in Draper's Hospital, that place that was called a refuge for "decayed housekeepers," and shuddered to think she might soon be forced to join its ranks!

To begin with it had been nothing short of miraculous that Mr. Mornay had approved her for the position of housekeeper in his establishment. Women of her age were seldom hired. Most people preferred younger, middle-aged blood. Of course Mr. Mornay did not. He avoided youthful women in fact—until he met his betrothed, that is.

Further, he was a generous master. Though known for his temper, she had never known him to be cruel or excessively out of countenance with his staff. The servants were uniformly attached to him, proud of him, happy to work for him. Indeed, it was the situation of her dreams. Mrs. Hamilton had gloried in her good fortune as housekeeper of number 25 Grosvenor Square. She now realized that she would unlikely ever retain such a position of esteem again if she lost this one and that Miss Ariana Forsythe would be to blame. What could be done to prevent such a calamity? There had to be some answer. And she, Mrs. Hamilton, must find it.

Ariana, meanwhile, had motioned to the servant, indicating she wished a private word with her. "Mrs. Hamilton, I hope you shall teach me what I must know to run this household successfully. I so want to please Mr. Mornay. Everything must be smooth as ever it was, for which I will very much rely upon your knowledge." Ariana's words, though meant kindly, were not received in kind.

"Ma'am, I am at your service, but there is no need to concern yourself, I assure you. Mr. Frederick and I shall maintain the running of the house. You are too great a lady, ma'am, if I may say so, to condescend to our concerns." She curtseyed as she spoke.

Ariana smiled. "I thank you, Mrs. Hamilton, but you must not spare me domestic concerns. It is my part to know these things and my intention, I assure you."

Mrs. Hamilton curtseyed stiffly and murmured, "As you please, ma'am."

But the colour that had popped up on her cheeks was not from pleasure. With a sinking heart, she was thinking, *And put myself out of a situation, that's what. So she's a sly one, is she? Her 'part to know these things,' indeed!*

She did not wish to think wrongly of Miss Forsythe—she was a pretty, sweetly countenanced girl—but her words were like the proverbial nail in the coffin. After this there could be no doubt. The young woman clearly sought to make Mrs.Hamilton dispensable. And why make her dispensable if she was not to be dispensed with? Miss Forsythe had made her intentions clear, and now it only remained to be seen what Mrs. Hamilton could do to prevent those intentions from being realized.

~

A group of London's premier shopkeepers came forward with their assistants, all bowing and speaking at once. Ariana was looking in confusion from one gentleman to the next until her aunt intervened.

"Gentlemen, please! One at a time!" Mrs. Bentley's authoritative voice never failed to produce its desired effect, this time bringing an instant silence. But it couldn't last: The merchants shared a passionate desire to be of help furnishing or decorating the home of the Paragon.

Mrs. Bentley had sent word to them, inviting them to attend. They could advise on the latest style, accept orders, and offer expert opinions. A new mistress might decide there were things she must have that were lacking in the house or at least wish to make her presence known with a few small changes, a few indications of her tastes and styles, particularly in a dwelling that had been home to only a bachelor for years.

Mrs. Bentley motioned to the butler, and he came and deftly ushered the shopkeepers and merchants into a ground floor sitting room. There he told them, in no uncertain terms, that they must wait to be called upon. And wait they would. It meant a lot to their business if they could include in their pattern books a little card with the words, "This item was purchased by the Paragon" or "Proudly in the morning room in the house of the Paragon."

"What are they here for, Aunt Bentley?" Ariana asked.

"For you, of course. To help you decide what you want for the house. Or may need."

"I could not conceive of—" she started to say, but already Mrs. Hamilton was leading them to the stairs to start the tour. And Mrs. Bentley walked off to take Mr. Pellham's arm. Ariana was troubled about her aunt's words. Not only had 25 Grosvenor Square been planned and built with particular care for architectural uniformity and classic styling, but Mr. Mornay himself had the better sense of fashion, style, and colour. Did he not choose her trousseau for that reason? And his house, in fact, was appointed with the same faultless taste, which had earned him the descriptive title of "Paragon." Everything elegant, the right fit, colours, and style, so that everyone bowed to his word on a matter of fashion or decoration. There was beauty and grace in his dwelling, everything placed precisely where it should be.

With a sigh Ariana followed the housekeeper, hoping her aunt would forget about the tradesmen. As the group made its way to the front drawing room, suddenly Mrs. Bentley was back at her side.

"Now that I think on it, I want to oversee the unpacking of your trousseau," her aunt murmured. "You cannot trust servants to do these things properly, you know."

"But do you not wish to see the house?"

"I do, of course. Which is why you must wait and offer your guests some refreshment until I return. I'll make quick work of it." Mrs. Bentley turned and went after the train of servants. *My niece,* she was thinking, *to be mistress here!* It was such a comfortable, encouraging thought that she left the room with a smile. In the hall a little chambermaid flitted past with a hasty curtsey. A little chambermaid that looked familiar.

It was Molly! Molly, the servant girl who had been an instrument in the theft of Ariana's letters only a few weeks earlier. Mrs. Bentley stopped and gave the maid a disapproving eye. The little traitor! She oughn't to be kept on here, not when she was involved with such spurious dealings in the past. She made a mental note to speak to Mr. Mornay's housekeeper.

Meanwhile she had reached the bedchamber which was to be Ariana's, and discovered quickly that there were communicating doors to Mr. Mornay's bedchamber. She examined his room as well. With her practiced eye, she quickly observed the artistry and expense of the rooms, taking in the smallest details as well as the massive mahogany furniture. And the ceiling? Mrs. Bentley had to smile. Her niece was going to *adore* this room.

She set about directing the servants and seeing to the wardrobe, completely in her element. But she did not forget about Molly.

The party took advantage of its time in the drawing room to look about with a rare lack of inhibition. Was this not why they had come? To see the place, top to bottom? The beautiful marble fireplace and elegant sofa and chairs. The frescoes and carved statues and portraits on the walls.

Frederick came in with two maids who carried trays of tea and a coffee service. There were also biscuits, seed cakes, and grapes. Men and women alike were happy to sit and chat while they sipped from their gilt-edged cups and enjoyed the "damper" on the trays. Each one was exceedingly gratified to have been included. They were in the house of the Paragon! They were acquainted with Miss Forsythe, the future Mrs. Mornay. The only person who did not feel thus was Mr. O'Brien, who had fallen into a decided dejection since entering the house.

Mr. Mornay was his competition, and it was all too evident that in material things Mr. O'Brien could not compete. Worse, his family hailed from Ireland while Mr. Mornay was solidly English. He ought never to have thought seriously of winning Miss Forsythe. Yet to see her, to hear her lovely voice—and she so recently his friend—made it impossible to give her up entirely. Since she was betrothed to Mornay, he knew his lingering hopes were pointless. Miss Forsythe had made her choice. But it was most assuredly not the one he had desired.

Frederick, meanwhile, had allowed a footman to carry in a stack of pattern books from the shopkeepers, showing the newest styles of furniture, silverware, and ornaments. Each catalogue was from a different shop, and Ariana could have bespoken new draperies, wallpaper, tile, or any number of things. Soon some of the tradesmen were there as well, for they had naughtily sneaked from belowstairs and found their way to the group.

Lavinia reached for a book and began flipping through the pages. "Ariana, join me. Look at these beautiful things!"

Ariana took a cursory look but said shortly, "I haven't seen the house fully yet. I'd like to admire what Mr. Mornay has, not pine for things he has not."

"Oh, but let us look just for amusement. Mama never enters these shops, so I seldom get to peek at such patterns."

Beatrice was sitting beside Mr. O'Brien and his mama, but at the sight of the pattern books, she came over in a flurry of curiosity. "I saw such books in the village once, when my mother was in want of a new tea kettle! Please let me look too!"

They leafed through page after page of furniture, all attended with the uttermost sighs of admiration from Beatrice and praises of "How elegant!" or "So commodious!" from Lavinia that even Ariana had to admit the modern styles of furniture—whether black, japanned tables or intricately carved chairs or plump sofas and settees—were all rich and luxurious and fine. She too enjoyed seeing the astonishing variety of pieces available. Grecian couches, desks with more drawers and cubicles and nooks than she could have imagined, and a vast assortment of chairs carved from mahogany or satinwood or rosewood, all rich with decoration. It was head-spinning.

The next pattern book was from a masonry shop and opened to numerous plasterwork motifs of the popular Greco-Roman mold. They saw dozens and dozens of figures, cartouches, vignettes, and busts. Greek nudes, barely clad Roman women, figures dancing, playing instruments, holding torches. Cherubs, pagan gods and goddesses; it was the sort of decoration that was all the rage, evident in the Romanesque pilasters and cornices and roundels in the very room where they sat.

"Did you ever notice, Lavinia, that the Greeks and Romans were shockingly pagan?" Ariana asked.

" 'Tis true," she said, "but I never gave it much thought."

"Imagine the beauty of these designs if they were to incorporate heavenly themes."

Lavinia gave an appreciative look at her friend. "What a novel thought! I wonder why there is no pattern book of such ideas."

"I suppose it would not be considered Greco-Roman, which is the ideal nowadays."

"Unfortunate, Ariana." Lavinia said, in a droll tone. "You would have much redecorating to do if there were such a book."

Ariana gazed off into space. Why should there not be such decorations? Why could there not be elegant winged angels in place of pagan nymphs? Or the twelve apostles instead of the Greek pantheon?

Suddenly it occurred to her that here was the very thing she could leave in the house—some small evidences of herself. Nothing too drastic or expensive, just a few small influences for Christianity rather than mythology. She felt as though a door of new possibilities had opened before her. Grosvenor Square was indeed a magnificent place, but it was all classical, all based on Grecian and Roman designs. If she could heighten the appeal of the house by incorporating Judeo-Christian artistry, might it not please Mr. Mornay? With a new excitement, Ariana started to look around as though she had never *really* looked before. It must have been providence that spurred Mrs. Bentley to send for the tradesmen. And now she, Ariana, would be able to show that she could indeed manage a fine house. Beginning with plasterwork, she was going to make changes such as would be impossible *not* to note. She would ensure that a visit to the Mornay establishment would be a memorable visit indeed!

Three

Half an hour passed before Mrs. Bentley returned to the drawing room and joined the others. She was full of praise for what she had seen of the bedchambers. They were so finely appointed that it felt soul-enlightening, even to her tenured eyes. Unlike some houses of the wealthy, nothing was overdone here. All was tasteful—bits of opulence, small accents of gold paint or filigree, a bust or painting just where it should be and enough to ensure that one felt surrounded by excellent quality in furnishings but was not overwhelmed by it.

Still excited by her new idea, Ariana trailed Mrs. Hamilton with bright eyes. Miss Herley came and squeezed her hand, and she smiled back at her.

"We shall begin at the top of the house," Mrs. Hamilton announced in a reedy voice, "and we'll work our way down until we've seen every inch of it."

"Your plan is fine, Mrs. Hamilton," Mrs. Bentley said. She was too used to being the one in charge and hadn't thought to allow her niece to give the approval.

"This is *so* diverting!" Lavinia gushed in a passionate whisper. "I cannot believe I am here, seeing Mr. Mornay's house!"

"You'll be here again, my dear Lavinia," Ariana reminded her.

"Yes! Because you will live here. When we first met, did I not tell you that you would be snatched up directly? But who could have thought, then, that you would make the most brilliant match? And after we collided into Mr. Mornay! Do you recall?" She laughed afresh at the memory.

Ariana smiled. "Of course. Could I forget that?" But she turned her attention to climbing the second flight of steps, still following Mrs. Hamilton. This floor, appearing as the third level from the street, held mostly servants' quarters, including a fine large chamber for the housekeeper and a suite of two adjoining rooms for the butler. They peeked into first one, then another, and Ariana inquired of the housekeeper whether she was comfortable in her chamber.

Mrs. Hamilton's interpretation of the question was that Miss Forsythe wished to know how *her* housekeeper would like it. Thinking quickly she answered, "We try not to mind the cold, ma'am, and the mattresses are as fine as any servant's, I warrant. I am certain all mattresses must be exceedingly hard on a body."

Lavinia and Ariana exchanged surprised glances. Mrs. Bentley's face puckered into thought, and though she moved on with the others to miss nothing, she made a little mental note to return to the housekeeper's chamber later.

Farther down the hall, the group was peeking into the rooms for the common servants, where two or three shared the same chamber. There was nothing unusual, but Ariana had never seen communal servants' quarters and said, "It must be difficult to sleep with the beds so close together."

Mrs. Bentley, with narrowed eyes, returned, "They are tired from a day's work, my dear. Servants fall right to sleep, I assure you." She gave Mr. Pellham a look as if to say, "The nonsense from this child!" Ariana believed that her statement was sadly all too true.

As mistress of Grosvenor Square, she would endeavour to be the kindest of mistresses. Not so much that the servants would be emboldened to take advantage of her, but she did hope to allow them what little acts of mercy she could, while maintaining decorum and propriety.

She would have a few words with Mr. Mornay regarding the comments Mrs. Hamilton had made too. Why would he, as wealthy as he was, not allow his servants more comfortable furnishings? She supposed, thinking while they moved on, that he must be unaware of such conditions.

They skipped seeing the garret, for Mrs. Hamilton said it was mostly used for storage and descended the narrow servants' staircase to the first floor. They had to go single file and made a bit of racket on the wooden steps, but they were all in good spirits when they reached their destination.

Here were the rooms of most interest, and which held the finest luxuries: fine art, expensive trinkets, rich draperies, exquisite wallpapers, plush and beautiful furniture. They passed through a sitting room, a parlour, a small armoury, and gallery. As each room's beauty unfolded before them, Ariana's eyes fluttered with surprise.

Such a rich house! Mr. Mornay was far wealthier than she had imagined. She took a long time in the gallery, viewing the paintings. Mrs. Bentley finally had to say, "Come, my gel. You will have plenty of time in the future for study." Farther down the hall were the bedchambers, and by now Ariana's demeanour had become quite serious. She was feeling downright daunted by her future home. Evidently people of great taste and knowledge had furnished it. How could she aspire to alter a single thing?

Mrs. Hamilton stopped at a door, her hand on the knob. "This is the Master's bedchamber," she said, beginning to turn the handle. Ariana's heart beat strongly. Miss Herley tried to make her smile by making a face at her and opening her eyes wide.

"Are we not," Ariana said to the housekeeper, "intruding on Mr. Mornay's privacy?"

The lady turned in surprise. "The Master instructed me to show you all of the house, ma'am."

"You will wish to see this room, my dear," said Mrs. Bentley.

Mrs. Hamilton led the way and then stepped to the side, as she did throughout the tour. She was not forthcoming with facts about the house or any of its possessions, and Ariana wondered at her lack of enthusiasm. There was no affection in her tone or manner, which was surprising. It was not unusual for upper servants to feel as if the house they served in was their own, and many would display all due pride when showing it. But not Mrs. Hamilton.

Thoughts of the housekeeper fled as Ariana entered the room and had to pull in her breath at the sight. In addition to watered-silk wallpaper and a large and glossy mahogany bed, the ceiling had a huge painted roundel. Against a rich blue sky with light puffs of clouds, there were heavenly angels and cherubs with musical instruments surrounding a centre of light in bright hues of yellow and gold and white. It was heavenly. It was glorious. It was—*religious*! Just the sort of thing she wished to see more of in the house.

Mrs. Bentley had been watching her reaction and had a little, knowing smile on her face. Miss Herley rushed and grasped her hand. "I should never have a night's poor sleep in such a room! You must endeavour to sleep here, Ariana, as much as possible!"

Mr. O'Brien did not turn to look at them but cleared his throat loudly. The two girls noted it and then looked at each other. Lavinia, with one hand to her mouth, stifled a giggle.

Beatrice had rushed around the room, saw the adjoining dressing room, and came back to say, "I think Mr. Mornay is as rich as the Regent! Or perhaps richer! For the prince, I heard my father say, is always in want of money."

Ariana was too in awe of the house—and its owner—to offer a reply. It was as though she had not known him, in a way. She had hoped to discover more about him by studying his house, but not simply that his wealth was vastly greater than she'd imagined. He was already too easily intimidating, and his recent disinterested attitude toward her only made him seem more so now. He was truly from a background that was surperior to hers, in a worldly sort of reckoning.

She looked back up at the ceiling. The angels looked serenely back at her. She tore her eyes from the room to pass through a communicating door to the next bedchamber. It was no less impressive. Whoever had designed the house had evidently understood that people liked to occasionally spend time in their bedchambers. A beautiful escritoire sat invitingly off to one side, and there was an adjoining dressing room here as well. It was lovely, indeed, but—separate bedchambers?

At home her parents shared one room. She looked back at the communicating door and felt an odd emptiness in her heart. Then a pang. Instead of feeling closer to the man she was going to marry, this day seemed to be accenting their recent lack of closeness. Did Mr. Mornay, then, not hold to the idea of a single bedchamber for the master and mistress? Despite her natural shyness of what the marriage bed represented, she felt disappointed.

Meanwhile Mrs. Herley and Mrs. O'Brien were enraptured, as they had been at every bit of the house. Mrs. Bentley was pointing out details to Mr. Pellham, who nodded and commented in turn.

Miss Herley was moving slowly around the perimeter of the room, looking over the wallpaper and furniture and accessories, as if she was in a museum. Her mother was all agog, to be sure, but there was also a slight frown between her brows, as she wondered why her Lavinia couldn't attract such a man of high standing and wealth. She eyed the expensive items in the room with a jealous eye.

Mr. O'Brien was trailing his mother and saying very little, watching Ariana a great deal but speaking mostly to Beatrice, and then only to keep her exuberance in check. And there was Mrs. Hamilton, stiff and silent, coldly watching everyone. Once again Ariana felt that strange sense of detachment. It seemed odd to her that it was close to the wedding date, and yet she had no feeling of *belonging* to the house.

Continuing on they went quickly through the remaining two guest bedchambers and then circled back to the first parlour. Ariana was keeping an eye out and now saw many pagan designs that she thought might be altered—but at the same time, she felt like a trespasser. How could she think of changing anything in such a dwelling? But then she knew she would feel more comfortable with less pagan designs surrounding her. Mr. Mornay had professed a newfound faith only two weeks earlier and at first had spoken with much enthusiasm regarding it. His love for God seemed to be growing steadily, had it not? Mr. Mornay, despite his recent reticence, would surely view the changes in the same light she did. He would welcome them. Just as he was welcoming her.

Just then the merchants came eagerly into the room. "May I suggest, ma'am," said one man, coming at her with a stare as though he was a hunter settling upon his prey, "a lighter wallpaper in this room?" Another said, "A new carpet is the thing needed here. An Axminster, I'd respectfully suggest, ma'am." Ariana met each remark with an expression of consideration, but she remained silent as she moved on through the room, followed closely by the merchants.

Her heart was beating palpably—if she failed to make the alterations right now, when the chance was before her, it would be because she was afraid that Mr. Mornay was indeed having a change of heart. Toward her, and even worse, perhaps toward God. Yet their history up to this time had been such that his love for her was clear and strong. She had to trust it. She had to trust that God had indeed brought them together and had good plans for their future as husband and wife.

With that thought in mind, she told herself that she had every right to bespeak a few new things for the house. The bevy of men were following her every move, suggestions ringing out regularly, but she ignored them.

A huge painted panel on the wall caught her eye, and she stopped before it. It was a masterfully executed pastoral scene, but the theme was an abundance of barely clad wood nymphs and a satyr. A picture of the Garden of Eden came to her mind. What a pleasing contrast it would be to this godless design. "Let me describe for you what I envision here," she began, and two men jumped forward, pencils and pads in hand, prepared to take notes.

Mrs. Herley, meanwhile, was overtaken with admiration for a little miniature portrait of the king, located on a section of wall in a corner among other small pieces of artwork. She never could believe the monarch had gone mad, though Parliament *had* voted in favour of the Regency. But such a good king! So upright a monarch! She could not help but to stretch out her gloved hand and touch the glass.

Across the room, the O'Briens had finished their inspection and were prepared to leave with Beatrice happily in tow. They said their goodbyes while Beatrice rushed at her sister for an effusive hug. Aunt Bentley said, "That's enough, Miss Beatrice! You will give your sister an ague!"

It was no longer a proper tour, as people began to scatter to areas of interest. Ariana slowly circled the first floor again, with the merchants eagerly following. She had no wish to make extensive alterations, of course. Just a few touches here and there would do. An artisan jotted notes whenever she stopped to suggest a new theme for a bit of statuary or bit of plasterwork—there were more nudes and pagan scenes than she had formerly realized. The men treated each of her suggestions with the utmost gravity and understanding.

Mrs. Hamilton tried to maintain distance from Miss Forsythe, but she determined to remain with her and observe her doings. She wished to know of any impending changes in her domicile—the master's domicile to be precise. It offended her mightily that the lady was evidently authorizing alterations in a dwelling that was already perfect. Moreover, she wasn't even the mistress yet!

In the dining room, Ariana noticed the medallions alongside the windows, all of which bore similar Romanesque carvings of goddesses in flimsy robes.

"I have just the thing to replace these," one man said, picking up on her tastes. "The same style of elegance and craftsmanship but with a decorated wreath surrounded by ornament and little cherubs."

"As long as the figures are properly draped, sir. I will not countenance," Ariana said, choosing her words carefully, "an absence of clothing, even in a cherub." Her cheeks flamed crimson, but there she had said it!

"Very good, ma'am." He made a note on his pad. "Shall we replace all four of these panels with the new design, then?" He eyed her expectantly. "You do of course want uniformity."

"Of course," she said sagely, though uniformity had never before occupied her thoughts.

"Ma'am, I have just the designer to meet your needs," said another man stepping forward. "Tell me which figures are acceptable to you; Moses, King David, or members of the Holy Family, perhaps?"

"Yes. Yes, any or all of them sound fine to me," she said with relief.

Eagerly he added, "My man does freestanding sculptures as well. Pointing to a corner that held a Roman bust of a soldier, with its style of peculiarly blank eyes, on a columnar pedestal, he continued, "Shall we say a bust of the head of St. Peter here?"

"Make it Mary Magdalene," she replied, without having known that she would have such a preference. My, but this was interesting. She was discovering her own tastes. And she did have them. She had preferences that had never been known as there had never been an opportunity to exercise them before.

A loud crash from the hall interrupted them. When they turned to see what had happened, they saw that Mrs. Hamilton, with a set mouth, was already investigating. Without missing a beat, the merchant added, "And in that corner, ma'am, we can replace that coldish looking statue with a very good bust of the mother of God. Wouldn't you agree?"

Did she agree? The mother of God? He meant the mother of Jesus. That would be Mary. She saw no cause to disagree and mumbled, "Yes, fine." The shopkeepers were making it all quite easy for her. "Very good, ma'am," was the standard reply.

Of a bas-relief Roman soldier in a chariot, she asked, "Can you make this Elijah in a chariot of fire? You need only add some flame effects, remove the helmet, and add hair and a beard." The man jotted furiously onto his pad, nodding his head.

In the study he suggested replacing the huntress Diana with the two hounds, pointing at a relief panel on one wall. Ariana looked thoughtfully at the area.

"Make it Nimrod."

"Nimrod the hunter? Oh, excellent, ma'am!" He eyed her with true admiration.

Where there were cupids or eros or mythical beasts, she asked for angels.

For every alteration suggested, the shopkeeper or artist suggested another. And all her decisions were met with praises of the highest regard—her taste was splendid, her choices, remarkable. The house would be a masterpiece and supremely fitting for the Paragon and his bride.

When Mrs. Bentley approached, Ariana asked, "What was the loud crash, Aunt Bentley?"

The older lady sniffed. "A bust, I'm afraid. Some soldier or statesman of

Rome, I warrant. Beatrice is too young for town. I was right on that account! Rushing around like a hoyden in this house. Mr. Mornay, I daresay, is bound to be out of countenance."

But Ariana had gone back to the pattern book before her, as though unconcerned.

"Does it not concern you?" her relation asked. "A fine sculptured bust, ruined?"

Ariana look up briefly. "We were getting rid of it, in any case, ma'am."

"We?" She gave the merchant a shrewd look, which he did his best to ignore. "Hmmm." She studied her niece thoughtfully. "I maintain it must be acceptable for a lady to make a few changes in her future abode, but pray, do not forget whose house you are in. Mr. Mornay should no doubt be consulted before you institute any grand—"

"But, Aunt, I mean to surprise him!"

"What? *You?*"

Ariana tried not to take offense at her aunt's tone. Surely she did not understand that just because Ariana didn't drool over fashion or millinery as her aunt did, it didn't have to follow that she had no taste at all.

"Everything is of the first water, my gel, and without Mornay here, I daresay you must be conservative in your plans." When Ariana did not respond, she added, with a little asperity, "Do you not think so?"

"Conservative?" Ariana smiled. "Aunt Bentley, I want above all things to be conservative." She pointed at bas-relief nudes on the wall. "I have ordered a new panel here," she said, with a satisfied look.

"You're replacing this? Why, what's wrong with it?" the lady asked, mystified.

Mr. Pellham had come in earlier, overheard some of the dialogue, and was smiling, understanding instantly how it was. And then Mrs. Bentley caught on and looked with alarm at her niece. "My gel, this is the classical style! No one thinks of this as anything but art. No one pays any attention to it at all, I daresay!"

"Then no one shall notice I've changed it," she replied.

Her aunt made a grimace. "What else have you authorized?"

"The addition of angels, a few paintings, and plasterwork. That sort of thing."

Mrs. Bentley stared at her niece. It seemed so unlike Ariana to take charge of anything so momentous as changing the Paragon's dwelling—even if she was soon to share it—that all she could do was stare for a moment. *The girl is growing up, that much is evident. All the better,* she thought. *Marriage and children will be easier for her.*

Resigned, Mrs. Bentley accepted Mr. Pellham's arm and followed her niece to the kitchens to complete their tour of the house. They saw a beautiful and very respectable library and Mr. Mornay's handsome study, a business office, the butler's closet, the wine cellar, and now the servants' hall and kitchens. Everyone was tired, and so Ariana requested a tray of cold meats and scones. They went back upstairs to a morning room to enjoy it.

The shopkeepers, all except the plasterers and sculptors, were disappointed with the results of the time they had spent at Grosvenor Square that day and left dispiritedly. The plate manufacturer had tried admirably to persuade the young bride-to-be that it was entirely fitting for a new dinner service to be made, but Ariana was growing dismayed at all the changes she had authorized. Thinking of the expense, she wouldn't hear of it. He flew to Mrs. Bentley, who offered the opinion that Ariana should indeed order new plates with a matching tea and coffee service, at the least. A fat catalogue of designs was produced. The Mornay coat of arms was suggested, but Ariana declined it. Too masculine.

Mrs. Herley and Mrs. O'Brien could not remain impervious to this discussion and offered their opinions. All three women tightly surrounded Ariana and strained to see the catalogue she held. Ariana could not stand up to the force of the three ladies and conceded to a Staffordshire set with a soft floral pattern, which she would customize by having the scrolling initials P and A incorporated into the design. Her heart beat faster at saying the initials. It was so exciting that she would soon be Mrs. Mornay. She, a married woman! Phillip, her husband!

Afterward Ariana dismissed all the merchants, thanking them for their time, and settled down to enjoy another round of refreshments with her guests before they were off. Mrs. Bentley, though she sorely needed a cup of tea, made some excuse and left the room. Mr. Pellham followed her. When she began to climb the stairs to the servants' quarters, he did likewise.

Mrs. Bentley continued on to the housekeeper's room and sat down abruptly on the bed. In fact she tried to bounce on it, all the while displaying a little, dissatisfied expression. Mr. Pellham looked on with no surprise whatsoever. Mrs. Bentley always had a reason for what she did. He might not understand it, but he knew if she deemed it necessary to bounce upon the housekeeper's bed, then it must be necessary.

Mrs. Bentley, frowning, rose and began to sternly examine the room.

She noted the size of the fireplace, the quality of the bedding and curtains, the fine desk, rocking chair, and carpet.

"Mr. Pellham," she said, "would you be so kind as to sit upon this bed for one moment?" With his usual amiability, he murmured, "But of course, Mrs. B." He went and sat on the bed.

"How do you find it?" she asked.

"Perfectly comfortable, Mrs. B."

"Humph!" said the lady. "Thank you, Mr. Pellham."

"Not at all, Mrs. B."

Before leaving the premises, Mrs. Bentley accomplished one more deed that had been on her mind. She took the housekeeper aside to tell her that Molly, employed in the kitchens, was a scurrilous, untrustworthy servant. She related what had occurred at Hanover Square and Molly's ignoble hand in it. Mrs. Hamilton was shocked by the disclosure and said she would keep a sharp eye on the little servant.

"Mrs. Hamilton," replied Mrs. Bentley firmly, "what you needs must do is dismiss her. I shudder at the thought of my niece being in the same household as that dishonest creature. Do you understand?"

"I do, ma'am." Her tone was apologetic. "I will speak to the master about it and, with his leave, do as you suggest."

Mrs. Hamilton watched the group leave, with a feeling of relief. This new information about Molly intrigued her. Under normal circumstances, she would certainly have dismissed the servant at once, but she remembered that the master had brought the girl to the household and would therefore need his express leave to do so. Perhaps (this made her smile inwardly), *perhaps* she had stumbled onto information that might be very useful in the future. Molly would surely want to keep her place. Though she was a scullery maid, there was the possibility of working her way up in such a household. Mrs. Hamilton herself had started in the kitchens as a young girl. Which meant Molly would be eager to do exactly as Mrs. Hamilton directed.

Four

Mr. Mornay came home early that evening to a house astir with servants.

"Good afternoon, sir." Frederick greeted the master with a mild look of trepidation. Mr. Mornay saw a couple of chambermaids go hieing from one room into another and looked in surprise at his butler, who said only, "Mrs. Hamilton would like a word with you, sir, at your soonest convenience."

When Mrs. Hamilton had been summoned to Phillip's study, he bade her come in and looked up from his desk expectantly.

"I beg your pardon, sir" she began. "But I thought you'd want to know." She hesitated, nervously wringing a handkerchief in her hands.

"Well?"

"After Miss Forsythe was here, I found, sir, that a silver candlestick has gone missing."

He raised an eyebrow. This gained his full interest and he put his head back to listen more attentively. "Perhaps it is being cleaned."

"I checked with all the servants, sir. That candlestick was there before I took her around, but now 'tis gone. I have the entire household searching for it, sir, but it's no good. It isn't here!"

He looked back down at the stack of papers on his desk. "I'll look into it, Mrs. Hamilton. Thank you."

"Yes, sir."

The woman remained standing there, so he added, "Is there anything else?"

"Yes, sir. I believe it might interest you to know that Miss Forsythe ordered new relief panels for the dining room."

This was a surprise, but he showed no change outwardly. "Very good. Thank you."

"And for the parlour and the gallery and library."

"*Very well.*"

"And the Roman bust in the hall near the drawing room was broken to pieces, I'm afraid, by one of the guests." She hurried on. "And statuary has been removed from the dining room and other areas for the purpose of measuring new ones."

"*One* of the guests? Who else was here? Mrs. Bentley, I suppose?"

At the sight of Mr. Mornay's mild scowl, Mrs. Hamilton's heart lightened. "There were eight people in all, sir."

"Eight?" He was surprised but said nothing, merely returning to his magazine before him, thinking for a moment. "You mentioned new sculpture. Did Miss Forsythe state her objection to the old ones?"

She cleared her throat. He looked up.

"They were immodest, sir. According to Miss Forsythe, they were pagan or lacking grace."

"Immodest?" He had to think for a moment, and then he quickly ducked his head down again.

"Very good, Mrs. Hamilton. Thank you. That will be all."

"Mr. Mornay, sir?"

He looked up again. She was waiting for him to lose his temper. Of course she had no desire for it to happen on her account, but on account of Miss Forsythe's meddling with his interior decoration. When he realized his housekeeper was waiting for some kind of encouragement, he asked, "What is it, Mrs. Hamilton?"

"Forgive me, sir," she said, "but I feel it necessary to inform you of this as well." She looked uncomfortable to the extreme but continued, "Miss Forsythe expressed an interest, sir, in occupying...the master bedchamber." She said this with a perfectly straight face, though her discomfort was evident.

"She wishes to oust me from my own bedchamber?"

"No. Forgive me, sir. She wishes to *share* your bedchamber."

His face didn't betray the least change, but inside his heart took a leap. Here was the biggest surprise yet. Didn't women always want their own bedchamber? The deep ache instantly accosted him. There was no appearance of the famous temper. "I'll speak to her about it." His eyes went back to his periodical.

Mrs. Hamilton's mouth pursed in disapproval, but there was nothing else she could do. In her opinion, and she had many of them, this business of sharing a bedchamber was evidence of ill-breeding. It was her understanding that the highest members of society kept separate bedchambers. It didn't mean that they always slept apart, but that they *could*. This had been further proof, in her opinion, of a serious shortcoming in the future mistress. Not that she needed proof.

She kept her eyes carefully averted from her employer's as she continued, "Shall I do anything about the broken sculpture?"

He looked up. "How did it break?"

"The younger Miss Forsythe was...scampering about like a hoyden, sir, and it fell."

He pushed out his chair and sat back, his arms behind his head comfortably. The idea of Ariana sharing his bedchamber had put him in a thoroughly optimistic mood. Far from being displeased over the broken statuary, or the apparently large-scale changes in his dwelling which were to occur, he was actually feeling quite generous. "Unless it can be fixed, there is nothing that can be done, Mrs. Hamilton. I'll see that your wages are compensated for the trouble today, however."

She stared at him stupidly for a moment. He didn't seem to understand that she had been reporting on his betrothed with the purpose of arousing his wrath. In fact he wasn't the least bit put out and had offered her extra wages! She remembered herself enough to curtsey and say, "Thank you, sir."

His placid eyes met hers, and he asked, "Is there anything else?"

"No, sir. Good day, sir." Her words were tinged with disappointment.

She turned to leave, but he called her back.

"You do understand, Mrs. Hamilton, that Miss Forsythe will be your mistress, and, as such, she has my complete authority to do as she wishes?"

She curtseyed again. "Yes, of course, sir."

"Is that a problem for you?"

"Not at all."

"Very good." As she turned to go once more, he said, "I'll eat supper early. Have Fotch ready for me, say, in one hour."

"Very good, sir. Will you be taking supper in the dining room, sir?"

This drew a mild scowl. "I'll take it here, as I often do." He looked at her searchingly again. She seemed a bit pigeon-headed today. When he was alone, he often ate in his study. The dining room, he reserved for company.

Mrs. Hamilton said, a little in her defense, "I thought you might wish to see what work has already begun, sir." The room in fact was rather a mess at the moment, for workers had gone straight to it, already removing panels and pieces of bas-relief for Ariana's changes. And she had forbidden the maids to clean up the area as yet, hoping that the disarray might upset her fastidious master.

"I'll see it when it's finished," he said, without lifting his head again. He set his magazine down and began to sift through the mail. More charitable requests? How was it that every asylum, hospital, or medical society suddenly knew his direction? It was as if attending the service at the orphanage had opened a floodgate leading directly to his house. He went through the latest stack quickly, picked out one he thought might use his donation to the best effect, and left a note for his man of business.

Disgruntled, Mrs. Hamilton made her way back to her chamber slowly. *Something* had to be done to ensure that life went on as before at Grosvenor Square. Not only was the master smitten with Miss Forsythe—that much was evident—the rest of the staff was too. Only she, Mrs. Hamilton, seemed to understand that situations were in peril. Life was about to undergo a vast disruption. And she would have to set things right. At least there was Molly, she reflected, to somehow use for her purpose.

Mr. Mornay had said nothing about her being replaced with a new housekeeper. She knew enough of her master to realize that he would give proper warning if such a thing were to occur. This should have softened her heart toward Ariana, but it did not. Mrs. Hamilton expected that the young lady was just crafty enough to keep her plans to herself until she was safely installed as his wife. *I am no fool. I know how the world works. Good thing I led the tour—it was a great opportunity to keep preparing for my future.*

She would need to survive on much less wages than she was making at present—perhaps none. The silver candlestick would fetch a pretty price, of that she was certain. But it wouldn't be enough. In fact, it would take a lot for Mrs. Hamilton to feel that she had been compensated for losing this situation. Working for Mr. Mornay had by far been the best paying and most gratifying work of her lifetime. Servants from other households treated her with great respect when they understood her prestigious situation. She would need good savings, not only to make up for its loss but to prevent ending up at Draper's, as her mother had.

Besides, even if the future Mrs. Mornay did not plan on dismissing me, no doubt my influence and authority are about to be severely diminished. It will never be the same. The mistress will now be consulted on all domestic matters, even if I am required to put them into effect. My own opinions are to be subject to that young chit's! How can it be borne? How do other housekeepers bear it? It was a mystery to her.

The candlestick had been a sudden brilliant revelation. There were plenty of pawn shops about. No difficulty should be encountered on that head, moving goods for cash. And, of course, in this house there were many, many goods available.

As Ariana stepped down from the carriage, arriving home after the visit to Grosvenor Square, three ladies who had been standing near the house hurried toward her. She stopped in surprise. Mrs. Bentley had gone off with Mr. Pellham on a small errand, and the others had returned to their homes. Even Beatrice was not with her, as she had gone to stay with the O'Briens at her aunt's insistence. (Sometimes there was just no changing that woman's mind!)

So when the threesome converged on her in front of the house, she was by herself.

"I say, Miss Forsythe!"

A footman had opened the door to the house, and Haines appeared. He saw the women and a worried look came over his face.

"Miss Forsythe! We beg your pardon," the speaker said, already breathing hard because she was not young, "for accosting you in the street this way. But you see," she continued, glancing at her companions, "'twas the only method we could find to gain audience with you."

"You might have called upon me at any time, I assure you," Ariana said, touched by their earnestness.

"Oh, my dear," spoke the lady in the middle. She was a bit plump in form, had a kindly, grandmotherly sort of face, but looked weary beneath a pretty bonnet. "We did try, you must know. Either I or my friends here left at least a dozen cards. I hoped you would return a call," she said, huffing a little, "but I am not often in London, and I suppose if you tried, I was not in residence."

Ariana glanced at the open door and said, "Please, let us talk inside."

The three women looked at each other with unreadable expressions. One spoke up. "Miss Forsythe, we beg your pardon, but we understand that our company is not welcomed by your aunt."

The girl's eyes underwent one of their intriguing colour changes, turning bluish-green. "Indeed?" she asked. "Are you certain?"

They nodded.

This was very surprising to Ariana, but she said blithely, "Well, my aunt is not home at present, and I am sure you are welcome at the moment. Now, please, follow me."

Haines, with a troubled look on his face, accepted their shawls, giving them immediately to a footman. "Ma'am, may I have a word with you?" He then looked at the footman and told him, "Show Miss Forsythe's guests to the *sitting room*, John."

The sitting room was never used to entertain callers, and Ariana looked at the butler in stark astonishment. She wanted to cry, "Haines! The sitting room?" but knew that there must be some reason behind it. "Orders," he said, in a low tone and with a look fraught with meaning.

Ariana felt more bewildered than ever.

Haines, perceiving her puzzlement, said in a low voice, "The mistress says that woman must not to be allowed to gain entrance to this establishment."

"There are three women, Haines."

"Yes, I was referring to the one in the middle," he said.

Ariana cocked an eyebrow at him. "But why? Who is she?"

Haines seemed startled. "That is Mrs. Southcott, the one they call a 'prophetess.'"

Ariana gasped, a strange light coming into her eyes. "Indeed."

"May I have your permission to show them out? You needn't face them."

But she was thinking. "By no means. I will see this Mrs. Southcott."

She left the poor man standing with the thought that he had utterly failed his mistress. Were Mrs. Bentley to arrive home with Mrs. Southcott under her roof—who knew what could result?

He checked his watch fob and, looking to heaven, shook his head worriedly.

When Ariana entered the sitting room, the ladies started to rise.

"Please, do not," she said with astonishment. Her cheeks flushed slightly with embarrassment.

"I daresay you know who I am now," Mrs. Southcott said, with a little sad smile.

"Yes." Ariana sat down upon a chair facing the women on the sofa. The fact that they had tried for so long to see her softened any suspicions the lady's reputation might have given her, and she asked, "May I offer you refreshments?"

Mrs. Southcott sat forward and replied, in a strong tone, "My bread is to do the will of Him who sent me. I have no appetite for any other."

"I see," Ariana said, appreciating the woman's zeal. "May I ask what you wished to see me about?"

"I wished to see you, Miss Forsythe, to give you a gift." Mrs. Southcott nodded at one of her companions, who drew forth a packet of letters sealed with ribbon. She handed them to Ariana.

"Some of your writings?" Ariana held out her slim hand.

Mrs. Southcott nodded. "For your perusal." She paused. "I have been told of your great sense of religion, Miss Forsythe. I am hoping to find a friend in you."

When Ariana said nothing, she continued. "I am afraid...I am in great need of support." She looked apologetically at Ariana. "I am sorry to put it to you so plainly, my dear. I hoped to nurture a friendship first, but as I have been prevented to wait upon you in this establishment, as we said earlier, I find that I have no recourse but to come straight to the point. No doubt you have seen the abuse that is hurled upon me in the papers." Her eyes widened with indignation.

Ariana nodded. The news had often been sprinkled with so-called *prophecies* of Mrs. Southcott's and then a barrage of letters, vindictive to her cause.

"I have *many* enemies," she said sadly. She looked questioningly at Ariana. "Must I count you as one of them? Be plain with me, I beg you."

"May I never be an enemy to anyone who seeks God in truth and according to the Scriptures, Mrs. Southcott."

For the first time, the lady smiled. She had a warm smile and her eyes twinkled in an agreeable manner, such as a grandmother's might. "Does that mean, Miss Forsythe, that I may depend upon you for support? I have recently lost a very great benefactor, the Marquess of Deane. He suddenly decided not to accept my last vision. I count it as a great shame—for his soul's sake as much as for my own welfare. May I hope, my dear ma'am, that you will consider supplying what he has ceased to provide?"

Coming from somewhere in the house, Mrs. Bentley's voice could be heard—she did not sound pleased. Ariana frowned, looked once more at the packet of letters, and said, "I have very little means at present, but I will read your papers and consider what you have asked."

The ladies looked at her in stark unbelief. She saw their expressions and added, "You have heard a rumour, I assure you, if you are thinking that I am a lady of means." They were still staring at her a little wide-eyed, and their looks wandered to the rich upholstery and the fittings in the room, all of which belied her words.

"Despite what appearances would have you think," Ariana added, "I am not a wealthy woman."

There was a moment's awkward silence until one of them said bluntly, "But you will be—soon. Is that not so?"

Ariana felt as though she had eager children in the room, and she smiled. "Why do you not contact me after my marriage? I may be in a position to do something for you."

"I have your permission to do so?"

"By all means. However, I cannot promise you, for I really must better acquaint myself with your writings. But I do plan to discover ways, as a lady of means, to do my best to aid in the comfort and welfare of the oppressed and the poor and, of course, to further the kingdom of God in whatever way He puts at my disposal."

"There are many evangelicals who are sympathetic to my cause," said Mrs. Southcott, a little defensively. But Ariana was being cautious. Her natural inclination was to help anyone who asked, but she was not at liberty to exercise such abandon—she had no money of her own. And what if the reports regarding the lady were true? She would certainly not support heresy! She said, "Send your correspondence to number 25 Grosvenor Square. I will soon be mistress there, and in the meantime, Mr. Mornay and I shall read your writings and study the matter together."

Mrs. Southcott looked at Ariana with a shrewd expression. "Do not allow fear of the opinion of mere man to interfere with godliness, Miss Forsythe. I daresay you would do everything in your power to aid me if you were to cast aside the fear of man!"

Ariana's large eyes were fastened on Mrs. Southcott's. She was not overly quick-witted, but she somehow managed to come up with an answer. "I have not had the pleasure of reading your words, Mrs. Southcott," she said gently, lifting the packet of letters in her hand slightly. "Even you must allow that we are told to 'try the spirits,' and then to 'hold fast that which is good.' You must give me time to try, to test what you have said here."

Mrs. Southcott nodded. "Yes, of course. Which is why I have tried to gain an audience with you heretofore, so that you could read the words for yourself and be fully assured of their divine inspiration."

"I do apologize on that account," Ariana acceded.

"We have encountered such things before," said another of the ladies.

"Nay, and will again, no doubt," added Mrs. Southcott, "as do all who truly seek to do God's will!"

Ariana nodded sympathetically. She could see nothing in this lady to make her doubt the woman's earnestness and wanted to read the letters very much.

A firm knock on the door was followed by the entrance of Mrs. Bentley. At her heels was Lord Horatio, a mutual friend of hers and Mr. Mornay's.

"Lord Horatio is here for you, my dear," said Mrs. Bentley, with a firm undertone that Ariana could not mistake. Neither, apparently, could Mrs. Southcott, for she and her companions stood up abruptly and curtseyed to Ariana. His lordship came over and bowed politely, smiling, and took her hand and kissed the air above it. Meanwhile, Mrs. Bentley had a footman at the ready to show the women out.

"Thank you for your time, Miss Forsythe. It was a pleasure to make your acquaintance."

"And yours, Mrs. Southcott." She nodded at the other ladies. One of them stopped before her.

"When you are Mrs. Mornay, I pray you—" she said, giving Ariana a searching, heartfelt look, "do not forget Mrs. Southcott!"

Ariana watched them leave the room and clasped the bundle of papers tightly, convinced that she should certainly read them. The newspapers and recent broadsheets had presented Mrs. Southcott as a lady who had begun well and with sound doctrine but had lately become severely deluded. Ariana, in all fairness, would discover for herself if what they said was true. She glanced at Lord Horatio, who was also watching the ladies leave, and noticed that his expression was startlingly disapproving.

But Mrs. Bentley hurried to the front door, thinking that she had to make certain all her servants knew never, never to allow those ladies beneath her roof again.

Ariana brought Lord Horatio to the first floor parlour, where he filled her in on the excitement of the morning's fencing match and mentioned that her betrothed had been in attendance. When Mrs. Bentley returned to the room, her face was still set in a frown, and she crossed her arms unpromisingly across her chest.

"My gel!" she exclaimed, the moment the conversation paused. "Do you realize who you brought into this house?"

"Three harmless creatures, I am sure, ma'am."

"*Harmless?* Tag, rag, and bobtail are more like it! Mrs. Joanna Southcott and her two minions! Do you realize the harm to our reputation if they were to be seen leaving our establishment?"

"Our reputation? How can it signify, ma'am?"

"I realize you may have a certain...fascination with the likes of Mrs. Southcott, but you are not at liberty to indulge that interest at my expense. Or at yours. It would not do, my dear, to form an association with such a disgraceful person."

"Disgraceful? I had thought her to be controversial—"

"My dear, she has been castigated from the pulpit! *That woman,"* she said, pointing out toward the stairway in the direction that Mrs. Southcott had left, "claims to have heard from God that she is to bear a son by the Holy Spirit! Like the Virgin Mary! And at the age of sixty-five, no less! It is outright blasphemy."

Ariana gave a patient look at her aunt. "My dear aunt," she said, in a tone that sent her relation's eyes to the ceiling with impatience, "that may be naught but buffle-headed hearsay. I found nothing wanting in Mrs. Southcott's manners or bearing. She seemed very kind. I again must say I think her harmless."

Her aunt looked at her, perplexed. "If she enlists your sympathies, it can do much harm! You are about to wed a high-standing member of society. You will drag his name down with you if you espouse the cause of this...charlatan!"

Ariana did seem to consider these words, but she was certain her aunt was exaggerating.

"If Mr. Mornay shares your opinion, ma'am, I will not grant the lady my sympathies, I assure you. But I shall read her writings for myself, you must know." She looked at the bundle of papers, which she had set on the table after bringing them up from the room below. Mrs. Bentley saw them, took them in her hands, and, without the least warning, threw them into the fire in the grate.

"Aunt Bentley!" Ariana rushed forward, intent on salvaging the letters, which she felt sure she could accomplish by acting swiftly. But Lord Horatio was on his feet and just as speedily wrapped his arms strongly about hers, not allowing her to get any closer to the flames.

"You will not touch your hands to that fire!" he cried.

"Then you must do it for me!" She turned on him. He glanced at the lady of the house, who was watching with a dubious expression but was silent. So he turned and took the iron poker from nearby the grate and began to inch the papers out.

Now Mrs. Bentley spoke up. "No, my lord! You will burn the carpet!"

"That was very bad of you, Aunt!" Ariana responded, shocked at her aunt's behaviour.

"Don't get up in the boughs over it, for pity's sake." Mrs. Bentley's manner was annoyingly offhand. "I have no doubt that you would give aid to the devil himself if he were to appear hungry at your door!"

"My dear Aunt!" Ariana replied in tones of indignation.

Lord Horatio tried admirably to save the mass of papers, but thanks in part to the wide ribbon around them, which had taken instantly to flames, there was little to salvage. Already the papers had become no more than chunks of layered ash and were rapidly disintegrating into cinders.

"I'm sorry," he said standing up.

"Thank you for for your efforts," Ariana said. She was still appalled by her aunt and disappointed because she had been genuinely curious about Mrs. Southcott's writings. She determined immediately to write the lady, asking for another set of copies. She had left her card, so Ariana would know how to contact her. She did not want to injure the lady's sensibilities by admitting that her aunt had burned her writings, so she wouldn't mention it.

It occurred to her that Mrs. Southcott might take her interest for an endorsement, but Ariana would have to take that chance. As soon as his lordship had taken leave, Ariana went to her chamber and wrote the letter at once.

Five

That evening at the O'Brien's house on Blandford Street, Westminster, the talk was more animated than usual. In addition to discussing the elegance of the Paragon's home, while they sat in the parlour listening to Miss O'Brien play the pianoforte from the next room, Miss Beatrice Forsythe was also regaling them with her most decided opinions. She was delighted to be the sole guest of the family and the centre, therefore, of attention. This, combined with the family's determination to be pleased with her, ensured an agreeable arrangement.

Feeling at home, Beatrice gave her audience a firsthand account of her fondness for Peter. It was her determination to soothe his dashed hopes for her sister by marrying him herself, at the earliest age of consent. All this caused Peter to purse his lips and shake his head at her fondly. If he had not already apprised his family of Beatrice's sentiments, it might have been a shocking pronouncement.

Mr. Ian O'Brien, the eldest son, was home on shore leave and perhaps derived the greatest pleasure of them all with their guest, having now discovered a pleasant way to plague his sibling at every turn. He had merely to hint to Peter of his future "engagement" and that it was now a matter of honour, and there would be no escaping it.

Ian, in fact, could hardly contain his laughter, which caused Peter to lean in closely to his brother and deny any such declarations. Beatrice had spoken so earnestly to Mrs. O'Brien that the lady could only nod, amused. The girl, after all, was only twelve. No sense in dashing her hopes when age and maturity would set all to rights.

And if it did not? Mrs. O'Brien would not object to her son's connexion with a Forsythe—her sister was marrying the Paragon. Her aunt was Mrs.

Bentley, well-known and respected. Beatrice was perhaps too outspoken for one so young, but was not her elder sister also known for her forthrightness? She could not wholly dislike the trait.

Before the night had ended, it was determined that Miss Beatrice's stay with the family was a triumphant idea. The invitation was extended to the end of the season.

Peter chafed at the thought of having his young admirer on hand day and night, but he felt her presence to be a link, however feeble, to that of the elder Miss Forsythe. With that in mind, he could countenance it with equanimity.

Ariana's letter requesting a new set of writings from Mrs. Southcott had some unforeseen aftereffects. Mrs. Southcott, not being told of the demise of the first set of writings, assumed that the young lady wanted another copy to give to someone else, which she was happy to provide that very day. She also provided her friends (those who had not abandoned her, in any case) with the news that a new benefactress had been discovered. Mrs. Southcott hadn't received a shilling yet, she had to allow, but Miss Forsythe had asked for another copy of her writings! What could be more apparent than that she regarded Mrs. Southcott's cause favorably?

The two ladies who had accompanied Joanna Southcott also did their part in passing around the *on-dit* that Miss Forsythe had been friendly toward them. With remarkable speed, they mentioned it to their little circle of nonconformists. From there, who knows how it spread? But within hours it seemed that every outcast from traditional religion, those whom the Church of England did not approve of or wholly embrace for one reason or another, sent a solicitor or an emissary to Hanover Square, seeking support for their cause.

In a matter of days, yet more charities and causes somehow learned of this new philanthropist, and then word spread further so that even many of the traditional and orthodox charities threw in their invitations to fund-raising events. The sparkling salver in the hall at Hanover Square overflowed with correspondence near twice a day. And many representatives of these places came in person to try to see Miss Forsythe.

Haines had been given an earnest combing for having allowed Mrs. Southcott in the door, and so he was more than prepared to handle solicitations when they arrived. Due to his authority as the butler, he easily fended off all such persons. Even if Miss Forsythe was in the breakfast room or ground-floor sitting room, she never knew of their attempts to see her.

For all his soft-heartedness, Haines was very serious about his role as butler. He was the gatekeeper. His was the best defense the household had against the wrong sort of people who might try to gain entry. To Mrs. Bentley's mind, ever since Mrs. Southcott had dared to call, anyone having to do with a charitable organization—of any sort—must be denied access. Therefore, no matter how legitimate the cause, such as when the British and Foreign Bible Society called, hoping to speak with Miss Forsythe, Haines replied, "Certainly not! Be off with you!" Neither would he accept a card.

Such a reception was not encouraging, to be sure, but neither was it sufficient in and of itself to completely dissuade charities from trying their luck in some other way. Therefore, letters went out to Hanover Square and, to be safe, Grosvenor Square too. Word on the street was that the soon-to-be wife of the Paragon was philanthropically minded, and somehow this message reached the ears that were most interested in it. More missives went forth, courtesy of messengers or the London mail.

It was easy to turn away letters that came by mail and had not been paid on despatch. At the same time, living emissaries, who had been turned away at Hanover Square, went in a determined course toward Grosvenor Square. A small ripple at first seemed to quickly become a steady wave. More and more gentlemen and women knocked at the door, seeking support for a cause. Not a one got past Frederick to the master, but cards and letters did.

Mr. Mornay deduced quickly that Ariana had a hand in his sudden popularity with the charitable institutions of the city (indeed, more organizations than he knew had ever existed!). He did not wish to upbraid her for it. But one afternoon, Frederick came in, carrying his salver of letters. He was followed by two footmen, each carrying a similar salver. The three emptied the trays onto his desk, right in front of him. At the sight of such a large pile of correspondence, Mr. Mornay's countenance took on an unpromising look.

At that moment, a knock on the door revealed a worried looking Mrs. Hamilton. She had come to report another missing item and that the workmen in the dining room had a question for him regarding some plasterwork details. Mr. Mornay closed his eyes and reminded himself that his wedding was soon to occur and that Ariana, who was bringing all these annoyances to his life, was the woman he adored. He then opened his eyes and stood up, without having lost his temper.

"What item this time?" he asked, as he rounded his desk.

"Your gold-handled letter opener, sir."

He stopped and returned to his former position and opened a slim desk drawer. His look revealed the answer. It was gone, all right.

His face finally took on the severe demeanour that could send people scattering. "How in blazes did anyone gain access to this room?" His eyes fell upon Frederick. The man swallowed uncomfortably but clearly had no answer.

"It was brought to the kitchens for polishing, sir." Mrs. Hamilton spoke up. "When I instructed Molly to return it to its place today, she said it was gone."

"*Molly* said it was gone?"

"Yes, sir." Her face was carefully void of feeling.

"Who was in the house besides the usual servants?"

"This happened yesterday, sir, during Miss Forsythe's second visit."

Mornay frowned at the thought of Molly being involved. Ariana had asked after the servant numerous times. She had kept up her personal interest in the little maid so that Phillip had given his word that he would keep her on indefinitely.

"Neither of you will say aught of this to Miss Forsythe. Do you understand?"

"Yes, sir," Mrs. Hamilton replied and left the room.

"Yes, sir," Frederick said. When his master dismissed him, he turned to leave but paused and picked among the letters on the desk, saying, "You'll want to know of this one, sir. It came by a footman from Merrilton House."

Mr. Mornay opened the elegant invitation and found that he was being asked by Lady Merrilton to appear on the following night. The lack of notice was explained by the fact that the Regent had suddenly agreed to show and Lady Merrilton wanted to ensure his comfort by having his friends present.

The invitation included Miss Forsythe—a rather daring move, he thought, since they were as yet unwed. But it meant he would see his future bride. Although his heart lifted at the thought, he knew caution would be the order of the day. She surely would look as charming and beautiful as ever, and he would need to remain aloof.

He sent word to Hanover Square so she would expect him to call, and then started on the stack of letters before him. The Mornay family had never shirked its responsibility to those less well-off. He tried his best to see that his tenants in Middlesex were not neglected and always held a large Harvest Home even making a quick appearance for the event. Mingling among his tenants was not something he particularly enjoyed. They were generally a cheerful bunch, and it had always intensified his own peculiar lack of cheer.

Looking down at the slew of requests, he felt no desire to be clutch-fisted now, but why in thunder was there such an onslaught of solicitations? He thought of Ariana's pleasure at the orphanage when she had been able to suggest the amount to give, and he knew she had a hand in this. He'd have to broach the subject with her. There were limits to what he could do!

When Mr. Mornay called at Hanover Square the following evening, Ariana was thrilled to see him. No matter that they had only been apart for two days, it was wonderful to be near him. He received her hands warmly, kissed them, and greeted her quite satisfactorily, and she could not help but notice that he looked even more handsome than usual in his crisp evening wear. When he caught her studying him admiringly, he laughed in response and then quickly turned her toward the street and his waiting equipage. To her surprise, he had come for her in an open curricle, very unusual for a formal event. He remarked breezily that the weather was fine enough for it, but barely looked at her throughout the drive.

The roads were clogged with the usual *ton* traffic as people traveled from one engagement to the next. Mr. Mornay drove as swiftly as possible, going from Hanover Square, across New Bond Street, and along Brook Street. He continued along Grosvenor Square, adjacent to his own house, and then onto Upper Brook Street, where many coaches were stopped, dropping off or picking up passengers. Once that avenue had been cleared, he made a westerly quick turn onto Park Lane and did an admirable job manoeuvering through equipages to bring them right up to Merrilton House.

Lady Merrilton was a wealthy Tory hostess whose palatial dwelling overlooking Hyde Park was often the scene of heated political debate. It was also a town mansion that Ariana had not yet seen. She soon discovered that the grandeur and elegance at Merrilton House made even Grosvenor Square pale in comparison. There were whole rooms full of rococo art of the past century. Gilded furniture, domed alcoves, roundels and statuary, pilasters and columns, and elaborately carved plasterwork were everywhere and in such quantity, they brought Carlton House to mind. To her surprise, she found that it was rather too elaborate for her tastes and that she began to appreciate the measured gracefulness of Mr. Mornay's house more than ever.

Ariana was delighted to find that the Herleys were there, Mr. Herley being a staunch Tory. The Regent, however, had fallen ill and was not expected to make an appearance after all. Lady Merrilton made sure all her guests were aware of his absence and that they were invited again to her house in two nights. The prince had promised to make up for tonight's disappointment by giving his word to attend the event on Friday. Even more astonishing and rare a treat, his daughter, Princess Charlotte, would also be coming!

Women couldn't vote or appear in Parliament, and Ariana had no stomach to listen to the latest debates (she was not like Lady Merrilton, who invited any member of Parliament to her table if there was the slightest chance of winning his vote on a certain issue), so she accepted Lavinia's invitation to play a rubber of whist at a small side table in the long gallery.

Phillip had already taken a seat at the long table, his presence receiving due pomp from Lady Merrilton, who, like most society hostesses, coveted it. The sight of pretty Ariana and her friend at a small card table drew its own little circle—stragglers, those who were growing bored with talk of politics, and latecomers.

"If you hear of Mrs. Tiernan performing, my dear Lavinia," Ariana was saying, "you must insist upon attending. Your mama and papa would be delighted by her. I daresay anyone would!

"A dramatic actress, you say, by name of Tiernan? I cannot recall the name. Where would I have seen her? Drury Lane?"

"Oh, I believe she only does her readings for churches or charitable causes. She's a missionary—"

"For charitable causes? Lady Merrilton is seeking a performer at this very time for a worthwhile cause. Tell me of what and whom you speak." This was a question from Mr. Howland, a well-known aspirant of dandyism, which, in his case, included an inclination to try to make himself as useful as possible to the upper class.

"May I ask what is the worthwhile cause you mentioned?" Ariana doubted that Mrs. Tiernan would want to perform at Merrilton House, one of the biggest London palaces owned by a politically powerful family.

"The cause is no less than the Regent and Her Royal Highness, the princess!" If Miss Forsythe knew something of an entertainer who might serve, he needed to know about it. Ariana told him quickly about Mrs. Tiernan and her dramatic reading of Scripture, giving her wholehearted endorsement of the lady. Soon Mr. Howland gained Lady Merrilton's ear, and by the time the game of whist had ended, her ladyship was above certain she would engage Mrs. Tiernan for the evening the royals were to visit.

In fact her ladyship was delighted to find she could offer an entertainment not only refined but with a pleasing moral emphasis that would gratify Her Highness particularly. She told the story of the princess coming upon a small lad once in a village (the name of which she did not recall at the moment, however) when Her Highness inquired of the boy, asking him who his father was.

"'Why, I thought everybody knows my father!' he replied, quite unconscious of whom he was addressing." Lady Merrilton did an admirable job of sounding like an indignant little lad, and the company laughed. "The princess was amused," Lady Merrilton said, continuing the story, "and further inquired if the child could read. His answer, that he could read the whole of Saint Matthew in the New Testament, pleased her exceedingly, so she asked, 'Do you have a Bible, then, my boy?' He told her that the family indeed had a Bible, though it was torn and dog-eared from handling. 'How many children does your father have?' she then asked and was given the number. Handing the boy a guinea, she pressed it into his palm, saying, 'There. Go and have your parents purchase a Bible for each of your brothers and sisters and inscribe them as a gift from the Princess Charlotte.'" There was a murmur of approval.

Lady Merrilton continued, at ease in the role of storyteller. "The boy, all agog then, stared at the guinea and then at the princess and wordlessly turned and ran off to do as she bade." She smiled at her listeners. "I think a moral reading ought to be just the thing that our warmhearted princess will enjoy. Miss Forsythe has recommended just such a woman to us."

Lord Merrilton opined his hope that the queen would accompany the princess, as she did on some occasions. He was anxious to hear any news regarding a possible improvement in His Majesty the King. "As long as there is life," he said, "there is hope."

Ariana made quite sure to take Lady Merrilton aside and confirm that her ladyship understood what sort of performer Mrs. Tiernan was. She was not purely an entertainer, but wanted her audience to experience Scripture in a new way. Her ladyship listened, but with a raised chin, replied impatiently, "Yes, yes. She's precisely what I want! Her Royal Highness will be delighted."

As Mr. Mornay drew up to them, Lady Merrilton turned to him and, hitting his shoulder lightly with her fan, said, "I'll depend upon you, sir, to get us our Mrs. Tiernan." To his questioning look, she explained quickly what she wanted.

Looking back to Ariana, she said, "Mornay never fails me." With that and a little knowing smile—a smile Ariana did not particularly like—she walked off to visit other guests.

"Don't look at me like that," Mr. Mornay said, though his expression was one of amusement. "I haven't the foggiest notion what she's talking about."

"But you're not out of countenance from her saying it," replied Ariana.

"Should I be? I thought you were in favour of a more forbearing attitude on my part."

Ariana admitted sheepishly, "Perhaps I only want you to be forbearing toward men."

He laughed out loud.

From that moment, word spread quickly that a dramatic actress was to appear at Merrilton House the night of the princess's visit. With only two days to find and secure the lady, Ariana hoped that Mrs. Tiernan would agree to appear and that her delivery would be as welcome to the pleasure-seeking denizens of the uppermost echelons of society as she had found it on Sunday.

While Mr. Mornay was engaged in talk with an MP, Ariana watched Lady Merrilton happily flitting about him, injecting herself into their conversation. She felt suddenly quite unhappy with him. No, it wasn't unhappiness exactly. What was it? Her ladyship flitted to someone else, spoke a word, and then turned, revealing her pretty face from behind a fan and nodding in Ariana's direction. Then she returned to Mr. Mornay, draped her arm inside his, and pulled him away laughingly, saying she must have his opinion on a matter.

Ariana was roiling with the thought that the marchioness was intentionally flouting her easy friendship with Phillip, as though to say, *You don't own him, you know. You never will.*

As she watched the lady laughing up at her future husband, all animated and very pretty, she was filled with an uncustomary jealousy that tore at her heart.

Never before had there been cause for jealousy. She tried to reason herself out of the feeling. But he hadn't as much as turned to look at her, and now he appeared exceedingly comfortable in a small group, her ladyship's arm still possessively on his own. Ariana felt humiliated.

She looked around and then quickly walked toward the wide doorway that led to an outer hall, beyond which was the grand staircase. She moved on, not sure what she wanted to do, but quite certain she wished to leave the room. She'd been looking forward to seeing her fiancé, but to find him equally as distant as he was on Sunday was disheartening. To find him enjoying another woman's company was beyond the pale! At the top of the stairs, Ariana hesitated for a moment. What was she doing out here? What was she doing at Merrilton House?

If Phillip had behaved as usual, Ariana could have entertained herself quite easily with conversation. There were many people she found interesting in the gathering, and some she even called friends. But she could not shake off the feeling of jealousy and pique. *I know it is childish, but why is he not attending to me first and foremost? It is ungentlemanly of him to abandon me!*

At the top of the staircase, she nodded to two ladies who were coming up the steps. Self-conscious about being found loitering about with no clear objective, Ariana descended the staircase. She felt a sense of relief. With the help of a servant, she soon picked out her lined cape and headed for the door.

In moments she was out on the street. Park Lane was really not so far from Hanover Square. She could walk home. But then the idea seemed rash and ill-advised. She took a few deep breaths of evening air, looked down the dark street, lit up only by the house, and decided against the idea of going home on foot. Surely it wasn't safe.

Reluctantly she returned inside and once again gave up her cape. She forced herself back up to the long gallery, thinking that she oughtn't indulge her pique a moment longer. As she entered, she almost lost her resolve. She found Mr. Mornay still with Lady Merrilton on his arm. He was searching the room, however, but stopped at sight of her. With a satisfied expression, he gave his attention back to her ladyship. It was all Ariana could do to stop herself from bursting into tears. *Why am I ready to cry?* She headed once more from the room and to the elegant stairway.

Mr. Mornay looked up and saw her leaving. He came to attention and spoke something to Lady Merrilton, who merely grasped his arm the more tightly.

Ariana, meanwhile, was taking the steps as quickly as she could. She did not want to be seen in her condition—ready to bawl like a child! She was jealous but knew that Mr. Mornay was not trying to make her so. *But what* was *he trying to do?*

She did not, at the moment, have the presence of mind to consider what his motives might be. In her heart she knew that Phillip Mornay loved her. He was going to marry her and share his life with her. Surely his recent aloofness could be explained. But here and now, it wasn't enough.

She wished she could go home for a few days. Her real home. Her own family. Not Mrs. Bentley's house. She was blinking back tears when she reached the street, without having stopped to even claim her cape. Across the street she saw a linkboy come to attention. Good. She could walk home, after all. She gestured to him, and he hurried to her, holding a lit torch. Thankfully, linkboys usually hung around the homes of the wealthy when a party was in evidence. She told him where to take her and fell into step behind him, not daring to think of what Mr. Mornay would say later about her leaving without a word to him.

She told the boy to hurry, wishing to get home quickly. She did not look back. Through a blur of tears, all Ariana saw was the boy's light and the dark streets of Mayfair at night. A carriage stopped in the street, but she paid it no heed. They must be nearing Upper Brook Street, she thought, where they would make a left and turn toward the house.

And then suddenly nothing was making sense.

Someone grasped her by the arm. At the same time, he pulled the boy roughly to a stop and moved his light nearer to her face. She could make out nothing in the dark, but assumed it was Phillip.

"By Jove, it's just the baggage I'm looking for!" the man declared in an aristocratic tone—a voice Ariana did not know.

Then someone else grabbed her around the middle. She let out a startled shriek as she was slung over a shoulder like a sack of grain. She tried pummelling the man with her fists, while yelling, "Let me go! Help!"

"Silence her, you fool!" A coach door opened.

Her captor tried to mount the steps with her still on his shoulder, but there was a scuffle. Ariana heard Mr. Mornay's voice. He shouted, "Not on your life, gentlemen!"

"Phillip!" Ariana called through her tears.

She heard the sound of running footsteps approaching and the voices of more men back by the house. And then the sound of a shot. At that Ariana was thrust into the arms of a different man, and she fought against him, trying to hit him with her fists. The linkboy's light was gone, and she could see nothing, but sheer terror kept her struggling. She cried again, "Phillip! Help me!"

The man's strong arms overpowered her. "I've got you! You're safe!"

It was Phillip.

The sound of a coachman shouting and the crack of a whip was followed by the hasty departure of the vehicle she had nearly been forced into against her will.

Ariana threw herself against her betrothed. Flooded with relief, she clung to his neck and allowed her tears to spill.

Six

Mr. Mornay lifted Ariana into his arms and turned back toward the house, while explaining to the men who had come running that there had been an attempted abduction of Miss Forsythe and the villains responsible had just driven off. Ariana was still clasping her beloved in fright, not able to forget the ominous words of that man. What had he meant? He'd said she was "just the baggage" he wanted. How could it be so? Thank God for the alert footman outside the house who had called for help! Mr. Mornay had already been on her heels and was just about to leave the house when the footman rushed in, saying there was some mischief on the street.

Later he had to admit that when the ruffian had thrown Ariana into his arms, he should have put her aside to catch the men. But he could not, though the action ensured their escape. With his arms full, he was unable to lift a finger as they scrambled into their vehicle and took off.

While Ariana clung to him, Mr. Mornay asked Lord Merrilton to quickly assemble a few men to pursue the carriage. Then he hoisted her up more securely and turned to make his way back to the great house.

"No, I must go home!" Ariana pleaded.

"I have to see that you're well enough first," he said.

"No, Phillip!" In such a weakened state, Ariana detested the thought of putting herself into the marchioness's care. Perhaps it was the urgency in her tone or that she had called him by name, but her words made him stop.

By now there was a crowd upon the street as the party found out what had happened.

Brummell and Worcester appeared. "Good heavens! Is she all right?"

"She will be. Fortunately I was in time to scare them off."

"What? Was she out here alone?" Brummell whistled loudly and ordered a servant to find Mr. Mornay's coach at once.

"It's a curricle," Mr. Mornay added, directing his comment to the retreating figure who was going round back toward the mews.

"You came in an open curricle?" Beau Brummell thought surely he was hearing things. His face was screwed up in distaste.

Mr. Mornay replied icily, "For lack of a chaperone, yes."

Brummell smiled. "But it wouldn't be the first time, would it?" Then seeing Ariana's stricken expression, he hastily added, "Right. Quite proper, Mornay." But before he raised his eyes heavenward for his friend's benefit, he gave Mornay an impish look. Brummel then proceeded to redeem himself by acting as a foot guard so that those who were joining them on the street were unable to accost Ariana or her rescuer.

"Miss Forsythe is fine—a couple ruffians abroad, that's all." Mr. Mornay continued to provide what few details he had; that the coves had a coach, no crest that he could see, and no lamp was lit. His own curricle was finally brought to the curb, but he realized he could not climb aboard without putting his charge down. Just then Merrilton arrived, quite indignant that a guest of his had fallen into harm's way.

"Use my coach, Mornay," he said. "We can't have Miss Forsythe put to any further discomfort." He issued orders for his coach to be brought and then turned to a nearby footman. "Where's the dratted beadle when ye need 'em? Seen 'im tonight?"

"No, m'lord."

The nobleman grimaced. "Not a beak in the street when ye need 'em!" He paused. "Isn't one supposed to be about?"

"I believe so, m'lord."

"Not even a dashed charley around!"

"No, sir."

"Good heavens!" Lady Merrilton came rushing out of the house. "Bring her in, for pity's sake, Mornay!" She looked at a servant. "Fetch a doctor at once!"

"Do call a doctor," Mr. Mornay said, "but send him to Mrs. Bentley's house in Hanover Square. Number 49."

"It isn't necessary," Ariana said. She was only sniffling now, but still quite terrified at her near disaster.

"Do it," he repeated.

The coach arrived, and he carried her up into the compartment and placed her on the cushion.

He stood with his head outside the door, saying, "I'll see her home and then perhaps take a look around. I'll see if I can recognize that carriage."

"Very well. There are a few men out looking now, but we'll wait on you, Mornay, and go together," said one of the men from the gathering crowd.

The Beau was already asking for a sword, as he didn't carry his own. Others were pulling out pistols or testing the strength of their walking sticks.

"When we catch them, they'll be sorry they tried their business with one of our ladies!" shouted Merrilton.

Worcester was practically drooling. "Teach 'em a lesson, that's what! And then give 'em an escort to the hulks!"

Mr. Mornay lit the interior lamp, sat down, and intently looked at the young woman crying quietly into her handkerchief. He might have lost Ariana to the hands of unspeakably vile men! His heart was still beating hard in his chest. She turned her eyes up to his, red-rimmed but pretty nonetheless. She wanted to throw herself back into his arms, but he made no move to take her up against him, and so she just looked at him, still sniffling.

"He—he said I was just the baggage he was looking for!"

"One of the men who tried to take you?"

"Yes."

"Hmm. I'm sure he didn't mean that exactly, but that you were just the right sort. They must have been intent on abducting a lady of good birth." He wanted to upbraid her for going forth alone at night while he was at it, but refrained on account of her teary-eyed state.

But she shook her head. "No. He had the linkboy's light in my face, and then he said, 'By Jove, 'tis just the baggage I'm looking for!' And he spoke like a gentleman! Not like a criminal. What could it mean?"

Mornay was silent for a moment as the carriage began to move. "No matter, now," he said tersely. "When I get you home safely, I'll take a look about to see if we can't find this man—the men, rather—who were involved."

"You'll be careful, won't you?"

"I won't be alone. The blue bloods detest any sort of violence or threat against themselves, and you are just close enough to their ranks," he said, with a little touch to her hand, "to make them feel threatened. They'll all help with the search."

"Good." She didn't move her hand from beneath his. And still her eyes were on him. She was trying to work up the courage to sink her head against him, to creep ever so slightly nearer. But he said, as if remembering suddenly, "What made you run from the house to begin with?"

"Oh—not now, Phillip."

"*Now.*"

"Nothing that signifies at this moment."

"What if I hadn't followed you? You see how dangerous the streets are at night!"

"I never dreamed—"

"Precisely. You mustn't go about at night unescorted." He studied her for a moment and then reached over and snuffed out the lamp. The carriage wheels began slowing, for they had reached her aunt's house. Ariana was once again suddenly blinking back tears. He should have taken her into his arms to soothe her—wouldn't he usually do so? Something was coming between them, and she had not the slightest idea what it was!

He escorted her to the door of the house. "The doctor will be here shortly. Will you be all right?"

Her heart sank. He was leaving, and there was an uncustomary chasm between her heart and his. She longed for that feeling of closeness they had been enjoying, it seemed, only a week earlier. What had happened? Swallowing the feeling of wanting to cry, she nodded at him and gave the briefest of curtseys. She would have turned, but he stopped her by taking her hand and lifting it to his lips.

It meant everything to her, the way he lingered his kiss upon her glove. Though there was fine satin between her skin and his mouth, her eyes began to dry up at once. He cared. He still cared. Seconds later he studied her with his dark eyes.

"I think it best if we limit our contact until the wedding. I'll escort you to anything at your request, but I have determined to pass the days until the wedding apart from you—" He stopped, seeing her face fall.

Three times Ariana had fought against crying that evening. Three times she had succeeded in quelling the tears, the sobs that longed to escape her throat. But now her eyes opened wide with a terrible feeling of finality—she'd been right! He was avoiding her. She burst into tears. He started, as if to speak, but Ariana turned and went into the house.

He entered behind her.

Haines was rather astonished to see the young miss come into the house sobbing and merely stood aside while Ariana rushed past, one hand to her mouth.

Mr. Mornay caught her on the stairs, ignored the servant, and took her about the waist. "Whatever are you crying about?" he spoke gently into her ear.

The sound of his voice, soft and intimate, brought forth a fresh sob, but she threw her arms about his neck and loved doing so. "You break my heart!" she said, in a shaky whisper. He had received her with a tight embrace, but at her words he pulled away, looking thoroughly bewildered.

"You are changing." She was trying admirably not to cry. "You are determined to avoid me! You have hardly looked me in the eye these past few days!"

He breathed a sigh, took her hand, turned without a word, and led her up the stairs.

He took her into the drawing room, his eyes upon hers in a look that she could not decipher. He did not appear angry. Neither did he seem sorrowful or upset. She tried to steel her heart against what she might be about to hear.

Mr. Mornay closed the door behind them and turned to face her while he completed the task, making sure it was closed firmly. He said, "Come here," and held out his hand to her. When she drew near him, he took her by both hands and pulled her toward him. "What on earth do you mean by saying that I am breaking your heart? Don't you realize, my foolish darling, that I am having a devilish time of it?"

"*You* are? On what account?"

He pulled her closer. "On account of wanting this marriage yesterday! I am *living* for our wedding!"

Ariana was greatly encouraged. This was more like the man who loved her. Then he hadn't meant to be so aloof. She put her hands up and clasped his well-shaven face, avoiding the snowy white neckcloth that edged out beneath his chin.

"Oh, Phillip!" They kissed, and then they stopped. But he pulled her closer and kissed her again more passionately. Then he showered her face and forehead with kisses, then her neck. Then—

He froze.

He released her.

"This is precisely why I must keep my distance from you, Ariana! Do not mistake my meaning, or lessen my resolve. I am only thinking of your honour."

She was frowning, but she nodded.

"Do not look so troubled," he said, almost smiling. "If I did not *adore* you, I would have no need for such caution."

These words filled her heart, and she impulsively threw her arms back around his neck. "I *love* you!"

He sighed, for her enthusiasm did little to help his state of mind, but his eyes sparkled when he answered, "And I love you, Miss Forsythe."

The use of her formal name made her smile. Still with her arms about his neck, she said, "I shall only allow us to remain apart until the wedding, if it is what you wish. I will bear it only for your sake."

He chuckled. "I have your permission? You little minx!"

Ariana drew back and then smoothed his snowy cravat with her hands. "I always want to touch your neckcloths. You do them so beautifully. Your face is framed perfectly and—"

He took hold of her hands and stopped her. "Unless you wish to leave for Scotland this minute, I must go." But he bent his head and planted a quick last kiss on her lips.

At just that moment, they heard, "What? *Where* are they?" It was Mrs. Bentley, and her voice was not far from the room.

Mr. Mornay touched Ariana's hair, taking a long last look at her. Then he took her hand with one of his, while opening the door with his other.

Mrs. Bentley was coming toward the room in a nightdress, robe, and mobcap. She was holding a candle in one hand, and Haines was with her.

"Why, Mornay, how do you do? I must say, I hadn't thought to see you in the house."

He bowed politely. "I was just leaving." The memory of Ariana's near-abduction came to the fore and that he was supposed to be searching for the criminals. "In fact," and he was speaking to Ariana now, "I'll never catch those dashed coves if I'm not off directly!"

Their eyes met, and a silent message of mutual regard passed between them. He reached down just to place a quick, chaste kiss on her lips and then bowed again at her aunt. He turned to leave. Mrs. Bentley was ready for her bed, or she would have stopped him to answer her questions, but instead she plied them at Ariana.

"What was he talking about? What dashed coves? Did something happen? He left rather hastily! You weren't alone with him very long, were you? A man gets bold before a wedding, I dare say."

"Aunt!"

"Well, what was he talking about? Come, tell me everything." She motioned for Ariana to accompany her. Thankfully the lady headed for Ariana's bedchamber and listened while Harrietta helped the younger girl with her clothing. Ariana wasn't comfortable until she had sent the maid away and was finished speaking with her aunt (who was indignant to be sure, at her niece's near disaster, but not nearly as vocal or reprimanding as Ariana feared). Then she was alone, in her bed, in a white chemise nightdress and cap. A single candle glowed softly from its perch on the table beside the bed. At last. Alone with God.

She hadn't read the day's collect, and so she started to now. She really needed to pray. Her soul felt dry, but of course, as such things are bound to happen, that is when the doctor arrived. He'd gone first to Merrilton House and then was directed to Hanover Square. After hearing the account of what had befallen Ariana, he did his usual ministrations: listened to her heart, felt her pulse, and recommended a diluted mixture with laudanum. Then, if she did not feel better with the morning, he said he would return with leeches for bloodletting, which was sure to do the trick.

Mrs. Bentley felt nearly in need of laudanum herself, but chose instead to order a late glass of bishop—a drink that often had soothed her tired bones in the past.

Imagine it—her niece, nearly abducted! The more she thought on it, the more it disturbed her. *Why was Ariana prone to difficulties? What if she had been abducted? And what if Mr. Mornay had then decided her purity was too compromised to have her as his wife? What if she had been* harmed?

Oh, would she never have this thing done? It occurred to her for perhaps the first time that her niece's marriage was not, in fact, *her* doing. Yes, she had dressed the gel and brought her into society. But Mornay had made her fashionable, and Mornay had fallen in love with her. Mrs. Bentley could take no credit for either feat.

She sipped her drink and tried to relax. A vision of Ariana on the street and in the hands of ruffians ruined her composure, however, and she had to sit up abruptly. Another thought intruded. *I can pray. That's what Ariana would bid me do.*

She folded her hands and thanked God that Ariana was safe in her bedchamber after such a close call. Her mind wandered...perhaps Mr. Mornay would think to elope! (She had never thought elopement respectable, but it was certainly superior to the ominous idea of Ariana being abducted.)

"Dear Lord," she added, with as much earnestness as she could muster, "keep my niece from mischief and—bring this wedding speedily, even if it takes an elopement! Amen!"

In all, two carriages of indignant lords and gentlemen spent near two hours driving around town, looking for the would-be abductors who had accosted Miss Forsythe in Mayfair. The Duke of Grafton had taken charge of the first vehicle, having always found Miss Forsythe exceedingly charming and wishing to be of service. Mr. Mornay, of course, was at the helm of the other—literally. He, with only Beau Brummell at his side, reverted to his curricle, feeling that it was easier to maneouver as they reconnoitered the neighbourhood. They saw plenty of coaches, most with only their drivers and a footman or two about them, at the curbs. They questioned the servants on how long they'd been there, who their masters were visiting, and so on, without uncovering anyone suspicious.

They stopped many a coach on the street, forcing them to a halt to avoid a collision by slowly crowding them out of space on the streets. This action elicited many reproofs from the occupants until they saw who it was and fell into an awed silence. But no one fit the shadowy figures Mr. Mornay had hardly been able to see in the night. By one o'clock, as the roads grew crowded with the moving of the *ton,* it became near impossible to hope for success, and they returned to Merrilton House.

Inside the long gallery, the talk returned to Miss Forsythe's near disaster and what ladies should do to avoid the danger of having such a thing occur to them. The overwhelming concurrence was that a lady must avoid being alone at all costs.

Mr. Mornay listened without comment, but made a mental note to speak with Mrs. Bentley. He decided, to be safe he must ensure that Ariana wouldn't be out of the chaperon's sight for the next ten days. Surely that wasn't asking too much. He couldn't do it himself, or he'd go mad from proximity to her.

Mr. Mornay assigned the task of reaching Mrs. Tiernan to his steward, Mr. Horton. An intelligent man, he made short work of the business. He reported that Mrs. Tiernan was gratified at the opportunity to perform before the Regent and Princess Charlotte. Certainly she would be available, asking only that Lord Merrilton would send an equipage to convey her there and back again.

Little reminder cards were hastily sent round about Mayfair and its environs, as Lady Merrilton feared that the incident with Miss Forsythe might serve to discourage the more delicate ladies who might not wish to risk showing up at her house. She needn't have worried, however, as no one wanted to miss the princess.

When Mr. Mornay saw the invitation he had a moment of indecision. Ariana adored Her Royal Highness, as most English subjects did. She would want to attend the evening affair. It took him only a minute to realize that he could not deprive her of the pleasure for selfish reasons, and he sent round notice to Hanover Square that he would be escorting her. So much for maintaining his distance!

Shortly after Mornay sent his message and left the house, Ariana and Mrs. Bentley arrived. The chaperone had sent for a seamstress to take measurements in the master bedchamber. The bed from the adjacent room had been placed next to Mr. Mornay's bed, as Miss Forsythe had requested. The little aisle between the two beds was there at Mrs. Hamilton's bidding. This afforded her some small relief—it was still not as proper, to her mind, as separate bedchambers, but at least there was some manner of separation.

While the seamstress measured the furniture for new matching counterpanes and drapery, Ariana made a quick detour to Mr. Mornay's study. She wished to leave a small wad of correspondence with him. On top of the pile she placed a note, written in her best handwriting. It read, "Please read and consider. Thank you, dearest! Your Most Affectionate, Ariana."

She left them squarely in the middle of the desk. How utterly satisfying it was to know that she might help the worthy causes being brought to her attention!

Back in the bedchamber, the seamstress had nearly finished. She needed to ask about bed curtains, pillows, a footstool, and a bench. If they were to match, she must know and measure accordingly.

Bed curtains were considered a little old-fashioned by some, but they were charming too, and Ariana felt aghast at sharing a bed with her husband in a house with so many servants (who might walk in when least expected!). She bespoke the bed curtains.

Her own little escritoire from Chesterton had been delivered just that morning and placed in the room. It was evidently not so fine a piece as Ariana had always considered. It looked out of place. Mrs. Bentley's decided opinion was that it had to go. Ariana's opinion was that it had to go *elsewhere* but not from the house. In any case a footman was sent off to procure a furniture maker's catalogue. No merchant in London would mind parting with a catalogue for the Paragon's establishment.

Mrs. Bentley's true aim was merely to keep the girl occupied and beneath her eye. Moreover, she enjoyed the town house and the fact that she was privy to its secrets now that her niece was to become its mistress.

Ariana, meanwhile, was struck afresh by being surrounded by the belongings of her future husband. It felt bitterly sweet—it was a joy and yet an ache at the same time. She hadn't noticed it when she'd been there with her friends on Monday. Now it struck her forcefully at every turn.

She hadn't anticipated the sudden strong shafts of affection that would strike her merely at the thought of him. Ariana lingered by the wardrobe, tempted to run her hands through the clothing he wore—indeed, might have worn just yesterday. She touched, sniffed, and stroked pillows and draperies. She stopped and studied every painting, roundel, and fresco in the vicinity—all the while marveling that Phillip had surely done so at one time or another. Everything she saw, he had seen. All that she was now admiring, he had either introduced to the house or seen fit to maintain.

She spied a pair of cufflinks upon a dresser top—something he might have picked up and toyed with that very day. Perhaps he had considered using them and then discarded the idea. In an impulsive gesture, she took one and clasped it in her hand like a treasure. It was made of gold and set with little diamonds, and since there were two, she decided instantly to keep one until their marriage. One for each of them. It would be a sort of "until we meet again" remembrance. She savoured the feel of it in her hand. It was merely a cufflink, but it was his, and now it was hers.

Then when a maid brought in a freshly laundered stack of Phillip's neatly folded handkerchiefs, though Ariana already had one tucked away at her aunt's house, she felt an irresistible urge to have another. She watched the servant put them into a drawer. After the servant left, Ariana crossed the room and opened the drawer. The top few handkerchiefs were made of soft silk and embroidered with a single *M* at the bottom corner—very fine and elegant. Beneath them were brown and red ones made of linen; "snuff" handkerchiefs. With a quickening of her pulse, she picked one up and sniffed it deeply. Yes, it had Phillip's scent, a mixture of snuff and clean linen.

With a little smile she tucked one into her reticule beside the cuff link. She would tell Phillip about it when she next saw him, if she was going to see him before the wedding. Oh, but it was coming at long last! Nine days more and she would be Mrs. Mornay! At times and in all honesty, a little cloud of fear accompanied the thought—after all, there were mysteries she knew precious little about. The sight of the beds in the room was a stark reminder of that. But she need not dwell on that right now.

She went and inspected her trousseau. Because she hadn't yet worn these garments, they didn't feel as though they were hers any more than the expensive furniture or decorations. Only her little escritoire from home was familiar, and it looked unhappily out of place.

She wandered down to the dining room, where the work she had authorized was underway. But when she got to the doorway, she stopped in shock. The room looked ghastly. It had been taken apart but not yet put back together, and she had a sudden sensation of having ruined the beautiful dwelling with her foolish ideas! She turned without having entered and nearly walked into the housekeeper, who displayed a very indignant expression.

"Mrs. Hamilton! My word, you startled me."

"I beg your pardon."

She did not seem sorry, and she had not curtseyed. Nervously Ariana asked, "Has Mr. Mornay given his appraisal of the work yet?"

"To my knowledge, no, he has not."

Mrs. Bentley entered the room, for the seamstress had just left. "When is Mr. Mornay expected to return home?"

"I cannot say, ma'am. I can ask Mr. Frederick, however."

"Yes. Do so."

"At once, ma'am." The housekeeper turned and yanked once on the bellpull and then left the room.

"I do not trust that woman," Ariana's aunt said, after watching the servant go. "She was staring at you with a look that should never be on a servant's countenance. First, they shouldn't stare at you at all, and second, they should always appear happy to be of service or, failing that, as if they had no feelings whatsoever!" Mrs. Bentley said this as she followed Ariana back upstairs to the bedchamber.

"But, ma'am, they are people and do have feelings."

Ariana threw open the wardrobe. Now they were alone in the room, and there was a little smile on her face. Phillip's servants kept his things in impeccable order, that much was clear.

"Pshaw!" Mrs. Bentley dismissed this with a toss of her head.

"And I mean to befriend Mrs. Hamilton. Indeed I will need her help as I grow accustomed to Phillip's habits and preferences. I understand she has not been here for much over a year." She wrinkled her brows, trying to remember. "Or was it less? Perhaps it was less. But you see, she has learned her duties. She can much benefit me as I seek to do the same."

"If you need help, you need only ask me or hire a new woman in her place. Not all servants can countenance a change in the household such as you are bringing, my dear. They get it in their heads that somehow the place belongs to them, and they resent what they feel is an intrusion. I have seen it, Ariana."

The butler arrived, after finding that the ladies had abandoned the dining room. He had Fotch, Mr. Mornay's valet, with him. Both servants wore looks of mild alarm, though they bowed politely.

"Ah, Frederick. Did Mr. Mornay mention when he would return today?"

"No, ma'am, except it is unlikely he will take his supper here."

Fotch stepped forward, with an apologetic air. "May I answer any questions for you, ma'am?" He looked behind Ariana to the open wardrobe as if to say, "I notice you are into my master's clothing. Is something amiss?" Being unable to resist assuring himself that everything was as it should be, he went and took a quick look at the wardrobe and then shut the door with a firmness that was perhaps a little unbecoming in one with a new mistress in the room. His loyalty and longtime care of his master's clothes were his excuse. Ariana could see the possessiveness, the protectiveness for his master, and she smiled at him.

Fotch then remembered that he liked Miss Forsythe, and he smiled back. But he noticed the single cuff link on the dresser, and he went and picked it up. He then looked questioningly about, as if it might have fallen.

Ariana, instantly aware of having the other, felt too embarrassed to say so to the servant.

Frederick cleared his throat. "Will there be anything else, ma'am?"

"No, Frederick. Thank you."

"Shall I instruct Cook to prepare a meal for you and Mrs. Bentley?"

Ariana's aunt answered, "No, we are to eat at Hanover Square."

Before leaving the house, Ariana quickly checked on the progress of all the changes she had authorized. She saw little that was finished, and the obvious work in progress made her uneasy.

Even Mrs. Bentley had to exclaim, "Upon my word! I do hope that you are not responsible for all of this upset, my dear." She stepped around bits of broken plaster and tools, looking as if the mess held the plague.

Ariana frowned but said nothing. She saw the place where a painted roundel had been, covered now by an opaque substance to prepare it for a new painting. So much grace and elegance erased, as though it had never existed! What if she had inadvertently ruined the house in Grosvenor Square? And what would Mr. Mornay say about it?

Seven

When the master of the house arrived home that evening, he had forgotten about the missing candlestick and the letter opener. Mr. Mornay was now informed about the expensive cuff link, which was missing its twin, and that a handkerchief—or perhaps two—were also unaccounted for, all of which had been noticed following the visit of a certain young blonde-haired woman.

Worst by far was that his valet came to him in tears—Fotch, with tears in his eyes! This was the first moment he felt real concern about the recent rash of missing items.

"Sir!" The agonized look on the servant's face was almost unbearable.

"Yes, Fotch?"

The man couldn't bear to speak. He held up a white linen shirt, a look of sheer misery on his face, and turned it so Mr. Mornay could see the front. There was a huge blotch of ink on it, running in a ragged bleed in all directions, even up to the collar points. The placket, where the three buttons were sewn on, was solidly black.

Mr. Mornay frowned but was not in danger of losing his temper. "What happened?"

"That's just it, sir! I 'ave no clue! I found it just like this, right and tight, hangin' in the wardrobe, sir!"

Mr. Mornay's lips were compressed. "Summon Frederick."

The valet didn't move from the room, and Mr. Mornay asked, "Yes?"

"If I could just say, sir, how sorry I am. 'Tis a rotten shame, sir!"

"Yes, thank you, Fotch." He thought of something. "You're not leasing out the laundry, are you?"

"Goodness no, sir! I washed this shirt myself, and I left it white as ever it was, sir!"

"Very well," he said, nodding.

When the butler arrived, he too was visibly upset. "Sir, I beg you to understand that neither I nor Fotch have the smallest notion of how this could have happened!"

"Set yourself at ease, Frederick. I don't intend to hang you on a gibbet for it." Mr. Mornay looked up from where he had been writing something at his desk.

"Thank you, sir." The butler relaxed somewhat, but of course a butler could not be expected to relax completely under the circumstances.

"However—" The master's word set a new flurry in his pulse.

"I do think I should be able to expect my butler to keep abreast of the comings and goings in this house. Something has been amiss, as you know. Missing items, possible thefts, and now my own clothing ruinously attacked!"

"Attacked, sir?"

"Do you see it as something less?" he asked.

"Well, sir—" he hesitated.

This made Mr. Mornay look at him expectantly. "Well? Do you know something?"

He looked down and then said, "Well, it's just a conjecture, sir." The butler looked at Fotch, who nodded his head in agreement. Mr. Mornay was losing patience.

"What *is* it, Frederick?" His tone dripped with exasperation.

"You see, sir, Fotch and I both saw—someone—looking in your wardrobe today."

"What! Why on earth didn't you say so?" He was growing more annoyed by the second.

"We assumed you knew."

"Knew! Are you mad? Who was it?"

"The lady, sir...Miss Forsythe. Our future mistress." Frederick's voice had trailed off, and Mr. Mornay's demeanour became unarmed. He seemed at a loss, in fact, and took a breath.

"Are you suggesting this was the work of Miss Forsythe?"

"Well, sir, we don't rightly know what to suggest. Or what to think. We only know we saw her at your wardrobe...and then Fotch found the garment."

"Where did you find it?"

"Hangin' up, sir, with your other clothing but pulled apart, so that it wasn't touchin' nothin' else."

Mr. Mornay held out his hand. "Let me see it." When he had the shirt in hand, he looked it over carefully, not really knowing what he was looking for but willing it to tell him something. Had it been stained deliberately or not? That was his question.

The three men examined the item, and there was no question in anyone's mind that it could have been an accident. Ink from a bottle had been deliberately poured on the garment and then allowed to slowly seep across it, in a spidery design that ended in uneven blotches all over the shirt.

Each of the men wore a frown. No one wanted to believe that the sweet-faced Miss Forsythe could be responsible. Mr. Mornay could not believe for a second that she was, but he certainly would speak of it to her.

He dismissed the servants and thought for a few moments. There were still nine days until the wedding, and now he would need to see her about this. There was no way for him to ignore that she had been in his bedchamber. The result of which he held in his hands, was so evident and deleterious. He looked at the clock on the mantel. It was nearly seven. If he hurried, he just might be able to catch her at Hanover Square before she accompanied her aunt somewhere for the evening. Otherwise he'd speak to her the following night as he escorted her to Merrilton House.

He called Fotch to help him change his clothing. Then before leaving the house, he stopped in front of Frederick.

"I want a footman or other servant at all times in the rooms where workmen are. Further, take all the items in these rooms that aren't closed up in drawers and lock them away somewhere until this infernal refurbishing is done! I want a man stationed at the door to my chamber at all times. And place another man at the next chamber since they are communicating doors, and make sure no one may enter either one without being duly noted.

The butler was nodding gravely.

"I also want a running tally of the cost of everything that has gone missing or been destroyed."

"Very good, sir."

"Tell Mrs. Hamilton what I've told you and see that my orders are carried out."

"At once, sir."

Mr. Mornay hesitated. The butler waited, sensing more was to come. "If Miss Forsythe comes again…"

"Yes, sir?"

Mr. Mornay fell silent for a moment, choosing his next words carefully. "Let Mrs. Hamilton or another servant accompany her."

"Yes, sir. Very good, sir." Frederick closed the door, troubled for his master's sake but inwardly proud of the man. The master was such a...*master!* He would see that there were no more dastardly goings-on in Grosvenor Square, that much was certain.

Lord Wingate drew a long, bony finger along the large map he had unfurled on a table. He tapped lightly upon Hanover Square and then let his finger run down the streets to Grosvenor Square, stopping abruptly at house number 25.

"'Tisn't a long distance but long enough for our purposes. I tell you, if we have to take her on the wedding day, we'll do it!" He looked to where his younger brother was stretched out on a worn sofa, eyes closed, one arm draped lazily across his eyes. Wingate's eyes narrowed. "Are you attending to me, Antoine?"

His brother slowly removed his arm from over his eyes and yawned. "I hear you, if that's what you mean. But evidently you haven't heard me. Did I not say," he asked, coming with difficulty to a sitting position and blinking at his brother who stood only a few feet away, "that I am not for trying again? I intend on dropping the scheme. I thought I had made that clear."

Lord Wingate grimaced. "What a cake you are. A prime gull." He paced with cat-like intensity to one end of the small room they were sharing, never taking his eyes off his brother. "This is a chance to get back what's been lost to us. The estate can be bought back. The trustees will be relieved to have it back in our laps. We can live there again, you know!"

Lord Antoine shifted and placed his booted feet heavily onto the floor. He looked tired. "Mornay had nothing to do with your bankruptcy. You did that entirely on your own!"

"As I am the legal heir, I fail to see how that concerns you." His eyes flickered angrily as he shook his long hair out of his face. "Mornay had more to do with it than you know. And his money will be sufficient to get it back. That's what matters."

"I thought what mattered was what he did to my wedding prospect. You don't really care a fig about that, do you?"

"All that signifies is that if we move ahead as planned, he will be willing to pay, and it will more than compensate both our losses."

The brothers stared at one another. Antoine hated to see the circles under Julian's eyes and hoped earnestly that his own did not mirror them. "Your losses, perhaps, not mine."

Julian smiled. "Both our losses, brother."

"After which I've no way of preventing you from gaming it away again."

Lord Wingate's demeanor changed. "I seem to recall that you enjoyed many a night's gaming as well, *brother*."

"I knew when to stop. You never did."

"Of course I did. You stop after you win. It's that simple." He dragged his fingers through his hair. "I had a run of bad luck, that's all."

"As I said, you don't know when to quit." Antoine stood up and made to leave the shabby apartment. It was the most they could afford, living off what they managed to eke out by gaming and other ignoble means. The family estate was "let to nurse." That meant it was in the hands of trustees until the debts Wingate had run up were fully paid. They had no regular income.

"Where do you think you're going?" Wingate's voice was slow and icy.

"What is it to you, sir? I see now that you were never in this on account of my ruined hopes, as you said!"

"I was willing to help, and now I will need your help."

"I said I'm not for it! I've thought it over. I'd have little chance with Miss Herley if I were to harm her dearest friend!"

"Don't be beetle-headed! Are you still harping about Miss Herley? And you say you know when to quit?" He faced his brother, his countenance snarling. "The game's up, Antoine! You're blocked at both ends. There is not to be a Miss Herley for you, and it is on account of Mr. Mornay! *And* his interfering little chit! Now you *will* help me in this matter. You have nothing to lose, and we both stand much to gain."

Lord Antoine stood grimly still, digesting what his brother had said. He was right, undoubtedly. There could be no chance of his marrying Miss Herley now. Her family was not rich, but they were utterly respectable—the very thing he was not. The very thing his family had not been for at least two generations. Mr. Mornay had been spot-on in warning her against him. But that didn't mean he had to just swallow it, did it?

He undid the buttons of his coat and walked over to where the map was laid out on the table. A single sputtering flame threw its light onto the paper, and when he bent over to study it, the light was partially blocked. Lord Wingate moved the candle.

"What is your plan?" he asked.

Perhaps it was the right thing to do, to help his brother. Even if Wingate was a knave, he was still his brother. Family. That had to count for something.

Eight

When Ariana awoke the next morning, a vague disturbed feeling rounded the edges of her consciousness. What was it? Tonight she would see Phillip—that was a good thing. She would see the princess—another good thing, to be sure. Yet something nagged at her. Something was wrong.

And then she remembered she'd nearly been abducted! Heavens, it felt like a dream, only it wasn't. She had very nearly been nabbed from the street by wicked, horrible men!

She reviewed the events in her mind but then determined to think only of the coming evening. The Lord had prevented harm from befalling her. She would not now repay Him by keeping her thoughts focused on an evil that had been avoided. With every remembrance of it, she would give thanks in her heart for her deliverance. For her fiancé.

Much better. Now she could focus on the coming excitement at Merrilton House.

For once Ariana was concerned about what she would wear to the event and wished she had asked Mr. Mornay to advise her. But she knew her aunt was capable of the task, and so she asked Mrs. Bentley to choose the gown. Her aunt did more than just pick out the lovely ivory silk gown, she also chose the accoutrements to match. It was all laid out and ready, and Ariana had only to wait for the evening to arrive.

As was rapidly becoming her habit (and to keep herself occupied), Ariana decided to stop by the house in Grosvenor Square. She felt a compulsion to be there, not so much due to a growing familiarity with the place as out of a nagging fear that she might have ruined it! Mrs. Bentley had squirreled off into her study to go over kitchen menus and shopping orders with Mrs.

Ruskin, so Ariana, determined to walk on such a gorgeous day, took a footman and set out for the house.

The street was busy with pedestrians, carts, carriages, servants on errands, and street hawkers. Ariana might have enjoyed the walk except for the hawkers, many of whom were evidently in need of more than just customers. She bought an orange from a girl, wishing she could allow her to keep the change, but it was all the money she had. Meanwhile, a black coach came down the street and slowed as it approached her, but Ariana was occupied with the girl and didn't notice it.

It rolled to a stop directly across from them.

Ariana's footman suddenly became aware of it. He hastened his steps so that he stood protectively beside his young mistress, between her and the street. Word had reached the servants, as it always did, of what had befallen her earlier that week. Mrs. Bentley had also warned them to be on their guard, and so the footman, Joe, was warily protective of her.

He watched with wide eyes, but no one came forth from the vehicle. Finally he had to speak up. "Mum," he said, making Ariana look up in surprise, just as she put away her change.

"What is it, Joe?"

"That carriage across the way." He never took his eyes off the coach. "Shabby, ain't it? Just as the one what tried to take you, mum."

She looked across the street and saw numerous dark coaches and carriages. Having no wish for another fright, she gathered her skirt in one hand and said, "Let us hurry then! I'll be safe at Grosvenor Square!"

"Wait. I know a way. They won't find you this way, mum."

Knowing his way around back alleys and hidden lanes, the footman hurried Ariana past Little Brook Street and across Bond, past the Venison Yard and South Molton Street. They then turned right onto the very narrow South Molton Lane, walked for a short distance, and turned west into another mews, this one with a sign saying, "Little Brooks Mews." When they came out onto Davies Street, the footman put out an arm to stop her and took a good look up and down the street. He motioned to her to follow him across Davies at the soonest opening of traffic. Once safely across, they ducked down another stable yard, across an empty lot, and into one more stable yard.

Ariana was growing doubtful of the wisdom of the route. She was wearing simple slippers, not half boots or walking shoes. Moreover, it seemed to smack of disrepute, following a servant in a furtive manner, and she had seen some people staring at her already. *I must be quite a sight, passing through stables in afternoon dress,* she thought. If only she'd had on a riding habit, it wouldn't have appeared half so odd.

They were getting closer to Grosvenor Square, however, and so she slogged on, eager to get there. Coming out on James Street, they turned south and then went west along Chandler to Duke. Finally they were heading toward the square, going north on Duke Street. Ariana was convinced they must have discovered the longest route to Grosvenor Square from her aunt's house that existed. She knew that Joe meant well and had her safety in mind, but she would welcome a rest when she reached her future home.

Lord Wingate peered out the window of his shabby carriage—a secondhand equipage that he'd won at cards—and watched while a liveried servant rounded the corner with Miss Forsythe behind him. He snickered. The idiotic servant had no doubt taken the lady on a circumbendibus route with the intention of hiding her from them. All he'd had to do was stop his coach at the square—and wait. He'd been guessing she was en route to her fiancé's home, and he'd been right.

The street was nice and quiet. "Here they are now."

His brother nodded. "I see them."

Wingate quickly unwrapped his neckcloth—he'd need it to keep the chit quiet—and held it, turning and twisting it in his hands in anticipation, as he watched their approach. Just then the footman noticed the carriage, and Wingate pulled his head back sharply to stay out of view, hissing at the same time, "He's noted us!"

In another second three carriages turned onto the square, moving slowly and blocking their view of the pair. The carriages stopped right there in the road, and still Wingate couldn't see his prey. Evidently Derby House, the residence next door to Mr. Mornay's establishment, was receiving guests. The door opened, and a butler came out, followed by two footmen. A groom appeared for the horses. People began stepping down from the carriages, and there was Miss Forsythe—stopping to greet an acquaintance. Wingate stifled an oath, his hands gripping the cloth in frustration.

Joe was still keeping a wary eye on their carriage. Wingate watched the proceedings but had to sit his gaunt frame as far back into the squabs as the cushions would allow to remain hidden.

Miss Forsythe moved on. The butler at 25 Grosvenor Square opened the door, and she was inside. The servant, after settling a last suspicious glance at them, went below stairs to the kitchens.

"Devil take it!" Wingate exclaimed. "We've bungled that chance, and that *deuced* footman is going to leak our presence!" He sullenly kicked the wall of the carriage with one angry movement, and they started off.

"There'll be another time," said Antoine. Though he didn't say so, he was relieved. His heart was not in this business. He'd tried to put himself into it. He'd come along for the opportunity, but no sense denyin' it, he wanted nothing more to do with the whole scheme. With any luck, Miss Forsythe would be married and gone from London before his brother was able to fulfill his plans. But of course, he'd never had any luck.

Never.

~

Ariana was relieved to enter the house, but not because she was convinced of danger without. No, she was merely tired. Her slippers were somewhat muddy—thanks to all the horse yards and mews they'd been through—and she hoped she had not picked up an odour. When she stepped inside, Frederick nodded and said, "I'll inform the master."

"Oh!" She hadn't expected Mr. Mornay to be home.

She wandered into the dining room while she waited but quickly left that room, not wishing to stay in it during its current state of upheaval. The men found her in the hall. Mr. Mornay had successfully kept himself elsewhere during her visits previously, and he seemed equally surprised as she to have encountered her here and now. His expression underwent a speedy transformation as he bowed, kissed her hand, and spotted her slippers. He said nothing, however, and asked her to step into the study with him for a minute.

She went, feeling a slight excitement to have found him home and wondering if he wished to discuss the charitable concerns she had left on his desk. Something was afoot, she felt sure of that.

"I would not have come, if I had known you were at home," she offered.

"I can believe that." His eyes sparkled, and that near smile was on his mouth.

He opened the door for her, and she, looking at him with a curious expression, entered the room. He made a gesture for her to sit in a comfortable wing chair, and he took a position against the adjacent one, studying her, his arms folded across his chest.

She folded her hands upon her lap, waited, and just looked at him with her large, pretty eyes.

He had to smile.

"What is it?" she asked, smiling back at him.

"You are enormously pretty, and because I hadn't expected to lay eyes on you until this evening, I am enjoying the unexpected pleasure."

Her smile broadened. "Thank you."

"You also appear to be in high spirits today."

"I believe I am, sir."

Suddenly he sniffed and then looked at her curiously.

With a blush she admitted, "I followed Joe, our footman, here, and he took me off the street, and we passed through horse yards, and—"

"What?"

"He saw a shabby-looking carriage on Little Brook Street. *I* didn't see it, but Mrs. Bentley warned all the servants to keep a sharp eye out—"

Mr. Mornay came sharply to attention. "Where? Was it following you? Where is your footman? Stay here!" And he disappeared. Ariana frowned. Here she had found him home, and now he was gone already. She hoped he wouldn't be long. She looked around and saw the family Bible, open on his desk. Her heart warmed. Phillip had been reading or studying it. *Good.* Rising and going round the desk, she saw there was also a book by Martin Luther, *Table Talk*. She picked it up and went back to her chair resignedly. She might as well do some reading.

∽∾∽

Lord Antoine wanted a diversion. He was considering a stop at one of his favourite lower-class haunts, a tavern called The Black Bear, when suddenly he noticed a familiar-looking young man on the street he'd been absentmindedly watching. It was Chesley! Harold Chesley.

He kicked the wall of the coach, and it began to slow.

"What the devil are you doing?" Wingate asked.

Holliwell looked at his brother. "I see a friend."

"You're not picking him up I hope!"

"No. I'm leaving." He prepared himself to exit the carriage as soon it had stopped completely.

His brother, the jaded aristocrat, put his head back and yawned. "Do as you like. Just find me later and don't get too deep in your cups to be of any use to me. The Forsythe chit ain't keepin' to her house, so we should have another opportunity soon enough."

"Right." Antoine jumped out of the carriage and hurried back the way he'd seen Chesley going. "Ho, Chesley!"

The man stopped, turned, and recognized Holliwell. He smiled and waved.

⸻

When Mr. Mornay was satisfied there was nothing further to pursue regarding the mysterious black coach Joe had seen, he returned to the study. He had gone outside and looked warily all around the square—as much as he could see of it—but saw nothing fitting the description of a shabby black equipage with sorry-looking horses.

Ariana shut the book. "I don't believe Mr. Luther is quite fit for ladies." She had read some rather shocking quotes from the man.

Mr. Mornay smiled. "Not that book, but other works of his would meet with your approval, I am sure."

"He was rather—" she hated to say it, "*crude*, was he not?"

"Perhaps *earthy* would be the kinder word." He was grinning as he gently eased the book from her hands and put it back on his desk. He turned again and surveyed her thoughtfully.

"Did you see the carriage?" she asked.

"No. They'd gone." His look changed. He went behind the desk, searched for something, and finally pulled out the ink-stained garment.

Her face changed to puzzlement.

He came back around the desk and held the garment out for her to see.

"What on earth happened?" she asked, looking up at him blankly. "Is this yours?"

"It is."

"I'm sorry for you. How did it happen?" she asked, noticing how intently he was looking at her.

He set the shirt on his desk and then held out his hands to her. He pulled Ariana up from her seat and said, "'Tis of no consequence. Come here."

"Of no consequence? After you took the trouble to show it to me?" But he was pulling her very close. "My dear sir, do keep in mind your good intentions to maintain a proper distance between us."

But even as she spoke, he began to kiss her face and nose and cheeks, and she couldn't help giggling. Then he kissed her mouth, his lips lingering on hers.

An onlooker would have seen an elegant pair of tall, well-groomed, and expensively clad people. His dark hair made a sharp contrast to her golden ringlets, which were held up with pins and adorned with a wide taffeta ribbon and one small ostrich plume.

Afterward and still holding her, he asked, "What were you looking for in my wardrobe yesterday?"

She pushed apart from him and tried to think. Her eyes fell upon the ruined shirt. "You think I did that! That I would be so careless as to—"

"No, I don't think you did that. But you must see the uncanny coincidence of your having been seen in the vicinity of my clothing and the fact that this shirt was later found in this condition."

She stared at him, understood the implication, and had no answer.

"So tell me...what brought you there?"

Ariana's eyes dropped. "I was merely...curious."

"Curious? About a man's clothing? About what, in particular, may I ask?"

Ariana blushed and sighed. "I was simply wanting to—touch something of yours." She suddenly remembered Mrs. Bentley's distrust of Mrs. Hamilton. "Who found your shirt, may I ask?"

"Fotch did, of course. He tends to my wardrobe exclusively."

She gave him a very concerned look, blushed afresh, and looked away and then back again. If she hadn't looked quite so adorably confused, he might have taken her reaction as an admission of guilt, but he knew her too well.

"Can there be an explanation, such as an accident, do you think?" Her perplexity of voice was second only to the agitation in her large eyes. Sparks of colour surfaced in them as happened when her feelings were provoked.

He turned his head, studying her sideways, appraisingly. "Could *you* have caused an accident? Don't be alarmed, I shan't be cross with you."

"I am not in the habit of carrying ink with me! And you need not speak to me as though I am a child. I remind you that I am not too young to be your wife!" She pressed her lips together in indignation. "You *do* think I did that!"

"No, I don't."

She searched his face.

He smiled a little. "Well, perhaps for a second or two, I might have. But I knew it was unlikely."

"Indeed!"

"But tell me what you were up to—"

"What was I doing? Oh, very well. I was just…enjoying…being near your things." She was still blushing, and she looked away from him, remembering. "I could smell your scent…"

His eyebrows rose. Then they stepped into another tight embrace, and he kissed her once more.

"You are my angel!"

"I look forward to being yours," she said and then blushed freshly, pulling away from him in haste. She wore a look of mortification, realizing how he may have interpreted that statement. He knew she had not meant it *that* way, but couldn't help, nevertheless, engaging her in another soulful kiss. Ariana pushed herself from him a second time. "We *must* go to a public room!"

He reluctantly released her. At that moment she spotted the correspondence she had left him, sitting in a neat pile on one corner of his desk. He saw the direction of her gaze.

"Yes, we will discuss those but not now."

She tried to read his features. "Please, let us talk of them today. I am so eager to—"

"You are eager to support every charity in England, I think."

She did not contradict his exaggeration. Adding to his conviction, she said, "And missionaries, you must know."

"I don't doubt it!"

She completely missed the sardonic edge to his voice. "Have you looked them over?" she asked again.

"I have, and if you must know, I have great reservations about supporting workhouses of any sort. They are heartless places, keeping people barely alive, while they work them to the bone and at useless endeavours like the tread mill. They ought to be abolished!"

She opened her mouth a little in surprise, paused after he spoke, but finally replied, "Which is all the more reason to help them. With proper support they would perhaps be more generous to their inmates. Kinder in their treatment."

"Unless there is a law in place to ensure it, Ariana, it would be foolish to expect it."

"Do you think so?"

"Yes."

They looked at each other deeply. She saw his earnestness and said, "Very well, but can we visit these places so that I may see for myself what their manner of operation is?"

"When there is time, after our marriage, yes. There is a workhouse not half a mile from here."

She gave him a little smile. "Very well. But what of the orphans' school? May we support that good cause?"

"I already sent something on your account."

"You are so good to me, sir!"

He smiled and took her back in his arms. He went to kiss her, but she turned her face away.

"I daresay the servants are already scandalized at our being alone in this room," she uttered into his shoulder.

"Not at all," he said, though inwardly he knew his behaviour was less than sterling. This was exactly why he needed to renew his efforts at keeping apart from Ariana until the wedding. But then he remembered there was still another matter he hadn't yet broached. "Ariana—"

"Yes?"

"Before we go, I need to mention that, since you've been coming by the house, a number of items have gone missing. And now my shirt has been ruined, with an appearance of it being done intentionally."

Ariana's face registered stark amazement. "Do your servants actually count your handkerchiefs?"

He laughed out loud. "Apparently. I see you *are* responsible for those, at least."

She reached for her reticule, still on the chair behind her, and dug in it for a few seconds. First she pulled out an orange, which seemed to amaze him. He said nothing, just watched while she placed it on his desk. Then she was brandishing the two handkerchiefs, which she handed him. And searching further, Ariana brought forth the cuff link.

"Here then! You may have them back. I wanted something of yours to be with me at all times, though I realize how utterly foolish that sounds—" She began to pace a little ways from him, peeved to have been found out in such a manner, and didn't notice that Mr. Mornay was at first mystified and then gratified.

He moved to her quickly, taking her by the arm, so that she faced him.

His eyes were full. But he also had that near smile as when he found her amusing.

"What?" Her hands were on her hips.

"You little mystifying minx!"

She had never heard him use that term before and didn't know whether he was scolding her or not. "I didn't *nap* them! I only borrowed them to have something of you with me at all times, as I said."

He held out his hand with the items she had given him and said, "Keep them. They're yours."

She slowly took them from him, feeling shy, but she did enjoy having them with her. They were a small token of his presence for when they were apart.

"As I'm yours," he said finishing his thought.

His words melted her cautious expression, which became one of undisguised affection.

With a speedy look toward the door to see that it was still safely closed, he took her for another kiss, and Ariana did not have it in her heart to deny him. Afterward she smiled and returned the articles to her reticule.

It was a relief to know that nothing sinister was behind the so-called thefts, but Mornay had to shake his head and smile to himself. That Ariana was so eager to be his wife that she needed to possess some of his things was strangely touching. But as he was thinking thus, she turned a troubled expression up to him.

"But what of your shirt? I assure you, I had no hand in that work."

"I'm thinking that one of the workmen perhaps wandered into my chamber."

"But why would anyone ruin a good shirt, when he might have taken it and sold it or worn it himself? Particularly one of such superior quality?"

He nodded. "I know. I've had the same thought."

Ariana's face grew cautious. "Do you think there is someone who does not want me here? Could it have something to do with me?"

He stroked the side of her face. "By no means. I should think my servants have been quite sincere in their huzzahs to me, and I believe they are actually eager to see how the presence of a woman will influence the household." He paused and then added, "But I'll have a talk with Mrs. Hamilton and Frederick if you like. If we have a *grumbletonian* in our midst, they'll know it."

To her still serious expression, he added, "Do not fret. Nothing will come between us. If I find that a servant has had a hand in this—" His look grew formidable.

"You shan't hurt anyone?" She was alarmed by that look on him.

"No, but I'll see them brought to justice."

"Oh, my dear. They could be hanged for less! You know as well as I do—that isn't justice."

"Thieving from one's master is a serious offense. In addition to what you had in your reticule, a silver candlestick, and a small portrait of George III have also been napped. I keep that portrait of the king merely to antagonize Prinny and should hate to have it missing when he next calls!"

"The prince calls upon you?"

"Occasionally. He may not again. But I did enjoy having it on his account."

"Do you not approve of the king for his own self?" she asked, a little chidingly.

"I have quarrels with some of his policies," he answered. "But more of that another time. The point here is that, if you didn't borrow these items, then someone else took them."

Her face looked troubled. "I didn't take them. I feel responsible, however. It seems as though my presence here has worked mischief somehow, and I don't know what can account for it." And then she grew upset. "I—I don't understand how this could be. Are you certain these articles were not missing prior to my coming to the house?"

"My servants appear to be certain."

"Well—"

"I'm sorry I mentioned it," he said, holding out his arm. "I thought it rather odd that you would borrow them. It's better you know about their disappearance so you'll be alert for anything unusual while you're here."

"Unusual? Like what?"

He met her eyes. "I cannot say. I've appointed more servants to keep their eyes on the workmen. If no other explanation turns up, we'll have to conclude it was one of their number. One of them may have wandered beyond where they should have been, but that won't happen again. And if I know my man of business," he added, "he'll charge the shopkeepers equally to make up for the losses. Don't fret—let us not talk any more of it today. I'll look into the matter. But now I must take my leave of you." His look became stern. "You are not to walk home. I'm leaving orders that you'll be taken in a carriage, if Frederick himself has to drive it!"

"Thank you, my darling." The words left her mouth so quickly and easily that she hadn't realized what she was saying until it was too late. He froze for the briefest second, wanting to take her right back into his arms but could not. She saw it in his eyes, and her blush deepened. All he could do was murmur, "My angel." And with a chaste kiss on her cheek, he strode hurriedly toward the door.

She was doing it again. She was driving him mad. He had to get out of there *now*!

Nine

After Mr. Mornay had gone, Ariana wished she had asked him to take her home. She no longer wanted to be in the house without him. She decided that she may as well make a quick survey of the work because she had bothered to come, and so she did. It was still looking terribly topsy-turvy. Good thing she and Phillip hadn't tried to look it over together. She wondered why he had said nothing of the upheaval, his displeasure at the mess, or of the expense. He was being enormously wonderful. Ariana was hoping to be proud of the results, but things looked worse each time she came. She hoped that when it was complete, the results might be worth all the trouble.

She noticed the footmen positioned against the walls, silent sentinels keeping watch over their flock, and found herself wondering which servant might be the one who did not welcome her coming to the household. Had Mrs. Bentley perhaps been right in thinking the housekeeper was hostile toward her? And if so, what could Ariana do about it? The last thing she wished to do was have to dismiss the woman. That could rile the other servants. She would need to pray about it.

She hurried on through the house to see every area being altered, hoping that something would have taken shape sufficiently enough to be pleasing in its appearance. Afterward she planned on returning to her aunt's house to finish a drawing she'd begun earlier in the season. It was a sketch of the courtyard behind the house, and once Ariana was married, she knew she'd have little chance to complete it.

She suddenly realized a footman was close behind her, as if he had been discreetly following her. She turned and addressed him directly, "Are you following me?"

"Yes, mum."

"Why?"

"Master's orders, mum."

"He said nothing to me about it," Ariana countered.

The man shifted uncomfortably on his feet. "Shall I get Mr. Frederick?"

"Please do."

He left to get his superior.

When Frederick came, he bowed slightly. "You wanted me, ma'am?"

"Yes." She looked at the footman. "You are dismissed."

He seemed uncertain about what to do and looked to Frederick, who nodded. The footman turned and left. Ariana and Frederick were in the gallery, standing among tall sculptures on pedestals and numerous grand portraits and paintings that lined the walls. "Freddie, why did Mr. Mornay want me followed?"

Normally Frederick would have gone to great lengths to appease his future mistress. He'd been fond of her all along. Unfortunately he had just come from the kitchens, where Mrs. Hamilton had finally shared her impression that Miss Forsythe was going to replace the staff—possibly the *entire* staff—with one of her own. Naturally this was a nasty shock.

He'd been butler in this establishment for over a decade. Although he'd been pleased at the news of a coming mistress, if Mrs. Hamilton was correct, it changed everything. Of course he would check her information with the master as soon as he returned to the house, but he couldn't do that now.

So he replied, "I believe, ma'am, it was Mr. Mornay's intent to merely keep abreast of your interests here."

"My interests?"

"Your...whereabouts, ma'am." He had to look down as he spoke.

Ariana's face stiffened slightly. *Mr. Mornay does not trust me!* A wave of pain swept through her. *He doesn't trust me, and he didn't even tell me. He hasn't been honest with me!*

Forcing down her indignation and shock, she kept her features purposely bland and said, "Very good. Thank you." Frederick bowed and turned to go.

He could see that his answer had been difficult for the lady. Yet what else could he do? Was it not the truth? Had not many items been napped beneath his own nose while Miss Forsythe was in the house? It was out of his hands.

As Ariana returned to Hanover Square in one of Mr. Mornay's carriages, her mind was still roiling with the thought that the man she loved did not trust her. With a pang in her stomach, Ariana realized that until they found out who was behind the ruined shirt and the lifted items, there could be no real peace at the house in Grosvenor Square. A candlestick, a small portrait, a letter opener, and an ink-stained shirt. The shirt seemed the worst thing of all in some ways. It was almost an attack on Mr. Mornay himself. His clothing—something worn on his person. The implication made her shiver.

Further, each mysterious disappearance followed her known presence in the house. And the shirt had been ruined after she'd been seen in the dressing room! Someone was behind it. Someone who did not mind implicating her in the business. But who? And why? She would need to speak with the housekeeper, but it appalled her that any servant could bring their hand against their master's possessions. She knew that sometimes servants would steal to lay up money for their retirement. That, to her mind, was in a sense excusable. It was at least understandable. But to deface property with no end or purpose except to plague the owner—or her—*that* was malicious. That was frightening.

Park Lane was blocked by an enormous crush of carriages around Merrilton House that evening. Inside, in the sumptuously rich long gallery and reception area, the house was buzzing with low conversations. The guests were in full sparkle this evening—the ladies in their evening gowns, white gloves, and best jewelry, holding pretty fans, little reticules, or lorgnettes. Peacock plumes adorned headdresses. Scarves and shawls were draped elegantly over shoulders and arms, ranging from the willowy limbs of young ladies to the heavily fleshed, gesturing arms of the dowagers.

The men were mostly in breeches with shoes, waistcoats and jackets, top hats, and buff gloves. Uniformed gentlemen were here and there, including the Duke of York in full regimental dress and admirals and colonels in naval colours. The Duke of Wellington was in Spain fighting the French, or he would have been present. Only a number of specially chosen Whigs were there for the purpose of being brought round to the Tories' side on an upcoming vote. Bonaparte had won two victories in May, and since the outcome of the Spanish campaign was still undecided, it was a good time to play on the vulnerability of the lords.

Frances, Lady Merrilton, a shrewd political hostess, shooed away the footman offering a fluted glass of champagne from a silver tray and said, "See to the guests, John." Other footmen had trays of like beverages or stood at the outskirts of the room, their faces aloof and stiff as statues. Lady Merrilton, looking about at the gathering of English luminaries, was momentarily satisfied. With the Regent and the princess promising to attend, she had done a commendable job of gathering the guests she wanted for the event, and more were still arriving each moment.

Mornay and his fetchingly pretty future bride had not yet appeared, and Mrs. Tiernan was being conveyed in one of the marquess's carriages. Lady Merrilton had long suspected that Mr. Mornay had more interest in political debates than he gave reason to believe. He had attended social engagements at the houses of Tory hostesses far more often than those of the mere "marriage-mart" variety. She was hoping to corner him this night and pinpoint his interests even though he was one well used to evading being cornered. Miss Forsythe might not like it, but Lady Merrilton was determined to have her answer.

What's more, the Regent had asked for it.

Ariana and Mr. Mornay were stuck in their carriage on Park Lane while awaiting an opening to Merrilton House. A surprisingly large throng crowded the pavement, even overflowing into the street. The crowd was held back from the entrance to the house only by the help of a corded off section, which was guarded by numerous footmen and a few law officers. Lord Merrilton was well aware that if word hit the street that the Regent or, even more significantly, Princess Charlotte was to make an appearance, crowds from the city would flock to catch a glimpse of royalty. The slew of footmen and other men on duty meant the house was prepared.

Sitting across from her beloved, Ariana locked her eyes on Mr. Mornay's inquisitive ones.

"Will you not tell me what ails you?" he asked, beginning to sound a little irked. Since he had called for her in his carriage a short time ago, Ariana had been keeping a petulant silence that was painfully obvious. He sat across from her during the carriage ride. Surprised and yet relieved at this seating arrangement, Ariana was still angry about him not trusting her.

He sighed. "I recommend you tell me the trouble now, before we must face the evening."

She stared away from him but suddenly turned and looked at him, and he knew she was going to tell him. Good. But instead she said, "Why are you seated across from me?"

He had been sitting beside her more and more of late, and so he knew what she meant. "'Tis only proper," he said mildly.

"You are suddenly much concerned with propriety!"

At this he almost shot out of his seat to sit beside her, but the crowds were in the streets and even attempting to peer in the little window in the back, and so he remained where he was.

She faced him accusingly but then dropped her eyes. Neither one of them could ignore the sound of the crowd, excited, jolly, all around the vehicle. His footmen had jumped off the board and were doing their best to keep people back, but it was a challenge.

"If you do not tell me the matter, I can do nothing for it."

She replied, "There, at least, you are perfectly wrong. You *can* do something, only you have done the wrong something! Pray, must we speak of it now?"

He leaned forward. "Speak of *what?* What is it I have done? Of which you do not wish to speak?"

The coach suddenly made some headway, advancing toward the mansion by the length of two carriages. The footmen hurried alongside. He continued. "Do you really imagine that I will allow you to avoid the matter, when it evidently distresses you?"

No answer.

"Do you intend to be my wife, yet without trust between us?"

"Ah!" she cried, leaning suddenly forward and surprising him greatly. Her eyes sparked with flashes of blue and green.

He felt a small relief. Something he had said had reached her at last. But he had as yet to learn the cause of the problem.

"Now there is a pertinent topic! Trust!" She stared at him wide-eyed.

"Go on," he urged.

"You speak to me of trust? Is that not the pot calling the kettle black? When you have had me followed about your house like a...a common street cull!"

It was difficult to take her seriously when she looked so adorable, but at her words Mornay closed his eyes for a second and sighed. "Ariana, you know full well I don't consider you a thief, common or otherwise."

She was now looking at him, her face expressing the hurt she felt. "You ordered a footman to follow me and keep an eye on me. Is that trust?"

"I ordered that for your sake and even before we spoke on the matter. I know you had nothing to do with the stolen things, but I lacked proof. I merely hoped to afford you a witness, so no one else could think you guilty!"

"No one *else*?" Her face was tragical. "No one *else!* You see what I mean!" She crossed her arms more firmly about her and removed her gaze from him to the door. She shifted to playing with her fan.

"You are determined to misunderstand me."

"How is that?"

"What I meant by no one *else* was that none of the other *servants* would think you guilty. Fotch and Frederick, both of whom had seen you in the dressing room, were afraid the ink must have been your doing. I suppose I may have given the impression that I distrusted you, but in fact it was to show the staff that you are up to no mischief. If something else had gone missing or been marred during your visit to the house, I didn't want a shadow of doubt regarding your innocence. Gossip among servants has a way of being magnified. I was merely trying to keep peace."

The carriage reached the mansion, and a footman lowered the steps. Mr. Mornay exited first to hand her down. Ariana had the feeling of living a fairy tale again, as when he had escorted her to Carlton House earlier in the season. Here she was, like a princess, taking the arm of the handsome prince before they together entered the aristocratic abode. One glance at the bystanders sealed the impression of great privilege she was enjoying. Wide-eyed, curious, or even jeering, their looks of admiration or envy made her more conscious of the high life she was beginning to take for granted. But she had other things on her mind just now.

She was relieved that Phillip apparently hadn't mistrusted her, but she still wondered about it. Had he really believed, when ordering that footman to watch her, that it was only for her sake? Was this misunderstanding the start of what would become a pattern of differences, of tiffs in their relationship? Looking at him now, while he held out his arm to her, she wanted nothing more but to fall against him, to snuggle into him, a warm pillar of strength. All she could do was give him an apologetic look and hold firmly to his arm.

For the rest of the night, she had to be her usual self, smile brightly, chat, and banter. After the couple was announced, they entered the huge, high ceilinged gallery. Ariana nodded and smiled as though nothing was amiss. But her heart was not at rest. She was realizing that anything involving Phillip tore right at the deepest part of her. If they weren't happy with each other, she could not be happy at all. If he was upset, she would be also. If he distrusted her, she could not be content.

It was disturbing. Her better judgment, which told her that of course he loved and trusted her, had no power to fight her heart when it concerned him. How could one be so foolish as to ignore what they must believe to be true? When the false light of a situation might cast it in doubt, how could she doubt his affections? She was sensing a chink in the armour of their love. A vulnerable place where her faith and trust—in Phillip and by extension God, for He had given him to her—wavered all too easily.

And then Ariana spotted Princess Charlotte, and all her dark ruminations fled. She found it difficult to take her eyes off the princess. Surrounded by people, smiling and shaking hands, the royal young woman looked eminently comfortable in her role. Ariana had never been in the same room as the princess before and had to struggle afresh with feeling like an out-of-place country miss. She had been getting inured to such gatherings, but this was different. Not only did she hope for an acquaintance with the famous royal, but she felt sure that, if ever she was able to begin a society to aid the poor, Her Royal Highness could be a staunch supporter.

The Princess was a tall and sturdy young woman, not stout but of a large bone structure, proud shoulders, and a large bosom, which the empire fashion suited admirably. Her hair was tastefully done up in a braided knot that could just be seen above a sparkling tiara. She had friendly, large brown eyes, was known to be smart, compassionate, strong-natured but well-mannered, and rather notoriously, treated shabbily at times by her father. Mr. Mornay noticed the direction of Ariana's eyes but said, "We must wait for her to request an introduction."

"Have you met her?"

"Properly introduced only once. I have been at gatherings where she was present as tonight, but knowing that I am a friend of her father's has not endeared me to her, I'm afraid." He spoke with that little hint of a smile, telling Ariana that he was not the least bit flummoxed by the princess's lack of approval.

Neither Ariana nor Mr. Mornay noticed that while they were talking, the very person they spoke of had taken note of them and was even now walking toward them. Lady Merrilton was with her, and suddenly Ariana was in the presence of the princess.

Keeping her eyes on the marchioness's, Ariana listened with a rapidly beating heart as Lady Merrilton said, "May I have the honour, Your Royal Highness, of presenting Mr. Mornay's fiancée to you?" Her words were merely a formality, as everyone already understood that the princess had requested the introduction.

The princess duly replied, "Please do."

"Miss Ariana Forsythe, ma'am, originally from Gloucestershire, I believe."

Ariana curtseyed slower and more deeply than usual, as was proper when greeting a royal, and looked up to see the friendly face of the princess.

"Miss Forsythe, I confess I have been eager to meet you. How do you do?"

"Very well, Your Royal Highness, thank you."

The princess turned toward Phillip. "Mr. Mornay, good evening."

Following a polite bow, he answered, "Your Royal Highness."

She looked back at Ariana. "I understand that you are to be thanked for arranging tonight's dramatic reading?"

"No, ma'am. Lady Merrilton arranged it."

"What Her Royal Highness means, my dear," the marchioness inclined her head to Ariana and explained, "is that we have you to thank for bringing Mrs. Tiernan to our attention."

"It may be that what I considered an admirable performance, in a chapel on a Sunday, may not be as well received here, Your Royal Highness. I pray you will still wish to thank me afterward."

The princess smiled. "I assure you I am fully prepared to be edified this evening." She looked at Phillip. "May I borrow your fiancée? I should like to be better acquainted with her." She slipped her arm inside Ariana's and led her in a walk about the room. In a confidential manner, the princess said, "I am very curious about you, Miss Forsythe. I have followed your romance with Mr. Mornay, you must know, with a mixture of admiration and curiosity. I am told of your great sense of religion, and yet knowing Mr. Mornay, I could not but be surprised that you would accept his offer. His consequence is great, is it not? I do hope you shan't take offense at my saying so, but we all know he is part of my father's set, and so I am certain I cannot say anything you have not heard before."

Ariana was smiling gently at the princess while she spoke, a little shocked at how directly she had broached the subject of Phillip's character. But then was not Princess Charlotte known for her forthright manner? There was no deceit in her. She spoke her mind and yet not in an unbecoming or disagreeable manner. And so Ariana replied, "I have indeed heard much on that theme, I assure you."

The princess smiled. "Then you must forgive my returning to it, but I must know your thoughts. I believe you are mindful of religion and matters of faith, are you not?"

"Yes, ma'am, I hope so."

The princess looked around. "More so than most in this room."

Ariana said nothing. Her Royal Highness studied her thoughtfully for a moment.

"I have been given to understand that Mr. Mornay is a changed man due to your influence."

"*My* influence? I could never take credit for anyone moving toward God, Your Royal Highness. It is entirely *His* doing, you must know."

"Mr. Mornay's?"

"No, ma'am. God's. I believe that no matter which route we use to come to the orthodox faith, it is God Himself who draws us along—until we find Him. Haply He has drawn Mr. Mornay, and I am most grateful." She looked over at him as she spoke, the gratitude she spoke of evident on her shining features.

"And is it true he accompanies you to church services? And that he himself recommended Mrs. Tiernan?"

"Yes, both are true. I believe that Mr. Mornay has discovered..." She hesitated, choosing her words. "That all men need God, and that he is no exception. I believe men come to these discoveries by God's grace—and only by grace."

The princess paused, then touched Ariana's arm and leaned toward her to say, "My dear Miss Forsythe, I am so glad to find you in such a company and at such a time as this!" With a look back at Mr. Mornay, she added, "And to think that Mornay has won you! I am certain you can only be exceedingly good for him." Settling her eyes back on Ariana, she added, "And for all who know you."

"Your Royal Highness is too kind!"

"Not at all. You must call upon me sometime, Miss Forsythe. I will send a card to your home."

Ariana curtseyed at this kindness. "Thank you, ma'am. I should enjoy that above all things!"

The princess then turned away, giving her attention to others who were waiting for her. Ariana made her way back to Mr. Mornay, who came forward to greet her and offer his arm.

Before she could tell him about her meeting with the princess, a flurry of excitement revealed that the Regent had now arrived. He entered the gallery, striding proudly and accompanied by two of his gentlemen. He slowed his pace to nod at the bowing subjects opening the way before him.

Ariana noticed the Lord Mayor of the city as he bowed, with his large medallion hanging about his neck and his wife beside him in a many-feathered headdress. Dukes, duchesses, marquesses and marchionesses, lords and ladies of all ranks gave due respect to the prince with formal correctness. The Regent was dressed in a sober dark twin-tailed frock coat, a top hat, and dark pantaloons. He stopped by various lords or ladies from time to time and addressed them as he wished. When he came upon Ariana and Mr. Mornay, he grinned at Phillip. Then recognizing Ariana, he stopped and smiled. Ariana held her curtsey for a proper amount of time.

"Have you tied the knot yet?"

"There are eight days until the wedding," Mornay answered.

"Ah, but we're not counting, are we?" He chuckled, and others joined him. He then turned to Ariana. "Delighted, Miss Forsythe."

"Your Royal Highness." She curtseyed again, and he moved on.

It took a long time for everyone to be seated for the drama. Ariana was anxious for the performance to start or rather to see how the audience would receive it. They sat through a short concert first, which she would have enjoyed more if she did not have a nagging concern over Mrs. Tiernan's performance. Finally the musicians let their instruments rest. Most of the candles in the room were snuffed. Only the footmen, who circled the edges of the room at intervals, held softly glowing tapers in a statue-like trance.

Mrs. Tiernan climbed upon a makeshift stage. She wore a white dress, making her appear luminous in the dark. A single lampstand near her gave off just enough light so everyone could see her facial expressions—very important to the overall effect. The Regent, sitting only two rows ahead of

Ariana and Phillip, turned his head, and Ariana could see, as he murmured something to a companion, that he was smiling.

The lady on the platform began to search the faces of her audience. It was dark, but she acted as if she could see and took every bit as long as she had done at the chapel. Ariana felt herself squirming. Did the woman not realize that one did not stare at the Regent? Or the princess?

"What the *devil* is she looking at?" someone said sharply.

Mrs. Tiernan maintained that look of distance in her eyes, and finally, taking a deep breath, began with the announcement that her words came from the book of Revelation, chapter twenty-two.

There was a great silence from the audience, and the actual reading began. Ariana did not feel the same thrill as she had on that Sunday morning at the London Orphan Society. The Word of God was being read with great feeling, as then, but somehow she could not enjoy it. It felt all wrong in this irreverent company. Was she hearing murmurs from the audience already? She tried to focus on the lady's words.

"And there shall be no more curse..."

"And there shall be no night there; and they need no candle, neither light of the sun; for the Lord God giveth them light: and they shall reign for ever and ever."

While she was speaking, a man carried up behind her a life-sized cross, but it was evidently not heavy as he lifted it easily. He stood it up directly behind her and then took his place behind the cross as its support. Mrs. Tiernan stretched out her arms. *"And, behold, I come quickly; and my reward is with me, to give every man according as his work shall be..."*

Then her voice grew passionate. *"For without are dogs, and sorcerers,"* she said, turning her gaze directly upon the Regent and with blazing eyes continued, *"and whoremongers, and murderers, and idolaters."*

It seemed as if the entire audience was suddenly holding its collective breath. Ariana certainly was. She felt faint, in fact, though she had never swooned in her life. Lady Merrilton came to her feet, but even she seemed at a loss as to what to do.

Mrs Tiernan continued. *"And whosoever loveth and maketh a lie..."*

Indignant murmurings started sporadically but grew louder as more people joined in. Soon Mrs. Tiernan could not be heard at all. The Regent was sitting ram-rod straight in his chair as the footmen hurriedly lit the candles around the room. Mrs. Tiernan at first ignored the unrest but then gave in and exited the stage.

The room grew lighter as the larger candelabras were lit. People were coming to their feet, and soon it was all confusion. Ariana noticed two footmen escorting Mrs. Tiernan from the room.

"What are they doing to her?" she asked alarmed.

"I'm sure they are merely returning her home. It is no doubt for the best," replied Mornay.

Then Ariana noticed that some people were giving her strange looks, hostile ones. The Regent had come to his feet and was speaking in clipped tones to his hostess, who was apologizing profusely.

Ariana's hand went to her mouth, but Mr. Mornay gently took it and held it fast.

"It isn't our fault," he said.

She looked at him worriedly. "Everyone will think it is. They will think I had a hand in this. I know it!"

"Then we shall set them straight."

"If they give us the opportunity."

The Regent and his retinue were leaving. Lady Merrilton was watching them go with a decidedly unhappy frown. She turned then, met Ariana's gaze, and began walking toward the couple.

"Here is our first opportunity," Mr. Mornay murmured. "Allow me to handle it."

By the time Lady Merrilton reached them, there were others in her train, and a small crowd was gathering around Ariana and her companion. Mr. Mornay held up an arm for silence, but Lady Merrilton was not about to be silenced in her own house, particularly when she had something of import to say.

"Mr. Mornay, you are no doubt blameless in this affair, and I am perfectly prepared to allow that it is so. Yet Miss Forsythe, I daresay, does owe an explanation!"

Lord Merrilton had joined them and was glaring at Ariana. "*If* there is one to be had!"

Others in the crowd expressed their approbation of this thought. Lord Horatio approached, looking concerned and meeting Ariana's eyes with compassion, but he was silent. What could he say? Fortunately Mr. Mornay had no qualms about making his sentiments known.

"Miss Forsythe had as much to do with that lady's performance as you yourself, Merrilton!"

"Me?" the man returned. "But of course I had nothing to do with it! As for her, it is a different thing as it was her doing!"

"Not at all! She merely spoke about her own pleasure at seeing Mrs. Tiernan in an entirely different sort of performance, and her ladyship, *your wife,* insisted she must perform here. Miss Forsythe went so far as to warn her to expect an exceedingly religious reading." He looked at Lady Merrilton, daring her to deny his words. She didn't, but her eyes were expressive of her resentment, and her mouth was set in a decidedly disagreeable frown.

The marquess looked at his wife. "You were rather keen on having her, I do recall."

Her ladyship balked. "Miss Forsythe painted her as being so wonderful! I was utterly misled into the opinion that she would make a proper entertainment for His Royal Highness."

She looked accusingly at Mornay. "*You* should have known better, I daresay, Mr. Mornay."

"How could anyone guess at her intentions? The only person who could answer for this night's work is the lady who presented it."

The marquess had heard enough. "All right then. Prinny will get over it. Let us not stand around arguing like a bunch of coves!" He relented and in a peacemaking gesture looked directly at Ariana. "Come, Miss Forsythe. Has anyone shown you the conservatory?" Then looking around, he added, "We have illuminations to go off shortly. The conservatory window gives an excellent view."

The crowd began to scatter. Her ladyship turned abruptly on her heels and stalked away, with a few other women hurrying to keep stride.

Mr. Mornay was grateful to Merrilton. Taking Ariana on his arm was the perfect gesture to convey he did not hold her a whit responsible.

Ariana too was grateful, but she did not feel certain that the worst was over. Lady Merrilton was a formidable woman. She could be immensely amiable, but her disapproval was daunting. Ariana was reminded of the feeling she'd had when she first discovered that Lady Covington had spread odious lies about her.

She hoped Lady Merrilton was not to do the same.

Ten

Princess Charlotte had not come with the Regent, so neither did she leave with him. However, when Ariana noticed how the marchioness hovered over the princess the rest of the evening, all her hopes for a future acquaintance with Her Royal Highness dissipated.

With a mere look, her ladyship let Ariana know that she was far from ready to forgive what she was determined to view as Miss Forsythe's fault. Even if Princess Charlotte did not hold Ariana to blame for Mrs. Tiernan's insult, Lady Merrilton did, and the Regent may well have felt the same. Further, it was not beyond the prince, she knew, to bar his daughter from keeping an acquaintance he did not approve of.

She thought too of the mysterious events at Grosvenor Square and felt sad. The illuminations from the conservatory were indeed as beautiful and spirit-lifting as promised, but the Regent's displeasure had left a pall over the gathering that nothing could erase. This only added to Ariana's regrets so that by the time she was back in the coach with her beloved, she had fallen into a melancholic mood.

She felt as tragic as Cordelia, the good but misunderstood daughter of King Lear. No, she was Ophelia, singing sadly and strewing flower petals as she glided down a stream, not knowing her very death was around the next bend. Better yet she was Desdemona, the wife of Othello, whose own husband was going to kill her under false suspicion of wrongdoing. Perchance she was Jepthah's daughter, a virgin dying before her time due to an ill-spoken oath. Oh, the slings and arrows of outrageous—

"Ariana?"

She was pulled abruptly from her tragic deaths.

Mr. Mornay was watching her with a little smile. "What *are* you thinking?"

She searched for how to answer, shaking her head. "I am exceedingly cast down from tonight's work."

"On what account? Nothing will come of it, I assure you."

"Nothing? I feel as though tragedy has struck me again without warning. As when Lady Covington spread her odious falsehoods about me."

"Which brought *me* to your parlour, recall," he said, his eyes warmly upon her.

She smiled reluctantly. "True."

"All is not lost. The marquess has shown his favour to you, and Lady Merrilton has ever courted mine and will continue to do so, I am persuaded. Her ladyship will not remain out of countenance with you, I am certain of it. She really has no one to blame but herself. Which is no doubt why the episode vexes her so!"

"But this is the second scandal you said my name could not survive!"

He chuckled. "No such thing. Your mind has a dramatic turn. Next time we ought to give you the platform. It would be much more to the company's liking than Mrs. Tiernan, I daresay. And the Regent has never disliked a beautiful woman to my knowledge. We will pay him a call, and you will win him over in a matter of minutes!"

"Do you indeed think so?" Her eyes came alight with hope.

"Of course."

On the following evening, the Herleys were having a card party. It was nothing like the card parties of the most *tonnish* families, for wagers were kept strictly low. Ariana had, of course, been invited and felt it incumbent on herself to attend. Mrs. Bentley had an invitation from Viscount Dickson and was much against the Herley party, so Ariana was in a flummox, not wishing to displease her friend or her aunt. Mr. Mornay saved the day by agreeing to take Ariana to the Herley's for a short visit (with the emphasis on *short*), and then join Mrs. Bentley at the Viscount's. With the usual footmen on the back of the carriage as chaperones, he came for Ariana in good time.

Somehow his idea of keeping distance between them was turning out to be untenable. He had meant to have it so, to stay occupied apart from her, but with the season in full swing and so many invitations for the two of them, it was impossible to fulfill the plan.

He handed her into his plush black coach with a greater feeling of contentment than he'd known in two decades. It was extraordinary—these feelings of satisfaction with life and of *love* for Ariana. He realized that he had not known what it felt like to be in love before. His youthful passion—and heartbreak—following an ill-advised, teen-aged liaison, he now viewed with the suspicion of maturity. It hadn't been love after all. It was merely an infatuation, which, coupled with his youth, inexperience with the world, and then the succession of deaths in his family—first his father, then Nigel his brother, and then his mother all within the space of eighteen months—had made him think himself heartbroken, heartsick, and world-weary. He realized now that he had mostly been grieving. But his grief had been pushed aside, and in its place he'd developed a deep distrust of women and the world in general.

Faced with the treachery of his youthful love-interest, he had avoided females—for years. He'd been quite successful at it too, feeling no need to change his conviction on that head until he'd met Ariana. Having charge of her now, tonight, felt very enjoyable.

He may have been failing to keep his distance from her, but he was at least doing better at keeping her out of his arms. But when she asked him point-blank to escort her somewhere, such as to the Herley's, how could he refrain? Did he want someone else doing so? No, most assuredly not—particularly in light of her near abduction! He moved into the equipage after her, sitting down across from her. He remembered the prior evening, how admirably he had behaved when he took her home, and was determined to do so again.

When the wheels began turning, she said, "Thank you for taking me to the Herley's."

"Not at all." He reached across and took her hand, and she allowed him to hold it firmly between his. For a few moments they sat that way. Then suddenly he moved and sat beside her. She gave a weak smile.

He kissed her hand.

"My aunt, I daresay, will expect us no later than ten o'clock!"

"No doubt." He turned her hand palm upward and kissed it again.

"May I take part in one card game, do you think, at Lavinia's?"

He paused for a second over her hand and said softly, "If you like." And then he kissed it once more.

"Thank you."

"Do not thank me. I delight in doing aught for you." He kissed her palm again more lingeringly, and just as Ariana was thinking what a good thing it was that she was wearing gloves, he took hold of the end of the glove at the fingertips and began pulling it off. Ariana snatched her hand away.

"Do not!" she chided laughingly, hiding the offended hand beneath her other arm.

He gave her a look of mild reproval, while taking back possession of her hand by prying it away until she was forced to relinquish it.

"Mr. Mornay! You are quite shocking!"

"Am I?" he replied, looking at her doubtfully. "If so, I am merely behaving in character, for I have always, I'm afraid, acted in a manner you find shocking on occasion. Can you disagree?"

"No, but in this matter you have ever been a gentleman."

"In what matter is that?"

She looked down at her hand, which was locked within his strong grasp.

"Am I not to be trusted with your hand? Only your hand?" He softened his hold on her, and Ariana suddenly felt that it *was* a bit silly to be so concerned.

"Very well. I give you my hand, but that is all—until you take it in holy wedlock Friday next."

"Which I am eager to do," he replied, looking into her eyes but pulling the glove off in one swift movement. He immediately put her hand up to his lips and kissed it on one side, then the other, and then lingeringly slid his mouth to her wrist. He pushed the fabric of her capelet aside, revealing her delicate arm all the way up to her elbow.

Ariana was decidedly unready for such an assualt upon her senses and pulled her arm away. "You are indeed shocking! I must beg you to cease your attentions to my arm at once!" She colored instantly for having said such a perfectly foolish statement, but she meant it, never mind.

"Do you indeed?"

"I insist."

"Very well." He released her hand and leaned over and instantly applied a direct kiss to her mouth. She made a sound of exasperation and pushed against him. He moved away but then went to pick her up and bring her onto his lap. She was just able to gasp, "No!"

Her tone did cause him to look in surprise at her face, after which and with a sigh, he released her.

Ariana moved away from him, staring with wide, wary eyes.

"You needn't look at me like that," he added with a sigh of resignation. "I just forgot myself for a moment. It won't happen again." In a much lower tone, she heard him add, "For now."

She turned her face away to hide a smile, which threatened to reveal her true emotions. Then she pulled her glove back on and smoothed out some imaginary wrinkles in her gown. They were both silent then, and she felt suddenly embarrassed. For the first time in recent memory, she was uneasy in his presence.

"Ariana."

"Yes?"

He chose his words. "Are you angry with me?"

She thought for a moment. "No." She could *feel* his eyes upon her. Slowly she raised her eyes to his. "I was rather…alarmed. But not angry."

He gave a defeated sigh. "I'm still a beast, you know. Never did have good manners."

Her face softened. "Nonsense. You have the finest manners. We—neither of us—are accustomed to being in love, I think."

His demeanor relaxed. "Very true."

When the coach began to slow, they prepared for their arrival. In minutes the Herleys' butler announced the couple. Ariana noted that Phillip had taken on the guarded expression he had by habit cultivated when having to do anything disagreeable. The prospect of spending the next hour in this less-than-exciting gathering of her friends was not something he was savouring.

"*Mr.* Mornay!" Mrs. Herley rushed ahead of her husband to greet their famous guest. "Only think how gratified I was to learn that you were to honour us by coming to our little gathering. May I invite you to sit at a table and play a game with us, perhaps?"

"I thank you, no."

At that point Mr. Herley came forward, hoping, as he thought, to rescue the man. "Allow me to offer our distinguished guest some refreshment, Mrs. Herley."

"Why yes, of course, Mr. Herley! The very thing I was about to suggest. A refreshment."

Mr. Mornay moved off with the gentleman, glad to be occupied while not having to mingle. He was still prepared to merely endure the next hour in the place, but with rare insight, his host suggested, "Might I take you to a quieter room of the house, sir? Where gentlemen can be expected to hear one another's conversation—the library perhaps?"

"Excellent." He willingly followed his host from the room, after taking a last look at Ariana, already sitting at table with Lavinia and other ladies. The cards were dealt. To his eyes she was like a star among the rubble, her hair shimmering even in the dim light of a single candelabra. Her evening gown draped beautifully to the floor as she sat. Her slim frame appeared quite pretty alongside the ladies who flanked her, both of whom were no longer in the blush of youth. Stopping to look, he was momentarily blind to the fact that his good-natured host was watching him.

Mr. Mornay was thinking that he must make it known among his friends that Ariana was not to be trifled with—neither now nor after the wedding. Many married women from his class, for some reason, were known to have illicit affairs, a few with the Regent himself. A mere scent of a scandal around a woman's name before marriage would ruin her completely. After marriage it was almost expected that she would eventually look to other men for her entertainment, just as most men also were unfaithful. But of course it would not, could not, be so for Ariana and him.

He followed the man of the house through a large double door, along a narrow corridor, across a drafty passageway, and into the library. It was more cozy than luxurious, evidently a room much used by the family, but Mr. Mornay took little notice. Just to be excused from attendance in the main card room was pleasure enough.

He tugged at his watch fob, checked his watch, and made a mental note to be in the coach with his beloved in no more than one hour. As Mr. Herley retrieved two glasses from the inlaid cupboard and chose their beverages from the bottles of port, wine, sherry, and brandy, Mr. Mornay walked idly about the room. He perused the bookshelves and paintings with mild interest. Stopping abruptly, he noticed that they had a small portrait of George III, exactly the same as the one that had recently gone missing at his own house. Curious.

He moved closer. By Jove, but if it wasn't very like! He wanted quite strongly to take it from the wall to examine it minutely, but good manners forbade that action.

When his host came over and handed him a glass with an amiable,

"Cheers—to the ladies," he received his beverage with a polite nod and raised it for the toast. After the first sip, he turned to the small painting and remarked, "'Tis a good likeness of the King. Is it an original?"

Mr. Herley placed his gaze on the portrait. He gave a short, uncomfortable laugh. "To tell the truth, sir," he said, his face colouring, "the place was furnished when we bought it. Because it is my wife's concern, the quality of the paintings and furniture and what...I couldn't tell you."

"May I look at it?"

The man gave a flourish with one hand, surprised but pleased that he owned something that had struck the interest of the Paragon. Mr. Mornay took it from the wall carefully and then turned it over. There, in an upper corner, were the initials, "M.M." He frowned. He didn't recall the portrait having initials. He had only learned of the portrait after a servant had found it among his mother's possessions during an annual deep cleaning. Frederick had seen it in the boy's hands and plucked it from him before he could replace it to the trunk where it had lain, forgotten, for who knew how long. He'd been quite pleased when the master, after looking thoughtfully at the portrait for a few moments, had thanked him for finding it and told him to put it in a prominent place in the first parlour.

Of course the servant had no idea that Mr. Mornay had instantly seen the picture as a nacky way to hector the Regent on his next visit. Nothing was more certain to raise a dust than for Prinny to think his friend was entertaining sympathies for the king! Publicly, of course, the prince took pains to appear as the loving son. But in private and with his friends, it was no secret he and his father shared little love between them, and the onset of his father's illness was a welcome circumstance for a man who lived in constant need of padding his purse. As Regent he enjoyed a greater income but still overspent what monies he had—at least there was no one to reproach him for it as gallingly as his father had often done in the past.

Looking at the painting, Mr. Mornay had to concede that the initials on the back fit his mother's married name, Miranda Mornay. But had the portrait from his house borne such initials? Was this his property or wasn't it? Why couldn't he remember? Also there must be many such portraits of the monarch in existence. As he stood there thinking, Mr. Herley had to smile with the thought that this prime fellow was an evident admirer of the king. He liked him the better for it.

Not wishing to be too hasty, Mr. Mornay carefully examined the wall where the picture had hung. This caused Mr. Herley to come and peer curiously at the painted surface himself. He had no idea what he was supposed to be looking for or at. It was just a wall. Mr. Mornay, however, appeared satisfied, gave him a brief, unrevealing smile, and then replaced the artwork to its former position. Curious fellow, this Paragon. Later on he would have to return and take a better look at the picture and the wall. There had to be something outstanding about both of 'em for the gentleman to have shown such an interest. He hoped he could discover what it was.

The men sat down, and Mr. Mornay took small sips from his glass at long intervals, allowing his host to regale him with the sort of chitchat men enjoyed; talk of the most recent show of pugilism, racing, and the newest equipages. He'd spent time doing worse.

Ariana was enjoying herself at multiplayer whist, while Beatrice, beside her, watched with sporadic interest. Although Beatrice wished to improve her playing, she had little patience to actually learn the tricks. Ariana had greeted her younger sister quite effusively, happy to see her. Beatrice still had a cold, but Ariana had never feared contracting it and paid no heed to it now. The O'Briens had dutifully kept the girl away in deference to Mrs Bentley's wishes, but tonight was an exception. And Mrs. Bentley wasn't around to know it.

Ariana was able to relax at the Herley's almost as much as if she'd been at her own house. Lavinia's lightheartedness was infectious and made the atmosphere jovial. Mr. O'Brien did insist upon settling a troubled look upon her now and then, which she studiously ignored, having no wish to engage in any sort of serious conversation with him. To everyone's amusement, Miss Alice invited Beatrice to practice a country dance while the adults played cards. Even Mr. O'Brien emerged from his brown study long enough to chide their errors and instruct them on proper form.

Here there was no formality such as when she had finally begun attending Almack's on Wednesday nights. The atmosphere there was stilted, and most of the young ladies were so agog with the idea of having to make a good impression that conversation with them was strained. Ariana, who had never viewed herself as being particularly at ease among society, saw that she did indeed stand in contrast to most of the other girls her age. When the patronesses addressed her, she answered them with no qualms. When the

Duke of York himself desired the honour of a dance with her, she accepted happily. Other girls looked fraught with unease, and some as if they would burst into tears at the least provocation.

Mr. Mornay had escorted her twice to the place. Even for Ariana he could little countenance the insipid atmosphere, despite the patronesses falling over themselves to make him welcome. On her second appearance at the establishment, Ariana had felt so sorry for a sad-looking young woman, by name of Miss Blenhem, that she had coaxed Mornay into standing up with the girl. Instead of raising the young lady's spirits, however, his surprising offer had caused her to swoon almost immediately. The experience (though not without humour) only added to his dread of the place. Which didn't bother Ariana. She much preferred more intimate, informal parties such as this evening at the Herleys.

They were playing the last rubber of a game when she spotted a silver candlestick on a table nearby. It seemed somehow familiar, and with a pang she recalled that a silver candlestick had gone missing from Grosvenor Square—after her visit there. After her visit, which *included* Lavinia and her mama. It was too jarring a thought to even speak of for a few minutes, and she grew quiet with distressing ideas running through her mind. Very casually, when it was the turn of a Miss Holden's, Ariana said, "Lavinia, I admire your candlestick."

"Say again?" Lavinia seemed confused. It was a little disconcerting to have an acquaintance suddenly admire one's candlestick. Had she said, "I adore your fan!" or "I must get some feathers such as the ones on Lady Gordon's headdress," Lavinia would not have been surprised. But to hear her friend say something about a mere candlestick struck her as so odd that she had to question her hearing.

"There," Ariana nodded in the direction of the table holding the item. "Your candlestick. 'Tis amazingly like one at Grosvenor Square." She kept her eyes on the candlestick, for she could not keep a reproach out of her expression, though she had managed to keep it from her voice. But Lavinia did not fly up into the boughs, as she had half expected. Instead the girl let out a tinkle of laughter.

"Did you hear that, Mama?" she asked. "Ariana says our candlestick resembles one from Grosvenor Square. Is that not amusing? That we should have anything on par with such a place as that!"

Mrs. Herley looked severely unamused. "Do not think it so impossible, Vinny. Why must you always sound as though you think we are all done up? I brought many a fine thing with me upon marriage to your papa, and that candlestick, well let me see, it may have been among them."

Lavinia took her first real look at the piece in question. "I cannot recall seeing it before," she said, "and if you do not recall it being yours, perhaps it isn't ours at all!" She collapsed into laughter, inviting all those around the table to join in. "How perfectly absurd! That we have a candlestick I've never seen before, and it mayn't be ours at all!"

Her mother cried, "Don't be ridiculous! Of course it's ours."

"But you do not recall?" Lavinia now seemed incredulous. "I daresay," she confided to the whole table, "I already know what my dowry may be, and I shan't forget a single part of it, ever, I am convinced!"

"You say that now," murmured her mother, while concentrating on her cards, "but you may surprise yourself—after a score of years in marriage."

Lavinia shrugged with a comical expression. She was such a guileless creature. How could Ariana have suspected her friend for a single moment? As for Mrs. Herley, however, Ariana was not so certain.

Molly reached out and took hold of the doorknob to Mrs. Hamilton's room, her face a mixture of timidity, fear, and curiosity. She'd never been in the housekeeper's room before. She wondered why the laidy wanted her and hoped it would be good news; a rise in her situation perhaps. Could it be? She'd only been in the place for just over a month—since that sweet laidy Miss Forsythe had rescued her and caused her to be taken on at Grosvenor Square. Such a fancy establishment! No one she had ever known had worked in such a fine place. The scullery was still the scullery, and she had many unpleasant tasks, but she was content.

"Come in," Mrs. Hamilton urged. Molly, naturally shy, had been creeping in slowly and looking about in wonder. The housekeeper's room was so cozy and well put up. It astonished her.

Mrs. Hamilton came straight to the point. She was sitting in a comfortable wing chair with a newspaper upon her lap. There was a small fire burning, and the laidy was even sipping a cup of some hot liquid. Molly wished she would be asked to join her.

But no such thing.

"I have learned that you are a wicked, disloyal servant, Molly! What do you have to say for yourself?"

Molly blinked at Mrs. Hamilton in alarm and surprise. For a few moments, she did not know what to say. "I ain't done nothin', mum," was her meager reply.

"Perhaps not yet, but do you deny that you were caught napping letters in your previous household?"

Molly instantly bowed her head in shame. She had thought that episode was behind her. She'd only done it for the extra money, which she used to feed her little brother, who was practically a street urchin.

"Well?" Mrs. Hamilton could be merciless at times.

Molly shook her head, *no.*

"Of course you don't deny it. You can't deny it. You're guilty!"

"The master knows, mum."

She seemed startled. "The master knows? What you've done?"

This time Molly nodded more confidently.

"I don't believe it. He would never hire you on."

"The mistress asked him to, mum."

"The mistress—do you mean, Miss Forsythe?"

"Ay."

"Does she know you took her letters?"

"Ay, mum."

This jarred with what Mrs. Hamilton believed of Miss Forsythe. It smacked of, well, *kindness* and didn't suit her mental image of the future mistress of 25 Grosvenor Square at all.

"Well I suppose in that case, she may even be planning to keep you on." Mrs. Hamilton's words seemed to be meant for herself, as though she were thinking aloud.

Molly did not understand them, in any case. Why wouldn't Miss Forsythe plan to keep her on? She certainly hoped she did! She had no reason to believe otherwise, as she had not heard Mrs. Hamilton's prediction, and no one considered a scullery maid of enough importance to repeat it to her.

After thinking for a moment, Mrs. Hamilton said, "Well in any case, I am going to keep a sharp eye on you, missee!"

The maid curtseyed. "Ay, mum."

"That will be all." Mrs. Hamilton took a slow sip of her tea, thinking hard. Her plans for using the girl would have to change. No matter. She was sure Molly would still come in handy. In fact—her eyes lit with a thought—she would come in very handy, indeed.

Eleven

Lord Antoine could not believe, now that he thought on it, that he had ever seriously entertained the thought of abducting Miss Forsythe. He'd always been a bit crass in his attitude toward women—frequenting East End flash houses with their ready supply of demireps could do that to a man—but certainly he never wished to harm a lady. And Miss Forsythe was a lady, indeed. Abduction, moreover, was a serious business, and he had to make it clear to Julian that he would have nothing more to do with it.

He thought back to the day when the whole nasty plot had been hatched. His brother, Lord Wingate, had come upon him unexpectedly as he had been nursing a wound in his favorite pub, The Whip. It was the worst sort of wound a man could sustain, he felt. He had hoped to marry Miss Lavinia Herley. The Herleys were not so wealthy that they could cover his debts, but Lavinia's dowry was not so small to be beyond temptation either. Besides, and perhaps most importantly, the Herleys had not been aware of his family's sinister reputation and had welcomed the young man into their midst as the best of suitors. It had been unfair and vexing to find that the Paragon had spoken against him, dashing his hopes, turning the Herleys into the same sort of cold and affronted individuals most members of the *ton* were when it came to his family.

These weren't the reasons that he had risen up against Mr. Mornay's fiancée, however. The thing that had catapulted him from a life of selfishness and debauchery into one of possible felonious crime—attempting to abduct a lady of quality—was that Lord Antoine *liked* Lavinia. Indeed, he missed her terribly. Not only was she bubbly and bright, the very opposite of his own morose disposition, but she enjoyed being with him. She found him witty and funny. And he liked amusing her. Indeed, he liked himself more in her presence than at any other time!

She was good for him, that's what.

Still it was with dismay that Holliwell had realized he had feelings for Miss Herley. He, a rogue, a rake, no less than his brother and father before him, had feelings for a gently bred young woman of no measurable consequence, except that she counted Miss Ariana Forsythe as her friend. It was daunting. It was unprecedented. It was...liberating! It meant that he had the capacity to love a woman—a simple thing, perhaps, for some, but a matter he'd nearly concluded was outside of his capabilities.

So, instead of thanking the Paragon for ensuring his release from further doings with the middle-class Herleys, Lord Antoine found his meddling unforgivable.

When he mentioned his woes, over a bottle of brandy that day in the pub, Lord Wingate, in a generous mood, vowed to get revenge for his brother's sake. They commiserated over the lost opportunities they had been deprived of: a dowry, a family connexion that would not harm their own (as if anything could further harm the family name), the progeny that might have resulted from the union, and finally the pleasures of matrimonial life (which neither of them had a clue about because their own sire and dam had not lived together since their conception). No matter, it was felt to be a major loss upon their sensibilities, and nothing but a good revenge would answer.

By the time a second bottle of the potent libation had been consumed, the brothers were feeling more brotherly than they had, perhaps, in all their lives. Lord Wingate, as the elder, felt especially protective of his younger sibling, and together they hatched a plan. They would get at Mornay through his weakest point, which happened to be Miss Forsythe. Exactly what they would do with Miss Forsythe once they had managed to get hold of her was not entirely clear. But the Paragon had deprived Lord Antoine of his intended bride, and so they must of necessity do the same to him.

Perhaps they would put her on board a ship bound for America. Perhaps Botany Bay. Perhaps they would hold her for ransom. Who knew? Who cared? The object at hand was simply to get her.

Lord Antoine remembered Mr. O'Brien was a friend of Miss Forsythe's. He was a trusting sort of soul—a real cat's paw. He might be useful in their cause.

It was Mr. Chesley who informed his lordship of the Viscount's ball, and Lord Antoine, though he no longer had a heart for felonious crime, who told his brother. He did it to silence him. To get him off his back. He also told him that he, Antoine, would have no hand in setting a trap for the lady on this night. He would be busy, he said, crashing the card party at the Herley's. He did not add that he had no desire or intention of waylaying Miss Forsythe upon any occasion or that he would henceforward refuse to help his brother if he persisted in that endeavour. He would face that confrontation another time.

Far too soon, it seemed to her, Ariana was collected by Mr. Mornay and was saying her goodbyes.

"I am so much better now!" Beatrice declared. "May I dare to call upon you, do you think?" She looked back at Mr. O'Brien. "I am sure Mr. O'Brien shall drive me to see you!"

Mr. O'Brien coughed lightly. He did not often use the family carriage in Mayfair as he preferred walking for his health, but he said, "Of course." It would be a good excuse to see Ariana again.

Ariana hesitated. Mr. Mornay, who stood beside her, said, "Perhaps in a few days. If your aunt sees the least evidence of ill health, I suspect you'll get a thorough combing that will leave your ears ringing."

Mrs. O'Brien added, "Beatrice will be accompanying me and the girls home now, as my son, I believe, is also going to the Viscount's tonight. Your sister will get the rest a young gel should and, I am sure, be fully recovered by the date of your wedding."

Ariana thanked her heartily.

No sooner had the couple started off for the Viscount's, when Ariana said to Mornay, "I saw your candlestick."

"I beg your pardon?"

"Your missing candlestick! I think the Herleys have it. I'm not certain, but I suspect that Mrs. Herley may have...she may have *napped* it!"

He then gave her an odd look, causing her to ask, "What is it? Do you know something of it?"

"I believe they may also have the missing portrait."

She gasped. "Upon my word! This is shocking!"

"It is unfortunate," he replied, "but alas, not shocking. I have heard of worse things occurring. You see now why I am careful of my company." She heard a silent reprimand, implying that perhaps Ariana ought to be more careful of hers.

"I am certain Miss Herley is above reproach," Ariana said. "I suspect only her mama."

When Mornay said nothing, she asked, "So, what is to be done?"

"Not a thing. I won't press charges against your friends."

"Thank you!" She looked at him adoringly, and he leaned over and placed a small kiss on her smooth, soft cheek.

Ariana sniffed a bit loudly.

"Yes, I have had a drink," he answered, guessing her thoughts.

"Mmmm," was all she said. She hadn't actually meant to imply anything but found his remark rather interesting.

"It is thoroughly to be expected that I will have a drink on occasion, Ariana. It has always been my habit."

"I understand."

"I do not drink myself under the table, as you well know, and I assure you it must not concern you."

"I am not concerned," she responded. "I *trust* you."

There was silence for a moment, while he ingested that pleasant thought. But he had to say more. "I have no intention of letting myself be bamboozled into drinking too much again, you know."

She was beginning to find his defensiveness amusing. "I know that, sir."

He shifted in his seat. There was another silence. This time it was filled with a fair amount of tension. Coming from him. "If you aren't concerned," he said finally, "then why the devil am I feeling compelled to keep apologizing? I hadn't the least thought of there being anything wrong with accepting a drink from a gentleman in his library until I entered this coach with you."

For a moment Ariana was silent from sheer surprise. Finally she said, "It is not *my* doing, I assure you. Perhaps *you* think you shouldn't have accepted the drink."

"I don't think any such thing!" He thought suddenly of the way his friends sometimes teased him, saying things like, "How can you stand to be in the presence of such a saint? Isn't it tiresome trying to behave all the time?" He had always laughed off such comments because he had never bothered to behave any differently in Ariana's presence than elsewhere. But now he suddenly felt he ought to. What an irksome thing! Then again if she had loved him before, when he had always accepted a drink without a thought, then she would continue to love him. He didn't have a thing to worry about. *But why the devil do I feel as though I do? Bother!*

When they reached the Viscount's house, the ball was underway. Ariana's hand was immediately taken for a dance.

Lord Horatio stepped forward and quickly asserted his rights to the next one. "You promised me at Carlton House. Both of you," he reminded her and her future husband. His friend could only nod and smile.

As Ariana was escorted to the dance floor, Mr. Mornay was approached by Lord Alvanley. "Come and join us, Phillip, and let some other men have the enjoyment of the angel for a while."

"The angel?"

"We can't keep calling her Lady Mornay, coz it puts the real ladies into a pet, moaning how every knight or sir's wife is called a 'lady' and every mistress of a house fancies herself 'lady this' or 'lady that.' Miss Forsythe is not nobility and neither are you, Phillip, though it ain't a secret that even Prinny defers to you sometimes! But that's the up and up of it. The members of our fairer sex are quite insisting upon a different term of affection for your soon-to-be wife. So it's 'angel.' Come, you aren't smarting about it, surely?"

"Don't be a muttonhead."

Alvanley chuckled. "I knew as much! And you have to admit, by face and reputation, you are marrying an angel of the first water!"

Mornay did not demur. It was true. He had thought so himself numerous times. But he wasn't about to make a cake of himself by discussing her that way with anyone. "Change the subject, Alvanley. Or are you so enamored of my future bride that you can't tear your mind from the topic?"

His friend smiled—and changed the subject. "Saw your new jacket at Weston's today. For the wedding, eh? It's all the dash, to be sure. I ordered one like it."

Mornay said nothing. He also did not discuss fashion.

"Ain't you going to complain that it's your new style? That I should steer away?" Still there was no answer. "Dash it! They told me you personally designed two extra inches at the wrists! I'm cinchin' it from you, and you say nothing?"

"Alvanley!" Mornay finally exclaimed, and the man's eyes lit, ready to celebrate that he had finally elicited a response from his unflappable friend. "You're wasting my time. Good evening." Mornay turned to go.

"Whoa, wait a minute!"

Mornay stopped and looked at him expectantly.

"When's the wedding?"

He hesitated. "You're not planning on coming, I hope?" But he smiled as he said it.

"Just want to know, dash it. There's bound to be a wager at White's tonight or soon enough. Thought it would be amusing to win one."

"Friday next," he answered. "You might have known if you'd heard the banns or read the papers."

At that moment a few men from the card room entered the corridor. "Here he is, and with Mornay! Come! We've got five minutes. Can we entice either of you gentlemen to join the game?"

"Not tonight," Mr. Mornay replied.

"I'll consider it," returned Alvanley, just to taunt them.

Mr. Courtney said, "We've got Argyll in his cups and out of half his estate! He'll be done up soon. But he's hocused. We need a witness before he's done up, or he'll challenge it later."

"Black-hearted coves, the both of you," muttered Mornay.

The man named Whipplehead took Mornay's arm, saying, "Sir, the man insisted upon the stakes! We were merely obliging him."

Mr. Mornay shook himself free and replied cooly, "Do that again, and I'll hang you by the tails of your coat." His voice had reverted to smooth-as-silk venom and had its usual effect.

Mr. Whipplehead quickly retreated behind Alvanley, who said, "Give it up, gentlemen. We're not for it."

The two men shook their heads and turned to head back to resume their game.

Ariana. Mr. Mornay wanted to see what she was up to. He headed back to the ballroom and looked around but did not find her. He asked the viscountess of her whereabouts.

"Oh but, Mr. Mornay!" she said, with a look of severe shock. "I was given to understand that you had decided to take her elsewhere. I thought the two of you had gone!"

His eyes narrowed. "Given to understand by *whom*?"

She thought hard for a moment. "I think it was...it was...oh dear." She turned to the Viscount, "My dear, what was the name of that young man who said he must take Miss Forsythe to Mr. Mornay?"

"What? The tall young blade?"

"Yes, the young man with the light hair. Do you not recall?"

Mr. Mornay, about ready to pop a button off his beautiful embroidered waistcoat, held his temper in check while he listened. But he clenched his fists with the effort.

The viscount, meanwhile, was rubbing his chin thoughtfully. "Yes, I know that boy."

"Yes, of course you know him," she said, giving Mr. Mornay a nervous glance.

"Wants to go into the church, doesn't he?"

"That's it!" The viscountess looked enlightened. "Now I know." She turned to Mr. Mornay with a reassuring smile. "Mr. O'Brien! I remember now. His mother has another son, I believe, in the Navy. We just talked of it tonight."

Mr. Mornay had gone, however, as soon as the name of Mr. O'Brien had left her mouth, and she was left speaking only to her husband.

"I hope I did nothing amiss in handing her to Mr. O'Brien. He seemed such an agreeable gentlemanlike sort of man."

Mr. Mornay continued his search. It was a footman, upon hearing him asking of Miss Forsythe, who offered the information that she had left the house in the company of a tall, light-haired gentleman not five minutes earlier.

With a severe look on his countenance, he went directly to the street, hoping to catch her with that addlepated youth before they could go elsewhere.

Out on the street, a few grooms and a passerby were huddled around something on the sidewalk. As he sent a boy to bring round his equipage, he caught a glance at the thing on the sidewalk. It was a man, and he was lying on the ground unconscious. For a moment he wanted to ignore this and go in pursuit of his wayward bride-to-be, but a tug on his conscience made him go and inspect the unfortunate lying there. If nothing else, he'd get him into the house where he'd be safe from thieves and hoodlums.

When the servants and other passersby saw him coming, they immediately gave way for him to inspect the person and told him that an officer had been sent for. Mr. Mornay nodded and bent over to get a look at the victim. He froze in horror for a second. It was Mr. O'Brien. A quick look around assured him that Ariana had not been reduced to the same condition, but what on earth had happened? Here was Mr. O'Brien, the man last seen with his beloved, lying unconscious on the pavement, and there was no sight or sign of Ariana.

Twelve

Lord Antoine and Mr. Harold Chesley had arrived at Burton Crescent for the Herley's card party just in time to see Mr. Mornay and Miss Forsythe leave in their coach. Mr. Mornay saw the young men as they alit from the hackney, recognizing Mr. Chesley at once. Their eyes met, but Chesley knew better than to hope for a greeting from the Paragon. He averted his gaze and continued up to the house with Lord Antoine, who stared at the Paragon and had caught a glimpse of the beautiful Miss Forsythe—and couldn't help feeling a little fascination. His recent repentance of the plan to abduct the lady had only strengthened the more he thought on it. He was above certain he could never take part in such a scheme. It was harebrained and too serious an offense for his liking. Indeed, he had no stomach at all for terrifying innocent ladies.

It didn't help that at White's, as he commiserated with Mr. Chesley about his brother's plans, the young man had replied, "Bravo! It's time someone gave Mornay his comeuppance! If I may serve in any way, do, I beg you, avail yourself of me at once!" Mr. Chesley had not understood that Holliwell was washing his hands of the business. But his friend's vehemence interested him. "Are you only the man's enemy, or do you have aught against the lady too?"

Mr. Chesley paused, taking a thoughtful moment while he swallowed a good amount of ale. "My argument with the lady is that she has accepted the man. I detest him. I will gladly help in any scheme against him. As long as Miss Forsythe remains in ignorance of my hand in it, o' course."

Holliwell nodded. He would keep his own determination—of being done with the business—to himself. He still liked Chesley though. He was an amusing chap. More, Chesley had a membership to White's, something

Antoine did not, and he liked the chance to be in the prestigious establishment, even if it was on the sly.

Ariana tried not to fall from her seat in the threadbare coach that was bulleting through the streets of London, heading toward the East End. She stared at her abductor and wondered whether she should attempt an escape from his clutches or not. He was not particularly frightening in appearance. That she was crying was more on account of the terrible sight, fresh in her mind, of Mr. O'Brien being struck down right in front of her! What if the man didn't survive? How had it all happened so quickly? And *why*?

Only minutes ago she had been at a glittering ball, enjoying herself quite satisfactorily and chatting with the viscountess. Then Mr. O'Brien had approached her with the startling news that he'd been sent by Mr. Mornay to take her back to Hanover Square. *We have only just arrived, but he wants me to go home?* Her first thought had been to find him and verify the matter.

But Mr. O'Brien's plea had been so eloquent. As he approached Ariana and the viscountess, he said, "I pray you, Miss Forsythe, allow me this honour, not only for your sake but for Mr. Mornay's. As you know he and I have never been friends, but he has elected to trust me in this, and I have every hope of pleasing him. It will constitute an excellent foundation for us to improve our acquaintance. Allow me to do this little favour for your esteemed future husband—I am gratified that he has asked it of *me*."

How could I have refused? She was starkly disappointed that her beloved was sending her home, however. Her mind filled with questions. *On what account? Does he want me out of the way so that he can spend his evening at cards without a qualm? Why wouldn't he himself come to speak to me? Has it come to this already, and we not even married yet?* Hearing the news from Mr. O'Brien had to mean it was Phillip's wish—Mr. O'Brien would never invent such a thing. So she questioned the matter no further. She merely sent word to Mrs. Bentley (who was enjoying herself as never before in society since Mr. Pellham was at her side), and left with Mr. O'Brien.

Under normal circumstances, Mrs. Bentley might have questioned this news. She herself might even have sought out Mr. Mornay to see what was what. But with her hand on Mr. Pellham's arm, and he so cleverly leading a little circle of her friends in a discussion of the Orient and amusing them with anecdotes gleaned from his travel books, she could only manage to nod when she heard the report. Thinking to herself, *If Ariana is agreeable to the idea, then I shan't raise a dust,* her only worry was that the girl might have taken ill. Why else would she be leaving so early?

Hearing the matter, the viscountess had also given her approval. If Mr. Mornay wanted a thing done, it must be accomplished speedily! She came away with the misunderstanding that Ariana was to join Mr. Mornay in leaving the party, as such things were bound to occur when the rooms were full and the hearing of the lady in question very compromised as hers unfortunately was.

At the curb, where a shabby black coach waited and a strange servant let down the steps, Ariana felt a sudden suspicion and cried, "This is not Mr. Mornay's equipage!"

"Are you certain?" Mr. O'Brien asked. The appearance of the coach made him sure, even as he asked it, that she undoubtedly was right. Unlike Mornay's gleaming black coach of the first water, this sorry-looking vehicle was old and weathered, with scratches and dents on its side. He had no sooner spoken, however, when something very hard came down upon his head, and he fell to the pavement like one dead. Ariana let out a shriek, but her mouth was quickly muffled by a pair of strong hands. She was lifted into the carriage, someone hastily shut the door, and the carriage took off posthaste. She was not released from the man's grip until they had traveled down a few streets, upon which she darted to a seat nearest the door and as far away from her captor as possible. There she sat staring at him through teary eyes and wondering what her next move ought to be.

"Who are you and what do you want with me?"

The man, unshaven and scraggly, looked at her unconcernedly. "Nowt. I don't want nowt at all with ye." He had very messy long hair, a sloppy hat that sat upon his head at an odd angle, and a patched overcoat. He calmly and carefully placed a pistol on his knee and said, "Be a good lass, and ye'll nowt get 'urt." He turned a crooked smile her way, revealing nasty-looking dark teeth. He wore a pair of ragged mitts on his hands, and his boots were mud-encased. His coat looked two sizes too large and had enormous pockets. Ariana remembered hearing tales of pickpockets and thieves who wore such garments to hide their stolen treasures within to escape detection.

"If you want nothing, then why am I here?" she demanded. Her feeling of horror at what had befallen Mr. O'Brien coupled with the unspeakable manhandling that had landed her in this predicament were giving her voice a hard edge that was not customary to her.

He eyed her, seemingly amused. "Ye're wanted, my laidy, but I don't ken what fer. It's five bob to me, that's what. That's all."

She eyed him doubtfully. "You're being paid five pounds to—to abduct me? Is that it?"

Surprised that she hadn't already understood that clearly, he said, "That's it, right an' tight! Jes' doin' me job."

"Your job? Do you mean you do this for a living?"

"I do what ah has to do, luv! No more 'n no less."

She gripped the seat as the vehicle swung around a bend in the road. They were leaving the West End of town, and with a little shudder at what might lie ahead, she gave her full attention to reasoning with this man, who seemed, in his own queer way, to be reasonable.

"My good man," she began, leaning forward to speak with all the earnestness she could muster but stopped in surprise when he burst out laughing.

"Ah, that's ripe!" he smirked. "Me, a good man!"

Ariana's lips pursed in impatience. "What I mean to say," she inserted loudly, "is that I can offer you more than five pounds. I can give you twice that amount—if you turn this equipage around and deliver me to safety."

This got his attention, and he raised his head with interest.

"Ten bob?" he asked, with a strange gleam in his eye.

"Make it twenty," she said, in case he was not impressed already.

"Twenty bob! Do ye have it on ye?" He eyed her suspiciously.

"No, but I give you my word that I will get it to you at once if you deliver me."

He scratched his head, pulled a dirty rag from one of his pockets, and began wiping the pistol. He worked slowly, in no hurry, and then said, "I tell ye, luv, if I only could, I would take yer twenty bob." He looked at her fully. "A pretty lass as ye are, I would take it if I could. More the pity, then, but I cain't. It would be ma life for it, luv."

"Why on earth do you say that?"

"It's that Wingate fellow. A right lord 'e is, but there ain't nothin' lordly about him, s'far as I can tell." His face took on a look of outrage and he put the gun down and cried, "'E's a right murderous blood, 'e is!" He looked at her as if she must certainly understand this. Shaking his head, he muttered, "Nay, it's five quid for ol' Whiddington, no more 'n no less."

Ariana felt a surge of alarm. She remembered that Lord Wingate was a man of terrible reputation, known for running up huge debts, gambling, drinking, and living a life of such debauchery that even the jaded *ton* had disowned him. For a titled gentleman—a *marquess*—to earn this judgment had to mean his conduct had been reprehensible to the extreme.

In addition, and this is what gave her especial pause, was that Lord Wingate's younger brother Lord Antoine had been forming an acquaintance with Lavinia. Miss Herley had hinted that this acquaintance might end in an event, but Mr. Mornay had put an abrupt end to it by revealing to her family his lordship's true character, which was little better than his elder brother's. Could her abduction be their revenge for interfering with the man's hopes? The Herleys were not known for having a fortune, and so this seemed unlikely. Yet, what else could explain it?

"Mr. Whiddington—that is your name, is it not?"

He frowned. "Did ah say that? Ay, I'm a right pudding 'ead! Jes' forget that name, luv! It'll do you nowt good! I'm nowt the one what's out fer ye. It's that Wingate what wants ye, 'e does."

The coach stopped suddenly, having encountered a narrow street and needing to make way for an oncoming vehicle. Ariana, without even thinking about it, jumped toward the door and yanked at the handle, but Mr. Whiddington was on her at once. He took her strongly by the arms and forced her back to her seat, saying, "'Nay, luv, cain't let ye do that! Ye wouldn' want ol' Whiddington to face a bullet now, would ye?"

The coach started off again. Ariana, suddenly teary-eyed, said, "But you will hand me over to Lord—Lord Wingate, who is a murderous blood! *I* may well be facing a bullet, and I haven't the least idea why!"

~

Back on Curzon Street, Mr. Mornay came to his senses rapidly, bent down, and checked to be certain O'Brien was alive. Thank God, he was.

Mr. Mornay pulled at Mr. O'Brien's coat lapels, bringing him to a sitting position. "Where is Miss Forsythe?" he asked sharply, though the young man's eyes were still shut.

Mr. O'Brien emitted a low moan and moved his head slightly. Mr. Mornay shook him gently, hoping to wake him but not hurt him. His moaning grew louder.

"Come out of it, O'Brien! Where is Miss Forsythe?"

The young man's face creased in thought, and he put one hand to his aching head. "What? What happened?" he asked.

"Ariana! Where is she?"

This brought him to, and he sat up abruptly, though in a great deal of pain. Holding one hand to his head where it ached, he drew it away only to see his own blood. His face took on a grave demeanour, but Mr. Mornay was at the end of his patience.

He lifted Mr. O'Brien so that their faces were not far apart. "Tell me where Ariana is, or I'll give you more to moan about!"

Startled, Mr. O'Brien blinked in surprise. Everything came rushing back.

"She was taken! In a coach! It wasn't yours. It was, eh, rather shabby, but I don't know whose it was."

"What do you mean, it wasn't mine? Of course it wasn't mine!"

"Did you not ask me to escort Miss Forsythe home? I was told that you wanted me to escort her to the house, that you were sending your coach to convey us."

Mr. Mornay's brows rose considerably. "Why on earth would I do that? You were told by whom?"

O'Brien grimaced. "Not sure. Goodby was his name, I think. Mr. Goodby."

Phillip looked thoughtful and let him go, thinking hard. Mr. O'Brien had regained his senses enough to assess his condition and tried to get up, the throbbing in his head notwithstanding. Mornay's coach pulled up then, and his groom hopped to the ready and lowered the steps. Mornay turned to him. "Did you see what happened?"

"No, sir. I 'eard a commotion, but when I got round to see, I just saw a coach movin' off."

A footman, who had elected to come along out of sheer boredom and who enjoyed a good game of cards while waiting for his master's return, piped up. "The coachman said somethin' was astir, sir." The master went to speak to his driver.

Mr. O'Brien staggered to his feet.

"Can you follow it, do you think?" Mr. Mornay was asking the man atop the board. "Good. On the double."

Ignoring O'Brien's presence, he made immediately for the door of the carriage, but just then Lord Alvanley—top hat, tailcoat, gloves, and cane in hand—came out of the house.

Mr. Mornay suddenly thought another hand might be needed. He gave way for a moment to his worst fears and yelled, "Alvanley, there's trouble and I need a hand. Come with me."

His lordship saw that he was in earnest and hurried over. He said, "Dash it, Mornay, I'm just headin' to White's!"

Mr. Mornay saw O'Brien staggering unsteadily toward him from the corner of his eye, and this, more than anything, made him feel the very life of his love might be at stake. He took Alvanley as roughly by the lapels of his very fine coat as he had Mr. O'Brien by his moments earlier. All thoughts of not making a cake of himself were forgotten.

"I say, Mornay! You've no call to—"

"I need your help. You're coming with me. Any questions?"

"No."

He pulled the man along roughly and pushed him into the coach, feeling he'd already wasted too much time. Two other peers of the realm had come out of the house just in time to witness that singular sight and looked at each other in astonished delight. Getting to see Mornay in one of his tempers was considered a treat—so long as you were not the one at the receiving end.

Mr. O'Brien was in no condition for heroics, but he hurried to follow the men aboard, preventing the groom from putting up the steps momentarily. He felt responsible for the disaster which may have befallen the angel—er, Miss Forsythe—and he wanted to be available, by all means, to do aught he could to rectify the situation. No matter that his head was still throbbing and bleeding. He was about to sacrifice a perfectly good handkerchief to stop the bleeding and hoped it would work.

"What the devil has got into you?" Alvanley fumed, trying to rearrange his disheveled attire. "Look what you've done to my coat! And I warrant my cravat needs tyin' again! And where the deuce are you takin' me?"

"Be quiet, you imbecile, and listen a moment. Miss Forsythe has been abducted just now."

"What! No such thing!"

"Yes!"

"And I've got the blood to prove it," put in Mr. O'Brien, holding out his deeply darkened handkerchief for Alvanley to inspect. The man took one look and pulled his head back in repugnance.

"Dash it! What happened?" Alvanley's tone of indignation had vanished, and he sounded downright contrite.

Mr. O'Brien told both men the story of what had happened as far as he knew it. That he had been standing around at the ball when a man approached him. He introduced himself as Mr. Goodby and continued on with a great deal of gratifying apologies for taking the enormous presumption to make his own introduction, but that it must be understood as acceptable inasmuch as Mr. Mornay had required it of him. He asked if he, Mr. O'Brien, would do Mr. Mornay a favour.

Mr. O'Brien was understandably surprised that Mornay would need a favour, first of all, and that he would ask it of him. But perhaps he liked the idea of being needed by such a personage. Perhaps he felt it suited him, as a friend of the family, to be the one to whom the Paragon might ask a favour. Besides, did not good manners require that he be as helpful as he could? So in a moment, he announced that he was at Mr. Goodby's service and asked what he could do for him.

"Well, it seems Mornay has joined a fast game and wants to finish it, but he doesn't relish having his bride-to-be alone out here. He begs to know if you would be so kind, Mr. O'Brien, as to escort the angel home."

"The angel? Oh, yes—Miss Forsythe?"

The man snickered. "Of course, Miss Forsythe, yes. What'll it be, lad? Will you oblige Mr. Mornay?"

"Are you seriously suggesting that Mr. Mornay would want me to escort Miss Forsythe to her house? And," he added, looking around meaningfully, "she is hardly what I could call 'alone.'"

"Well, she ain't with him, an' he knows you're a friend of the family, sir!"

"Well, yes, I am." Mr. O'Brien was flattered by that. But he suddenly came to. "Look here, sir, Mr. Mornay knows I have not brought my equipage. I cannot think he would want me—"

"O' course he knows that, sir, as you say. He's sending word for his coach to be brought round directly, and he's given instructions that you may use the coach afterward to go to your own house or, if you like, to return here to the ball. Now, may I tell him that you are happy to be of assistance? Or should I say that Mr. O'Brien is unwilling to oblige? If you are, best say so, so's I can pass on the tidings. What'll it be, m' boy, eh?" With a confidential air he leaned in toward Mr. O'Brien. "Here's your chance to get in 'is good graces, y' know. Not likely to have a better one! I advise you to take it right off, sir, and give the man a reason to be in your debt."

Well, that was putting things in a new light. The idea of Mr. Mornay coming forward to thank him was irresistible bait, and suddenly he was agreeable to the idea. He sought out Ariana, letting it be known that he had been commissioned by Mr. Mornay himself to take his bride-to-be home. He admitted that Ariana had not been enthusiastic to the idea, but had no wish to displease her betrothed.

Mr. O'Brien finished the story; how the wrong coach had appeared and how everything went black directly following the whopping blow to his head. He touched it gingerly, feeling the wet blood on his hair, and reapplied his handkerchief.

Lord Alvanley was troubled, but after a few moments of thought, he said, "Hey! It might be someone playing a trick, you know."

"Would a trickster have nearly done me in?" Mr. O'Brien lowered his head sufficiently so that the blood-reddened, nasty-looking gash could be seen in the lamplight.

Mr. Mornay took his first real look at the injury and grimaced. "You'd best be taken home where your mama can do something for you."

"No, sir!" His energetic reply drew their attention. "I am to blame in this matter, and I will not go to my house until I know that Miss Forsythe is safe."

Mr. Mornay looked appraisingly at him. "You'll be little good to us in your condition. In any case, because we haven't a clue as to the whereabouts of my fiancée, I think it better we leave you out of the business."

"I must insist that you do not," he replied looking very grave. For the first time since their acquaintance, Mr. Mornay felt the slightest twinge of respect for the young man. Perhaps he had some bottom after all. The matter was dropped.

The coach halted and the groom jumped down, came round, and rapped urgently on the door. He had been atop the board with the coachman just in case he might spy anything giving a clue of Miss Forsythe's whereabouts. He had seen her on many occasions and could recognize her—if they could find her.

Alvanley opened the door.

"Beggin' pardon, sir, but where do you want us to search?"

"Head toward the East End!" Mr. O'Brien cried in exasperation. He felt it did not take a man of much education to realize that most of the criminals in town came from that region of the metropolis.

The others looked at him in surprise, and Mr. Mornay felt his second little twinge of respect for the boy.

The groom looked to his master who said, "Do it."

Thirteen

Mr. Whiddington eyed Ariana uncomfortably. Apparently he hadn't considered that he might be delivering a young woman of gentle birth to her death. But he shifted in his seat and then said, "Lor', I ain't supposin' it's a bullet 'is lordship's wanting to put into you, if ye' get ma meanin'."

She gaped at him, horrified. The thought turned her lovely white face a deep red. Her countenance dropped so completely that Mr. Whiddington, seeing her response, said, "Oh, that's how it is, eh? You are a young'un. Well, I don't see as I quite got the choice there, now, do ah?"

"Of course you do! Lord Wingate might have picked a hundred other men to do his dirty work for him, but he chose you on account of your being available, that's what! It was your choice entirely, and I pray God you suffer for it!" She felt terrible as soon as the words left her lips, but Mr. Whiddington seemed, if anything, more uncomfortable than ever.

"Nay, ye needn't bring *Him* into it!" he muttered with a deep scowl. And then in an irked tone repeated, "Ah do what ah needs to do for me livin'! No more 'n no less!"

Ariana felt a sudden hope. "I shall pray to God this very minute for my deliverance!" She closed her eyes on the spot, tried to envision herself sitting in the pew at St. George's on a Sunday, and began a prayer, speaking loudly to impress her hearer with the words.

"Almighty God, we thank and praise Thee for Thy great might and power. For Thy omniscience! That Thou *seest* all! And *knowest* all!" She had decided to pray in the formal speech that the Anglican church used, even though her parents had always modeled the use of everyday language like the Methodists, sensing instinctively that it would better impress her audience.

She peeked one eye open to see that Mr. Whiddington had indeed given her his full attention and was sitting there with a look of utter horror on his face.

"Nay, there's no call for that sort o' thing!"

"Of course there is!" she interjected, returning at once to her prayer. "We know, O God, that Thou art just and wilt do with us as we deserve on that great and coming day of judgment!"

"Oh now, did ye have to go and say *that*?"

Ignoring this, she added, "I heartily ask your forgiveness for *my* wrongdoings, O Lord." She peeked and saw Mr. Whiddington now in a serious slump, his face quite dejected. His only sound was a low, drawn out, "Oh."

She then began to pray in earnest. Lord Wingate had taken the trouble of tricking her into leaving the safety of the house, forcing her into the carriage with this vulgar ruffian, and had cruelly injured Mr. O'Brien. What, then, could he have in mind for her, except some horrible fate too unspeakable to contemplate? She forced her mind to focus on Mr. O'Brien and prayed very hard for his welfare. It gave her some peace to pray for someone other than herself, for it helped keep her mind from any thought of what might come. When Mr. Whiddington once again placed his pistol upon his thigh, holding it with one hand, it distracted her.

But his face was still dejected, filled with sorrow, in fact. There was just enough dim light from the glim he had with him to see faintly. The coach had very small windows, and she could not even see a street sign—nothing well enough to know their whereabouts. She eyed the pistol. She was in dangerous hands, indeed.

She thought of Mr. Mornay and how he would wish to protect her—if he knew! Oh, but he probably didn't. *Why didn't I verify that he wanted me to leave without him? He has never requested such a thing before. Why was I so willing to believe this of him?*

Feeling herself ready to cry, she began to pray again, more fervently than before. It was the only way of keeping her emotions in check. She suddenly decided to try once more to sway the man with the one thing he most definitely wanted—money. With a curious look at him, she ventured, "I suppose you aren't interested in earning fifty pounds? This nasty business can still be avoided, and God Himself will look favourably upon you if you grant me your aid."

The man looked over at her, but she could not make out his countenance. Then he grunted. "'Ow do you ken ought about God? We go back a long ways, ma pretty mort, and I got a long list o' things He didna like!"

"We all do, Mr. Whiddington. But God is forgiving." Her calmness of manner impressed him more than her words. She seemed so utterly and entirely certain of what she was saying.

There was another silence and then a bitter guffaw. "Your list ain't nowt to the likes o' mine, depend upon it! I cain't be 'elped! An' I gots to do what I gots to do!"

"That is nothing to the point," she returned, as calmly as before. "You mistake the matter. Size, quantity, quality, manner or matter of wrongdoing—it makes no difference to whether He can forgive you, sir! If you do the littlest misdeed you may as well have done the worst—either one keeps us from heaven!"

He was listening but with a look of doubt and suspicion. "Then it's all spades for me, luv—and for everyone else too! We're all done up!"

"We would be, you're absolutely correct, but for Christ who died for us. He died for *you*, sir! He *died* for you! He died to pay for every sin, big or little. Again it makes no difference to God, Christ's forgiveness covers all!" She stared at him accusingly. He seemed to have a conscience for God. He knew, somewhere in his being, he knew it was true. He wasn't ignorant. She felt no pity, just a cold anger. Suddenly just a cold anger. "You are giving yourself to a life of misdeeds when you might find mercy and help and forgiveness and *heaven* after all! How *can* you be so…pigeon-headed?"

Her large eyes were visible to him in the dark. They were filled with such indignation and righteous anger that for a moment Mr. Whiddington wanted to drop his head in his hands. Oh, why was this dratted bleached mort managing to render him useless? He was rapidly filling with self-reproaches so violent and unavoidable that his entire being was shaken. She was destroying the great wall he had carefully put in place to remove him from just such thoughts!

Other than removing his hat or cap when passing a gospel shop, he had managed for quite a long time to keep *Him* out of his thoughts altogether. Why did this laidy, so innocent-looking, indeed a right white ewe, have to remind him of all his sins? And then it hit him, and he felt alarm to the bottom of his holey boots.

"Ye're the Black Spy, ain't cha!"

"The *what*?"

"Old Nick! Old Harry. The devil 'imself!"

"Oh, don't be such a gull!" Ariana was finding herself saying the strangest things—*pigeon-headed, gull*—words she never used. Soon she'd be speaking "St. Giles' Greek," if she wasn't careful. "Would I be telling you to mend your ways and that God will indeed forgive you utterly, if I were?"

"Ay," he answered flatly, "'coz I cain't do it! Yo'r 'ere to torture me with it!"

"Of course you can't. Not on your own, but you won't be on your own. All you need do is ask for God to help you, and He will. There's nothing impossible about it!" She was really out of patience with him. "If you indeed wish to repent and have a home in heaven, then you must abandon your lawless ways. And I suggest you start right now!" She saw he was listening, giving her his curious but wary attention. So she added, "All you must do, right this minute, is *stop* being a vessel for evil. Do not take me to Wingate! Take me, first of all, back to the West End, and I, in turn, will see that you are rewarded handsomely. I'll...I'll find you a situation!"

"What, *me work*? I ain't never worked a day in me life!"

Impatiently she responded, "You, Mr. Whiddington, have had to work your entire life! Scrimping and scrounging. Napping other people's articles and effects at peril of your life. Then selling them to rogues for less than they're worth, no doubt."

"Eh, 'ow'd you ken that?"

"It's what you do, sir. It's what hundreds of you do."

He looked at her darkly, weighing her words. "What sort o' situation?"

Ariana stared at him, thinking for a moment. "I could take you on! You will be a man-of-all-work. Surely you are capable of helping cook, or—"

"In the *kitchens*? *Me?*" He wrung out the words to great effect, and his face took on a look of such abhorrence and aversion that Ariana saw her mistake and hurriedly added, "The stables then! The fields. Whatever you like, Mr. Whiddington!"

His countenance lifted at those words. "I kin drive a coach," he offered, his eyes revealing a faint light of hope.

"We may need another coachman!" Her words were more encouragement.

"Or I—I could be one o' those fancies, what 'angs on the back o' the carriage."

"A footman! Of course!" She smiled at him. *So he sees himself wearing livery, does he?* "Mr. Mornay's livery is splendid! Crimson and gold. You'll look *so—*" Here her words died on her tongue, for what could she say? Handsome? That would be flummery. His was not the sort of physique that was favoured for footmen to begin with, being quite large of girth. His calves alone were absurdly unfit. Footmen in the best households were often hired by the look of their calves. They had to look good in the old-fashioned knee breeches and waistcoat, which livery required. Finally she said, "Dignified!"

He smiled, revealing a lopsided grin. She breathed a sigh of relief.

The carriage pulled up to the curb just then, and he said, "Wait 'ere, ma good mort!" The man then got out of the carriage and she was left alone.

Ariana strained to look out the window and was daunted to see they were in a little side alley in a seedy neighborhood. There were doxies standing about, eyeing the carriage with hardened, sullen looks. Ariana sat back quickly when the gaze of one fell upon her. Her headdress alone would inform anyone that she was a change from the usual fare of women on that street.

Fortunately Mr. Whiddington returned in a trice. The carriage began moving while he sat down heavily across from her. Then she heard the sound of flint striking stone and watched as he lit the lamp and extinguished the glim.

With the better light, she could see all the more why the man would have agreed to nap a girl for a mere five pounds. His clothing was ratty, the boots worn, and his unkempt hair scraggly. He had a large, bulbous nose, and his skin was reddish and unshaven. His eyes were deep in his face, rather large, and looking at her just as curiously as she was studying him.

Perhaps more so. His eyes lighted on the area above her chest, and she realized he was staring at her necklace, probably wondering how large a sum it could fetch him. It was an emerald surrounded by little diamonds, a gift from Mr. Mornay after his return from Chesterton.

"'Ow do ah ken ye'll keep yer word, if I bring ye back, eh?"

The carriage was turning around! She began taking off her necklace and said, "If I do not keep my word, you may keep this."

He received it with glowing eyes, held it up closely for inspection and then shoved it down deeply into a pocket of his voluminous coat.

"Since I do mean to keep it and appoint you a footman," she said, "you will return it to me when you don your livery."

He nodded. "Agreed."

"And now you will kindly give me your weapon."

He looked at her askance with great alarm. "No such thing!" A sheepish look. "Beggin' yo'r pardon." But his face was pained. "But I cain't do that! Give up me barkin' iron?"

"Mr. Whiddington, I shall return it you when I've been delivered to safety. And then I will buy it from you. As a footman you'll really have no need of it."

"No *need*?" he was incredulous. "I know the blokes what naps coaches, and they all got barkin' irons, mum! Aye, a footman needs 'is bull dog, all right."

Ariana blinked. "A bull dog?"

He held up his pistol. "Me barkin' iron, mum."

Ah, well. That was a thought! She would speak to Mr. Mornay on the matter.

He was rubbing his chin thoughtfully. "O' course, bein' a fancy 'anger-on won't buy back me skin from 'is lordship! That cove'll be devilish puckered when he finds out ah've bilked him! What good is the fancy duds to me if I was to have my throat slit afore mornin', eh?"

This was alarming. The man was already having second thoughts. "I assure you, Mr. Whiddington, Lord Wingate will be brought to justice," she hastily replied, "and he won't have the satisfaction of having made you a cat's paw!"

Mr. Whiddington slowly digested this point and then agreed with a hearty, "Ah-men to that, luv!" But then he added, "But lordships are never brought to justice! We ken that, all right."

"Oh, you don't know my fiancé," she returned calmly. "This one will be."

She would instruct him later on how to address her properly. No footman could call their mistress "luv" or any other such thing.

The light in the coach was still on, and suddenly another carriage came abreast of theirs, as if trying to pass them. Only instead of passing it remained side-by-side. It was precarious, and Whiddington's coachman tried to rid himself of the unwelcome neighbour by speeding up. The other coach did likewise. The carriage was beginning to sway, and Ariana and her captor were forced to hold onto their seats, their heads bobbing with the suddenly violent movements of the vehicle. The noise from the other coach's horses was loud, and Ariana had to yell, "What is happening?"

In response Whiddington cried, "That lunatic whip'll have us feedin' daisies yet!" They both hung on grimly. Little by little the other coach was forcing theirs to the side of the road. Whiddington blew out the light and had to place his hands against the side of the coach for support. Ariana gripped the worn cushion of her own seat in order to remain upright. The carriage rocked as it dodged the other coach, which with seeming indifference appeared bent on causing a collision.

A loud report suddenly pierced the air. Ariana gasped.

Whiddington stuck his fat face at the tiny coach window just as the other vehicle finally drew ahead. The carriage immediately slowed down, and Ariana sat back with relief. She was no longer frightened of Mr. Whiddington, but this episode had given her new frights. Also she was anxious to get back to the viscount's to see her beloved, to find out how Mr. O'Brien fared, and, perhaps most of all, to simply revel in being *safe* again. What if this other coach was Lord Wingate's?

They continued to slow down, which further mystified and frightened her. Whiddington seemed to know what was afoot. "Blast! We're gettin' comp'ny!" Whiddington sat back in his seat and cocked his pistol. Then to Ariana's surprise, he dug into an inner pocket and pulled out another one.

"Come 'ere, luv, and sit behind me," he said. Suddenly her abductor had become her protector.

"Do you think it's Wingate?" she asked in a fright.

"Cain't say. 'E's ridin' a wave, if it's 'im," he replied, for he had noted that the coach was a real bang-up specimen, far richer than the one they were in, which *was* Wingate's.

"'Ere," he said, keeping his eyes steadily on the door of the coach. They could hear footsteps on the street, rounding the vehicle.

"Ah 'ave yo'r word on those fancy duds, eh?"

"I promise you! Upon my word!"

"Awright then." He pointed his pistol so that it faced the coach door.

In the next moment, the door of the carriage was pulled open from the outside and Mr. Mornay, with a thunderous expression, appeared holding a pistol. When Ariana saw him, she jumped at Whiddington's right arm, the one nearest her, screaming, "Don't shoot!" But it was too late. A report rang out, loud and leaving a cloud of smoke in its wake. Ariana's scream turned to, "*Nooo!*"

Whiddington had used the weapon in his left hand just as she screamed for him not to. The shot was excrutiatingly loud. Ariana's mind instantly filled with horror at the thought that her beloved had just been killed. And so despite all the hardiness and resourcefulness she had displayed since being taken and despite the fact that she had never done so before, she fell at once into a faint, slumping senselessly to the side.

Fourteen

Freddie always waited up for the master. He had little to do in the middle of the night, however, so he sifted through the morning's mail, which he had left in a pile on Mr. Mornay's desk. Already there were letters from Christ's Hospital, Bridewell Hospital, Bethlehem, and St. Bartholomew's. Just yesterday he had carried letters on the silver salver to his master's study. Those letters were from such places as St. Thomas's Hospital, the National Benevolent Institution of 1812, the Orphan Working School, and the London Orphan Asylum at Clapton. He had longtime standing orders to cover all postage when necessary, but he would make it a point to see Mr. Mornay on this matter. Never had so many charitable solicitations been seen in the house! The family, of course, had always supported St. George's in Middlesex, the local poorhouse, and even Westminster Hospital here in London. But the recent influx of requests—for he was certain that's what they were—was entirely beyond the pale.

Haines, at Hanover Square, was experiencing a similar puzzling onslaught of mail. A sudden stampede of letters, most of them addressed to Miss Fosythe. Haines too could hardly help but notice that the letters were nearly all from charitable institutions—more letters than he'd remembered arriving at Hanover Square before. It started suddenly one day and to date showed no sign of abating.

Today there had been letters from Guy's Hospital in Southwark, London Hospital on Whitechapel Road, St. Luke's, Small-Pox Hospital, and even from an ophthalmic hospital in Moorfields! Yesterday's deliveries had origins such as the London Fever Hospital, Lock Hospital, the City of London Lying-in Hospital on City Road, an infirmary for diseases of the skin, located on Blenheim Street, an infirmary for diseases of the lungs on Artillery Street in Bishopsgate. Why were they all targeting Hanover Square? It mystified him.

Much as he hated to endanger Miss Forsythe's mail, he would have to inform the mistress. Most of these letters came with postage to be paid on receipt. Normally he paid all such expenses without question. In this case it wouldn't do. Letters were coming in the early and late mails. Some days there were three deliveries, and it was adding up. Surely Mrs. Bentley would not approve.

"Hold your fire!"

"Stand down!"

"You're outnumbered, sir!"

The firm voices of the men outside the coach were daunting. Mr. Whiddington, shaken because his shot had not landed where he had aimed it, namely at the forehead of the man who had swung open the carriage door with such force, slowly lowered his weapon. He pulled his other arm loose from the weight of the laidy who had swooned against him. If it had not been for that, he would have rapidly followed his first report with another, but she had prevented it.

He saw two pistols pointing in at him and said, "Awright then," in a voice that conveyed his ire.

Mr. Mornay, with one leg on the steps and holding his pistol so that its barrel pointed squarely at Whiddington's heart, said, "Get out!" His manner, look, and tone were all sufficiently awesome so that Mr. Whiddington rose to do as he was told. Mr. Mornay quickly shouted a second order, "Put your weapons on the floor!"

Whiddington stopped, set the guns down, and then moved past the severe-looking bloke on the steps. As he exited the coach, he noticed that the coachman was already bound at the wrists and was wearing a mean-looking expression. The coachman was a fellow rogue known as Blighter, so named for his foul odour. Even among those for whom being odoriferous was not uncommon, Blighter's stench was thought to be so severe that it was capable of causing a blight.

"Why'd ye stop, ye greenhead?" Whiddington hissed at Blighter.

"I did me best!" Blighter spat out, following it with a real spit of some dark substance. "We'd 'ave capsized for sure, if I 'adn't."

Mr. O'Brien took out his last handkerchief, rolled it up, and tied

Whiddington's hands behind his back, like the other man's. "On your knees!" he said to the men, using a tone of authority that became him. The ruffians dropped down.

Meanwhile inside the carriage, Alvanley watched as Mr. Mornay picked up Ariana and sat down with her in his arms. Sitting across from the two of them, Alvanley, a man of endless surprises, handed Mornay what looked like a little nosegay of cloth bound with ribbon. "Smelling salts," he said.

"Obliged." Mornay's brows were raised with surprise, but he took the little package and held it under Ariana's nose for a second.

She came to with a short gasp and a sudden start. One hand flew to her head. She grimaced, but then seeing her beloved, she threw herself against him. "Oh, Phillip! I thought—I thought you'd been killed!"

He was holding her equally tightly. Alvanley, with a little smile, turned his back on the couple to give them privacy.

Mr. O'Brien glanced into the carriage and saw that the angel was unharmed. He sighed with relief but felt his aching head all the more.

Ariana and Mr. Mornay finished a passionate kiss. "Come, let me get you to safety," he whispered to her.

She rose with his help, surprised to find herself feeling shaky and woozy. He helped her from the carriage with one hand and then tucked her arm inside his. Ariana could just make out Mr. O'Brien. "Oh! Thank God! I thought he may have been killed too."

As Mr. O'Brien turned his head, she knew at once that he had been hurt, but his presence meant that it could not have been too severe. He was looking vastly relieved, standing there with the rogues on their knees beside him. Lord Alvanley was holding a small torch, his face a study of fascination and enjoyment. He was delighting in the opportunity of being witness to such a momentous event involving Mornay and his angel. He would have excellent fodder for conversations in the highest drawing rooms of the *ton* for weeks. All of his pique at Mornay's earlier bullishness had vanished.

Mornay turned to Alvanley and said, "Take their coach and drive these men to the magistrate. Tell him I want them taken directly to the hulks."

"Not the hulks!" shouted Whiddington. Every criminal was imbued with a fear of the hulks. They were retired war vessels that were in perpetual dock. Originally opened to ease overcrowded prisons, they housed those awaiting transport—and never closed. They were cramped, dark, filthy, miserable places, and many prisoners didn't survive them to be moved on to a permanent place.

Whiddington's voice got Ariana's attention. She turned to see him again and remembered that she had made an agreement with the man. "Oh! My dear sir, Mr. Whiddington was helping me!"

"What?" Mornay looked at her in surprise.

"Really, dearest! I promised him a situation for his help. You can see we were heading back to the West End. He agreed to return me to safety in return for a situation with our staff!"

The coachman heard Ariana's words and sneered at Whiddington. "Well, are you not the turn-cat!"

"I'm not a cat's paw at any rate!"

"Yes, you are—to that mort!" He nodded toward Ariana.

"She's a right gentry mort!" returned the other.

"Hold your tongues!" It was Mr. O'Brien, to his credit, who interfered.

Mornay glanced back at the malkintrash and tried not to grimace. "He nearly killed me," he said to Ariana calmly.

Alvanley added, "If your betrothed hadn't jerked his head aside before you could say 'Jack Robinson,' he'd a been a goner!"

Ariana shuddered and drew closer to him, at which he covered her hand with his other, but she said, "We thought you might be Lord Wingate in pursuit!"

"Wingate? Whatever for? Is he in this?"

"He hired Mr. Whiddington to take me! But I convinced Mr. Whiddington to work for me," she said earnestly, making Mr. Mornay smile at her and shake his head.

"So I'm not the only one you can beguile, eh?"

She smiled. "I prayed a great deal too."

"So did I."

Alvanley had overheard this remark and his eyes bulged for a moment. Then he chalked it up as something his friend had to say to please his bride-to-be. There wasn't the least possibility, to his mind, that Mornay might have meant it.

Suddenly Whiddington nodded at Mornay and cried out, "I gots to speak to the fine bloke—alone!"

Mr. Mornay turned, saw Whiddington looking at him, and said, "Very well. Put him in the carriage."

After O'Brien told him to rise, he walked back to the coach, stopping by Ariana to say, "I 'av yo'r word, mum?"

"You do!" she assured him, even as Mr. O'Brien pushed him along. After

Mr. Whiddington had entered, Mr. Mornay hopped in and sat across from him but kept his pistol at the ready.

"See, guvnor," Whiddington said, wary of the pistol, "I didna want to deliver the little white ewe! She's as sweet as a saint, so 'elp me, God!"

"But you took her from safety—you took her from me. You also nearly killed our companion with that blow to the head."

"That was nae me, m'lord!"

"Governor will do," he said sardonically.

"Well! I 'av to make me livin', same as you," he said, trying to sound reasonable.

"Yes, and you'll go to Newgate—or the hulks for how you've chosen to do so."

This got him mad. Whiddington made a move as if to dig in a pocket, but Mornay said, "Ah, ah, ah," and held his pistol up.

Ariana now climbed up into the carriage and sat near Mornay. She tried to speak, but Mr. Whiddington cut her off with, "It's no good, mum. 'E won't 'ear me at all."

She turned to her beloved, who only glanced at her, wanting to keep an eye on his foe. "I gave him my word," she said, watching his face.

Mornay continued to watch the other man but said, "Giving your word to a man who has abducted you is completely understandable—but not binding."

"To me it is!"

"He deserves Newgate at the least—if not for today's work, then for many another, I'm quite certain."

"But people can change! He wants to! He wants to wear livery!"

The raised brow. He had to turn his face and give his love a look of incredulity. "That's not possible," he said firmly.

"Why not?"

He shook his head. "You don't realize what you're asking. This man would have access to our house. Our very lives could be at stake. I can't do it. You know I want to please you, but I'm afraid that in this case, it would be sheer lunacy."

Whiddington interjected, "I ain't done nothin'. I was returnin' the laidy to ye."

Mr. Mornay said, "I'll see you to a compromise." He looked quickly at Ariana, who was listening intently.

"Yes?" she said.

"I'll give him his freedom. With the understanding that if he dares to come near you again in this life, it will be the end of it."

Whiddington looked visibly relieved. It was a disappointment but far better a prospect than City College, as they called Newgate, or even worse, the hulks.

Ariana frowned and looked sadly at Whiddington. "I'm sorry," she said. "I meant every word I spoke to you."

He looked away uncomfortably. She felt so guilty that she had to say something else. Something to cheer the man. "You may keep the necklace."

"What?" Mr. Mornay saw her bare neck and knew immediately what she was offering him—a costly piece of jewellery, which he had bought for her only a sennight ago. Ariana clapped a hand over her mouth. Then, knowing that Phillip would surely try to get the necklace back, she turned to him again, took hold of his arm, and put her face nearer his. "Darling," she wheedled, "we must let him keep it! I promised that if he did not become a servant, he could keep it."

His mouth was set in a firm line. Even her use of the word *darling* did not soften his resolve. Instead he called to Alvanley, who was standing outside nearby.

When Alvanley opened the door, Mr. Mornay said, "Call O'Brien to escort Miss Forsythe to my coach, while you guard the other man. I will join her shortly."

"Phillip!" she cried. "I gave my word! Pray, be reasonable. The man must have some reward—he was bringing me back to safety. Lord Wingate will cut his throat for it! He quite deserves it."

Mr. Mornay, with his eyes on the prisoner, murmured dryly, "I'm sure he does."

Lord Alvanley by now was taking Ariana from the coach, easily overpowering her and leading her gently but firmly from the vehicle. Mr. O'Brien stood at the bottom of the steps, keeping his eyes on the other fugitive, but poised to help Alvanley if necessary.

Ariana did not have much fight in her. She was ashamed at the behaviour of her betrothed and of her inability to keep her promises to Whiddington. But she'd been through quite a lot, and at least she was safe now. She accepted Mr. O'Brien's arm without a word and allowed him to hand her up into Mr. Mornay's coach. Inside she sank gratefully onto the cushions and took some deep breaths, trying to calm herself.

Finally she looked over at Mr. O'Brien, who was watching her with a rapt expression.

"I am greatly relieved to find you well, sir."

"Miss Forsythe, you cannot be nearly as happy as I am to find you so."

Then she noticed that some of his hair was matted with blood, and she sat up with a gasp. "Oh, you *are* hurt!"

"It's stopped bleeding," he said, but he couldn't help but to enjoy her concern.

"I was praying very hard for you," she confided, "after we took off, leaving you like that."

"As soon as I came to my senses, I was praying for you," he admitted, not looking at her.

He rubbed his hands together and played with the fringes of his sleeve while he said, "I felt dreadful about having put you into such a position. It was all my fault, I'm afraid."

"Your fault? That there is such evil in the world? No, I cannot blame you," she said gently.

He looked fully at her and shook his head. "I should never have believed that Mr. Mornay would ask a favour of me—I should have known better. It was my vanity entirely that persuaded me to credit the idea."

"Vanity is forgivable, Mr. O'Brien."

"It is a twin, Miss Forsythe, of pride." They looked at each other. "And pride, we both know, is what occasioned Lucifer's fall. I am as guilty of pride as the next man, who, I daresay, has much more to be proud of than I!" He spoke a little bitterly, and it touched Ariana's heart. She was distracted by her concern for Mr. Whiddington but tried to give her attention to Mr. O'Brien. He did not deserve to blame himself for what had occurred.

"*Dear* Mr. O'Brien," she said, leaning forward in her seat. He looked up, from where he had begun to hold his head in his hands, thoroughly ashamed of himself for his role in the events of the night—and noticed how earnestly beautiful Ariana looked.

He raised his head.

Back in the East End, Lord Wingate, that tall, thin, ne'er do well of an old ne'er do well family, was pacing while he waited at an appointed place for the return of Whiddington—and Miss Forsythe. He might have been a remarkably handsome man except that his life of debauchery, coupled with his meanness of character, served to lessen the natural appeal of a well-shaped head and fine features. Instead of the proud nobleman he should have been, he was merely a "beau-nasty," a slovenly, gaunt shadow of a man, with few reminders, either in his person or apparel, of having had prior wealth.

His eyes, narrow but sharp, scanned the dark street. A carriage or two went by from time to time but not his own. He went back to pacing. Where the devil was Antoine? Despite what he'd said earlier, Julian was certain his brother would appear. After all if their scheme worked, Antoine stood to gain as much as he did.

As the minutes passed and no coach arrived, Lord Wingate could endure it no longer. He slammed his fist against the nearest building and cried out, "Where is that deuced Whiddington? The devil, but something's gone amiss!" He wondered if that man, O'Brien, hadn't been gullible enough for the scheme to work. But then wouldn't his men have been back by now? He cursed himself for sending idiots to do his own work. He should have known better. He wouldn't make the mistake again.

Sitting across from Whiddington, Mr. Mornay fixed him with a steady stare. "The necklace," he said, "let's have it."

"Y'or mort promised it to me!"

"Unfortunately it is me you are dealing with now, not her. Hand it over."

"Will ah get nothin' from ye then?"

"I've already said, you'll get your life. Your freedom."

"Free to be done in by Wingate!"

"The company you keep, sir, is your own doing."

"When I was seein' ma way to save yer mort!"

"Hand it over." He cocked his pistol.

Mr. Whiddington dug deeply into an inside pocket of his voluminous coat. He was keeping a disgruntled eye on Mr. Mornay as he did so, searching around with his hands. Finally his face lightened, and he pulled out—not the necklace, but yet another pistol! The men's eyes met in a deadlock for the merest split second. Mr. Mornay had sensed that something was afoot, watching him intently. Immediately upon glimpsing the pistol, Mornay kicked out his foot, knocking Whiddington's hand that held the gun. The gun fired and went flying, the bullet missing Mr. Mornay's head by only an inch.

The horses, meanwhile, had been stamping impatiently. This rude, startling noise sent them into enough of a panic to take off pell-mell, whinnying in alarm. Mornay's groom was holding the reins to prevent just such an occurrence, but he was surprised nearly as much as the horses. He could not contain his hold on them. The force of those two frightened animals overpowered him, and he had to give up, releasing the ribbons before he was pulled along to his death. With deep remorse, he watched as the vehicle disappeared quickly from sight on the dark road. There was no coachman, no one in charge of the horses, and his master was inside. Moreover, the shot may have meant Mr. Mornay was in danger—or worse.

Inside the vehicle, Whiddington dropped all pretense of bravado and hid his head in his arms shouting "Don't shoot! I didna mean to shoot it! I was nae goin't shoot ye!"

Alvanley watched the rapidly disappearing carriage with a look of surprise—and then unbelief—on his face. Good heavens! Mornay was in that coach! He looked at a loss for a moment, but his eyes settled on his friend's coach, and he quickly handed a pistol to the groom saying, "Guard this cove with your life! We'll be back for you. You have my word!"

He hurried over to the coach and jumped up without using the steps, shouting to the coachman, "After them!" But when he landed inside and had closed the door, he turned—and was struck dumb with a shock of a different sort.

That dandy-prat O'Brien was holding the angel in his arms!

To make matters worse, when the coachman took off abruptly, Mr. O'Brien found himself pitched forward, so that he fell upon the cushion and was practically on top of the lady.

Alvanley glared. While Mr. O'Brien scrambled to gather himself, Lord Alvanley noticed Miss Forsythe's mantle had been removed! There it was on the floor, as though discarded with great haste. Once Mr. O'Brien had managed to move away from Ariana, Alvanley could see that she lay unconscious on the cushion but was slowly sliding toward the floor. O'Brien picked her up and sat her on the seat, letting her rest against him. He quickly put an arm around her to keep her from slumping forward onto the floor.

As her head fell against his shoulder, he looked protectively at her but then back at Alvanley, who was still glaring at him. Mr. O'Brien gave a great sigh of relief. "I thought she'd been shot! She's fine," he said and almost laughed.

Alvanley regarded him warily. "I should think not! What the deuce made you consider elsewise?"

"I didn't realize she'd swooned! I heard the report, and then she fell against me directly. I thought she'd been shot!"

"Well, now you know she wasn't. I say I think you should unhand her, sir."

"She's out cold! I dare not."

"What happened to her?"

"Fainted, I daresay, after hearing the report. Poor creature. She's been through so much tonight. But I can't tell you how relieved I am that she hasn't taken a bullet! She gave me a bang-up fright."

Alvanley felt for his smelling salts but remembered he'd not got them back from Mornay earlier. "Dash it!"

"So who fired the shot?" O'Brien asked.

"I haven't a clue. I heard it like you, and then those deuced horses took off as though all hell was at their backs!"

Mr. O'Brien's eyes filled with understanding. "With no whip?"

"No whip." Alvanley paused and added, "Unless it's a ghost driver! You'd think those horses never heard a pistol before!"

"And Mr. Mornay?"

"He's in there, all right, with the fat one. Let us hope we can catch up and that he hasn't overturned!"

Mr. O'Brien was silent a moment. "Mornay might have been shot then."

Lord Alvanley faced the young man. It was a thought he had shared but had no wish to believe. "Don't get your hopes up," was all he replied, with another glance at Ariana.

Mr. O'Brien felt little affection for Mr. Mornay, but this was unworthy of him and his eyes flared with anger.

Alvanley continued, "'Tis more likely the other fellow that was shot, if anyone was. Let us hope it is so!" His eyes fell on Ariana once more. He hated to think of facing her if something terrible had occurred. He looked back at O'Brien. "Why's her mantle on the floor?"

Startled, Mr. O'Brien looked down and picked it up, putting it gingerly beside her. "It fell, I suppose."

"Not by itself."

Mr. O'Brien felt the hair stand up on his neck. "What are you suggesting, sir?"

"What did you do when Miss Forsythe fainted, sir?"

"I do not care for your tone, sir."

"Answer the question, sir!"

"I thought she was shot! I told you so! I was looking to see if she'd been wounded!"

In a caustic tone, Alvanley replied, "Which is why you were cinching her clothes."

Mr. O'Brien was almost speechless. "I was looking for the wound, sir!" There was a pause, while neither one spoke. Mr. O'Brien's eyes flicked back over Ariana, still propped up in his arm. "She fell over directly following the sound. How was I to know she had merely swooned?"

"That is a poor excuse for manhandling Mr. Mornay's betrothed!"

Suddenly Mr. O'Brien was inclined to agree. *What a thick pate I am! What an idiot to remove her mantle.* But he'd been so worried. His only thought was that he had to find the wound, to know how badly she was hurt. *Why didn't it occur to me that she might have fainted?* With a growing discomfort, he realized how things must have looked to Lord Alvanley. It had all happened so fast, and he'd had no time to think about propriety or how things would look.

He and Ariana had been commiserating over the night's events when suddenly they both heard a very loud report close by. Ariana shot up from her seat. Mr. O'Brien thought she was going to try to leave the coach to investigate and immediately put out a hand to prevent her. But instead of moving toward the door, she collapsed against him. Right into his arms. His fevered brain immediately *knew* she'd been shot! Why else would she have jumped at the sound, only to collapse directly after?

In a panic his only thought was that she was injured—possibly mortally—and he had to do something to help her. It was such an alarming, terrible thought that all he could do was investigate, hoping to yet save her. He heard the other coach take off but could think only of the tragical beauty in his arms. In a great deal of trepidation, he laid her down and undid the fastenings of her mantle. He had tears in his eyes. But there was no blood on her gown, nothing on the bodice—all was white, beautiful, her skin unmarred by a wound. Thank God! It hadn't gone straight through her!

But he had to be certain, and so he turned her over, pulling the outer garment off the rest of the way and dropping it thoughtlessly to the floor in his haste. And there—no blood! Nothing! Her gown, perfectly clean. He was ecstatic. He pulled her impulsively up against him, holding her in his arms with vast relief when the door was pulled open and there stood Lord Alvanley, scowling in at him like a man come upon a thief.

The same scowl he was directing at him now.

Mr. O'Brien knew himself innocent of evil intentions. But he certainly felt like a fool.

Fifteen

Mrs. Hamilton was tossing and turning, unable to sleep. The day had been distressing on account of yet more workmen in the house, more changes being made to what, in her opinion, had been near perfection to begin with. It made her shudder to see a man with a tool prying a lovely dado from the wall or removing a piece of elegant sculpture or, worst of all, using a paintbrush to obfuscate a work of classical art to prepare it for a new one! She felt each change as an assault, for they served to remind her that *she* was coming and that *she* would be getting rid of her. Mrs. Hamilton feared ending up, still and all, at the Draper's Asylum for Decayed Housekeepers.

No matter that the artwork in progress was beginning to appear as though it might be superior to its predecessors or that the new sculptures were indeed masterful. It truly didn't matter. All that mattered was that her life was being ruined.

She gave up tossing and turning, lit her bedside candle, and, holding the sconce in front of her, made her way down the stairs. Reinforcing her earlier discomfort, Mrs. Hamilton walked through the rooms, empty of workmen now, and looked at the sorry state of affairs. Sheets draped much of the floor and furniture in the main rooms. Plaster shards had not been completely removed from areas of work, and the familiar statuary was gone. In some places the new piece had not yet arrived, and so the area looked eerily empty, lacking—*needy*. There was an odour of paint, of plaster, and this too added to her feeling of unrest. Incompleteness. The trembling shadows, cast by her small flame, made the rooms look even more unfamiliar, and it was disheartening.

Mrs. Hamilton kept thinking how she would hate to leave, how it was such a shame that things had to change. She started to feel almost panicked at the thought of being ousted, thrown on the street, no doubt. A small voice reminded her that Mr. Mornay would certainly be fair, give a few months' extra wages or better, if his new wife wanted to be rid of her. But small voices had little power against dark thoughts during the black of night.

She could see that change was coming. She could smell it. She could *feel* it.

She ought to have begun spreading word that she would need a new situation—to avoid Draper's if nothing else! She was pessimistically positive that she would never secure so good a situation again, and that thought only added to her resentment.

With a sorrowful eye, she traversed the rooms where work was being done and looked for anything amiss that she could possibly report to the master—if he ever got home. She hadn't heard him come in yet, and it was nigh dawn. She wandered down to the kitchens and saw Molly at work, as she was supposed to be. It was the fate of the scullery maid that she had to be one of the first servants to rise in the morning and prepare water for cooking, washing, and so on. But Mrs. Hamilton then turned and went toward the servants' sleeping quarters. On the way she popped into the master's bed chamber and opened a few drawers, looking for something small. She found a pile of guineas and a gilt-encased timepiece and took them. She stopped afterward in the parlour, took a porcelain figurine, and then finally proceeded to Molly's room. When she appeared again and returned to her own chamber, she had left all the stolen items in the place she had long ago found for hiding them. It was the perfect spot, and if they were found by chance, Molly alone would be blamed. Molly, who already had a history that proved her a thief. It was providential.

"Hand me the pistol!"

Mr. Whiddington, looking meek and trying not to give way to dismay, peered up at the fine bloke. He knew the horses were running wild with no whip atop the board, felt the precarious rocking of the carriage on the road, and did as directed.

"Now give me your coat," demanded Mr. Mornay.

"Me coat?" Whiddington said with a deep grimace.

"Your coat directly! You've likely got more weapons in it."

Both men had to hold onto the cushions just then as the carriage began swaying. The horses, still running in a blind panic, were precipitously close to the edge of the road. If they didn't straighten their course, the carriage could overturn or end up in a ditch. Mr. Mornay knew there was danger, but didn't know what to do.

Whiddington began to remove his coat with an exceedingly unhappy countenance, taking his time about it. While he was doing so, the horses began slowing. They were either growing tired or their terror had worn off. Mr. Mornay noted it with relief and could see from the small back window that another coach was coming fast on their heels, probably his own equipage.

As soon as Whiddington gave up his coat, he quickly felt inside the pockets to determine if there was another weapon, but there were so many bulky items and even extra patch pockets to hold more that he could not tell for certain without emptying the contents. He chose instead to open the carriage door and toss the coat into the night. As soon as he did, he remembered the necklace! Dashed if he hadn't forgotten all about it!

Whiddington watched his coat disappear into darkness with an expression that was reminiscent of a man having an apoplexy. Mr. Mornay stayed near the door, preparing to jump out to grab the reins the moment the horses slowed sufficiently and preventing the huge man from jumping out to recover his great coat—and its contents. Mornay's pistol was the only thing that stopped him.

They were quickly losing momentum now.

"I am going out to manage the horses. If you run for it, I will shoot you."

"Whatcha want me for, guvnor? You got yo'r laidy."

"We have further business, sir. Stay put!"

It was a small miracle that the team had kept to the road—perhaps there was an advantage to using older horses. Long years of being driven made them keep to the road by habit. In any case, Mr. Mornay was relieved when he finally was able to jump out, run along 'til he caught the reins in hand, and bring the team to a full halt. He quickly looked for a tree to tie them to so that he could get back to Whiddington, in hopes the man could lead him to Wingate. The only way to truly put an end to the business would be by settling the dispute between his lordship and himself—if that were possible.

⁂

Mornay's coachman drew the vehicle up behind the other and stopped. He saw his master and felt a great deal of relief. Inside the equipage, Alvanley and O'Brien were in the dark, literally. Who had been shot earlier? Was it their companion?

"If Mr. Mornay has been shot," O'Brien said ominously, "it may be that we're about to face an armed ruffian!"

Alvanley thought to see if Mornay kept a pistol in the coach. He groped beneath the seats and found the box and opened it. "Dash it! It's empty!" They heard the sound of footsteps and gave each other helpless looks of apprehension. Then the door opened and there stood Mornay.

"Thank God!" exclaimed his lordship, pulling forth a very white handkerchief to swipe his brow. Mr. O'Brien was relieved as well, but he had unwittingly pulled Ariana closer to his side protectively. Mr. Mornay revealed that he was holding Whiddington by the scruff of his shirt and then pushed him forward and into the carriage. He then jumped up himself, his shoes landing on the floor with a hollow thud. He looked rather the worse for wear from the night's work. His neat cravat was askew, and his polished footwear downright muddy. His gaze fell on Ariana, whose head had fallen against Mr. O'Brien's shoulder, and his eyes narrowed.

He handed Alvanley the pistol, motioned at O'Brien to move, took the unconscious girl into his arms, and sat down with her across his lap.

"She swooned, sir! At the sound of the shot."

Mornay looked fleetingly at Lord Alvanley, who shrugged and frowned, as if to say, "I don't know anything." But aloud he said, "That was a deuced business with the horses! Gave us quite a fright for you!"

"Here's the thing," Mornay said. "I threw this man's coat out of the carriage when we were still moving, for he has endless weapons in it."

Here Mr. Whiddington grumbled in his gruff, deep voice, "I gots to make me livin', right and tight!"

Mornay continued, "But Miss Forsythe's necklace is in one of its many pockets." He glared directly at Whiddington when he mentioned the pockets.

"I gots to make me livin'!"

"How far back do you suppose it to be?"

"Not so far that you shan't find it." He looked at O'Brien and Alvanley. "Take the lights and the servants and start looking, if you would."

Alvanley was suddenly in a chipper mood. "We'll find it for you, I warrant." He gave the pistol back to Mr. Mornay saying, "Just keep an eye on this beastly fellow."

The two men left the carriage. Mr. Mornay looked squarely at Whiddington. It was cold, and he was tired to the extreme, but he had Ariana, and that gave him renewed energy.

"Tell me all you know about Lord Wingate."

Forty minutes later Mr. Whiddington was a much happier man, having his coat back, although he had lost the necklace. Mr. Mornay had revived Ariana, but his next concern was to get her to safety and pursue Wingate.

"We left your footman with the other cove," Alvanley reminded him. The second footman drove the rogue equipage, and they turned round and went to collect them. Afterward Mr. Mornay released Whiddington, keeping his word to give him his freedom. He sent Alvanley with a pistol and one of the servants to give Blighter a personal escort to the nearest magistrate.

His eyes focused upon Mr. O'Brien. The young man was a sorry sight due to his injury. Further, he looked exhausted. He'd see him home, do the same for Ariana, and then go after Wingate.

Ariana rested her head against his shoulder, trying to rest. She had a prodigious headache. Mr. O'Brien tried not to stare at Miss Forsythe, but he had to ask, "Are you quite well, Miss Forsythe?"

"I will be," she breathed, snuggling closer against her betrothed. She hadn't even bothered to lift her head to speak. But she could see that Mr. O'Brien did not look well. "How are you? Does your head ache?"

"I am sure I only need some rest, and I'll be as good as new," he said, although he was not sure of this at all.

Mr. Mornay, eying Mr. O'Brien's wound, had to wonder. But the young man was kind not to worry Ariana, and he had to appreciate that.

"Be sure to call a doctor to clean the wound properly," she instructed.

"My mother will be content at nothing less, I assure you."

When they reached the West End, Mr. O'Brien became obsessed with the thought that he would be leaving Miss Forsythe alone in a carriage with Mr. Mornay. It irked him.

"It would be most efficient for you to take Miss Forsythe to her house first. You may leave me anywhere you wish afterward. I will find my way to my house, I assure you."

There was a long silence. Even Ariana, who loved to jump in and rescue people from awkward statements or situations, found herself speechless. For some reason the real motive behind this suggestion seemed embarrassingly obvious. She did not relish what she instinctively felt would be a harsh response from her fiancé, but she could think of nothing to answer for it.

"That won't do, Mr. O'Brien, as you well know," Mr. Mornay answered finally. His voice was light and lazy, as it tended to get when he was annoyed but not quite at the breaking point.

Mr. O'Brien swallowed, but he glanced at Ariana and continued, "Sir, even though you are betrothed to marry—"

"Do *not,*" said her beloved, "continue on this topic. I am in no mood for it, for one thing, and if you're thinking that I am not to be trusted with my future bride, I would like to say that you have no idea what I can or cannot be trusted with. And if you persist in conjecturing, I shall take it as an accusation—in which case you might just as well ask to meet me on the field."

"*Sir.* Mr. O'Brien is injured and not himself," Ariana offered.

"Thank you, Miss Forsythe, but I am in my right mind. I only speak on your account."

"'Tis on her account that you are able to speak at all," Mr. Mornay instantly replied.

Ariana was far too raw from fright and worry to countenance the burgeoning argument a moment longer. "Gentlemen! I beg you both, be silent!"

The ensuing quiet minutes, where only the sound of the carriage wheels and the horses hooves were heard, she greeted with relief. Mr. O'Brien had been forced to withdraw his indignation, but he was even now eying Mr. Mornay with stubborn remorselessness. Ariana was surprised at his bravado but knew it was hopeless. After what he'd been through that night, worrying on her behalf, she knew there was no one, save the king or queen, who could likely hold sway against Phillip right now. She placed her hand on Phillip's sleeve, and his hand quickly covered her own. This little movement awakened Mr. O'Brien's fears—or was it jealousy? Once again he had to say, "I shall be pleased to send a servant to return with you, Miss Forsythe, if you would allow it." Since his family only had one manservant, a parlourmaid, and a cook, this was truly the voice of desperation.

Mr. Mornay sighed with annoyance. "What *are* you thinking, sir? You do a disservice to Miss Forsythe that is completely beyond the pale. No matter what you think of me, you must do this lady the honour of recognizing her character and good sense."

"He doesn't mean any harm," put in Ariana, trying to diffuse the situation.

Mr. Mornay had an instant rejoinder to this, which at most times he would not have failed to deliver himself of. The look on her face, coupled with his recent scare of losing her, caused him to keep it to himself, however, and so he only nodded stiffly and vowed silently not to speak another word to the man, if he could help it. And he was very practiced at helping it.

Mr. O'Brien was grateful that Ariana had championed his cause. His disgust of Mr. Mornay was acute at the moment, but it was a relief to know that he would soon be at his own house. His head ached terribly, as it had all night.

When Mr. O'Brien had first reported the story, Mornay's worry about Ariana was greater than his disgust at Mr. O'Brien's foolishness. Now, however, having her safely back at his side, Mr. O'Brien's fault in the matter stood out more clearly, or so he feared. Perhaps he had ought to keep his mouth shut for now.

When they arrived at Blandford Street, Mr. O'Brien turned to Ariana and could not help but say, "I am eternally grateful that you are safe from harm, Miss Forsythe. I wish you a safe return to your own house."

Mr. Mornay said, "Out!" between gritted teeth.

Mr. O'Brien left that way, in disgrace with Mornay, with himself, and soon, he knew, with most of society. They would likely share the view that he was a fool. He had seriously been considering giving up fashionable society because it had brought him nothing but heartache, of which every encounter with Miss Forsythe was a fresh reminder. And it cost a great deal to be accepted. He had no chance of saving enough money for his own equipage, if he continually frittered it away on the latest style of topcoat and boots. So perhaps it was a good thing, this night's business. Of course he wished, for Miss Forsythe's sake, that no ill had befallen her. But she had come through unscathed. She always did, didn't she? Then he thought of little Beatrice and her pretty, childish ways.

The girl had rashly promised to marry him without his asking her, of course. And he had no intention of holding her to a childish passion. Best if he put her out of his mind, in fact. If he forgot about Beatrice or could forget about her, then his contact with Miss Ariana Forsythe would be brought to a minimum. Indeed, after the wedding there was a good likelihood that he would not see her again. Not for a long time, perhaps.

Of course he could no longer retain even the slightest romantic hopes of her, but he couldn't help that he reveled in her presence. Why was it so difficult to give her up entirely? He must concentrate on his vocation, the living that had been promised to him.

When afterward he dropped off to sleep in his bed, having been helped by their one manservant, Edwards, with his clothing, it was with true-to-his-soul weariness. He was still in pain, but he managed a single feeble prayer for Miss Forsythe's deliverance from Mornay, followed by a heartfelt wish to learn to forget her, utterly and entirely.

Little Beatrice, in her white chemise and stockinged feet, crept back to the chamber she shared with Alice and quietly took her place beneath the covers. Alice had not awakened at sound of her brother's return, but Beatrice had heard the noise and risen to investigate. She sighed now, satisfied that she could truly sleep. Mr. O'Brien was returned home and in his bed. All was right once again with the world.

Sixteen

In the Regent's apartments at Carlton House, the prince was reclining on a lounge chair as comfortably as was possible, considering that he was suffering a terrible case of the gout. His foot was wrapped in cloths and appeared many times its natural size. It was elevated, in hopes of easing the pain, by a pile of pillows propped securely in place. The Marchioness of Hertford, sitting in a small chair at his head, was feeding him spoonfuls of broth.

Princess Charlotte had received word from the Regent that she was not to further an acquaintance with Miss Ariana Forsythe. In response the princess sent word that she needed to speak to him urgently. As he did at times, he responded that she must not come that day—he was unwell, unable to receive visitors, in no state of mind to countenance a discussion of any sort, and likely to be taking laudanum, which would render him totally useless to her.

On rare occasions the princess defied his wishes, showed up at his house, and demanded to be seen. It was little known that Princess Charlotte, while equal to state tasks with equanimity and grace, could also behave in the most shockingly spoilt manner. She was terribly emotional at these times, in fact, and even her father, a master at displaying emotion himself, could barely constrain her.

On this day Her Royal Highness was fully prepared to stage a tantrum if the situation warranted it. She appeared at Carlton House and demanded an audience with her father. She *knew* one of her ladies had brought the parental stricture against her, as the princess had been so indiscreet as to have freely spoken in favour of Ariana Forsythe and of her particular wish to further her acquaintance with the future wife of the Paragon. This, she was sure, had been reported to her father just at the time when he had been feeling greatly abused by Mrs. Tiernan, a thing he did feel Miss Forsythe must be to blame for.

After putting off the inevitable encounter for as long as he could endure, the prince gave leave for his servants to allow his daughter in.

The princess came heavily into the room, with determined long strides. She curtseyed to her father and looked at Lady Hertford pointedly, until that woman got reluctantly to her feet to curtsey to the princess. The two were not friends.

"Sir," she said to her father, "I am deeply grieved that once again you have seen fit to forbid my acquaintance with a young woman of quality! May I ask why you treat me as a child? I am of sufficient age that you wish me to wed but not given leave to choose my friends! How is that just or fair, Sir, I ask you?"

The Regent was in no mood for another scene involving his daughter, but he asked, knowing full well whom she was referring to, "What friendship have I denied you?"

"Miss Forsythe! Miss Ariana Forsythe who is to marry your friend Mr. Mornay! I am sure one of my ladies let it out that I desired to further our acquaintance, and I would like nothing better than to dismiss her directly—"

"Except that I won't allow it."

"No, of course not. I may not choose my friends, I may not choose my ladies, and I will likely not get to choose my husband!"

"You are England's princess," he said, reminding her that her life was one of sacrifice to her country, without having to say so. They had had such discussions before. Numerous times.

"And you are the Regent, and yet I daresay I see little of sacrifice in *your* life!"

"Do you dare speak to me thus?" he asked, making as if to sit up in anger, only the pain in his left foot was so severe that he ended up collapsing back down in a paroxysm of pitiful moans. The princess was one of the few things in the Regent's life that he could exert a most determined control over, and he wasn't about to give that up easily.

"Leave us!" he snapped at her. "You are evidently in one of your moods, and I refuse to have a conversation with you. I will call for you when I deem the time appropriate."

"Sir!" she said, her tone low and strong. "I cannot be treated thus! What harm is in it for you if I take tea with Miss Forsythe? I fail to comprehend how this could be displeasing to you or why it should concern you at all!" In truth it was not so much the loss of Miss Forsythe as it was the loss of so many things, so many times, in so many battles of will against her father. Why could she never win?

"Everything about you concerns me," he replied. He looked at Lady Hertford, who instantly fed another spoonful into his mouth. He squeezed her hand and gave her a short smile. The princess looked on fuming. But she had a thought.

"My Lady," she said, getting that woman's full attention. "Can you think why my father has forbidden me to see one of our most famous saints? Seldom do we hear of such piety as Miss Forsythe is said to possess among the *ton*! Wouldn't you suppose, to the contrary, that he would wish me all the more Godspeed in making and keeping her acquaintance?"

Lady Hertford sensed she was being baited. With a look to her royal admirer, she slowly replied, "Are you asking me to question your father's authority?"

"Only as his friend, ma'am. As a true friend—who will not allow fear to blind her eyes to what is right but will give her honest opinion when it may help. Can you believe for a moment that my father will be served by alienating Mr. Mornay from his circle?"

Lady Hertford seemed to think on the matter for a moment. "This situation really concerns Miss Forsythe—and I should think the young lady must keep to the ranks of her religious friends, Your Royal Highness. She has displayed a severe lack of judgment, as you know, in bringing that dramatic lady to the fore!"

"Keep to the ranks of her religious friends?" The princess looked at her father. "Does Mr. Mornay comprehend that you hold his lady in such a thought? Does he know, Sir, that you are forbidding me to keep an acquaintance with his future wife?"

"I care not what he knows!" he shouted vehemently, as though he might have banged his fist upon a table if he'd been in position to do so. Yet, the very force of his pronouncement tended to belie the words he spoke.

The princess began to slowly circle the room, thinking. She stopped and asked him this, "I have heard you say that Mr. Mornay would make a fine addition to your cabinet—if only he had a heart for it. Have you since changed your opinion of him then?"

"No. I believe he would, or so I did think. How is this to the point?"

"The point is your own best interest, Sir. You are still in need of true friends in your government. I cannot see anything but trouble ahead between you and Mornay if you alienate his wife. I thought you actually mentioned ennobling him at one time."

The Regent was listening, almost with a smile. "You do begin to remind me of myself," he said, raising his glass to her.

She nodded, accepting the dubious distinction, and added, "In fact, now that I think on it, with this Parliamentary session nearly over, it would be an advantageous time for you to do so—strike while the iron is hot, and all that. The lords are all getting itchy to return to their country seats, and with his popularity, who will dare speak against him?"

Lady Hertford had to smile. Her smiles were not the warmest, but this one warmed the heart of the princess. She knew she was making an inroad.

The Regent made a dismissive gesture with his hand. "I've never even broached the subject with him! 'Tis out of the question."

"What title did you have in mind for him, Sir?" Lady Hertford was curious.

The Regent hesitated. "Oh, a baronetcy, I suppose. See if it raises a dust."

She looked at the prince. "That might flatter him, but it wouldn't put him in the house."

The Regent explained, "I'd follow it with a barony if there's no strenuous objections."

"There will always be strenuous objections when men see another man profit," said the princess, "but I daresay you can manage them." The intended flattery was well received.

"Well!" Lady Hertford fanned herself. "The Whigs will surely oppose you in it. Why not encourage him to seek election to the Commons?"

"Because I know he'd never do it. Mornay try to appease a crowd? Exert himself to win favour? Devilish unlikely!"

The princess was listening, her face controlled, her demeanour nothing but polite attention. Inside, however, she churned with the thought that Lady Hertford herself was inadvertently championing her cause!

"Blast it all! The Whigs oppose everything I do! Everything I *want* to do, in any case."

"I daresay Mr. Mornay could worry about the Whigs, if need be. He does have a way of getting things done!" Lady Hertford seemed to like the whole idea of creating him "Sir Phillip." Of course she was also pleased with the fact that Mr. Mornay had never shown a sympathy, publicly anyway, for the Regent's wife, the Princess of Wales. It might be very advantageous to see him in the House on the prince's side. He was an intelligent man, capable of swaying a vote, if need be. Indeed, quite capable.

Later that day the young princess happily instructed her secretary to make room on her calendar for tea with Miss Ariana Forsythe. A card must be sent to Hanover Square directly. Or was the wedding, perhaps, too close? On second thought, Her Royal Highness gave different instructions on what sort of correspondence to send Miss Forsythe. It was a singular idea and would no doubt draw criticism from some corners. But Princess Charlotte smiled at the thought. She so rarely got to do things of her choosing and merely for amusement. This was going to be an exception.

Seventeen

After the O'Brien's manservant, Mr. Edwards, had helped Master Peter into bed, he went to his mistress's chamber and knocked firmly at the door.

Mrs. O'Brien soon came awake in an instant alarm and pronounced, "Who is it? Come in!"

When Edwards, an old man, approached with a look of apprehension, her fear grew even greater. "What is it, Edwards? What has happened?"

"'Tis Master Peter, ma'am. He has taken a blow to the head, I believe."

"What? Goodness gracious!" She hurried out of her bed, grabbed her robe from a chair as she passed, and wriggled into it while walking hurriedly to her son's room. Edwards had closed the drapes in the room, and it was dark as they entered, but she took the servant's candlestick, held it over her son's head, and moved him gently to get the better view. She gasped and covered her mouth in horror.

She met Edwards's eyes. "Send for the doctor."

"The apothecary, ma'am?"

"No, not this time. I want a real medical man! Call for Doctor Henderson. He's a bit further and much dearer, of course, but I trust him." The old man nodded in a sort of bow and turned to go. "Edwards—"

He looked back at his mistress expectantly.

"Hurry!"

When the door shut quietly behind her, she was on her knees beside her son's bed, with her eyes shut and her hands clasped together in prayer.

Mr. Mornay suddenly realized that Ariana would not be safe enough at

Hanover Square. Tonight's business had been proof that she was truly in serious peril. How could he allow her to be out of his sight after this event?

He was still supporting her with one arm. He kissed the side of her face and then her forehead. "I haven't prayed with such difficulty since the night I gave myself up to God for the taking. O'Brien was praying too. I could tell. But I couldn't bring myself to speak to him, much less pray with him."

She pulled herself away a little and said, "You missed an opportunity. Prayer is more powerful when believers unite together in it."

"Yes, so I've learned. But I'm afraid I was not at my best. I'm still not. I'm feeling positively venomous, and if anyone dares cross my path again tonight—"

"Shhh." She put a finger to his lips. "All is well now."

"Not quite. Not until I've settled this business with Wingate."

Her eyes widened. "That's the name Whiddington mentioned!"

"I know. And I'll see him about this."

"Oh, pray don't! He called him a murderous blood! I couldn't bear it if something should happen to you—"

"Not another word," he said soothingly. "Nothing for you to fret about. I shouldn't have mentioned it." He stroked the sides of her face. But Ariana was not put at ease.

"You mustn't seek revenge, you know. It isn't given to us to seek revenge. 'Tis God's affair." She paused, giving him an earnest look of such utter sincerity that he was touched. She was so close, so sweet—and he had almost lost her. He bent his head as if to kiss her, but she said, "Mr. O'Brien was right. We should not be together like this."

"Yes, by Jove, he *was* right! I'm sure that's why I was ready to box his ears for it. I can hardly stand this any longer!"

Ariana bit her lip so as not to giggle at him, never imagining she'd see him so boyishly vulnerable on her account. He gave her a sideways look. "Forgive me. I haven't fully recovered from my fear of losing you." She put her head against him while he added, "Until I see to this business, I must have your word that you won't leave your house."

"Not at all? I cannot promise that!"

"Not without two footmen then. In fact," he said, thinking it over, "I'll send some men or hire extras for the purpose."

"I doubt that is necessary."

"After tonight anything could be afoot, Ariana. I won't take a chance. I don't know yet what Wingate has in mind that he would dare to do anything involving you. It's considered thoroughly poor form, you know, to involve a woman in a man's quarrel. But he's got no principles, and so there's no telling what could result with him. I will do whatever I can to see that you are not put in harm's way again."

Staring at her earnestly, he said, "To think I could have lost you!" He kissed her again, and as they pulled up to her aunt's house, Ariana was kissing him back.

Afterward he said, "I'll take you in." And when they were in the house, he added, "I may have to insist upon awaking your aunt, for I must speak with her." But Mrs. Bentley suddenly appeared at the top of the steps.

"Oh, thank God!" she cried, hurrying rapidly down the staircase. "My dear!" The old woman came up to Ariana and reached to put her hands around the girl's face. "Thank God! You are unhurt?" Her eyes were filled with more caring concern than Ariana had ever seen her relation display toward her before.

"Yes, Aunt, I'm not hurt!"

"My dear, you are aging me, I am afraid." But she blinked happily at her relation. "And now that Mr. Mornay has ensured your safety, I think we must both get some rest. You will tell me all about it later."

"I want two of your best footmen outside her chamber door," Mornay insisted.

"I just sent two men off with Mr. Pellham—to see him safely home. He stayed here with me all this time. We hoped and prayed that Ariana would be safe—"

"In that case, I must take Ariana to Grosvenor Square," he interjected.

"Your house? Whatever for?"

"For safety. With two of your men gone and those who would harm her at large, I dare not risk another opportunity for them to lay hands on her."

"Mr. Mornay, this house is every bit as safe," she began, but her tone was weak even to her own ears. Ariana's abduction had been a terrible fright for her, and the old lady wasn't feeling strong. But she raised a reasonable argument. "The servants would be thoroughly scandalized, I assure you! No such thing! She is safe enough here."

"I cannot agree." His look was calm but firm. "There is nothing of consequence that can prevent her coming with me. Any reasonable person must see the wisdom in my wishing to keep her beneath my own eyes under the circumstances."

But even Ariana did not think it proper. "'Tis no good, sir. I cannot stay at your house, and I am astonished that you of all people should think it possible—"

He turned her to face him fully. "Our wedding is in six days. You may live in my house, and I will remain in the servants' quarters if I must! But I shall not leave you here. Indeed, the more I think on it, I am astonished it did not occur to me sooner."

She reflected on his words for a moment. "Six days. I think I can promise to keep to the house since you feel so strongly about it."

"No. I realize that I suggested that earlier, but it is not sufficient."

Ariana was tired and had no will to argue. Not at the moment. She saw by his eyes and tone of voice that he was determined to have his way in this. Mrs. Bentley said, "She will go later when I can find a chaperone for her."

"Are you not her chaperone?" he asked.

Mrs. Bentley blinked at him. "I am, but when I am not well—and I maintain I am not well after this vexatious night, worrying over Ariana, not knowing what might befall her—I simply cannot abandon my house in this condition. I can only be comfortable in my own bedchamber, I am sorry to say, but it's the truth!"

He looked at Ariana. "Shall we send for Miss Herley?" Remembering that he knew full well that the Herleys were in possession of two items from his house made her gratitude for him swell to a billowing peak of affection.

"I do love you!" she responded. He instantly took both her hands, basking in her approval. Mrs. Bentley blinked again. She had missed something of that exchange, she was sure of it. How could sending for Miss Herley have elicited such a response?

He turned to Mrs. Bentley. "'Tis settled then. I will leave it to you to send for her friend while I get Ariana settled at my house."

"*You* get her settled? I should think not!" She turned, strode to the bellpull, and gave it a few good yanks. "I will send two maids with you. Harrietta is out for the day because she slept at her sister's house last night, but at least I'll know my niece has my own servants for chaperones."

"I will have my housekeeper stationed outside her door," said Mr. Mornay, for he had had enough and was intent on moving things along.

"Your housekeeper! Sir, there is no one who would accept the word of your own servant in a matter such as this! That will not answer! You will take two of my own maids to stay with her."

"I have adequate servants—" he started to say, but Mrs. Bentley took the extraordinary measure of interrupting him. Her concern over the situation was her excuse.

"If these men find that Ariana is at your house, will it not prove as easy to waylay her at some hour there as here?"

"No."

His short response did not satisfy. "Why not?"

"Because I live there. And I will see that it is not."

It took courage, but Mrs. Bentley persisted. "But you will be gone, at least some of the time, trying to apprehend these men yourself, did you not say so?"

"I will never leave her without a proper guard. I have more men in my household than you."

Ariana quipped sleepily, "I feel as though I were the crown jewels!"

Mr. Mornay looked at her. "No. You are much more valuable." To Mrs. Bentley he added, "No one will expect me to take her beneath my own roof, as you have already perceived. Therefore it stands that she is safer there."

Mrs. Bentley had one last qualm. "Sir, I am her relation and her chaperone, and I cannot like this arrangement. I feel it is too likely to spawn rumours and suspicions!"

"I don't care a fig about rumours!" stated Ariana, too tired to care.

Mr. Mornay met the eyes of the old lady, who cried wide-eyed, "I am responsible for her!"

"Not anymore."

"You are not yet her husband, sir!"

"Then send for Mr. Hodgson this moment, and I'll be her husband! He is number 15, Grosvenor Street."

This alarmed the lady. Mr. Hodgson was the rector of St. George's. "There is no need for that! Do not disturb the rector at this hour." Her look changed. "You *will* wait six more days, sir! And you *will* behave yourself if she is beneath your roof!"

Mrs. Bentley sounded so severe that Mr. Mornay, who never minded when other people gave him a comb, had to smile ever so slightly. "You have my word."

~~~

Taking her hand, Mr. Mornay led Ariana firmly from the house and into his carriage. The coachman had fallen asleep atop the board and had to be
~~~

awakened. And then two maids came rushing out, holding onto their caps with one hand and small valises with the other. They looked very alarmed but stowed their luggage and jumped on back of the board for the short drive.

Mr. Mornay gave a sigh of relief and settled back to allow his weary future bride to rest against him. He allowed his hand the liberty of running through the strands of her hair, which had come free during the evening. He let the loose strands fall between his fingers and then slipped his arm back around her shoulders, letting her rest. The strangest feeling came over him. The most unusual thing. And for a few seconds, he did not know what to make of it. What was happening to him? He didn't recognize the emotion that was welling up so suddenly. It came to his mind, his consciousness, his very throat, in a wave that nearly took his breath away. And then just when he realized what was about to happen, what the feeling was, it was already too late. The sensation of a wet drop on his cheek appeared as evidence.

I nearly lost Ariana. I might have lost *her!* Now that he had her back safe and sound, it was occurring to him that it might just as easily have gone another way. *She might have been hurt, abused, or possibly murdered!* He thought of his new faith in God, and questions flew at him.

Why has God allowed this to happen? Why have I got along just fine for nigh three decades with no need for a woman like Ariana, only now to be utterly shaken at thought of losing her? Am I growing weak as I age? He had to shake his head to blink away the water in his eyes. *Perhaps I am tired?*

No, it was more than that.

Dashed if he wasn't a love-sick puppy! He'd been too busy searching for her earlier to focus on the growing unrest within himself, but now it was coming at him in a flood. He gently lifted Ariana onto his lap, and she, half asleep, smiled weakly and nestled her head back against him. The carriage pulled to the curb in Grosvenor Square, and he heard the maids jump off the back and scurry toward the house. There was no other sound for a minute, and he didn't move. Then footsteps grew louder, and the steps were put down, and the door opened.

Mr. Mornay was immobile, however. Sitting there with Ariana, he felt himself almost sick with what might have happened to her. Thank God, he'd been too busy to give thought to these feelings earlier, or he'd have been utterly useless. He felt as if he'd just suffered a severe blow, and what was it? That once again, just as when he was young, he was at the mercy of the love he felt for someone. For Ariana. It was a terrible feeling. And yet she was in his arms, and that was wonderful.

What a paradox! How he wanted to deny it. It was indeed a blow to see himself for what he really was. Not the Paragon, the cavalier, confident society favourite. Not the friend of the prince. Not that person who could care less about whom he offended. No, this man was vulnerable. This man loved deeply. And he was frightened. This was the man who had folded like a house of cards years earlier when he'd lost his family—mother, father, brother—within eighteen months. The man who had tried to swallow the pain and get on with life, only to find that in denying his grief and rage, he was rapidly losing his interest in all humanity. He made quick work of most people, deciding in seconds whether to give them his time or not, or whether they would bore, tire, or exasperate him.

Then to his own surprise, his increasing irascibility had the uncanny effect of enlarging his reputation, his consequence among the *ton*. Strange, indeed, that he had neither sought their approval or took pains to preserve it, once given. This too only added to his aura. Couple that with a natural tendency toward fastidiousness in dress and a figure people insisted upon calling handsome, and it resulted in his being called the Paragon. Once spoken—and no one knew who said it first—the label stuck.

For years he had lived this way and quite comfortably too. When he was in the mood, he spent the night about town, visiting Carlton House or other aristocratic dwellings and engaging in a bit of gaming and a bit—a very little bit—of port or other wine. He could spend evenings going from house to house in this manner—remaining long at none, giving few his attention, and enjoying some bantering here or there. Hostesses were delighted by his appearance, and he enjoyed the greatest attentions from them, the best of everything they had to offer. And at times they offered everything.

He didn't know what it was that had kept him from succumbing to their offers. Or what it was that sent him to hire a hansom, if need be, to remove himself from a neighborhood where his companions had taken him and were intent on enjoying the company of light-skirts. All except him. He had a disgust of loose women. This was perhaps the best result of his teenage tragical romance with Miss Larkin. This, and that it led him to disavow women for so long, kept him unwittingly and unpurposefully pure for Ariana.

How glad he was now that he had not dallied with other women. Somehow it made his attachment to this one, this precious one snuggled against him, all the more precious. Again he was assailed with the thought that he might have lost her, and that same awful feeling filled him, tightening his throat and making him blink. He pictured Wingate, that reprobate aristocrat, impoverished in mind and pocket, and thought of what he could do to rid himself of his menace.

No one must be allowed to threaten this newfound happiness. No one who has proven dangerous to Ariana can be left alone. Least of all a dissolute, reckless peer with a grudge. I'll have him arrested, and locked up until he can be tried and sentenced to transportation. Hanging would be better yet, but it's seldom done for a peer unless treason could be proved. Yes, transportation—and only permanent transport—say, to Botany Bay, will answer.

Eighteen

When Mr. Mornay came to grips with himself, he carried Ariana into his house. Dawn had arrived. Frederick's quiet "good morning, sir" carried with it no evidence of surprise. The two maids had evidently informed him of their guest. "The third bedchamber, sir?" he asked. He took his master's hat, but that was all he could get before Mr. Mornay moved to the staircase and then proceeded up the steps, all the time with a look of deep concern on his face.

He lay his charge upon the bed and gave her a kiss on the forehead as she murmured a sleepy "good night." After telling the maids they were not to leave the room, he left. He felt that he had done the right thing. It might have been unusual to keep one's future wife in one's house, but it certainly gave him greater peace of mind than any other arrangement would have.

Back downstairs he considered whether to leave at once to search out Wingate but then decided to rest first. He was sorely tired. But he fell to pacing, considering his next move. He had to ensure Ariana's safety and be rid of Wingate with no fear of his return. In addition—and this made Miss Herley's coming of double importance—he wanted to know what that young woman's feelings regarding Holliwell actually were. Had he inadvertently prevented a love match? He had to look into the possibility. He would wait until her arrival, speak with her, and then go on to search out the arrogant marquis.

He headed toward his bed, intent on resting, but hesitated. He had a sudden urge to check on Ariana.

At the door of the room, he hesitated, then knocked quietly and turned the knob. One of the maids had jumped at his knock and was coming toward him.

"Is she asleep?" he asked.

The girl looked back toward the bed, and Mr. Mornay followed her gaze. He nodded at the maid, who went softly to the chair she'd been resting upon across the room in a sitting area. He stopped beside the bed and peered down at Ariana, whose hair had been let down, and she wore a nightcap. Evidently the servants had thought to pack a nightdress for her too, for he could see that it was ruffled and reached her neck. Her face was smooth and lovely. Every fiber of his being wanted to protect her, to settle this disquiet in his being. *After the wedding I'll take her from London, and she'll be safe. But there are still six days before the ceremony. Or is it only five now?* He couldn't even think straight.

What if I can't find Wingate? What if Whiddington's information about the man's whereabouts is false? While he mulled over these thoughts, Ariana stirred and eyed him sleepily. "Why do you look unhappy? I am safe now."

He started, as if wakened from a reverie, and then bent down to place a kiss on her forehead. The darkened room did not conceal the shadow across his face. He looked worried, drawn.

She came more awake. What had brought him to her bedside? "Is something wrong?" When he looked away, his visage unreadable, she whispered fiercely, "Phillip! What is it? Is there new danger afoot?"

She started to rise up beneath the covers, but he said, "No, no, I promise you."

But the unusual hardness she saw in his face belied his words. "Do tell me what ails you then! It is something. I can see it!"

He stared down at her for a long moment or two. "I might have lost you!" He hated to reveal the depth of his feelings. He hated the weakness in himself, which had produced an actual tear on his cheek earlier.

She reached for his hand and held it tightly. "But you did not."

He returned the hard grip on her hand.

She murmured, "I love you, my dear Mornay. And you must know I never doubted my deliverance."

This surprised him. "Didn't you?"

She shook her head. "Not truly. I felt God's presence with me. It kept me from hysterics, I am certain."

"I wish I could have felt it thus!"

"You are still new to the life of faith. It is for times such as this that our practice of knowing God and our familiarity with His Spirit must give us hope and strength. In time you will experience Him more and know the Scriptures so that remembering them can strengthen and comfort you."

Her words encouraged him. He took a tender leave of her and instructed the maids to remain in her room throughout the day. He appointed two footmen outside the chamber door as well and sent a servant to tell Mrs. Hamilton to stay with Ariana from the moment she arose. Outside the sun was rising, but the thick drapery did an admirable job of making the bedchambers as dark as possible. Ariana was exhausted and fell into a heavy sleep. The maids stretched their legs and tried to rest as well.

Lord Wingate was furious. Whiddington and Blighter had disappeared with his coach, and now he had no help, no equipage, and no Miss Forsythe. So when he came upon his brother the following morning in the Black Stag near St. Giles, he was in a thoroughly foul mood. Antoine, on the contrary, had been admitted to Miss Herley's house the prior evening and was in a remarkably good frame of mind. Because he had accompanied Mr. Chesley, a family friend, Lavinia's parents did not wish to insult the man by barring his companion from the party.

His contact with Miss Herley had been sufficient to be assured of her unchanged feelings concerning him. He had, in turn, been able to make enough small gestures and statements to her so that she too could be in little doubt of where his sentiments lay.

Lord Wingate was too sensible of his recent disappointments to be much aware of his brother's good spirits. "I'll kill those worthless culls the moment I lay eyes on 'em," he hissed, after ordering a pint of ale. "They're dead men, both of 'em, and if you happen to lay your clappers on them before I do, then the job falls to you to do the business, Antoine."

The young lord said nothing, and there was no indication from his expression to give a clue to his feelings on the matter.

"In fact," Lord Wingate continued, "I need your help to find a new carriage. I can't lose another day—that wedding is in six days!" When there was still no reply, he added in an acid tone, "If you'd gone along as I suggested, I might have entirely better prospects today!"

"I had other business," Holliwell said simply.

"But you are acquainted with Miss Forsythe and could have lulled her into compliance."

"It was *your* deuced idea to begin with, and I have no intention of lulling Miss Forsythe—" He lowered his voice at that moment, looked around to see if anyone was listening, and continued, "or any other lady to comply with your schemes."

"It is *your* bloody honour we are supposed to be defending, and *your* lost bride we are avenging!"

Antoine turned in his seat to face his brother. "If it is only on my account that we are abducting a lady of quality from a man of great influence and means, then why is it so deuced important to you?"

Lord Wingate shrugged. "I suppose I've nothing better to do now that we're both ruined and nigh well bankrupt!" His appearance was stark evidence that his circumstances had been accurately described. His face, though of a handsome cut, was unshaven and unhealthy looking, and his clothing only a remnant of the finery it once was.

"You've been ruined for years and managed to get along. I've had second thoughts, sir. It is perhaps providential, if I have the slightest claim to providence, that your plan was blocked up last night. I saw Miss Herley, and my hopes are high in her regard. I am determined to have nothing more to do with knavery or smuggling or abducting a lady, or any of your scatter-brained attempts to make a fortune. They never work, Julian! And if you're taken in this, you'll hang for it."

Lord Wingate's steely grey eyes narrowed prodigiously. He came to his feet, paced a little ways, and then returned, taking the chair and coming down on it so that his arms rested atop the back and his legs straddled the sides. He rested his cold eyes upon his brother. "See here, Antoine, and understand this!" His eyes glinted in the light that was filtering in through the grimy windows. "I mean to finish this. I will have revenge, and I will exact enough money from Mornay to get myself—and you too—out of this rat's hole we've dug for ourselves. Do you hear? We are noblemen of the realm, and we are not going to live out our lives in this flea-ridden 'holy ground.' Do you understand?"

His brother heard him out and then turned deliberately and faced his pint. Wingate shot up from the chair and came at Antoine, who jumped to his feet. They scuffled with each other, and Julian pushed his brother so that he had him against a wall. Others in the room made sure to be out of their way, but no one seemed to think they ought to interfere. The fight was looked upon as a natural event, nothing to be surprised at.

Antoine had his back to the wall, but he hissed, "*You* listen to *me*, brother! I *understand* that we are depraved and deserve what we've created for ourselves, utterly and entirely!" His eyes were equally as fierce as his elder brother's, and his nose flared, giving him an almost heroic look. "Miss Forsythe is Miss Herley's dearest friend. I will not have a hand in bringing her harm! It would ruin any chance I have to win Lavinia, and I have no interest in causing such distress to a lady!"

"You're a dashed coward!" Julian released him and snickered, causing Antoine's face to glower and his nose to flare again. "I don't mean to harm the lady as long as Mornay comes through with the blunt. And what's more, you don't stand a chance to win Miss Herley! Mornay called your bluff there. When will you cease to be so bottle-headed and realize when the game's up? You've become a lily liver!"

"What I've become, sir, is *sober*." The brothers stared at each other, and Wingate's glare lost just a token of its strength. Antoine's eyes were calmer but with a firm resolve in them that did not portend well for his brother. "What is your next move?" the younger one asked.

There was a moment of wary silence and then, "I'm off to Hanover Square." Wingate's tone was grim. "If I have to wait a fortnight by her house, I'll do it until I get that blonde mort!"

"What if Mornay sees you hanging about?"

"What's that to me? He knows nothing of my plans. He and I have some old business, but I doubt he'll be eager to face off on it. Probably forgot all about it, though I have not."

Holliwell was silent for a few moments. "So this is why you took up 'my' cause to begin with. To revenge yourself on the man."

"Don't be such a gudgeon! I'd always intended on revenge, but your little matter merely served to hasten me." Wingate drank down his pint, wiped his mouth, and turned to go. "It's not too late, Antoine. I'm going to win this time. I'll have Mornay on his knees!"

The younger man had taken his seat. He watched the other but did not reply.

Wingate seemed reluctant to leave. Antoine, after all, was the only family he had. The rest had been done with him long ago, and he was no longer welcome in any of their homes. "Don't abandon me, Antoine." There was a hint of a plea in his tone, spoken more softly than usual. This did have its effect, and the younger man rose and went and stood in front of his brother.

"Give up your revenge!" His tone was heart felt. "Let us think of a better way to regain our fortune."

Lord Wingate snorted in derision. "There is no better way!" He took a deep breath. "I'll ask you once more. Come with me, and let us do this thing together. We can get your Miss Herley, leaving her no recourse but to marry you if her virtue is compromised." His glittering eyes stared at his brother's face. Shortly Antoine's look became determined. Without another word, he turned and went back to his seat. It was not easy for him to walk away from Julian, but he felt it was absolutely necessary. He might have ruined his young life with dissipation and keeping poor company, but he was not lost entirely to his conscience. He was not such a cove that he'd participate in this addle-brained idea of revenge—and especially not when it involved the likes of a Miss Forsythe and a Mr. Mornay. And he would sooner lose Lavinia than sully her! Julian evidently knew nothing of love.

Lord Antoine had gone against his better judgment from the beginning. He may have been careless, reckless, and selfish. But not so much a son of Lucifer that he could terrify a young lady of good character to no purpose. He knew, even if his brother did not want to admit it, that Mr. Mornay had only done what any upstanding person would. He was right to warn the Herleys, dash it! And they had no one to blame for his being right except themselves.

Lord Wingate released a torrent of oaths at his back before finally leaving the place. As soon as he stepped out of doors, he saw a man he knew he could hire for his cause, and in a few minutes had done so. A short time later, they found a carriage at the curb and persuaded the coachman to abandon it by brandishing pistols in his face. It was only a short time then, since Wingate had come upon Antoine, that he found himself heading once more to Hanover Square—his mind set on extortion more than ever.

He was in a rage over Antoine's betrayal. He let his head fall back—he had to think, *think*! In minutes he realized that his brother's assistance was not vital for his plan to work. *I have a little money left; enough to pay my new "coachman" to help me confiscate the girl. Once I have Miss Forsythe in my power, Mr. Mornay is certain to open his purse. My brother is a cork-brained idiot, and when the deed is done, I'll give him nothing. Not a shilling!*

When Ariana left the house with Mr. Mornay, Mrs. Bentley released a disheartening sigh. She was not comfortable with Mornay's decision, but she did not have the energy to go with them and serve as chaperone herself. It would mean no sleep for her, and she was utterly fagged as it was. Miss Herley! She had to send for her!

About twenty minutes later, Haines was on his way to fetch the young woman and bring her back to Hanover Square. He had orders to say that Mr. Mornay had requested the girl for the sake of his future wife. Mrs. Bentley wanted to see Lavinia before sending her off to Grosvenor Square. Miss Herley had to understand the utter seriousness of what was expected of her. She was to be not just a friend to Ariana but her companion, a chaperone. As such she could not go traipsing about town or doing anything apart from Ariana. That Ariana was staying in the house of her betrothed before the wedding was rather extraordinary. Every effort must be made to ensure that it was not made to seem even more so by adding a hint of scandal.

The Paragon had sent for Miss Herley? What could be afoot? How exciting it seemed to the family that Mr. Mornay had called their Lavinia for Miss Forsythe's sake! She was speedily dressed and packed and on her way to Hanover Square in little more than an hour.

She had no sooner entered and was standing in the hall removing a light shawl when Mrs. Bentley came toward her saying, "Do not remove your shawl, Miss Herley!" She seemed a bit breathless but explained, "Mr. Mornay has already taken Ariana to Grosvenor Square—you must join her there. You are to be a companion to her—a chaperone actually. On the way there, I will tell you everything you must know to do it properly."

Miss Herley stood there blinking. "A chaperone? Me? But you are also coming?"

"I am only seeing with my own eyes that you get there, my gel. After that I am returning to my house and going to bed directly! And I want no interruptions for the rest of the day! I have had precious little sleep this night—and worry and vexation—and I am determined to get my rest later. That is why I had to call for you, my gel. I cannot be Miss Forsythe's chaperone at Grosvenor Square. She must have you." She had finished tying on her bonnet and said, "Come! Let us go!"

"I do not understand," said the young woman, as they left the house. "Why has Mr. Mornay taken Ariana to his house?"

"Oh, my word! You haven't heard! Come, come, into the carriage, and I shall tell you all."

Inside the vehicle Mrs. Bentley said, "I am grateful to you for being available, I must say."

"Not at all," Miss Herley replied politely. "I am happy to be of service, I assure you." She took her shawl and draped it around her head, as she often did when trying to preserve an especially nice hair design. Last night's card party had given her mama incentive to have Lavinia's hair done. A local lady allowed her maid, who was exceedingly talented with regard to the latest styles, to be "rented" out, so to speak, just for such occasions. A good shawl around one's head, Lavinia had learned, helped much to maintain the style for at least an additional day.

"You see, it is like this—Ariana was abducted last night!"

"What! How?" Lavinia's composure was shaken.

"Oh, I don't know the particulars yet myself. Someone named Wingate was behind it, I think." Miss Herley's features froze. Lord Wingate was Lord Antoine's brother! Could it be the selfsame man she referred to? But why would he do such a thing? Mrs. Bentley noted her expression but misinterpreted it. "Yes, exceedingly horrid, isn't it?"

"Upon my soul, yes!" Lavinia couldn't have meant it more. "Was Miss Forsythe harmed?" she asked with great trepidation.

"Not bodily though she swooned, you know, for the first time in her life."

"Perfectly understandable!"

"Indeed! But this is not to the point. I am not able to stay at Grosvenor Square with her, though I will come by as often as possible. But your presence is necessary so that there is no question of impropriety. Mr. Mornay could not feel that Ariana was quite safe with me at Hanover Square, though I daresay she would have been. Why *do* men take these strong notions into their heads? But the thing is you must be on hand at all times. You are not to be her friend only for your own amusement or pleasure, Miss Herley. You must be more than that. You must be a chaperone. You must rise above the call of mere friendship." She stopped suddenly. The older lady looked at her questioningly. "Do you think you can manage this?"

Miss Herley was listening very intently. She had never heard Mrs. Bentley speaking quite so quickly and with so intense a manner. "Of course!" She was a bit taken back by the question. Why shouldn't she manage? Ariana was not some spoilt child to give her difficulty. "I see no reason why I should have any difficulty whatsoever, Mrs. Bentley."

"Very good. That is precisely what I hoped to hear from you." They were just nearing the Square at the end of Upper Brook Street when a carriage shot out rather suddenly and then had the audacity to block the intersection.

Haines hurriedly reined in the horses and gave his most disdainful look to the driver of the vehicle in his path.

A man exited the carriage and came toward Haines. In an aristocratic tone, he said, "I say, but this *is* Mrs. Bentley's coach, is it not?"

Haines's look changed to one of wary curiosity. "It is."

"Excellent. Will you hold your horses for a moment while I have a word with your mistress?"

Haines glanced at the carriage still in his path. "I have no choice but to do so, sir."

The man smiled. "Indeed. No, I suppose you do not." He moved on to the door of Mrs. Bentley's carriage, where she had been looking out the window and wondering what on earth was holding them up. Giving her his most charming smile, he opened the door and said, "Mrs. Bentley, I beg your pardon. I'll only take a minute of your time."

"Who are you, and what do you want?" she demanded.

He pulled out a pistol and pointed it right at her heart saying, "I am a man who has been wronged, and what I want is this young woman." He looked at Lavinia. "Come with me this minute, or this old lady dies!"

Nineteen

Miss Herley was too agog for a moment to move or do as he said, despite the very real pistol pointing at Mrs. Bentley. She merely grasped the ends of her shawl as if for strength and swallowed in distress.

To the older woman's shame, the moment she saw the barrel of the weapon aimed at her heart, she was instantly filled with a most sickening feeling. She had just been about to open the door of the carriage to give Haines a good comb on stalling for so long, when the man had appeared at the window.

She was now staring down the barrel of his gun, and the sickening feeling was becoming worse, violently worse. *Oh, my word, I am going to be shot!* And then all went black.

Lavinia gasped when Mrs. Bentley slumped over, but the man said, "Come, come, we haven't got all day!" As she began moving toward him and the door, he said, "Now wear a smile and keep it on until I tell you otherwise." There were people about, and the coaches in the road were beginning to cause a crush of traffic. When the driver saw his accomplice leaving the plush carriage with the young woman, he moved his equipage out of the way, pulling it over to the curb.

Haines, meanwhile, had grown suspicious of being stopped as they were. He couldn't release the horses and couldn't abandon his perch atop the board, or he would have climbed down to check on his mistress. He heard the carriage door open again, however, and then saw Miss Herley and that shabby gentleman leave.

"Hey there!" he shouted at them. Lavinia's look of utter distress mixed with hope—for she was encouraged that Haines had noticed her—was enough to cement his suspicion that something was amiss. He had taken the precaution of bringing a pistol with him and now pulled it from his pocket.

Lord Wingate moved Lavinia along but revealed his own pistol. He then pointed it back at Lavinia's side, so that the butler, who wasn't fluent with the use of weapons in the least, could not risk taking a shot and had to lower his. For a second or two, Haines watched the couple leave. He grew angry, then pointed his gun in the air, and fired a report. He jumped at the loud noise, but the ensuing panic on the street unfortunately only resulted in giving the criminal even more freedom to hurry his victim along.

Haines cracked his whip, intending to waylay the other vehicle with Mrs. Bentley's coach and perhaps stop this outrage, but then something happened that made him turn off Upper Brook Street instead. As he approached the rogue's coach, the man with the pistol pushed Miss Herley into it and then turned and pointed his weapon straight at Haines, approaching head-on! With eyes widened with fear, the butler turned the equipage onto Grosvenor Square and sighed with relief, though it was only a partial relief. Miss Herley had been nabbed right from under his nose, and he had still to ascertain that his mistress was safe.

To the footman who came forth from house number 25, he yelled, "Move sharply! Take these reins!" Haines jumped down hastily and opened the carriage door. For a moment he froze with dread. There was Mrs. Bentley, slumped on the seat unconscious! Was she dead? Haines was all aflutter, but he had the presence of mind to feel for a pulse and found one.

He breathed a sigh of relief. Someone inside ran for smelling salts, and soon Mrs. Bentley was awake. She came to with a start saying, "What! What happened?" But then she remembered and, seeing no sign of Miss Herley, fell into great distress. Haines himself had to insist that Mr. Mornay be summoned. Mrs. Bentley had her head in her hands and was sitting in the carriage rocking with regret.

"Oh, my word! Miss Herley abducted! Right from my own carriage! Her parents will blame me, I warrant! That odious man had a pistol!" Freddie at first refused to wake the master, but Haines reminded him in no uncertain terms that Mrs. Bentley was the relation of his future mistress. Not only that but Mr. Mornay had sent for Miss Herley, who was now abducted!

When the man finally went to inform his master, Haines went out to coax his mistress from the carriage and into the house. Instead, she saw him and cried, "Haines! Take me home! On the double!"

"Ma'am, Mr. Mornay is on his way to receive you."

"Haines, are you quite deaf? I want to go to my house *now*!"

Under normal circumstances such a reprimand might have made the butler stiffen with wounded pride, but as he climbed atop the board, taking the reins from one of Mornay's footmen, he felt relief instead. Mrs. Bentley was returning to her usual self.

~

"What do you want from me?" Lavinia's voice was tense, and her tears were threatening to spill over. She had just learned that her dear friend had been abducted the night before, and now it was happening to her! Why should it be so? It was absurd, but it was true! She remembered that Lord Wingate had been named as the perpetrator, and she wondered now if it was him whom she was dealing with.

He led her to a serviceable carriage and ordered her to embark. When she hesitated, he pressed his weapon, which he was hiding beneath his coat from the scope of onlookers, into her side, so that she had no choice but to do as he bade. Lavinia knew she was not equal to this. Ariana had somehow survived her ordeal and was safe again. Could she hope to do the same? She did not have Ariana's pluck or nerve—or faith.

~

Mr. Mornay had fallen wearily into bed not two hours earlier. He couldn't remember the last time he'd felt so tired, and yet he was conscious of the nagging restlessness that made him wonder if he could sleep. Not only was Ariana in a bedchamber down the hall from his, but he was still disturbed by the close call she'd had. The close call *he'd* had. The thing was he needed to know for sure what Wingate's motives were. Was it truly revenge? He'd never given much thought as to whether his curmudgeonly ways were creating enemies—he hadn't cared. But now it mattered. Now it involved Ariana. If there was something in his power that he could do to make things right with the man, he needed to find out what it was. And if not, the man needed to be arrested at once.

Far too soon he heard a firm knock, and it took a few seconds longer for his groggy brain to come awake. Freddie entered his chamber and approached the bed. "Sir, Mrs. Bentley was on her way here when her carriage fell into mischief. She requires to see you at once, sir."

"Has Miss Herley arrived?" he asked.

"No, sir. Miss Herley has been abducted."

"What? Miss Herley?"

"On her way here, sir."

"Where did it happen?" He was already out of bed and pulling on pantaloons, though his weariness from the previous night and the worry concerning his bride made him feel as though he moved at a snail's pace.

"On Upper Brook Street, sir."

With a repressed oath, Mr. Mornay muttered, "Get my carriage ready—the closed curricle. Put a second footman outside the guest bedroom." Frederick waited, recognizing when his master had not yet done issuing orders. "Be certain, if I delay long, not to allow Miss Forsythe to leave the premises. You must tell her that it was my express wish that she stay here until I return. Is that clear?"

"Yes, sir."

As an afterthought Mr. Mornay added, "Have Mrs. Hamilton keep company with her. I don't want her alone for a second." Mr. Mornay had to get dressed quickly. Miss Herley had been abducted on the way to his house, for Ariana's sake, so he had no choice but to try and help the girl.

He checked that his pistol was loaded and ready for firing. He put it in a pocket of his coat, as well as a few extra bullets and his loading kit.

When he arrived at Hanover Square twenty minutes later, he was tired and not in the best of dispositions. When he saw the state of the unflappable Mrs. Bentley, however, his heart sank even more. There could be no mistake that Wingate was serious. What really worried him, however, was the thought that Miss Herley had probably been mistaken for Miss Forsythe. In which case, it was his beloved they were really after.

It was his beloved that he must never allow them to get.

Once safely inside her own house, Mrs. Bentley had made her way to the ground floor sitting room—she was too weak to reach her chamber—and the nearest sofa. Haines quickly put a groom in charge of the coach and horses and hurried into the house after her. He sent one footman for a doctor; another for Mr. Pellham. He sent for the local constable and the nearest beadle. He sent a man to the houses of the night watchmen and the known charleys. Even the rare policeman might be around and should be sent for. He sent for anyone he could think of sending for until nearly every servant employed at Hanover Square, save Cook and the scullery maid, were to be found running on the streets of Mayfair in search of some personage or other.

He was also considering whether to notify the Lord Mayor when men started arriving. He had sent a cordial to his mistress and ordered a bracing breakfast of cold meats and coffee for her, but soon the ground floor sitting room was bustling with officials. Mr. Mornay and the doctor, Mr. Peabanks, had arrived. The food was left on a side table and was picked upon by the assembled personages, who finished it all off neatly in no time.

Mr. Pellham, dear soul, had been reading his newspaper. When word arrived from Hanover Square, he knew only that Mrs. Bentley was unwell and required his presence. He immediately flew into a frightful discomposure. What was her complaint? How long had she been ill? Had the doctor been sent for? The footman knew none of the answers to these questions. This caused Mr. Pellham, who barely had a moment to locate his snuff box and shove it into a waistcoat pocket, to hurry from his house with a great deal of worry on his brow.

He made his way as quickly as his legs and cane would allow but grew more alarmed when he caught sight of several of Mrs. Bentley's servants scurrying in all directions. Perchance his love was dying! His own breath came out swiftly, and a sweat broke out on his head and neck. He must hurry! Mr. Pellham was not a man given over to much fretting, but he was certainly fretting now.

When he finally reached the house, he was breathing heavily, and Haines, with a concerned look, took him directly to the sitting room. When Mr. Pellham saw that Mrs. Bentley was in the ground floor sitting room, this strange happenstance only added to his fears. He turned to Haines and asked, "Will she make it, do you think?"

Haines raised his brows in surprise. "Do you mean Miss Herley?"

"Miss *Herley*? Why would I mean Miss Herley? I mean your mistress, of course."

"Mrs. Bentley was unharmed, sir."

"Unharmed? Is she ill or isn't she? Why was I sent for, man, if she is unharmed or not ailing?"

"Oh, she is ailing, sir. I daresay you will be a great comfort to her."

Mr. Pellham was no fool, but he could make heads nor tails out of the conversation. He looked at Haines evenly. "Open the door, Haines."

"Yes, sir." He went in and rushed to the side of the languishing lady. "My dear Mrs. B., whatever is the matter?"

"Oh, Mr. Pellham! Thank God you are come! Such goings-on! You will not believe your ears!" In the ensuing minutes, he had taken her hand and patted it often while she poured out her tale of sorrow. Mr. Mornay took the opportunity of overhearing the detailed account—as did the constable, beadle, one watchman, and one officer, so that they all understood what had happened.

Mornay was able to supply the further information that Lord Wingate was definitely behind the abduction and that his brother, Lord Antoine, might also be involved. He quickly related all that had happened to Miss Forsythe on the previous day.

One or two of the men were familiar with the name of Wingate, and the officer knew him by sight. Lord Antoine was less known, but the brothers were acknowledged to be noted bluffs, scoundrels, blackguards of the first order.

Mrs. Bentley called for the arrest and imprisonment of the impudent ruffians. She was still in a rare pet. Seldom had she been so put upon as she had this day. Never had she been forced to endure such brutality! A pistol—right in her face! She had looked down the barrel, expecting any second to breathe her last! And she feared to think what Miss Herley must be suffering! Oh, it was unendurable!

The doctor had also been listening, allowing the lady to tell her tale, but he stepped forward now. "Gentlemen, I beg you, allow me to see my patient privately. She must not continue to relive this distressing experience. I daresay you have all received adequate information to begin your investigations into this matter and recover the unfortunate young lady." (This elicited a fresh moan from Mrs. Bentley.) There were murmurs of agreement, wishes for her recovery, and thanks for her help, and then finally it was only Mr. Peabanks left with the lady and Mr. Pellham.

He prescribed a dose of laudanum, but the patient, though she knew it would help her sleep, was not quite ready for it. She had an illness no doctor could fight. She was absolutely ill with the thought that she had sent for Miss Herley only on account of her own refusal to accompany her niece to Grosvenor Square. And harm had befallen the girl simply because Mrs. Bentley didn't wish to endure the discomfort of staying somewhere other than her own house. She had always preferred to stay in her own home; so much so that she had not visited the Forsythe's in Chesterton since they'd left London! But this was too vexing. She needed to *do* something about the situation. She needed to know that something was being done to recover Lavinia! She needed—oh, what *did* she need?

She had a sudden thought. "Randolph, please summon a maid for me."

"Of course, Mrs. B.!" He went toward the bellpull.

To the chambermaid who appeared, Mrs. Bentley said, "I need my prayer book. Run to my chamber and get it from the night table near my bed." She looked at Mr. Peabanks. "Sir, I must have a few minutes with my betrothed."

He bowed. "Of course, ma'am," he replied and went out to the hall where, to his surprise, all the gentlemen who had previously been in the sitting room were now gathered. They were still speaking of the abduction, other crimes of late, what could be done to prevent such things, and who should be in charge of searching for the brothers. Mr. Mornay listened to the talk only long enough to ascertain whether or not it was going to help him in his own search for Wingate, but hearing nothing of moment, he left.

His intention was to follow up on Mr. Whiddington's lead, which was that Wingate often stayed at what was called the *Holy Ground* of St. Giles' parish, where criminal nurseries were common and criminal minds congregated. He hoped the man had been truthful—there were other criminal nurseries in the city, and without a proper lead, he could search for weeks without ever uncovering Wingate's hideout.

Back in the sitting room, Mrs. Bentley looked plaintively at her future husband. "Randolph, may I ask—may I ask you to pray with me?"

Her voice was greatly subdued all of a sudden, and his surprise at the change in her tone was second only to his surprise at her request. But he instantly responded. "Of course, my dear Mrs. B." And when the maid returned with the little leather book, Mrs. Bentley took it and flipped through the leaves impatiently until she had found the collect she wanted to read. She gave him the book, and Mr. Pellham got heavily to his knees—not so easy as once it was—and there on the floor, beside her where she lay on the couch, he read from its pages quietly and with conviction. When he got to the prayer, Mrs. Bentley closed her eyes. "*Hear our prayer, O Lord...*"

Afterward, for the first moment since Miss Herley's abduction, Mrs. Bentley felt an easing of her vexed spirit. Had a mere prayer really accomplished so much for her?

"Thank you, Mr. Pellham," she said, patting his hand most gratefully and affectionately. "I daresay I will be able to get some rest now. I just *know* that God has heard us!"

"I am inclined to agree with you, Mrs. B.," he said, and he went and started dragging a wing chair closer to where she lay on the couch. They could both use some rest after such unnerving events.

⁂

When Mr. Peabanks had the temerity to knock softly on the door a few minutes later and, upon hearing no response, quietly enter the room, he took a look about him. His expression softened at what he beheld. Mr. Pellham was asleep in a wing chair that was adjacent to the bed, close enough so that one of his hands still held one of Mrs. Bentley's. The lady, meanwhile, was asleep on the couch, and both souls looked perfectly peaceful. He left a sample of medicine, in case it was needed, and instructions for Haines to call upon him at the first hint that his assistance might be needed.

⁂

After Mr. Mornay had gone, Frederick sent for Mrs. Hamilton. She was supposed to keep company with Miss Forsythe, which he understood to mean that she ought to join her future mistress in the guest bedchamber and personally keep an eye on the lady, as the master had wished.

"Mr. Frederick!" she exclaimed, after he gave her the orders. "Are you not shocked that Miss Forsythe has agreed to remain beneath the roof of this house before the wedding? And without a proper chaperone? Are you not disappointed in her character, sir?"

Mr. Frederick knew nothing of the abduction attempt, and he had to admit that expressed thus, Miss Forsythe's presence in the house did sound rather questionable. But the master surely would not sanction the thing if it were not proper, and he begged to remind her that the young woman did bring two maids with her. He supposed they were companions of a sort, which made her presence more digestible.

"Bless us, she's gone and brought her own servants already! Did I not warn you, Mr. Frederick, of her intentions? She'll have us turned out directly, I've no doubt! It's the Draper's Asylum for me, I fear, for I am nothing but an old, decayed housekeeper."

Frederick's face softened, but he had not had the chance to check with the master regarding his future or any of the servants, and he could offer her no consolation.

"I wouldn't be surprised," she whispered in a confidential manner, "if Miss Forsythe turns out the lot of us now that she's here. She won't go back to her own house, I assure you. Whatever her pretext is for coming here, the master, I fear, is sadly deceived in it. I daresay I will find her well and strong, and all this fuss about footmen at the door and myself in the chamber—all for what? For what I ask you? Not for *her* sake, I warrant! Perhaps our master realizes the thieving that's gone on has coincided with her visits one time too often, eh? We are to keep an eye on her, indeed! What think you of that?"

Mr. Frederick's face was troubled. "Mr. Mornay did say not to leave her alone in the house for a second."

"Just as I feared, sir! We must nail down the house now before she carries off anything more! Trouble, trouble, trouble," she said shaking her head.

"But I must think she is ill, Mrs. Hamilton. The master did carry her into the house, you know, in his arms, and she has been asleep since. I daresay she has some malady or illness."

"He *carried* her in? That is shocking, Mr. Frederick. Shocking, indeed! I am above certain," she said with great feeling, "that our Miss Forsythe may well have been *foxed,* sir! As I say, she is trouble for this household!"

"Surely not that," he returned. He was remembering the incident when Mr. Mornay was foxed and how Miss Forsythe had clearly disapproved of such a state. That was only weeks ago. Could the lady have changed so drastically in character? He doubted it.

"I am afraid the master was quite clear in that he wished you to stay in her chamber with her, nevertheless," he said apologetically.

"Humph!" she responded. "I'll get my shawl and a book. Make no mistake, sir. I will do my duty, for the master's sake—but not for *hers,* mind you." She sniffed loudly. "When is the master to return?"

"Only God knows, Mrs. Hamilton. There was an abduction of a lady who was on her way here with Mrs. Bentley from Hanover Square—he has gone to be of assistance in recovering her, I think."

"The master is gone to help recover her? Why should he do that, I wonder?" She shook her head and gave Frederick one of her most severely disapproving looks. "It gets worse an' worse. Nothing but trouble. That's all we've had since Miss Forsythe appeared."

Frederick merely nodded. "Very good, Mrs. Hamilton." But when he turned to leave, his face remained troubled, and his thoughts were uncomfortable to the extreme. *Is Miss Forsythe's presence in the house evidence of a loose character? Why would the master wish to wed an* impure? *And what reason could she have for napping items from the house, when all will soon be hers? Even Mr. Mornay does not trust her enough to let her roam the house alone. Worst of all, am I to lose my situation as butler after serving nearly twenty years? Will Mr. Mornay, always such a strong and sensible man, give way to Miss Forsythe's wishes to have her own staff at the expense of his own? And here we've welcomed her with such high expectations! Her sweetness of countenance and her kindnesses are all for nought. She has no intention, alas, of becoming our mistress!*

Twenty

The man who had abducted Lavinia was giving her an exceedingly strange look. He was sitting across from her in the shabby carriage with his pistol on his lap. Lavinia's heart was racing, and she was afraid that she was going to swoon, just as Mrs. Bentley and Ariana had done. But, oh! That would leave her too much at this fellow's mercy!

"You look different," he said. "Remove that shawl."

"Sir?" This was a startling request.

"Remove it, I say!" She hurried to do so, watching him fearfully all the while. When she'd revealed her dark locks, his look changed to anger. "Who in blazes are you?"

"Miss Herley!"

"Miss Herley!" He seemed struck to the core. "Miss Lavinia Herley?"

She nodded. "And you are Lord Wingate, are you not?"

"Ah, she knows me. Indeed I am." He started to laugh lightly, but then he turned a terrible eye upon her. "Where is Miss Forsythe?"

"At Grosvenor Square. I was to join her there."

"Devil take it! Just my luck!" His every word made her jump, and so he added, "I have no intention of harming you, so do try to contain yourself."

"Now that you realize who I am, sir, may I hope that you will release me? There is nothing to gain by detaining me. My family cannot pay you a ransom—"

"Not so fast, Miss Herley. I'll have to think about this. You may be of use to me yet. I daresay your friend Miss Forsythe will pay a pretty penny for your safe return."

"Miss Forsythe has no money of her own!" gasped Lavinia.

"That's my eye, she doesn't't!" He considered the matter. "But even if she does not, her future husband does. And I hear he has every intention of being exceedingly generous with his new little wife."

They said nothing after that, and Lavinia simply sat there in despair watching the streets go by and knowing she was being taken farther and farther from home and safety.

When the carriage slowed to a stop, Lavinia looked out, saw they were on a narrow and dirty street, and she started crying. Wingate hissed, "Be quiet, or I promise you, I'll give you something more to cry about!" Then she heard only whispering as he disembarked and consulted with another man. He looked back in, waved his pistol at her, and said, "Come along, then."

She stood up a little shakily, but when she reached the door and went to step down, Lord Wingate took her forcefully by the arm.

"I know your brother!" she cried, hoping this might soften his manner toward her.

"Of course you do," he replied. "Antoine is no stranger to the demimonde."

"The demimonde? But I am, sir!"

"You mean you were," he said ominously.

"If you harm or abuse me, you'll have to answer for it!"

By now they were entering a building that smelled strongly of liquor, smoke, and stale perfume. A few women were lounging on sofas and blinked stupidly at her, and one look told Lavinia she was in a place of demireps, for sure. The ladies were bedizened with too much face powder, lip colour, tawdry costumes, and cheap-looking jewelry. A man strolled in from a corridor, appearing more properly dressed, but his look at her, settling hungrily on her flesh as though she were a piece of meat to be eaten and enjoyed, turned her blood cold.

A woman greeted Lord Wingate familiarly and gave Miss Herley a smirking look, and from somewhere inside came the sound of coarse laughter. Could this woman not see, Lavinia wondered, that she did not belong there? Could no one see the repulsion and fear on her face? Or was it simply that they did not care?

A certain young man awoke from a drunken sleep on a sofa and saw Lord Wingate moving a woman along. My word, it was Lavinia Herley! He came sharply to attention, seeing that she wasn't happy. He knew Wingate and also recognized the cove with them. His brain clicked—he knew instantly what was up. *Dash it, why hadn't Wingate got Miss Forsythe, as he was supposed to have done?*

With an irritated grimace, Mr. Harold Chesley came to his feet, awakening the lady beside him. Before she could protest his leaving, he produced a few coins from a pocket and tossed them to her. He then quickly strode to the door. There was something he had to do.

Mrs. Hamilton dismissed the two maids who were with Ariana, telling them to go and ask Cook for some food. They were happy for the relief and did so unquestioningly. She took a look at the lady, still asleep—*good.* Circling the room quickly, she searched it as if looking for something in particular. Then with a final furtive glance at the sleeper, she pocketed a silver snuffer from a table. She went quietly to the door and opened it.

"I've remembered something I must do for the master," she told the two footmen, who were standing against the wall but looking at her curiously. "Let no one enter or leave this room. I shall return shortly."

"Yes, mum."

Mrs. Hamilton disappeared down the hall and went up the servants' stairs to their sleeping quarters. She went into Molly's room, deposited the snuffer with the rest of her stash, and returned to the guest bedchamber.

About an hour later, for it had taken him that long to locate Lord Antoine, Chesley plopped down beside him at a small table in one of the many "flash" houses of the East End. The establishment was known to cater to men who had fallen from grace, those who had started out well but found themselves in "low tide" from one circumstance or another—mostly of their own doing. Although Mr. Chesley himself was not in disgrace, he frequented these houses because it was more affable to his pocketbook. Much more affordable to spend a night gaming here, say, than White's or Boodle's—he simply didn't have the blunt to compete there, much as he enjoyed those places.

There were other gentlemen about, and Mr. Chesley did not want to blurt the thing in their hearing, and so when he sat down, he simply gave his friend a *look.*

"What's on your mind, Chesley?" Holliwell took a good draw on his pint of ale.

Chesley looked around a bit and frowned, but he said, "I just saw a young woman whom, I believe, you are acquainted with."

Lord Antoine looked at him sardonically. "Well? I know plenty o' morts around here. What of it?"

"This one isn't a mort—and she's not from around here. Come with me a sec and I'll tell you more about her." He was gesturing with his head and eyes, but Antoine was being cork-brained or too deep in his cups, and it was only morning!

Lord Antoine leaned forward. "Did you not take note of Miss Herley last night? Her little kindnesses to me and all that?" He paused. "I ain't your man, Chesley."

"Don't be such a gudgeon!" he returned with fervour. Then in a fierce whisper, he said, "This is about Miss Herley!"

"What? You saw her hereabouts? Why didn't you say so, you lackwit!"

Chesley had risen. Antoine did the same, and the two moved to leave the place. "I wanted to, you hulver-head," said Chesley, "but your friends are all so chummy with your brother, and he's the one who's got her!"

Holliwell halted abruptly. His face had frozen in an ominous look. "Explain your meaning!"

"Just what I said. I saw him bullying her into Mrs. Wood's, and she didn't look too chipper. He also had that nasty jarvis with him. What's 'is name—Campbell, and I don't doubt he had a pistol at her side."

Holliwell's face hardened, and his nose flared, and he was quickening his steps. "I'll kill him if he lays a finger on her! I swear I'll kill him!" Their eyes met. Chesley nodded.

In tandem they began running down the street. They'd have to hoof it to Mrs. Wood's house, but both men were young and had the speed-enhancing benefit of a noble cause. They made it in record time.

Lavinia had stopped crying, but she wouldn't accept a drink from her captors, and she was terrified that Lord Wingate would return and something terrible would happen to her. She knew she was in a brothel, what the lower classes called a *monastery*. Thoughts too horrible for words were going through her mind, which was a shame because she found the place utterly fascinating. (It was a shocking thought, and if her mama knew, Lavinia would have earned an instant combing. But if she hadn't been so frightened, she would have been intrigued to see such a place firsthand.)

Lavinia had read about such establishments and heard of the rare police raid, but to actually *see* these women, to see that such places existed *really*—it was so curious! She was studying the woman she liked to think of as the "abbess," (another cant term that she wasn't supposed to know) when the sound of agitated voices came to her ears and grew louder.

The abbess heard it too and at first reacted with a look of sheer boredom. But she grew suspicious as the sounds grew closer, and she got up and went toward the door. Stopping to look back at Lavinia with a leer, she said, "Sit tight, luv. I'll be back in a wink." Lord Wingate's earlier companion, the driver, had been dozing for the past ten minutes. The lady left, locking the door behind her.

Lavinia scrambled to her feet and searched the room to see if it adjoined with another, but there was no other doorway. She rushed to a window and threw aside the curtain, but the street below, scarcely populated, held no beadle or officer of the law who might come to her aid. It was too far to jump—it would be the death of her, being three stories at least. But she could still shout—yes, scream if she had to!

She tugged at the window, but it was no use. The weathered wood had expanded or perhaps was painted with the sill, and it wouldn't budge. Loud thuds at the door got her attention, and she spun around. The voice of the abbess angrily shouting…then another voice. Oh! Could it be? It sounded like Lord Antoine! Without thinking she rushed at the door crying, "Antoine! I'm here! It's me, Lavinia! I'm here!"

The door opened then, and her hopes dropped abruptly. It was Lord Wingate, not his brother. He sneered at her, "*Antoine! I'm here, it's me, Lavinia!*" And then he snickered and was joined by the abbess. He held up a piece of paper. "I've got it, my little lamb, the thing that will earn your freedom." She eyed him warily but said nothing.

"Are you not curious? Oh well, here it is then. A detailed account of your fate, unless Miss Forsythe can persuade her heart's admirer to pay the price I've named. It requires only your signature." He shoved the paper at her saying, "Here. Read it if you like. And sign it."

Lavinia didn't take it. "You will not get a great sum for me. Mr. Mornay cares nothing for me!"

He took a breath. "Do not tax my patience, Miss Herley. I am determined to deliver this letter tonight. So, you see, you must sign it now, or I will be forced to deal with you." His tone was light, but there was a dangerous glint in his eye. He had picked up the paper and now held it out to her again. She took it. The abbess was on hand with a quill pen and ink.

Lavinia hated to do it, but she was relieved that at least it meant they would know something of what had happened to her. And by whose hand. She signed it a bit shakily and handed it back. Lord Wingate took it eagerly and nearly pranced to the door, stopping only to say a few words to the abbess, and then he was gone. His exit gave Lavinia some relief. Unlike Antoine, whom she was in love with, his brother filled her with unease. He was handsome in his own way but far too frightening to truly hold any appeal.

Downstairs Mr. Mornay had arrived. He'd been searching systematically through house after house, pushing away people—men or women—who got too close, asking questions of some and constantly keeping a sharp eye out for either of the brothers. At Mrs. Wood's he asked for Wingate and gave the usual information: that he owed the man money from a wager and was there to pay up.

This earned him the information that he had just missed the man! Where did he go? He was given only the direction, but that was enough and in seconds Mornay was on the street and running after the tall, thin figure quickly moving across the street.

Chesley and Lord Antoine came at Mrs. Wood's from a different direction and saw Mornay just as he left the building.

"Him?" Chesley cried, stopping his companion.

Antoine said, "I ain't afraid of 'im. Maybe he'll serve to help us!"

"Well, I don't like him," replied Chesley. "If your brother had appeared with his lady, I wouldn't have raised a finger to help her."

Lord Antoine said, "But she is a woman of gentility and done you no injury."

Chesley was still staring after the man he detested. "She's marrying him."

Before entering the house, Holliwell took out his pistol and cocked it. He hid it again while he used his familiarity with some of the regulars to ascertain whether or not his brother was in the building. He was informed that Wingate had left not long ago. Was he alone? He was. *Good*. That meant Lavinia was still in the building.

His lordship sought out the proprietress, Mrs. Wood. She was an overweight woman with sloppy hair, wearing very white face powder and dark lip color that made her look garish. Mrs. Wood was no rattle-trap and always tried to protect her patrons, but she knew Antoine. Therefore when he asked which room his brother had rented, she said, "Last room on the left at top o' the stairs, luv." She eyed the young noble a moment and added, in a leering tone, "Don't you want your own room now?"

"Not this time," he answered, and she shook her head disapprovingly. But he had found out what he needed. They reached the room Mrs. Wood had specified and stopped outside the door. There was no sound from within.

Antoine knocked, pistol in hand, his muscles tensing of their own accord. The next minute would decide if the business was going to be a simple matter or, God forbid, a bloody one. Chesley too was at the ready, his eyes riveted at the door, his hands balling into fists.

When Lavinia heard the knock, her eyes opened in hope. The abbess turned to her and hissed in a low tone, "Not a sound out of o' you, missee, or Wingate will know of it!"

The sleeping man came to with a start. "There's someone at the door," the woman said to him, just as the knock came again.

"'Ere, who is it?" She had gone close to the portal and spoke through the wood.

"Antoine! Open up, Mrs. Smith!" Her brows cleared, and she went to open the door.

But the man cried, "Not so hasty, luv! I don't think 'is lordship's on terms with 'is brother."

The lady hesitated, looking at him, but in an irked tone, replied, "What's that to me?" She opened the door, was met with a pistol, and said hurriedly, "I let you in, didn't I? You don't want to shoot ol' Mrs. Smith now, do ya?"

With a look of alarm, the man in the room hurried to get up and get to his coat with its pistol, but Antoine came in forcefully, understood his object, and went and stood between the man and his overcoat saying, "Not another inch. Sit back down, and you won't get hurt." The man reluctantly did as told.

Lavinia was in tears with joy and let out a relieved sob. Antoine's eyes met hers, and she rushed to his side and threw herself against him. With his one free arm, he held her, and the look on his face became by turns tender, then angry. His eyes glared at the man and woman to blame.

"Are you hurt?" he asked, leaning down enough to speak into her hair.

"No, I do not think so!"

"Get the key," he instructed Chesley, who obediently went toward Mrs. Smith, who didn't fight him at all. She held it up in a matter-of-fact manner, and he took it.

"Check his coat," Holliwell added, nodding toward the crumpled garment, which had been tossed over the back of a chair. The man on the floor frowned severely as Chesley obeyed the order. Soon Mr. Chesley was brandishing a pistol, which he had pulled out of a deep pocket of the coat. He also pulled out a flask of some liquid, but Antoine shook his head, and it was returned. Chesley took the pistol to his friend, who had motioned for him to do so. He tucked the gun safely inside his waistcoat.

"Over here, Mrs. Smith, if you please," Lord Antoine said, pointing to the far side of the room.

The lady promptly began to move. "Your brother will want your 'ead for this," she said warningly as she went.

"I do not doubt it." But he was in high spirits with Lavinia near, and he added an impish wink to the statement, so that Mrs. Smith smiled and instantly forgave him all.

In moments the threesome backed out of the room, locked the door behind them, and hurried down the stairs of the establishment. They had no idea when Lord Wingate would be returning, and they needed to get as far from Mrs. Wood's house as possible. When they'd gone a few streets away, Antoine said, "We'd best split up." Chesley agreed. He said his farewells to Lavinia, who thanked him tearfully for coming to her rescue, and walked away from them. Shortly afterward his lordship engaged a hack and was comforting Lavinia in his arms until they reached Burton Crescent. His brother was indeed going to be in a rage over the day's events, but Antoine was now more certain than ever that he loved Lavinia Herley. Somehow, someway, he would have to prove his worth to her parents so he could marry their daughter in a respectable, traditional fashion. The question was how to do it? How?

When Ariana finally awoke near four in the afternoon, the two maids from Hanover Square had fallen asleep in their wingback chairs across the room, and Mrs. Hamilton was reading a book by the light of a candle in a chair closer to the bed. Ariana was blithely unaware of what happened to Miss Herley that morning and was feeling much restored from her own misadventures. But her mind did wander to the events that had befallen her. She thought of Mr. O'Brien and remembered the awful gash on his head. He had been injured on her account.

What if he was to develop the fever? What if he failed to heal or if his brain were somehow affected? Oh, my! Such gruesome thoughts. *I will have to ask Mr. Mornay to send a servant to find out how the man is doing. Surely a doctor has been by to see him and has given his opinion regarding Mr. O'Brien's recovery. I simply must know!*

"Good day, Mrs. Hamilton," she said.

"Good day, Miss Forsythe." The lady looked up from her book. "Shall you want something to eat, ma'am?"

"I need to speak to Mr. Mornay. I should like him to—"

"I'll see if the master is home," she said, rising and going at once to the door. Ariana was certain that Mr. Mornay was home—why would he leave when he had taken such pains to have her beneath his own eyes? Hadn't he said she would be safest with him in the same house? The servant had been short with her, but she shrugged it off. Her only concern right now was to ascertain the state of Mr. O'Brien. She awakened one of the maids to help her dress.

After washing and dressing, the housekeeper still hadn't returned, so Ariana went downstairs. The footmen she discovered at her door instantly followed her, which this time she found amusing. She knew it was not because she was distrusted, but loved!

She stopped in the morning room, hoping to find tea or coffee available, but nothing was in evidence. She spotted Mrs. Hamilton passing in the hall and called out for her.

The lady barely curtseyed, mumbled that she was sorry, but Mr. Mornay was indeed not in the house at present.

Did she know where he had gone?

"No."

Did he say when he would return?

"No."

"Has Miss Herley come to the house?"

"No, ma'am." (This was the truth, Mrs. Hamilton reassured herself!)

"Please send Frederick to me," she said, thinking that she would learn more of Mr. Mornay's business from that man, who always was nothing but helpful to her.

After waiting for some minutes for Frederick, Ariana finally left the room in a huff, causing the two footmen to scramble hastily from their places flanking the doorway. They had been leaning against the wall a bit lazily but quickly came to attention to follow her.

"Freddie," she said, after coming upon him in the hall, "do you know where Mr. Mornay has gone?"

"No, ma'am. His whereabouts are unknown."

"Did he say when he would return?"

"No, ma'am."

"Has he left no message for me?" She was a bit shocked.

"He wishes for you to remain in the house until he returns."

Ariana nodded. That, at least, made sense. "Freddie, I need a footman or boy to run an errand for me." He seemed a little nonplussed, so she said, "Is there a problem?"

"No, ma'am—except that these two," he replied, motioning to her bodyguards, "are not to leave you, and the boy is already out to market for Cook."

"Surely Mr. Mornay has other footmen," she said reasonably.

"He took a few men with him, ma'am."

She turned to the two who had been stationed at her doorway. "One of you must go."

Frederick cleared his throat. "Ma'am, they would face the master's displeasure if they were to leave you for any errand."

He seemed to be looking at her pointedly. Not with an ounce of affability, as was his usual attitude. Perhaps she had scandalized the servants by spending the night in the home of her future husband? Oh, dear! Servants with poor attitudes were not to be borne! She wished suddenly to be back at Hanover Square. If Mr. Mornay's footmen must follow her there, so be it. Then she remembered Mr. O'Brien. She had not dismissed Frederick, but he was turning to leave!

"Mr. Frederick!" Now she looked at him with a little asperity. She considered defending herself. She wanted to say, "You must know there was no impropriety in my spending the night here! Mrs. Hamilton herself was beside my bed!" But one did not explain oneself to the servants. They were expected to behave as their station required, regardless of their judgments.

"I will need use of a carriage. A closed carriage. These men may accompany me on back."

Frederick hesitated. "Ma'am, may I remind you that Mr. Mornay wished—"

"Yes, I know what he wished. I shan't be long."

The butler cleared his throat. Mr. Mornay had told him in no uncertain terms to keep Miss Forsythe in the house. What was he to do? In a minute his confusion cleared up. It was his part to obey his master—not a future mistress and certainly not one who was intent on parting him from his situation!

"I am afraid, ma'am, that I cannot allow it."

She opened her mouth a little in surprise. "I am not asking for your permission," she said, her face flushing with anger. "I am giving you an instruction. Which you *will* obey!" When he still hesitated, she added, "Or shall I go on foot?" She was determined not to allow the servants to think they did not need to respect her wishes, even if she was new to the household and even if they did think she was scandalous! Ariana knew enough of how new households were run to know that if the servants didn't respect you, they would never be in line. They had to know from the outset who was in charge.

Frederick looked at her for a minute, but his face grew unsettled, and he dropped his eyes.

"As you wish, ma'am." He was not going to fight the woman. He had tried to obey his master's orders, but Miss Forsythe had seen fit not to. It wasn't his fault.

"You may inform Mr. Mornay, if he returns, that I have gone to Blandford Street to check on Mr. Peter O'Brien's condition."

In a few minutes, Ariana was being handed into a small, closed carriage by a footman. He put up the steps and jumped on back, beside the other liveried servant, and the vehicle began moving away from the curb. Once they were out in traffic, Ariana finally relaxed and thought to pray. *Why are the servants at Grosvenor Square suddenly so off-putting? By rights they should be eager to see to my comfort. It is beyond the pale the way Mrs. Hamilton has kept me waiting with no word for so many minutes. And then Frederick didn't even come to my room when he was expressly requested to do so.* She had not mentioned these gaffes to the servants, not wanting to appear too particular, but when Frederick had challenged her authority—that was too provoking!

She forced her mind to calm down and started to pray for them. She prayed that, yes, her relations with the servants of her new house would be affable. That Mr. Mornay, whatever he was doing, was safe and sound. That she would find Mr. O'Brien well on his way to recovery and not in mortal danger.

The drive went fast, and soon she was alighting in Blandford Street with the two footmen around her like a king's guard. As she approached the front door, she wondered briefly what had prevented Lavinia from coming to her. Then the door was opened by an aged manservant who took her card and welcomed her inside.

Ariana hoped she would see Beatrice while she was here. The servants she would worry about another time.

Twenty-one

Lord Antoine slowed the horses and drew his curricle to the curb. Miss Herley was much restored from her ordeal and had been smiling, but now her smile faltered. She was home, and she was happy to be home, but it would mean having to say goodbye to Antoine.

The young man climbed down, tied his horses to a post on the street, and then came around and handed Lavinia down. They eyed each other a moment. She smiled shyly.

"My parents will be surprised that I am returned home."

"I hope you will tell them that I helped bring you back."

"Oh, yes! They must know of it!"

They slowly moved toward the front door, just looking at each other very wistfully as they spoke.

"Do you think, perhaps, they may allow me to call upon you?"

"Please do! I'm sure when they comprehend just how central you have been to my safe return, they cannot do otherwise but welcome you."

"I hope you are right," he said awkwardly. They had reached the door. "Allow me to see that you enter your home safely."

Pleased, Lavinia turned, lifted the knocker, and rapped it firmly two times against the wood of the door. It was already afternoon—her nightmare had lasted less than one day, but it felt much longer. She glanced at her companion and then away again and then back again. She was desperately hoping he'd say something more, something that would sound like marriage intentions. When noises from within indicated that time was short, something in Lord Antoine's brain clicked—he was running out of time. He grasped her hand. "My dear Miss Herley—Lavinia! Know that you are in my heart. When I can offer you a comfortable arrangement as my..."

She held her breath. He was about to offer for her! But the door latch was opened, and it creaked and swung wide. And there was the family servant, Hobbes, looking at the pair.

Lord Antoine bowed slowly and then walked away. "God bless you!" were his last words.

Lavinia watched him go with full eyes and much regret. She hoped he would call upon her soon. She had asked him to go to Hanover Square to give news of her safe return and then to Grosvenor Square. Mrs. Bentley and Ariana must be wild with worry on her account. Antoine was so good to allay their fears by calling upon them! She hoped that Mrs. Bentley would not be too distraught that she had not been able to serve as chaperone—but what could she do? After the fright of her abduction, she simply *had* to return home.

Around four thirty in the afternoon, there was a knock at the door at Hanover Square, and when Haines opened it to a young man of dubious appearance (shabby genteel at best) he said nothing but merely raised his brow at the man.

"I must see Mrs. Bentley," he said. "I have a message for her from Miss Herley."

This statement earned him an immediate entrance to the house, where he was told to wait in the hall. Despite the young man's lack of a calling card, Haines was given his name—Lord Antoine. Realizing Mrs. Bentley was asleep, Haines went directly to the man appointed by the local constable, who was in the kitchens at the moment, eating heartily, having hit it off famously with Cook.

When he gave the name of the young man, the officer stopped eating abruptly, wiped his mouth on his sleeve, and sprang to his feet.

"The blackguard himself! He has the nerve to show up here!" The man cocked his weapon, spoke some words into Haines's ear, and then the men proceeded cautiously back toward the young lord, who was waiting with no clue of what was coming.

Haines assembled a few of the footmen and gave instruction to rush round the house to block the front entrance—the young man's only means of escape. In minutes they had him in custody. He protested violently, but he was severely outnumbered and handcuffed.

"Miss Herley is safe at her house!" he cried. "I brought her there myself!"

"Indeed! After abducting her? You'll tell it to the magistrate, sir!"

"This is deuced unfair!" he said. "I came at Miss Herley's request to inform Mrs. Bentley of her friend's safety! Am I to be treated as a criminal? When I am the one who saved her?"

The butler and the officer looked at each other. Neither man believed him.

"You knew where she was to save her. I call that convenient." This was said dryly by the official.

"Ask Miss Herley herself!" he cried. "Ask Mr. Chesley! They will verify my innocence in this matter!"

The officer said to Haines, "Send word to Grosvenor Square, will you? Mr. Mornay will wish to know that I have one of the trouble-making pair in custody."

"Why, Miss Forsythe!" Mrs. O'Brien sounded much surprised. "I never dreamed of seeing you out and about. My son told us what happened last night. My poor gel, you must be dreadfully fagged!"

"I am sure I feel far better than your son, ma'am." she answered smiling gently. Her expression changed to one of concern. "How badly is Mr. O'Brien injured? I am aware of how unusual it is to call upon a gentleman, but my sister is staying here, and I had to know his condition. I am fully conscious of the fact that his injury was sustained on my account."

"Oh, my child, not at all. Peter has confessed his foolishness to me, and I am convinced you are the last person in the world who can be blamed in the matter."

"You are very kind."

Mrs. O'Brien smiled and led Ariana toward the stairs saying, "His wound is rather severe, but it is well dressed and the doctor assures us that with proper rest and a strict regiment of changing the dressing—to encourage the noxious elements that may have contaminated his blood to come out, you know—he should be fine, given time." She stopped and turned to face her guest. "We said nothing to your sister about your abduction, knowing how frightfully upsetting such news would have been. We told her Mr. O'Brien sustained an injury trying to put a stop to fighting on the street."

"That was thoughtful of you. Thank you. Now that I'm safe and sound, I suppose we can tell her the truth."

"Yes, but I sent her and Alice out with Miss O'Brien for the day. They are to take in some shopping and visit a park or garden. I thought it would be beneficial for Mr. O'Brien to have quiet at home."

"Of course." As they progressed through the house, Ariana hoped that what she would see of Mr. O'Brien would help relieve her fears for him, not exacerbate them. They reached the first floor drawing room where the invalid was resting comfortably, propped in a half-prone position on a sofa, with many pillows and blankets cocooning him. His head was wrapped in cloths, giving him the appearance of a wounded soldier. Hair hung limply beneath the dressing, and his face was pale. His eyes were closed, and he looked sadly frail.

"My dear, you have a visitor," said his mother.

His eyes fluttered open. "Miss Forsythe!" He gave a weak smile.

Ariana went and stood close by the sofa so that she could speak gently. She put her reticule on a little table near his head. "Mr. O'Brien, I came to tell you how dreadfully sorry I am for your having taken such a nasty blow on my account."

"Oh, my dear Miss Forsythe," he said looking embarrassed, "when it was all my doing and resulted in danger to your own person, I pray you, not another word about it. I am exceedingly grateful that you are safe!"

His voice was not at its usual strength, and she noted that his face, though pale, bore dark rings beneath his eyes.

"You must know," he said, with a bit of a twinkle in his eye, "that my mother and Miss O'Brien are attending to me handsomely. I feel as though I've reverted to childhood. You needn't add your own efforts to theirs, or I shall have no desire to recover whatsoever—being indisposed garners me the most felicitous female attention I can recall having the good fortune to receive."

She let out a little laugh. "I am sure you quite deserve and require it," she returned.

"Please, have a seat." He took a cup of tea from his mother, though his hand seemed to shake a little, and then he eyed her again. "My mother took the notion into her head that she might have lost me." He stopped and gave his mother a patient, affectionate look. "She was, I dare say, overly alarmed, and then the doctor only added to her fears by insisting I was liable to catch my death, not from the wound itself, but from the danger of infection."

"Oh, dear!" Ariana grew pale and looked at Mrs. O'Brien in alarm.

"Don't be alarmed, Miss Forsythe," Mr. O'Brien said, seeing her face fall. "I am young and strong and have every hope of recovering, I assure you. Indeed, I can expect nothing less because my heart tells me that God has work for me to do yet in this life."

Mrs. O'Brien added, "We will know his prospects of a full recovery better tomorrow when Mr. Henderson returns and removes the bandaging."

"I see," Ariana said.

Mrs. O'Brien poured Ariana a cup of tea. She took a little sip, but could not help but stare sadly at Mr. O'Brien. Far from feeling reassured by this visit, her worries were stronger than ever. "Well, I shan't stay and weary you, sir. You need your rest."

"Do not go," he said quickly and tried to sit up but winced and put his hand to his head. She looked at him sorrowfully.

Mrs. O'Brien said, "Miss Forsythe, my son is glad of your company. I pray you, stay a bit longer. I warrant you are a tonic of health for him."

"Last night I was quite the opposite," she said ruefully, but out of politeness she decided to stay a little longer. The parlourmaid came in and curtseyed. "Beggin' yer pardon, mum. There's a fine gentleman at t'door t'see you, mum."

"Oh?" The mistress of the house looked in surprise at her son. "Are you expecting a gentleman friend of yours?"

"No. I suppose it's possible that word has spread of my injury, however."

The maid curtseyed again. "It's you, mum, he be wantin' to see."

"Indeed. Very well." She looked at Ariana. "Excuse me, Miss Forsythe. I'll be back directly." But she hesitated before going and asked, "My dear, would you be so kind? He only needs you to hand him the cup, so that he doesn't strain himself reaching. The doctor insisted he wasn't to strain himself at all."

"Oh, of course." Ariana hurried from her seat and took the place where his mother had been, realizing belatedly that it was going to feel awkward. Mr. O'Brien may have been injured, but he wasn't helpless. Yet how could she refuse to see to his comfort? She took the seat where his mother had been, near the patient's head. A little table had been pulled up too, so that everything was handy.

"Would you be so kind?" he asked, with a nod at the cup of tea on the table.

She handed him the teacup. He took it gratefully, sipped the warm tea, and gave it back momentarily. It was just about empty.

"Shall I refill it for you?"

"Please."

She poured him another cup from the teapot and handed it to him carefully. He touched her hand on the cup as he took hold of it. Had it been an accident? Ariana was too embarrassed to say anything about it.

After taking a good sip, he remarked, "Very good. Nice and hot."

Suddenly they were like strangers. It was their proximity, Ariana decided. She looked around and saw a book. "Shall I read to you?"

He smiled. "I would enjoy that a great deal. You are very kind."

She stood up carefully, so as not to disturb the table, and in a minute had come back with a dog-eared copy of *Gulliver's Travels.* She stopped in her tracks, however, as she caught sight of the bandaging on the back of his head. There were deep stains of blood on it, and it set her heart pounding. She sat down and started reading from the page where the bookmark was.

There were tears in her voice. It wasn't just that Mr. O'Brien looked frail and sick. It was everything: her abduction, her rescue, his injury, the changes she'd ordered in the house that so far made only a great mess, the servants' poor treatment of her, and, behind it all, the wedding. The biggest event to happen in her young life, growing so near. As happy as she was about it, there could be no doubt that it was just a bit nerve-wracking. She wished her mama was with her.

Meanwhile, Mrs. O'Brien reached the front hall, where there was indeed a fine gentleman standing. He was impatiently slapping one glove against his hand and looking disinterestedly at a portrait on the wall.

When he turned, Mrs. O'Brien, who was not easily disturbed, gasped in surprise.

It was Mr. Mornay.

Mr. O'Brien looked pitifully at Ariana. "I...I wish I hadn't been so eager to believe your betrothed had required my help. I must admit that my...

continued love for you moved me to do it. I cannot resist any excuse to be near you."

"Oh, do not…do not speak of that! I will leave you this instant if you persist!" To his look of penitence, she said, "I shall read to you."

Mr. O'Brien was startled by her sudden nearness. He sensed how upset she was—and how solicitous of him. He studied her face and could have held his breath. Miss Forsythe's face, her beautiful face, was only a foot from his own. He froze for a moment, not wishing to change a thing.

Her lips pursed prettily in concentration as she turned her attention to the book.

Mrs. O'Brien's hands clasped together nervously. "Mr. Mornay! This is quite the surprise! I beg you'll forgive my servant for not seeing you to the parlour at once."

"That is of no matter," he said lightly. He had returned home to check on his future bride. He had not found Wingate when he followed the tall man, but a stranger. Fearing that his lordship may already have been in Mayfair to further his cause, he took himself back at once but discovered his wayward girl had left the house, despite his clear orders to the contrary. He was not in the best of moods.

Mrs. O'Brien's eyes grew wider with surprise—and wonder. Having heard from her son the full account of matters from the prior evening's adventures, she had little thought to have seen this man in her house. Was he angry at her son? Was he there to call him to account? And more, did he know that his betrothed was at that moment in their parlour? How would he react when he found out?

"Is Mr. O'Brien well enough to receive visitors?"

At that exact moment, it struck Mrs. O'Brien that the presence of Miss Forsythe in the parlour with her son was bound to further aggravate this man. For the slightest moment, she hesitated.

"How is he faring?"

She blinked at him. He was acting quite gentlemanlike. "He's comfortable, sir. We won't know his prospects really, until the doctor returns tomorrow. He'll remove the bandages then and have a better idea, he says, of what's to come."

He listened nodding. "May I see him?"

She blinked up at him, her mind moving quickly. There was no shame in Miss Forsythe having called under the circumstances. But would he see it in that light?

"Actually, sir, my son has already received a visitor."

Here his look changed. He seemed to be weighing his words.

"Yes?" he finally replied.

"Miss Forsythe—" Mr. O'Brien pulled her from her reading.

"Do you not like the book?" she asked.

"No. I mean—that isn't it." He could stand it no longer and made to sit up, but of course his head ached instantly and he winced.

"Do not sit up!" she chided, at the same time pushing his shoulder back down gently with one hand. This was altogether too much for Mr. O'Brien, who, ignoring the explosion of pain in his head, clasped first her hand, then reached for her in a swift movement and pulled her about the middle until she came right off her chair.

"Come this way, sir. I daresay you are acquainted with the lady."

"I daresay."

Oh, dear, thought Mrs. O'Brien, *Mr. Mornay seems to know that Miss Forsythe is here.* As she led the way toward the staircase, she hoped he was not provoked by it. She would dread it if Miss Forsythe was to get a combing on her son's account. But Mr. Mornay's manner seemed mild, not formidable. That was something.

In the parlour Ariana's chair fell against the table, making the tea spill. With a cry of surprise, she was yanked from it and onto Mr. O'Brien. Just as suddenly as his move had been made, his mouth was upon hers. For a single second there was nothing but silence, and for Mr. O'Brien it was a blissful single second. But Ariana wrenched her head away saying, "Let me up this instant! You are incorrigible!"

Her face had turned rosy, and her large eyes were reproachful. She was pushing against him, and he said, "Yes, of course, I must." He looked as though he meant it too, but instead he pulled her back for another kiss.

~

The two people approaching the parlour heard the noise, and with a look of alarm on Mrs. O'Brien's face, they rushed to the door and opened it. At first they saw no one and heard nothing. Mrs. O'Brien looked puzzled. But then there came a muffled sound coming from the small circle of furniture, and then the top of Ariana's head popped up and could be seen over the back of the settee, which faced the door.

"Impudent man! Shame on you!" she cried. "Will you never learn that I am marrying Mr. Mornay?"

"I don't mean to behave badly—surely you realize I am in love with you! Only say that you will marry me instead, Miss Forsythe! Only say you will! It's not too late, you know!" Meanwhile she was fighting to free herself.

Mr. Mornay had frozen for a second listening. His expression underwent a frightful change. He sprang to action, quickly rounding the settee, and stood there for a moment, his eyes burning with fire that could never be met by anyone with equanimity. Nor did Mr. O'Brien greet it with such now.

His hands dropped abruptly, releasing Ariana's arms, and she immediately scrambled to her feet, collecting her wits and glaring at the patient there. But then she noticed that Mr. O'Brien's demeanour had changed completely. Following his gaze, she turned and saw her fiancé. Different emotions flashed quickly across her face in succession: first delighted surprise, then, with a sudden remembrance of what had just taken place, a measured sobering, a bit of a fearful look.

Mr. Mornay, for his part, looked her over quickly, then moved as if to harm Mr. O'Brien, who was cowering against the settee with a fearful look on his face. Mrs. O'Brien was standing silently, her hand covering her mouth, for she was as horrified as their dignified guest at what she had just seen. She couldn't say a word, though she thought surely she was about to witness the murder of her child.

Mornay moved toward him, but Ariana grasped his arm.

"He is injured!"

He seemed to consider this. He glared at Mr. O'Brien silently for a few moments while he grappled with his emotions. Then Mr. Mornay placed a firm arm about Ariana and led her quickly from the room, without having said a word.

As they passed the matron of the house, Mrs. O'Brien gave Ariana a most heartfelt look of sorrow. She was utterly, utterly afraid that Mr. Mornay might vent his wrath on the poor girl, and she felt herself to blame for leaving the two young people alone together. She herself had asked the young woman to sit by her son! She was at fault! Then she turned her mind to Peter, the sad patient. She came around the circle of furniture and looked at him. All her pity was gone, erased by the shame that filled her for his behaviour, and in its place, she felt a sudden cold antipathy.

She stared him down for a moment, shaking her head in disbelief of his enormous impropriety. Then without a word, she turned and left the room.

He sat back against the cushions with a bit of relief—it hadn't been so bad after all. Mr. Mornay hadn't accosted him. His mother hadn't upbraided him. And, despite his failure to win her, he had actually kissed Miss Forsythe! He had kissed the angel! He would savour the memory. Or would it serve instead to remind him of his rash and ungentlemanly behaviour? He considered the matter and soon felt a slow sense of shame begin to creep upon him.

He knew he would need to repent of what he'd done. He would also need to apologize and ask forgiveness. Exhausted, Mr. O'Brien lowered his head slowly back upon the pillows on the settee. Why could he not maintain command of himself when in Miss Forsythe's presence?

For her part, Ariana knew her "friendship" with Mr. O'Brien had finally been put to an end. She would never risk being near him alone again. Never.

Twenty-two

Far sooner than Mr. Pellham expected her to, Mrs. Bentley awoke groggily from her sleep. She had been dreaming that Mr. Mornay had eloped with Ariana to Scotland, and that London was abuzz with crude insinuations and remarks as to what had caused the Paragon to take such an infamous step. She awoke all aflutter. Mr. Pellham was at her side at once and offered the information that one of the ruffians had been arrested, and that Lavinia was safe. Mrs. Bentley's face registered relief, which she expressed with a grateful sigh. But her expression quickly changed to one of concern.

"Dear me!" she cried. "Ariana has been at Grosvenor Square all this time without a chaperone! How could I not think of it sooner? Miss Herley never got there! Oh, Randolph. This is precisely what I never wanted to happen."

She rang the bellpull. "I must go to Grosvenor Square, where I shall remain if I never sleep another wink again!" To Haines, who came quickly, she said, "Haines, get the coach at once. You will drive me to Grosvenor Square and then drop Mr. Pellham at his home. I will remain at Mr. Mornay's house until further notice."

Haines was surprised, but of course it wasn't his place to question a command. "Yes, ma'am," he said and set out to take the precaution of loading again the little travelling pistol that usually sat, almost forgotten, in a small recess in the carriage.

Ariana did not know what to say. She allowed Mr. Mornay to scurry her to his carriage, and then, as he took his seat beside her, she looked at him searchingly.

Does he know I did nothing to intentionally dishonour him? Does he know that Mr. O'Brien (that formerly gentle soul!) took cruel advantage of me? What is he thinking?

"You know that I belong to *you*."

"I made it clear you were to remain at my house."

She swallowed, thinking about what had caused her to leave. "Your servants despise me!" Tears formed in her eyes. "It is easy to see they think my presence early this morning in the house was scandalous!"

He frowned. "What makes you say so?" She went on to tell him of her afternoon at the house, of their insubordination, and how unwelcome she had felt.

"That is hardly reason to take my wishes so lightly. Is this what I am to expect throughout our marriage? That you won't do as I bid? That, at the least provocation, you'll fly up into the boughs and do what seems best to you without my approval? Against my expressed wishes?"

"I cannot tell you how wretched I felt about Mr. O'Brien's wound and how I had to see how he fared, though I am heartily sorry now that I did. I am sorry. I can and will do better. I promise you!"

This seemed to help.

"I must tell you," he said in a different tone, for he had just remembered, "Miss Herley has been abducted."

She gasped. "What? Oh, my poor Lavinia!"

"I spent hours looking for Wingate or Holliwell but without success."

"Did you? Oh, my darling!" She grasped his hand. "And to think how she adored Lord Antoine!"

He was startled. "Did she?"

"I believe so."

Mr. Mornay thought for a moment and rubbed his chin but said nothing. He was wondering if the "abduction" was merely a ploy to force a marriage between them. Perhaps he'd underestimated the man's intentions toward Lavinia.

"We'll speak to the servants," he said, "regarding this morning and see what's what." But he was still bothered by the memory, fresh in his mind, of seeing her rising off the sofa upon which Mr. O'Brien was reclining. "And perhaps you can explain to me," he added, in a caustic tone, "how I came to find you in such a compromising position with that endless pest, O'Brien!"

In no time at all Mrs. Bentley was raising her hand to the knocker at 25 Grosvenor Square. Haines prepared to take Mr. Pellham home, waiting only long enough (as any thoughtful butler would) to be certain his mistress gained entrance to the house.

Once inside Frederick informed Mrs. Bentley of the astounding fact that neither Ariana nor Mr. Mornay were at home. Her hand flew to her heart with the thought that they'd absconded to Scotland, just as she'd dreamt! She feared the answer, but had to ask where they'd gone.

Frederick thought for a moment. It was not his duty to give people the whereabouts of either his master or anyone staying in the house.

He did not know.

Had he no idea whatsoever? What time had they left the house?

He offered only the information that they had not left the house together.

Did not Miss Forsythe say where she was going or when she would return? Frederick's house of cards began to crumble. He had no loyalties to Miss Forsythe at the moment, since she was soon to part him from his situation, so he said in absolute honesty, "I believe Miss Forsythe said she was going to Blandford Street."

"Blandford Street?" Mrs. Bentley's face wrinkled in confusion. *Oh! The O'Brien's.* She then remembered that she had sent Haines away, and now she could not go to Blandford Street to collect her niece. *How vexatious! Why did Mornay allow my niece to leave the house? And why, especially, apart from him, after raising such a dust about her needing his protection?* The more she thought on it, the less sense it made.

"Will you be waiting for the master's return, ma'am?" Frederick asked, interrupting her ruminations.

Mrs. Bentley was very tired. But Ariana was not here. No reason, then, why she might not just as well go back to her own house and get some rest. At least there she *could* rest.

In moments she was back on the street, faced with the tiring prospect of walking home. She, Mrs. Bentley, was going to walk! Too vexing to wait for a message to reach Haines to bring the carriage back. The horses would, no doubt, have just been unharnessed. With a sigh, she started down the street, wondering if she ought to call upon Mr. Pellham. *If I do I might have his company for the walk. But then why disturb the man when I will just return to bed upon reaching my house? I do not feel well and will not feel well until my niece is securely married.*

Ariana stared at her betrothed, no longer blinking back tears but angry now. She crossed her arms. "I was *astonished* by Mr. O'Brien's behaviour! You cannot think—that I welcomed it?"

"How does a man get that close to a woman if she does not welcome his attentions? How came you to be on that settee, Ariana, when Mr. O'Brien was indisposed?"

She told him exactly what had happened, but only silence ensued. Even though they were sitting together, she felt they had never been so far apart. How could he think she had encouraged the man to impose on her? But the longer she sat there, the less she felt she had any right to be angry. She herself had given sway to jealousy for much less cause.

She took his hand again and turned to face him completely on the seat. This got his attention, and he looked at her. She reached for his other hand. Then holding them up, she kissed them. First one, then the other. Slowly and with love and sorrow in her eyes, watching him as she did. She saw feelings flit across the handsome face and dark eyes, but he kept himself in check. Still holding his hands, she inched closer to him and then raised one of his arms so she could put it around her shoulders. She quickly scooted into the spot against his side. She leaned up and whispered. "I love you!"

Then he turned and pulled her up against him, and they shared a good embrace. She clung to him, holding him as hard about the head and neck as she could. And then they were kissing, and it was wonderfully different than what she had felt in Mr. O'Brien's arms.

"I ought to take you to Scotland right now!" he said, keeping her right up against him. "I feel I dare not let you out of my sight for an instant, lest you run into some form of mischief."

She smiled weakly. "I shan't. I'll be ever so careful."

"One more episode with you, young woman, and I shall—I avow it—I shall take you directly to Scotland, and we'll be married before you can blink an eye!"

"I think I should like that."

This earned her an additional kiss.

"I have property there, you know."

"In Scotland?"

"Yes. My grandfather acquired it by fighting in some royal cause."

"Amazing! Where do you *not* own property?"

He smiled. "Park Lane."

She laughed. "But you own the approval of all its inhabitants."

He grinned, but then his face sobered, and he moved his arm and touched her below the neck in the area of her heart.

"Here. Here is where I most wish to own property."

"Foolish man." She leaned up and kissed him again. "It is there where you own all of it."

They pulled up to his house, Mrs. Bentley having disappeared around the corner only minutes earlier.

Traffic was cluttered, as it often was on Upper Brook Street. Mrs. Bentley kept a sharp eye out for a break in traffic and an opportunity to cross the road, as she would have to sooner or later to reach her own house. Suddenly she heard a voice calling her. A distinctly French voice. She looked ahead and saw that Madame LaCroix had stepped out on her doorway and was waving at her with a handkerchief.

Madame LaCroix had been looking out of her first floor bow window when she saw Mrs. Bentley coming down the street. Her brows knitted together. Madame LaCroix had once been a great beauty, and, even now in her golden years, was not unbecoming. She was a tall Frenchwoman living in Mayfair because her fortune had survived the Revolution—though her husband had not. There was a companion in the room with her.

"Mon Dieu!" Madame LaCroix said beneath her breath. "Clarisse," she called out, while motioning to her companion with one hand. Clarisse came and stood beside her at the window.

"Is that Madame Bentley?" she asked in French.

"*Oui*, madame. It is she."

"*Biensûr!* How odd that she is alone and on foot. She seems to be in a hurry."

"*Oui*, madame."

"I must speak to her. I must know what is happening!" In a trice Madame LaCroix hurried to her front door, opened it, and stood, waving an expensive silk handkerchief.

"Madame Bentley! Helloooo, Madame!"

Mrs. Bentley came to a halt. "Oh, dear! Not Madame LaCroix. However will I explain my walking on the street alone?" As she approached the house, the Frenchwoman went so far as to step out onto the pavement to meet her.

How provoking! Everyone knew Madame LaCroix loved to gossip, and Mrs. Bentley had no wish to supply her with fodder. But wait. Perhaps Madame LaCroix knew something. Could it be that she might know something of Ariana and Mr. Mornay? Mrs. Bentley should have realized the great unlikelihood of this, but she was too tired to think better of it.

Madame lived in a three-storey Georgian structure like most of the houses on Brook Street, except that it sported the addition of a jutting bow window on the first floor.

"My dear Madame LaCroix!" she said, as she came up to her.

"My dear Madame Bentley!" She used her handkerchief to motion Mrs. Bentley into her home, saying, "Come in. Do come in!"

"Alas, madame, I have no time for a visit today."

"But, madame! You must rest. Allow me to offer you some tea. You are tired, yes? And hungry? I have just the perfect thing for you, madame." In the next minute Mrs. Bentley found herself sitting in the lady's opulent French-style parlour, in a well-stuffed chair, and already with a tray of French crème mints before her.

"I long to speak with you," said madame, which was really no surprise to Mrs. Bentley for the woman always longed to speak with someone—anyone—who might share an *on-dit*, a secret, perhaps, or the latest news item. But on this occasion, Mrs. Bentley was hoping that madame would be the one to enlighten her.

In addition to the mints, madame rang for a tray of delicate French pastries that made even Mrs. Bentley's jaded tongue water. Madame was treating her with proper respect, at least. Not that *this* was any surprise. Mrs. Bentley's importance in society had certainly risen to a crest since her niece had won the hand of the Paragon.

As her hostess chattered about this and that, Mrs. Bentley began to relax. Indeed this little break was precisely the thing, now that she thought on it, that she needed in her vexed and worried state. The tea was excellent—madame had the same suppliers that she did. And somehow she ended up, between bites of very fine pastry and sips of that tea, sharing her latest errand and her recent experience. Imagine it, an abduction attempt on her niece!

Then, before her very eyes, Miss Herley successfully nabbed! Mrs. Bentley herself had swooned, and she could not, in all her memory, remember having ever swooned before.

"Oh, but of course, *mon amie*!" sighed madame, displaying the very essence of understanding and concern. She was, in fact, an excellent, rapt listener. Why had Mrs. Bentley never realized it sooner? Madame could never be a gossip—she was a friend, a well-meaning, empathetic friend. She found herself revealing that, at Miss Forsythe's terrible disappearance, "Mr. Mornay was nearly beside himself!"

"Yes, beside himself! Of course! And what did he do?"

"What *could* he do?" she asked, as if there had never been a whit of doubt regarding it. "He insisted upon packing her off to Grosvenor Square, under guard, of course, to ensure her safety!" It sounded, as she told it, so very reasonable. So very like the thing any man would have done for the woman he was soon to marry.

But the next thing Mrs. Bentley knew, the lady was exclaiming that she didn't doubt they had eloped. This was the reason Mrs. Bentley found the house empty of its occupants just now. This was the solution Mr. Mornay must have seen was the only remedy to answer such a threat—of losing his bride!

"Oh, not at all," Mrs. Bentley said suddenly and sharply. No matter that she had suspected the very same thing herself.

The Frenchwoman turned her head sideways and looked pityingly at Mrs. Bentley. "Oh, I think so, madame! Mr. Mornay, he does not take chances. He is a man who gets his desires!"

"And so he shall after the wedding, of course!" Mrs. Bentley did not like the direction the conversation had suddenly turned. "Mornay would never elope. The wedding is settled, and Miss Forsythe's family will be in Mayfair any day now for the event. There is no question of an elopement!"

But Madame was not to be deterred. "But when Mr. Mornay sees what scandal he started, how can he not elope? And you say they are gone? And you do not know to where? I think they elope!"

"You are severely mistaken, I assure you!" Mrs. Bentley stood up to leave.

"Do not take offense, madame," said the foreigner. "I think elopement is...ah...the romantic thing. Very romantic. And who could not forgive a man who fears that his bride might be snatched from him at any moment."

Mrs. Bentley blinked scathingly at the lady. "Your experiences in the revolution have affected your brain, madame! I assure you, there has been no elopement!"

"But you say that Miss Forsythe spent the night at Grosvenor Square, yes?"

"Well, yes, but—" Suddenly Mrs. Bentley saw this admission in the light of day for what it was—scandalous! Madame LaCroix was exactly right! What did two house maids count for as chaperones? Miss Herley, who should have served as chaperone and would have shut the mouths of gossips such as madame, had never arrived. Instead she'd been abducted!

"Madame—I must go!" The ladies walked to the front door. Mrs. Bentley was suddenly in a great hurry, and Madame La Croix accompanied her, wearing a little, curious smile.

Mrs. Bentley had barely received her things from the butler as she was rushed out the front door. Behind her she heard, "*Bon jour*, madame! I thank you for stopping!"

Thank her for stopping, indeed! She halted and turned to give her hostess a knowing stare. "Before you rush out with your tale, madame," she said, in a warning tone, "recall that it is the Paragon you may slander! And when you have been proved wrong, you will appear foolish, indeed! Not to mention you may get a public set-down!" These words did seem to have an effect on the lady, as her little smile vanished at the thought.

Dusk was approaching. She resumed her hurried pace toward home as fast as her aging feet could carry her. *Elopement, indeed!*

She was still blustering to herself when she arrived at her dwelling, angrier than ever at herself for stopping at madame's. *Make no mistake*, she thought grimly, *I will find out exactly what is underfoot with Mornay and my niece, and if I am not perfectly satisfied, I will* want *them to elope! Perhaps I should have encouraged madame to believe that's what happened after all. It would mean they are married, that no impropriety has occurred. Why, I will take the couple to Scotland myself, if need be! Better an elopement than a scandal!*

How exceedingly annoying that Madame LaCroix had to spot her on the street on this day of all days. *How foolishly I went, like a lamb to the slaughter, into her French dwelling. It is a lesson I will not soon forget.*

Twenty-three

"I would rather return to my aunt's house," Ariana told her betrothed for the second time.

"You will on no account allow servants to intimidate you. I am with you now, and there is nothing for you to dread. On the contrary, if I have to give the boot to the whole lot of 'em to keep you comfortable and happy, I will do so."

"Really? You would do that for me?"

Mr. Mornay hesitated. "Except for Fotch."

"Really?"

"And Freddie, of course."

"Freddie! Hmmph!"

Mornay looked around for any sign of ruffians, and then he hurried her to the door of his house. Dusk was approaching and a lamplighter was working his way down the street, leaving small dots of fuzzy light behind him.

"Does Freddie vex you?" Mornay asked. "I had the impression he was fond of you."

"Until this morning, I was rather fond of him," she replied.

His eyes narrowed. "Come. We'll get to the bottom of this right now."

"I realize we must do this, but I am frantic to hear word of Miss Herley!"

Inside the hall Mr. Mornay eyed Freddie with a little extra attention. What on earth could have caused him to mistreat Ariana? Frederick knew immediately that his master knew all, and his mouth was set in a little, apologetic frown that he could not help. He felt a little guilty, if truth be told, but what could be expected of a man who was about to find himself on the street?

"Come to the study shortly, Freddie."

"Yes, sir." Now he'd get it! And then he'd give it! Why hadn't Mr. Mornay given notice to his staff? On what pretext was Miss Forsythe to base their dismissal? What provisions would the master supply for them between situations? Yes, he too had questions.

Madame LaCroix spent some time considering whether or not to spread word of a possible elopement of Mornay and his young bride-to-be. Despite anything Mrs. Bentley said in her objections, she kept returning to the fact that Miss Forsythe had been taken to Grosvenor Square before the wedding. It was simply too improper to the English to expect that the couple had any other respectable alternative! That was her case.

She called her manservant, Bouffant. "Prepare the carriage. I have places to go." She went to her toilette and, with her lady's maid, prepared herself. Even at her age, Madame was still a willowy figure and could wear an evening gown to good effect. Moreover, she believed that a lady on a mission did not go forth in shabby attire. Besides, her affluence tended to lend credence to her gossip, though being French was a detraction because their countries were at war.

She started off in early evening, therefore, dressed in rich silk, satin, and lace. Her companion, Clarisse, was at her side.

Mr. Mornay was eager to question his servants, beginning with the butler, but first he had to know if there was news of Miss Herley during his absence.

"Any messages?" he asked, as Freddie received his hat, coat, and gloves, and then Miss Forsythe's articles. Ariana was still anxious to hear the servant's answer with trepidation. Had Miss Herley been recovered?

"Mrs. Bentley called while you were out."

They both looked on with interest.

"Did she say what her errand was?" Ariana was unable to contain her curiosity and had to ask. Servants could be so slow to impart news.

"She asked for you, ma'am. She said that it is believed Miss Herley is safe—"

"Oh, thank God!" Ariana touched Phillip's arm, and he quickly put his hand upon hers.

"That's excellent!" he murmured. "Is Miss Herley returned to her home then?"

"She didn't say, sir."

"Was there anything else?"

"That a Lord Antoine has been taken into custody—temporarily to Newgate."

"Lord Antoine!" Ariana gasped. "My goodness! You were so right to warn the Herleys against him! And to think that Lavinia hoped to marry him, when all along he was indeed an *errant knave*!"

Mr. Mornay nodded. "I'm glad to learn of it. I was beginning to think I had spoiled a love match."

"Evidently not!" she said, still blinking at the thought of what a scoundrel the man was to have abducted Lavinia, who admired him so.

"Mrs. Bentley also wishes to inform you, sir, that she wants her niece 'returned to Hanover Square, directly.'" He paused and added, "She was most decided upon that point."

"You see?" Ariana said. "I must go home."

"You've slept here already. It no longer signifies if you do so again. Your aunt is welcome to join you, but I am determined to keep you here. I am certain you are safer here, and that's all there is to it."

When they were alone except for a single servant who stood against a wall awaiting a small supper in the second parlour (because the dining room was in disarray and the morning room was not comfortable enough for their tired bodies), Ariana became suddenly aware that she had Mr. Mornay to herself. She turned to him and snuggled into his arms.

"I am so relieved that Lavinia is safe!"

"Of course you are," he said. At first he reveled in the embrace as much as she did—or perhaps more—and then he gently extricated himself, just as a maid came in, added wood to the fire, and left again.

Ariana pressed herself into his chest, saying, "And now I am safe, and I am with you!" She snuggled her head against him and was very happy, but he pulled her away from him. After stroking her hair once and then the side of her face, he turned and quickly went to a wing chair, where he sat down tiredly.

She looked after him, studying him. He felt her gaze and said, "After we get some food in us, I think it will be high time for both of us to get some sleep." He rubbed his eyes wearily, and for the first time it occurred to Ariana that he might not have slept well for near two days.

"Did you get any sleep this morning after we arrived?"

He met her eyes. "A few hours. 'Tis of no consequence. I'll make up for it tonight, I'm certain."

"You've been up since yesterday morning! You spent all of last night searching for me and rescuing me. And now you've been out all day on my account!"

"Not entirely. I went out to try and find your friend."

"And then you had to fetch me from the O'Briens, and now the whole day has passed, and you have had no opportunity to rest at all!"

He gave a little smile. "Am I getting a set-down for my trouble?"

Her eyes melted. "Not at all. I am sorry for it, that's all." She started toward him, but there was a sound at the door, and then Freddie was there.

"I have a note by special messenger—from the Regent, sir."

~

When Madame LaCroix set out from her house with her companion, she chose to stop first at a nearby soiree and speak to a few choice characters of a *rumour* she had heard, and then she left the house. Afterward she stopped at a ball she would have happily ignored but needed to drop a few words—it was only a *suspicion* she had heard, and of course, she had no proof—into the right ears. She used her box at Covent Garden—madame was popular—to tell everyone who dropped in of the outrageous report (which just could *not* be true, she was certain!) she had heard at the soîree and then at the ball. By the time she was back in her own house near eleven o'clock—an early night, but an effective one—she knew her *on-dit* was secure. Ah, now she could sleep well.

~

The news of the Paragon eloping with Miss Forsythe was such a delicacy that the *bon ton* wished to share it with their neighbors. Such a stir of excitement in ballrooms across the West End! So many disapproving sounds of the tongue from ladies of upright character! Such a flurry of moving carriages, more activity than usual, so that the roads were crowded all evening instead of only during the usual busy hours. Messengers delivered hastily written notes to friends and acquaintances, and, as was inevitable with such a thing, word reached Carlton House. The Regent was regaled with the news by his mistress, who had just heard it from a most trusted source.

Mrs. Bentley, of course, had opted to remain home this night, still recovering from the undue excitement and nervous strain she had endured. A flurry of messages did arrive at her residence, but Haines was putting them on her desk for another time, as ordered. The mistress needed to sleep and had even taken that dose of laudanum to that effect. She wanted no interruptions unless it was Ariana herself come home.

Freddie entered the parlour and handed the note from the Regent to his master, who opened it and asked, "Is the man waiting for a reply?"

"He waits for you to accompany him to Carlton House, sir."

"What, now?" came the startled reply.

"Indeed, sir." The servant's tone said that he agreed the summons was a nuisance.

Mornay read the contents quickly, while Ariana waited frowning.

"Thank you, Freddie. Tell the man I'll come shortly."

After he'd gone, Ariana asked, "You will go with him then? To Carlton House?"

"Prinny seems to require my presence, though I can't imagine what for."

She shook her head. "Can you not send a note in return? You are not fit to go, sir."

This made him raise his head. He thought for a moment. "I'll have to go, I'm afraid." But he was frowning. "I don't like to leave you alone again."

"I am not disturbed by that," she replied. "But I suppose I should return to my aunt, as she wished."

"That's out of the question," he interjected sharply.

She said shyly, "Phillip, I am still without a proper chaperone. Lavinia could not come. This won't do at all. Think of the talk."

At that moment the servants arrived with their meal. First they put down a white linen cloth and then their place settings. All the food arrived in covers, and glasses were filled. Ariana just watched her beloved, waiting to speak privately once more. When they'd gone, she sat across from him, but the table wasn't meant for eating at, and the height was a bit awkward.

"Do as I do," he said, and he actually sat down on the carpet. She had to giggle, but she came and sat beside him rather than across from him.

"Shall I say the blessing?"

Their eyes met, and his were intrigued. "Is that your habit?"

"Of course!"

"Then do so, please. In the future I will." She was so pleased, she could have kissed him, but remembered how he had pushed her away from him earlier. She had been thoughtless then. She needed to help him maintain propriety—even if she was staying in his house against all reason.

Ariana purposely made their first shared mealtime prayer short, and then they ate together. The food was excellent, but she could scarcely give heed to it, though she did eat. He was tired, she knew, and so she contented herself just to eat with him and get to look at him as much as she liked until he had to leave to see the prince. They were comfortable together even though they said nearly nothing throughout the meal, and even that brought her contentment.

The candelabra on the table threw comfortable shadows around the room, and she had a sudden strong wish that they were married, already. For a moment she thought she understood exactly how he must feel at times. Just then he said, "Are you aware that you've been staring at me since we sat down together?"

She smiled. "Yes. And I'm quite enjoying the view, thank you."

His face froze for a moment.

"Have I shocked you?" she asked.

"You little minx!" he finally said. "Are you trying to drive me mad? Didn't your mother ever tell you not to say such things?"

"No, I'm afraid not."

He sat up and leaned over and kissed her cheek. They were close to one another, and their eyes met. He leaned his head down again but heard a sound at the door and pulled abruptly away.

"Sir, the prince's man says the horses are restless."

"Yes, I'm coming. Thank you, Freddie. Send Fotch to me directly."

"He is waiting for you, sir, in your dressing room."

"Very good." Once again they just looked at each other. Finally he said, "I will have your maids sent to your room, and I want two men at your door. I hope I don't have to say that you are not to leave the house."

"No, you do not." She was still looking at him with that little smile.

"I'm afraid I must tell you to stop looking at me like that, or—or I will forget myself entirely."

~

The prince's liveried messenger was waiting, holding the reins of two horses. Mr. Mornay came out in fresh attire, and only someone well acquainted with him could have told that he was going on so little sleep for two days. With astonishment, he realized he was expected to ride to the prince's house—at night! And on a strange horse. What on earth was Prinny thinking? Was he short on carriages?

He took a minute to pet the horse, speaking gently until it nudged its head against his arm. Thank goodness, it was good-natured. He petted it some more, then nodded to the groom, who held the reins to steady the animal until he had mounted. He wasn't wearing riding boots, but he didn't care. He had no time to. He had other things—like the beautiful girl he was leaving just now—to think of.

With a gentle kick to the horse's side, he started off, following the servant. On an impulse he glanced up at the house and found her watching from a window. He felt an unfamiliar tug at his heart, which increased as she waved gently. He nodded at her and then headed toward the corner of the square, where he lost sight of the house.

~

Mr. Mornay looks exceedingly handsome on the saddle, she thought.

~

Mornay was quickly ushered into an inner room of the prince's private apartments. His Royal Highness was seated at a table and beckoned for Phillip to join him. He motioned for his glass to be filled from a decanter, which a beautifully liveried footman did. Mr. Mornay knew it would be excellent quality wine.

He sat down after bowing to the Regent, who was giving him a wry look.

"Dash it, Mornay! You kept me waiting so long that I was beginning to credit that deuced report they're saying about you!"

He took a sip from his glass and replied, "What report is that?"

The prince seemed surprised. "That you've gone and eloped, of course. I knew it couldn't be true, but I had to check, nevertheless."

"You needn't have dragged me out. You could have asked me through a note, you know."

"Seeing is believing, old chap, and I had to know for certain."

"And what's the business with the horse? I'd have much preferred my carriage."

"Well, that was on your account. I've heard the streets are crawling with traffic because everyone's bursting to share the news of a certain man's elopement." This brought a familiar scowl, and the prince looked knowingly at his friend. "I've seen you looking better. What the devil are you up to? Something, I've no doubt, that started the rumour."

Mr. Mornay sighed. "Someone has been trying to abduct Miss Forsythe—wants to pluck her right from under my nose. There have already been two attempts on her, and I insisted on having her beneath my roof—with chaperones present to ensure her safety."

The Regent's face revealed his shock. He set his glass down and wiped his face hurriedly with his napkin. "Well, I can't blame you, old man, but beneath your roof? I begin to understand why there's talk!" He had to laugh. "Sorry, Mornay, but to think of *you* being in such a position!"

"Miss Forsythe has two servants with her from Hanover Square, and we sent for her friend, a Miss Herley, to come as a companion, but *she* was abducted en route. I am convinced she was mistaken for Miss Forsythe because Mrs. Bentley was with her."

The Regent could be a very feeling man at times, and this occasion found him so. "Dashed coves! A Miss Herley, you say? Any news of her since?"

"I got word that she is returned safely. I suppose they discovered their mistake."

"And your Miss Forsythe? Is she safe? Where do you have her?"

"She is still beneath my roof. My Aunt Royleforst would have come already, but her doctor advises against her leaving her bed just now. Apparently she has been ailing, though I've yet to learn the details."

The prince wiped his mouth again delicately with the linen napkin and gave his friend a thoughtful look. "Perhaps we should find a different house to keep her in. A safer place, where they won't be looking for her."

"Such as?"

He shrugged. "Above all, the place and people must be respectable. I could have Lady Hertford take her in."

"You said 'respectable.'"

"Don't start with me, Phillip!"

"Any other ideas?" Mornay knew Ariana would be miserable if asked to stay with the Regent's mistress.

"I'll think on it and send a note when I've hit upon it. That's all you need, you know, the presence of a good matronly dame, and that'll shut every 'bone box' in London."

"In the meantime, sir, I think I must return to the house speedily. I trust no one at this point but myself to keep her from harm's way."

"Well, of course." His Royal Highness still looked thoughtful. "One other thing, Phillip. I've been told I should create you a baronet. What think you of that?"

Mr. Mornay was taken by surprise. "I cannot think why."

The Regent laughed. "Because you're so devilishly fashionable that you ought to be a title. It will make your lady a real lady, and then when people say 'Lady Mornay,' it will be accurate and not send the other real ladies up into the boughs!"

When Mr. Mornay was still silent, he added, "I'm sure I could find you a place in the household fitting your station, so you'll perform proper 'service to the crown' and so forth. I'll give you a turn at being the gentleman of the wardrobe—that ought to suit you, eh?"

"A dignified valet?" Mr. Mornay seemed amused.

"Well, dash it, yes! To your future king! I'd like you to do it, Phillip. I'm taking a great deal of slack lately with regard to my costume, and I'd like to end all that. I'm confident that you are the man to transform me in the eyes of the dashed press!"

Mr. Mornay folded his arms. "I am about to be married, sir."

"Precisely! It will be my gift to you. Miss Forsythe should be pleased, I daresay."

"Let me think upon it."

"Of course."

"Can you offer me any help with regard to protecting her until we wed?"

This was a daring request. The Regent had no obligation to do any such thing, but he was, after all, a personal friend. "What do you need?"

"Two of your guard. Well trained with arms."

He was silent for a moment while he thought. "Done. You go on home to your Miss Forsythe. I'll send them along."

"Excellent! Prinny, you're quite the thing...at times."

The Regent was gratified. He smiled and shook his hand. "Glad to help, my friend. And I will appreciate your accepting the baronetcy. Let me know, *Sir Phillip*, will you?"

Mornay exhaled a little laugh. *Sir Phillip! No doubt the prince means it as an honour, but never for a second have I wanted a title or any of its traditional responsibilities either. Gentleman of the wardrobe, indeed!*

The *Morning Chronicle* wasn't nearly as considerate as Mrs. Bentley's butler, who had kept the rumour out of sight on her desk. The newspaper, in contrast, printed the elopement on the front page. The small print acknowledged the news as yet an unsubstantiated "fact," a typical oxymoronic statement by the paper. There were, it said, "the most excellent" sources for the veracity of the statement. It was printed again in the "Announcements" column, directly above the "Auctions" listings.

Mr. Pellham never missed his paper, and with a heavy sigh, he took it in hand when he set out that morning to call at Hanover Square. Mrs. Bentley, he thought, was going to be in rare form.

Twenty-four

Lavinia Herley finally prevailed upon her parents to allow her to call upon Miss Forsythe. Her services as a proper companion might be needed for one thing. And she did not want to miss the opportunity of staying at Mr. Mornay's beautiful house and being with her dear friend for the last four days before she was wed. It would be exceedingly diverting.

Her father had to let fall a heavy blow, however. He held up his copy of the *Chronicle* and let his daughter read the headline for herself. "The Birds Have Flown!" Beneath it was a caricature of Mornay and his pretty wife, both styled as costumed birds. The male bird was replete with top hat and coattails, and the female with a bonnet and gown. The two were flying off with an arrow pointing ahead to a banner reading "Scotland." The bird representing Mr. Mornay was saying, "I'll keep you safe, my love!" While the she-bird responded, "Heaven help us! This is shocking!"

Lavinia was speechless. Having herself suffered an abduction, she could understand what had driven the couple to such an extreme measure, but she was unaccountably disappointed at it. She was quick to note the line, "unsubstantiated fact," but in her heart, she felt it must surely be true. Mr. Mornay would not suffer his love to fall into the paths of evil again. She was sure of it. And she was glad that her friend was safely married to the man she loved! Pity it had to happen in such a way, but Ariana was finally Mrs. Mornay now. She thought of herself and Lord Antoine. If only they could find a way to persuade her parents to allow the match. She would settle for an elopement in a second if it made her Lady Antoine!

While she was thinking thus, Mr. Chesley called, wearing a look of great unrest.

"Miss Herley," he said, while they were still in the front hall. "Antoine is in Newgate!"

"What! On what account?"

"They've pinned your abduction on him!"

"But that's ridiculous!"

"I know it and you know it, but devilish little good that will do him. They took him at Mrs. Bentley's house."

"Oh, no! I sent him there to tell her I was safe!"

"Well, he's under the hatches now. They'll send 'im across the herring pond if we don't do something—if they spare him the gibbet, of course!"

"Transport—or the gibbet? Oh, my soul!" Miss Herley covered her mouth with one hand. "And Ariana and Mr. Mornay gone! What am I to do? If I tell my parents, they'll only believe him more guilty and deserving of what he gets!" She turned her earnest eyes to her friend. "We *must* help him!"

Mrs. Bentley had finally achieved a good night's sleep, but she awoke knowing she was not at her best. She had endured having her niece abducted from the best neighborhood that existed in London. She had endured the further horrifying experience of having Miss Herley abducted from her own carriage. She had swooned—for the first time in her life—and little liked the experience. She had been through the ups and downs of the romance between her niece and the Paragon! And now she was tired. She was tired of planning, scheming, hoping, wanting, and striving. In fact she was just plain tired.

But today she had one last important task to accomplish, and she wanted it done speedily. She was going to correct the insanity of the situation with her niece. It was absurd, utterly, that it had been allowed to go on as long as it had. She would put her foot down with Mr. Mornay and insist upon Ariana joining her at Hanover Square, or—or she'd get the magistrate! The law would certainly be on her side. It wasn't proper or right that he should be given leave to keep a lady of quality in his house unchaperoned!

Now that one ruffian was in custody, she was certain that brother of his, Wingate, would keep a low profile. Which meant it was no doubt safe for her niece to return to the house. There were a mere four days until the wedding. Her brother and his family would be arriving at any time. They would expect to find their child with Mrs. Bentley, and rightly so.

Imagine if they were to find that she was residing in her future home prior to the ceremony! There would never be another niece for her to sponsor—not that Mrs. Bentley was sure she would ever wish to sponsor another niece after this higgledy-piggledy season with Ariana! How scatter-brained she had been to allow Mornay to take her relation from the house. Then she thought of her recent stop at Mornay's house when the couple was out. Well, they would be home this morning.

She rang for Harrietta. "Quickly, Harrietta! I cannot rest a moment longer until I see my niece!"

Mr. Pellham was just turning the corner onto Hanover Square when he saw a carriage that looked much like Mrs. Bentley's leaving it. He had his cane and his newspaper, and he stopped in consternation. If Mrs. Bentley was going out, his mission was in vain.

Yet he was not certain it had been her carriage—they all looked frightfully alike—and he could always wait at her house for her to return. He continued walking.

Miss Herley was taking a drive with Mr. Chesley. This is what she told her parents. She did not mention that the light curricle was borrowed—without permission—or that their destination was Mrs. Bentley's house on Hanover Square. Drastic times demanded drastic measures, she told herself. When Antoine was safe, she would tell her parents everything.

As soon as they pulled to the curb at Ariana's aunt's house, Lavinia could not contain her impatience. "I'll go ahead, sir. Come inside when the groom appears." She scrambled down, in a rather unladylike manner, eager to enlist the aid of Mrs. Bentley. Once that lady understood that her Antoine had not been involved in her abduction—not in the least—she was certain Mrs. Bentley had the wherewithal to obtain his release.

Haines recognized the young lady, or he would never have parted with the information that his mistress had just left for Grosvenor Square.

"Grosvenor Square! Whatever for?"

He believed she was going there to see Miss Forsythe.

But hadn't she eloped with Mr. Mornay?

Eloped? Haines looked utterly shocked. Lavinia turned on her heel and hurried back to the carriage.

~o~

There was a great hub of people and carriages around Mr. Mornay's house when Mrs. Bentley's coach tried to approach it. In the end she had to leave her equipage and walk from the corner of Upper Brook Street to house number 25. It was only natural she should inquire what all the fuss was about.

"Mornay and Miss Forsythe have eloped, ma'am! Have you not seen the paper?" The young man offering this information immediately produced the *Chronicle* from beneath one arm and unfolded it as best he could, in front of Mrs. Bentley's face. She saw the headline, "The Birds have Flown!" and quickly scanned the caricature. Her mouth dropped in astonishment, and her eyes opened wide with horror. She was mightily thankful for her bonnet at that moment, as her reaction was therefore largely hidden from the bystanders, of whom there were many.

"If this is true," she said, trying to speak in a normal tone, though her heart was beating painfully in her chest and her legs had gone all weak, "what is the purpose of this crowd? If the couple has eloped, there is naught here of interest!"

The young man smiled. "There are more bets on this at White's and Boodle's than any man of my acquaintance can recall seeing on an issue before. I am here to protect my wager, ma'am. I will know the truth, you see, if I must remain here all day and the next! I've a thousand pounds on it!"

"Upon which side is your money, sir?" Her face had taken on a look of wary disdain. The young man did not notice that the hands gripping the newspaper had tightened ominously.

He smiled, as if speaking to a child. "Surely you do not doubt the *Chronicle*? If they have slandered Mornay, there'll be no end of it! No, I am convinced the report must be true." Mrs. Bentley quickly folded the paper again and moved as though she would thrust it sharply back into the hand of its owner. Instead, giving in to a sudden strong righteous indignation, as though this young man was to blame for all, she stared into his uncomprehending eyes for one moment. Then she lashed that paper down upon his head, his hat, and his shoulders, at which he began backing away. Looking at her as though she were the devil incarnate, he turned and took off as fast as the crowd would allow. Mrs. Bentley watched him go and stood there catching her breath a moment.

She realized that people were staring at her. Her action had caused the crowd to grow oddly silent about her, and now all the faces were looking curiously at her.

"Spurious lies!" she pronounced to the whole crowd. She threw the paper to the ground and continued on. Her legs were feeling weaker yet. Was she in danger of another faint? What on earth was happening to her robust constitution? She walked on, blindly moving among the milling crowd, making her way woodenly toward the house. Had she really thought that an elopement might solve something? Faced with the possibility, it no longer held the least appearance of rational judgment! Was she going mad? She was no longer certain whether to condemn the action or to give it her approbation! What was the world coming to, when a body could not tell whether something was good or bad? Was this not *precisely* what she feared, what she *knew* must happen?

Madame had launched the *on-dit* onto society, had she? If only Mr. Mornay had listened to her to begin with, none of this would have happened. Well, she, Mrs. Bentley, was not going to set things right. Leave it to Mornay to clear his own name! He was the one who insisted upon making the arrangements—keeping his future wife in his house! Little wonder there was such a fuss! She continued on toward the house and was given way by those who knew and recognized her. Of course many wished to speak to her. ("To get her beneath their heels long enough to savour the sensation of crushing her in the dust," she would later say to Mr. Pellham.) But Mrs. Bentley would have none of it. Soon she was knocking decidedly upon the door of the house. In a second she was faced by uniformed soldiers—the prince's colours!

"I am Miss Forsythe's guardian and chaperone," she exclaimed, "not to mention, her relation. Now take me inside at once." They looked at each other but hesitated.

"You know as well as I do," she said, in a shrewd undertone, "that my niece and Mr. Mornay are at home in this establishment! Take me in, I say!"

One of the men nodded at the other. Mrs. Bentley was brought inside. She sighed inwardly, greatly relieved. So they hadn't eloped! And then she grew worried because they hadn't. Oh, it was all too provoking!

Lavinia and Mr. Chesley had no hope of getting into the square at the rate they were going. It seemed that Mrs. Bentley's carriage had made it just before that crucial time when a crush turns into a complete hubble-bubble, when no one can make headway in any direction.

"You'd think Napoleon was captured!" Chesley exclaimed.

Lavinia's face was creased with worry. "Do you think Mrs. Bentley was able to get through?"

"She may have been. But it might be best to wait in her parlour for her return than to try and squeeze through this."

"No, I couldn't stand it," she cried. And with that, Lavinia once again scrambled down from the equipage without help, straightened her gown, and with one hand on her bonnet, rushed into the milling people on the street toward the square. No one must stop her from getting help for Antoine. Had he not rescued her? It was her chance now to do the same for him!

At the house, the soldiers were still guarding entry.

"I am Miss Lavinia Herley! Mr. Mornay sent for me, and I was abducted yesterday when I tried to get here!"

"No, I have no note, but I was to be Miss Forsythe's chaperone!"

"But I know Mrs. Bentley! She wanted me for her niece's companion! You must tell her I am here!"

"Please, I beg you!"

Tears ran down her face. Lavinia was utterly cast down. *Oh, dear Lord, Ariana prays to you and is helped. Please, help me, now!* But still the stern faces of the soldiers blocked her from the house. She turned to go. But wait! The door of the house opened, and one of the soldiers scooted over for a word with someone behind it. Next he turned to look at her and wonder of wonders! He motioned for Miss Herley to come, and the next thing she knew she was inside and sharing an embrace with Ariana.

It couldn't have been a result of my prayer, could it? Lavinia thought.

"Lavinia! Thank God you are safe!"

"And you, my dearest! You *didn't* elope!"

"Of course not!"

"But Ariana—oh, it is so terrible!"

"*What* is?" Her friend's eyes were large in her face. Mrs. Bentley was suddenly there, looking on with interest. She wanted to express her satisfaction that Lavinia had been safely delivered but paused to hear this.

"Antoine has been taken! They've got him at Newgate!"

Ariana gave a worried look to her aunt. "Oh, my dearest!" was all she could say.

And then Lavinia saw Mrs. Bentley. She rushed toward her.

"Mrs. Bentley! You know he had no hand in what happened! It was all Lord Wingate! You were there!"

Mrs. Bentley's face went blank. "I daresay I do not know who took you, my gel. I never saw the man before."

"Ma'am! It was his brother, Lord Wingate. He crossed his own brother to rescue me! Mr. Chesley saw me in Wingate's power, he told Lord Antoine of it, and they came together and got me out! They freed me from the man, don't you see? Lord Antoine put his own welfare and safety behind my own! Wingate is bound to seek his harm, as soon as he learns his brother caused my escape." Lavinia's eyes were tearing up, and she shook her head sadly. "Mrs. Bentley! You are my last hope! You must say you will aid me in getting his release! They'll transport him! Or hang him! Please, I beg you, tell me you will help me!"

Mrs. Bentley had put one hand to her heart. She was amazed to discover that Miss Herley was in love and that it was with a man she had no doubt whatsoever was a criminal. What could she say?

"I will help you." It was the voice of Mr. Mornay.

Twenty-five

"I do not know what to say, sir!" Lavinia blinked up at Mr. Mornay gratefully.

"You can start by telling me this. Is it not true that while Antoine had no hand in your abduction, he helped to plan the attempts on Miss Forsythe earlier? That her incident at Merilton House and her abduction from the viscount's house were on his account as well as his brother's?"

"Only the first attempt. He had no hand in taking Ariana from the viscount's. I have spoken to him at length regarding all of it! He fully repents of his wrongdoing and was sorry for it from the start!"

To Mr. Mornay's look of doubt, she added, "His brother is the *real* villain! All Julian cares about is money—for gaming and drink. Antoine tried to dissuade him from taking Ariana, but he was adamant. Antoine feels certain, sir, that there is something in your past history with his brother that is fueling his resolve—"

"I am aware of my history with the man," he said, making Ariana look at him with curiosity. Was there something between the men she did not know about?

"Nothing fuels his resolve so much as spleen and depravity," he continued.

"I am sure you are right," Miss Herley agreed sadly. "But I warrant you that Lord Antoine intends on nothing in the future but to live lawfully. I am certain he wished to—" and here her voice broke again, "to get a special license so that we could marry. I am hopeful that his helping me has made my parents view him with more favour." She looked at him pleadingly.

Mr. Mornay walked up to Miss Herley so that he could see clearly into her eyes. "Tell me, Miss Herley, are *you* convinced of his worthiness? Do you have any doubts regarding his intentions whatsoever?"

He studied her face and eyes keenly. And for a few moments, the question hung in the air while everyone waited for her response.

"I trust him, sir. I'd trust him with my life!"

Mrs. Bentley came forward. "Miss Herley, forgive me," she said, "but I must speak." To Mr. Mornay she said, "The constable told me both brothers had a long list of offenses against the Crown. What do you make of that?"

Miss Herley watched Mr. Mornay, fearful of what he would make of it, indeed.

"Is that news to you, Miss Herley?" he asked.

She hung her head a little. "No. I know everything, I daresay, there is to know about Antoine's past activities." Here she raised her head again, and her eyes were glowing with conviction. "That is all in the past, sir! Unless we are on the street starving, I am convinced there is nothing that could induce his lordship to act in such a manner again!" To Mrs. Bentley she added, "He rescued me, I tell you! He'd have done the same for Ariana!"

Ariana walked up to the girl and gently took her arm. "Come, Lavinia, here we are, standing in the hall all this time." She met the eyes of her beloved, looking at him with her own silent plea. She hoped he would help Lavinia, as he had said.

He said, "Go to the morning room," a bit automatically, as he had not yet eaten.

En route and despite her distress, Lavinia could not help noting that the house appeared to be in quite a shambles. "What has happened here?" she asked Ariana, who did not wish to supply the information that her own hand had caused the mess. In the room while they all sat at table, it was evident that Miss Herley was unable to relax.

"Sir," Lavinia said, with a flattened voice, "I am sorry to ask you, but I must know. Will you help us? Do you intend to give us your aid?" The tension in the room was palpable.

Mr. Mornay put down his coffee and looked at her squarely. "Of course. I said I would, did I not?"

"You may not be able to free the man, Mornay. Not even you," said Mrs. Bentley.

Ariana frowned at her aunt. To say that in front of Miss Herley—now of all times!

Lavinia nearly dropped her plate. "Do you think so?" she asked very earnestly. "That Antoine's innocence and help in this matter shan't be enough to gain his freedom?"

Mrs. Bentley shrugged and met her eyes. "I do not know."

Mr. Mornay didn't betray the least concern but asked, "Did his lordship say what started their hare-brained scheme against me?"

"He said, for his part, it began on account of your interference between us." She looked at Ariana and couldn't help but to smile. "That made him realize his love for me! When he was crossed in the matter!" She looked back to Mr. Mornay. "But later, after sobering up, he came to view the scheme differently and wished to drop the plan, but Lord Wingate refused!"

Mr. Mornay fell into a pensive gaze. He finished eating and stood. "You're certain he's at Newgate?"

Miss Herley looked to Mrs. Bentley who offered, "That was where the constable said they would take him."

"Was it not unfair," Lavinia added, "that when he called to bring the news of my safety, at my bidding, that he was snatched into custody?"

"His lordship was discovering the consequences of his past choices," put in Mrs. Bentley. "But if he rescued you, then he has my gratitude. I felt sick with the thought that harm had come to you on my account, Miss Herley."

"On your account?" Lavinia asked Mrs. Bentley.

"Because I was too foolish to come here with Ariana in the first place! It would have settled all! You would have not suffered your abduction, and there would be no rumours of an elopement," she said, looking in the direction of the street, where traffic still moved more slowly than usual as everyone stopped to gape at the house of the famous eloper. "And none of these upsetting events would have taken place."

"Nevertheless, Wingate's plans would still be in place," Mornay said. "And regarding the rumour—if the marquess hears it, perhaps he may withdraw his claws, at least for the time being. Long enough for me to get to him before he tries again to get to us." He went round the table and gave Ariana a kiss on the hand. "I'll return as soon as I can," he said, looking into her eyes. Turning to Ariana's friend, he said, "In the meantime, remain here as Miss Forsythe's companion, if you would." To Mrs. Bentley he said, "Would you prefer to be in your own house now that Miss Herley is here? I can take you home if you like."

"I would prefer to take Ariana with me to my house, sir. Her family will be arriving any time, and they will find it most irregular that she is here! No, she must come with me, or I believe I'm staying here as well."

"Then you are my guest," he said settling the matter. "I'll smooth over any concerns the Forsythes have regarding this arrangement."

Mrs. Bentley was frowning. So much for putting her foot down with the man. "Do give word to your house guards that they must allow Mr. Pellham entrance, if he comes."

"The prince's men," he said, "are coming with me, but I'll tell Freddie."

"Obliged."

"Be careful, darling!" Ariana cried, alarmed that he felt it incumbent on him to take the soldiers.

He stopped once more and bent down to kiss her cheek. "I will. Stay in the house. Do not cross me in this."

"I have no wish to cross you in anything, sir."

Miss Herley smiled into her teacup, and Mrs. Bentley sighed.

At Newgate it wasn't difficult for Mr. Mornay to get an audience with the prisoner. To his repulsion, he found that Holliwell hadn't enough money to get into the state area but was in the commons. Further, the area for felons was past the women's section and then the debtor's section. By the time he finally came upon the man, he'd had more than his fill of odours and sorry-looking prisoners.

Mr. Mornay had paid the warden so that he could sit in a quiet spot with the prisoner, and after they'd been shown the way down a narrow corridor and brought to a small, empty cell, Lord Antoine looked interestedly at his visitor. Mr. Horton, Mornay's steward had remained at the entrance of the place, ready to make another financial transaction if necessary.

Mr. Mornay met Holliwell's eyes but said nothing. He was determined to ascertain the man's character by his own words and actions rather than relying chiefly on Miss Herley's opinion. She may have been sincere, but women were known to be sincerely wrong about men, weren't they?

"What is your business with me?" Holliwell asked.

"I might ask you the same," came the smooth reply.

The prisoner turned his head. "I have no business with you, sir, that I know of." His face was bland.

"I believe you do, sir. You and your brother have twice attempted to abduct my future wife. That gives us business."

Antoine made a small grimace but was silent for a few long seconds. Then he said, "So you're seeking a confession? To ensure that they hang me? Surely you realize I shan't say a word to further incriminate myself. At least I've a chance at transportation then!"

"That is not my errand."

This got the man's attention. "Then what?"

"You'll need to be frank with me. I need to understand the situation entirely. Is it true that the scheme against Miss Forsythe was for revenge? For my interfering with your hopes of Miss Herley?"

The young man gave him a resentful stare. "If I answer, that's as good as a confession! You'll have me hung by the neck before I can say 'Jack Robinson'!"

"I thought we settled that. I am not here to see you hung."

They stared at each other.

"*Was* the cause of your revenge my interference in your hopes?"

"Yes, dash it! But I was in my cups! I thought better of it afterward."

"Did you? And when did that happen? Miss Forsythe was twice approached and once taken. That doesn't support your thinking better of it."

"I realized it was sheer folly shortly after the night of our first attempt. I've broken with my brother over the thing. He is acting entirely on his own. When he sent that pigeon Whiddington, I had nothing to do with it."

"You knew about it though."

There was a pause. "I knew something of it, yes."

"You could have warned me."

"You have not been my friend, sir!" This, with great feeling.

"Neither have I been your enemy."

Another few seconds of silence passed. Antoine said, "It seems you understand the whole business. So what do you hope to accomplish here? What do you want with me?"

"Explain to me your disappointment when you lost the prospect of marriage to Miss Herley."

"Eh? Why I was disappointed? *That* is what you came here to discover?"

"It is part of what I hope to learn, yes. Miss Herley's family is not wealthy. She has little to offer you. Tell me why her loss prompted such a drastic revenge."

"I can't see how it signifies, sir, but I will tell you." He swallowed hard, thinking carefully. He had been taking restless steps in no particular direction throughout the conversation. "My brother undoubtedly has his own reasons for wanting to cross you, and I do not know what they are. For my part, yes, I wanted revenge. I wanted very much to marry Miss Herley." He swallowed again, and his gaze drifted toward the walls. He then shook his head with discomfort and finally forced his eyes to meet the other man's. "I love her, you see. It is that simple."

"And your intentions were honourable?"

"Yes!" His face changed. "Not at first, I grant. But when I came to realize my feelings for her—I was astonished, you know—I had only honourable intentions. Unfortunately I could not accompany them with an honourable name! I know why you did what you did to discourage our union, and I cannot fault you for it. If I had been in your place, I would have done the same. I am responsible for my own troubles. I know it only too well."

There was silence. Mr. Mornay eyed the young man keenly. "Do you still wish to marry Miss Herley?"

The prisoner gave a bitter laugh. "Yes, if she'll move to Newgate! No, sir, I fear that avenue has been closed to me for good. I saved her from my brother, and that is my only consolation as I sit here. I did something right for once in my life—and now I pay for it, by God!"

"You are not here to pay for doing something right. You are here for all the wrongs you've done in the past."

Antoine merely looked at him, fuming inwardly.

Mr. Mornay took a breath, looked out the barred window, and then turned back to the young man. "I can get you out of here, you know."

His look changed. He was disarmed but wary. "You would do that? For what in return?"

"For your help in assuring that your brother will cease being a threat to my bride. Further, I can convince the Herleys to allow your suit with their daughter. But for that you must promise to live a decent life, henceforward."

"I *want* to do that, sir! I would like nothing better! I give you my word!" The young man's response had been so strong and earnest and heartfelt that Mornay almost smiled. But there was more to settle.

"You cannot game away your allowance."

"I have no allowance. I don't see how we'll manage, if you must know."

"I will arrange one for you."

Lord Antoine was speechless with surprise—and wonder.

"I will allot a stipend to your wife. If you squander it by gaming or being often in your cups, it will cease. You will be ruined. Do you understand?"

"I do! I don't know what to say. Your generosity and goodness to me... to us...I cannot fathom it!"

"One more thing," Mornay added. "I'll expect you to be at my service, if I ever require it."

"I can live with that," he responded.

"And one thing more," added the Paragon, having just thought of it.

"Yes?"

"You must faithfully attend church in whatever parish you reside."

At first Antoine was silent. He smiled a little. "Really?"

"Yes."

"Do you attend yourself, may I ask?"

"I do."

The man looked surprised but nodded. "Very well. You have my word."

Mr. Mornay hesitated, as yet another requirement came to mind. Would the lad stand for one thing more? He had to try. "I have thought of one more thing."

Now Holliwell looked wary, but he recognized the humour of it and said, "You'll have to put them in writing for me to remember them all at this rate."

"I most certainly will. All the arrangements will be in a legal document for referral at any time."

"What is it?" He almost held his breath. It must be some great thing, he felt, for he noted how Mornay was hesitating, choosing his words.

"When the matter is settled with your brother, meaning he is no longer a threat to me, I want you to agree to pray with me. For your salvation."

Lord Antoine just gaped at him for a moment. "Did you say '*pray*' with you, sir?"

"I did."

"Pray— as in 'Our Father, who art in heaven'? That kind of prayer?"

"Something like that."

Lord Holliwell was very tempted to laugh but did not want to insult his deliverer. He turned to him with a grin and said, "I think I can manage that."

"Good." Mr. Mornay held out his hand and then smiled that rare, handsome smile that most people found irresistible. Lord Antoine was no exception, and he smiled back, vastly relieved, and shook Mr. Mornay's hand effusively.

"I don't know how to thank you!"

"I'll give you an opportunity, my boy. You must help me locate your brother and settle whatever matter he holds against me."

"Are you not aware of it, sir? What he has against you?"

Mornay sighed. "I believe it must be the fact that I was present on an occasion when he lost a fortune, some thirty thousand pounds."

"I remember that!"

"Do you? Do you also remember that your sibling tried to kill the man who'd won against him rather than surrender his losses?"

Antoine shook his head. "No, sir. He said nothing of that to me. What stopped him?" And as soon as he asked, he knew. The look on Mornay's face confirmed it. "I see."

"I could hardly allow him to kill a man to avoid a debt of honour."

"Of course not."

"Your brother has blamed me for the loss of his circumstances since then, though I wasn't a part of the game, and God knows I never encourage a man to play so deeply in his pocket."

"Julian knows no restraint when it comes to gaming, sir. That wouldn't have been the first time he lost a large sum, nor was it the last. I fail to see why he has set upon you for revenge."

"Very likely it was nothing more than opportunity. Your grudge against me coincided with his own, and it was a scheme he thought you would share in." Mr. Mornay looked at Lord Antoine gravely. "But he doesn't give it up without you. He keeps to his purpose, eh?"

The young man nodded. "It appears so. He even took Miss Herley, the blackguard!"

"The thing is we have to halt his activities. Do I have your word that you will help me find him? I will push to see him transported, of course. I doubt there will be any settling with him."

As they walked back, joined by the man who had escorted them down the dank corridor and provided the light, Antoine warned, "Beware, Mr. Mornay. If Julian thinks you'll pay him off, he'll accept the arrangement. Only you can't trust him in future. If he games it away or even spends it, he'll want more."

"I have no intention of settling financially in that way with him."

"'E stops 'ere, guvnor."

The voice of the jail keeper startled Mr. Mornay. They stopped and shook hands again. "I'll see to your release at once."

Mr. Mornay turned to go, but Antoine had a troubled expression and said, "Sir?"

Mr. Mornay turned to face him.

"I am very grateful for your help, believe me, but I must know. What made you trust me? What made you willing to settle with me so generously, when you won't do so for my brother?"

Mornay thought for a moment. "I'm not certain," he replied, to his own amusement. "Perhaps it was Miss Herley. She spoke so eloquently of your innocence."

Twenty minutes later, after which a bank note had changed hands and papers were signed, the young prisoner was fetched and presented to Mr. Mornay.

Lord Antoine was a free man.

Twenty-six

In the second parlour where Ariana and Miss Herley were engrossed in rapturous conversation about men and marriage and other such taboo subjects, Ariana's head popped up in sudden alarm. She looked to the large double doors of the room saying, "My aunt is coming. I'm afraid our topic of conversation will have to change, Lavinia."

"Alas, yes." And then she gasped and covered her mouth with her hands.

"What is it?" Ariana asked.

"I forgot! I never told my family I was coming here! I was afraid they'd prohibit it."

"We'll send a messenger," Ariana replied.

"I have no money for such."

"I'll have Freddie do it. He keeps a purse for such things. All butlers do. Doesn't your man?"

Before she could answer, Mrs. Bentley had opened a door and was already speaking. "My dear! Haines has just sent to inform me that your family has arrived! They are waiting for us at my house. We cannot demand they all come here. Let us go at once and, if Mr. Mornay wishes you to spend the night beneath his roof, then so be it. But for now, we must go! The carriage is at the curb, my gels. Quickly now, and be smart about it!"

Ariana came to her feet agitated. "My word! I haven't seen my family for near three months! But I dare not go! What would Mr. Mornay say?"

"He is an understanding man," opined Miss Herley, "on occasion. Not to mention that he adores you." She smiled. "I think you are perfectly safe in this. How could you refuse to see your own family?"

"Lavinia, only recall his words to me. He forbade me to leave the house!

I dare not, I tell you." She looked at her aunt. "You must bring my family here, Aunt."

"My dear! With the work going on? That won't answer. Recall that we are in the second parlour because the workmen have taken over the other. And the dining room is equally unfit for guests. We shall see them at Hanover Square."

Ariana seemed to be considering the matter. She brought her hands together in thought, strode to the window, and stood, looking down at the street below. She saw that Mrs. Bentley's coach was indeed at the curb. The thought of her family being in Mayfair was such a happy one!

But Mr. Mornay is soon to be my husband. I can not shirk his wishes, not after such a disaster as resulted when I called upon Mr. O'Brien. He had said, "Is this what I am to expect when we are married?" And today his words were loud and clear: "Stay in the house. Do not cross me in this." I will stay.

She turned to her relation, who was watching her impatiently. "I cannot accompany you." Ariana's voice was low but firm.

Mrs. Bentley waved her hand at her. "So be it! Do as you wish. But when Mr. Mornay returns, you must come to my house at once. He can convey you there himself. And you too, of course, Miss Herley."

Lavinia nodded her thanks.

"Goodbye, my gels," said her aunt, and she closed the door and was gone.

Ariana turned and said, "Let us tell Freddie to send a man to your parents before they begin to think you've run into more mischief."

"Thank you, dearest!"

When that was done, Lavinia looked at her friend. "Shall we go to the parlour? I recall that we had started a delicious conversation." The girls shared an impish smile.

"Yes, let us!"

Mr. Mornay's coach had been making the rounds of the East End, from St. Pancras to Cripplegate, stopping at every flash house, tavern, and other places of ill repute where Holliwell thought they might find his brother. They had begun the search in the shabby, rundown room the brothers were calling home at the moment and had continued to find him absent from every other haunt he usually favored. They questioned demireps and Corinthians, sharpers and high kicks, tavern owners and chambermaids, but the man was nowhere to be found. It wasn't a matter of being blocked by friends who were protecting him because Holliwell knew the same friends. His brother was known as a "here or thereian," and no one knew his current location.

"I don't understand it," Holliwell lamented, returning to the coach after checking the house of Wingate's favorite doxie. "He should have turned up by now. Word is he's got new wheels, so perhaps he's gone somewhere."

"How does he manage to keep a coach?" Mornay wondered. It was expensive to do so.

"Well, he wins 'em every so often from the occasional greenhorn. Then he sells 'em or rents 'em, if he can get by on it."

"So he takes advantage of inexperienced young men who get in over their heads and lives off his winnings."

"That's about the size of it. Along with an odd job here or there with other fellows."

"By 'job' I take it you don't mean 'work.'"

"Good heavens, no! Can you see Julian working? Though I think he went body-snatching once. That reeks of 'work' to me. Not to mention being devilish disgusting!"

Mornay shook his head. Why had he asked? Dash, he was getting restless. "Leave messages that you're looking for him," he said, "and we'll come again later. Perhaps tonight we'll fall upon him when he's had a chance to get deep in his cups."

His lordship nodded his head. "Oh, he'll know I've been looking for him, no fear there. He'll hear it everywhere he goes." He met Mornay's eyes. "He ought to be eager to find me actually. He knows by now I had a hand in getting Miss Herley from his grasp, and he'll feel wronged by that. Julian, as you well know, does not forget when he's been wronged."

Mrs. Bentley settled back into the carriage as they pulled away from Grosvenor Square. The streets were no longer clogged with traffic but much alive with commerce and pleasure vehicles as usual. Mrs. Bentley looked tiredly at the empty seat across from her, staring blankly and seeing nothing. Only a few more days must pass before her niece would be safely wed! Ah, the comfort she would take in that. Secretly she had been quite pleased by the early arrival of her brother and his family—she hadn't expected them for another day at the least. But she was, no use denying it, happiest in her own house, and despite all her bravado about staying with Ariana come what may, it was a notable relief to be heading back to her own bed.

She did not relish having to explain to her brother Ariana's absence. But she was certain, with Ariana's father in her house, Mornay could no longer insist upon keeping the gel at Grosvenor Square. She would keep her niece under lock and key, if necessary, until the ceremony! The strain of these past days was too provoking. Abductions and rescues and shootings on the streets! Mrs. Bentley had always thought her nerves to be of the strongest constitution, but she was nearing her limit of what was tolerable.

The coach pulled up to the curb, and Mrs. Bentley looked out at the familiar house with a sigh of relief. How pleasant to be back home. In a moment the steps were let down, and Mrs. Bentley left the carriage.

When she opened the door to her home, she started to call for Haines, but she was taken by surprise by two ruffians who pulled her roughly into the house. She couldn't believe her eyes. Before she could speak, a third man appeared. "Oh my word!" It was the man who had pointed a gun at her! The man who had abducted Miss Herley right from her carriage! Lord Wingate, wasn't it?

"Where is your niece?" he demanded approaching her, his face mean and angry.

"Where is my brother and his family?" She asked in return; greatly affronted. Miraculously she seemed to have lost her fear of the man. She was too provoked at finding that her own house had been infiltrated, too busy adding up her intolerable misfortunes at his hands or on his account, to feel the least fear of him.

"Why did you leave your niece behind?" he demanded again.

"What have you done with my servants?" she responded.

"Allow me," he said with derision, "to ask the questions. Your life is in peril if you do not answer them." He was surprised to find this lady staring him down so boldly. Was this not Mrs. Bentley, who had swooned at the sight of his pistol only two days earlier? "Why did you not bring Miss Forsythe with you?" He gave her a sneering look and held up his pistol, pointing it at her head.

Mrs. Bentley no longer believed his aim was to do away with her, however, and so she merely responded in kind, with a voice fraught with disdain. "Miss Forsythe has a mind of her own, sir," she responded. "She refused to come. And I must say, it is providential that she did."

Without answering Lord Wingate turned to his men. "Put her with the rest of them and on the double! We'll have to get Miss Forsythe before Mornay returns to his house."

Mrs. Bentley gasped. "You wouldn't dare!" And then she recalled that here they had dared to enter and command *her* house. They had somehow rendered her servants helpless for none were in sight. As one man led her off toward the kitchens, she looked back at Lord Wingate, hoping to sound ominous. "Mornay will have you hung if you harm that gel!"

About twenty-five minutes after Mrs. Bentley's carriage had driven off from Grosvenor Square, another carriage pulled to the curb in front of the house, and three men appeared from within it. They strode rapidly to the house, one man looking around warily as he did so. Freddie answered the door and a moment later backed away, his eyes bulging as the men forced their way in by lieu of a pistol in the butler's face.

"There's no need for alarm," said Lord Wingate, his long face curling into a chilling grin. "As long as you do exactly as you're told."

The man who had spoken and seemed to be in charge nodded at his companions, and they took off toward the stairs. Freddie's heart sank, remembering how low on men he was at the moment. One servant had gone off for Burton Crescent to deliver Miss Herley's message. Two were with the master. Oh, if only Mr. Mornay was home! And only two more on duty. Thankfully they were the men charged with keeping an eye on Miss Forsythe. He hoped they were on the alert! The man turned to him. "Sit here."

"Upon the floor?"

"Yes, upon the floor! I am pointing at the floor, am I not?" Without another word, Mr. Frederick sat himself down, sighing inwardly. He had his back against the wall and knees pulled up against him. He eyed the stranger resentfully. If only the master were home!

Meanwhile Lord Wingate was eyeing the expensive wallpaper and furnishings, and his thoughts turned to the practical matter of theft. Why settle merely for taking Miss Forsythe? There were numerous doors adjoining the rich hall with its marbled tiles, and he suddenly realized he might do well to avail himself of some treasures. The sound of his men on the next storey floated down from the direction of the staircase, however, and he pointed his pistol at the butler with renewed focus.

At that moment Mrs. Hamilton walked innocently out of a doorway, evidently coming from the kitchens. She stopped in alarm, her mouth opening slightly. Lord Wingate had not seen or heard her, and she slowly backed away, her eyes filled with a knowing alarm. The butler saw her but quickly removed his gaze so that he would not alert his captor to her presence. He prayed the woman would somehow quickly summon help. *Where was Mr. Fotch when he was needed?* He hoped Mrs. Hamilton had the presence of mind to run to a neighbor. There were footmen enough on the street to make up a small army, and he was certain the dwellers on the Square would willingly lend their men when they understood the threat. But would the housekeeper think of it?

Suddenly sounds came from the stairwell, and then the young women appeared, faces quite fallen, each held by one arm by a rogue with a weapon. When Wingate turned and saw them, his eyebrows rose and he smiled. "Well, well, this begins to make up for all, does it not? What do you call it? Two birds with one stone?" He gave a wicked laugh.

~

Mr. Mornay and the other men were leaving the East End to return to Grosvenor Square. He had to bring his steward back, for one thing. He would allow Antoine a short time to see his love—chaperoned, of course. And he would write a letter to the girl's parents, a recommendation of the marriage between their daughter and the young nobleman. Then after the pleasure of seeing his own future bride, the men would return to the East End to put Wingate in his place once and for all.

He was getting married in four days. He wanted to be done with this nonsense. Tonight would be an end to it even if it took him all night!

~

"Do not scream or raise your voices in any manner, or I will use this weapon."

Lavinia said, "Listen to him, dearest!" Wingate had locked the butler in the pantry and pocketed anything he could quickly grab. He also threw some things hastily at his other men, who shoved them obediently into the great pockets of their coats, which, like Whiddington's, were fashioned expressly to answer that purpose.

He motioned for the men to move the young ladies out of the house, and in a moment they were being hurried, rather brusquely and at gunpoint, into the worn black equipage. Ariana was tense, but she could sense that Lavinia was terrified, and she held her hand bracingly. Two of the ruffians jumped on back of the equipage, so that only Wingate entered after them. A small relief but nothing to ease their tension.

"So this is Lord Wingate," Ariana said, managing to keep her voice calm, although she remembered only too well that Mr. Whiddington had called him a "murderous blood." The contempt in her tone was barely disguised, however. She was surprised to find that the dark-haired, finely featured man might have been considered handsome but for a mean glint in his eyes and a gauntness of features that spoke of hard living.

He studied her in turn. "I'm happy to see that you are as attractive as I've heard, Miss Forsythe. Mornay will pay a pretty penny for his pretty lady, I've no doubt."

Mrs. Hamilton had run down to the kitchens in a flutter after seeing Mr. Frederick on the floor with a pistol pointed directly at his head. Upon telling Cook and the kitchen maids the situation, these ladies fell into such fits of fright that the housekeeper had been forced to quiet them before deciding what she ought to do.

It only took another minute or two to reach much the same thought as Mr. Frederick's—to approach the neighbors. She went out with just a shawl over her gown and headed next door to Derby House. She had to stop at the pavement, however, for upon coming up from the steps to the street, she saw that she was perfectly parallel to an unremarkable black coach, whose driver sat atop the board and would see her emerge.

When finally she saw him turn away and watch a passing wagon and its working class passengers, she darted from the service entrance and dashed to the next house, not daring to look back. Then she was forced to wait minutes to see Lord Derby. Her protestations that it was of the utmost urgency, that ruffians were in the house, and that ladies were in danger seemed to have little effect upon his servants or his lordship himself. By the time she emerged from the house with Lord Derby's footmen and his lordship, who brandished a pistol, it was just in time to see the back of the carriage leaving the square.

"What is your quarrel with Mr. Mornay? Why are you doing this?" Ariana asked.

He studied her for a moment, perhaps weighing whether to tell her or not. "That is not your concern."

"As you are abducting us, I think it is. What is it you want precisely? We know it isn't us."

Lavinia said, "Must you point your weapon at her? If the carriage bounces you may kill her! We are only two women, and surely you are not so frightened of us that you cannot put it aside!"

Ariana wanted to say, "Bravo, Lavinia!" but didn't dare. She squeezed her friend's hand instead.

Wingate smiled, but he rested the weapon atop his thigh.

"You look like a gentleman, sir," Ariana said. "What is it that makes you abduct women who have done you no harm?"

Lavinia remembered her earlier encounter with this man and how frightened she had been. She would never have had the presence of mind that Ariana was displaying! How *did* her friend possess such courage? It was a mystery.

When Mrs. Bentley had been duly delivered to the servants' hall, where the staff was sitting, bound and gagged, her indignation reached a crest. Even Mr. Pellham, poor man, was among the prisoners and looking none too comfortable. It was not to be borne! The mouths of each person, furthermore, were stuffed with her own expensive handkerchiefs and table napkins. It was distressing, indeed.

At the sight of Mrs. Bentley, the servants began a stream of indignation, making sounds from behind their gagged mouths as best they could. The man who had brought Mrs. Bentley looked around in surprise and then hastily tied the lady to a kitchen chair, though she rapped his arms and hands with her fan until it was no longer possible to do so. She berated him with her mouth all the while too, reminding him of his certain fate on a gibbet. Surprisingly he did not bother to gag her but turned and fled as soon as she seemed securely bound in place.

The men were in a hurry, and she knew why. Her servants were all looking deeply sorrowful. With their mistress a prisoner like themselves, their hopes of rescue seemed to sink. Mrs. Bentley knew she must free herself. Her binds did not seem as tightly done as the others, and she was determined to break free. She set about wriggling in her seat and straining at the cloths that had been twisted in a rope-like fashion to tie her to the piece of furniture.

"Do not fret," she said aloud. "We are not harmed, and I *will* manage to free myself!" As an afterthought she added, "If it is the last thing I do manage!"

Mr. Pellham nodded at her encouragingly, and he even winked.

This gave her renewed strength, and as she twisted and strained, she felt certain she was making headway and that the "chains" felt looser. Moreover, her determination gave others more hope so that soon the roomful of occupants began to work at their own cloth binds with the same zeal. It was only a matter of time until someone broke free.

It was just growing dark by the time the Paragon's coach pulled to the curb in front of the house. The door opened before he'd even stepped down from the carriage, and he could see Freddie's face looked drawn and unhappy from where he stood. He hoped there hadn't been more trouble between his future bride and his staff—if it wasn't painful for the people involved, including Ariana, he'd have laughed at it. He just couldn't figure out *why* trouble should have started between them. His staff was well-trained, and Ariana was agreeable to everyone. It made no sense.

Lord Antoine and his steward joined him as he started toward the house. It felt unbelievably superb to know that he was soon to greet his love. It meant so much to him, more than he knew it would, to have her under his roof. It was a feeling he wanted to grow very familiar with.

Freddie's face at close range revealed more than tension. He looked agonized.

"What is it, Freddie?" he asked.

"Miss Forsythe, sir—" He choked on what he had to say, and Mr. Mornay felt his blood run cold. "She's been abducted—again, sir!"

Twenty-seven

An awful energy, a pain of shock, ran through Mr. Mornay's whole being. His mind, heart, and limbs all rebelled at the words he'd just heard: *It's Miss Forsythe, sir. She's been abducted—again!* Every last bit of him wanted to yell *nooo!* Instead he took a deep breath to steady himself and forced his brain to remain calm. "What happened, Freddie?"

The butler had sent a man to Hanover Square already and had the whole story. Mornay's heart sank while he listened to it, but he also felt a determination and anger growing within him so that he flew into action. No wonder they had failed to find Wingate. While they'd been scouring his neighborhood in their search for him, he'd been plotting and planning in theirs! It was the perfect irony.

He turned to Lord Antoine, who had heard the explanation and whose mouth was set and hardened in as firm a line as Mornay's. He stifled an oath and instead vowed, "We'll find them. I promise you!"

"Good," Mornay said. He then turned back to the butler. "Open the armoury." They walked to the little inner room with no windows. "Take these men to the kitchen so they can eat. Quickly! Tell Cook to give them something for the drive."

"Yes, sir. Will you be eating, sir?"

"No." He had no appetite for anything except possibly murdering Wingate. He knew he wouldn't do that, of course, unless the man attacked him. But he would see him hung for this! Transportation no longer seemed severe enough for his crimes. He had struck too great a blow by taking his beloved yet again. It would not, must not, be borne.

In fifteen minutes Mr. Mornay was back in his coach with Antoine, his steward, who had elected to stay on in case he could help, and the two soldiers. He took them first to Hanover Square, where an assortment of local law officials were gathered, as he thought they would be.

Mrs. Bentley wanted to speak to him, of course, but he told Haines to send the men out, and soon he was back inside the coach again. Now the small group was larger with the addition of two stocky, strong-looking men. One was a night watchman, and one a policeman. Antoine sat atop the board with the coachman to direct him because he best knew the neighbourhood and his brother's likely whereabouts.

Mr. Mornay occupied himself by loading three separate pistols and placing them about his person. One went in a waistcoat pocket, one in his boot, and one in his coat pocket. Afterward he still felt a nagging concern that he was *not* prepared. Then it hit him—he hadn't prayed!

"Gentlemen," he said, looking around at the assorted men in his carriage. "Before we arrive and separate or anything can get out of hand, please join me in a word of prayer for the safety of the ladies, the capture of Lord Wingate, and no harm to our persons."

The faces around him showed surprise, but these were followed by grateful nods of agreement. "Mr. Mornay, sir, if you like," offered the watchman, "I've a proper Bible 'ere, sir."

He accepted it gratefully and with no small surprise. There truly were more devout people in the world than he had ever realized when he wasn't one of 'em!

"Thank you." He cleared his throat and bowed his head. "Almighty Father…"

Back at his house, Mrs. Hamilton was in her room, filling a traveling trunk with her effects. She knew her days were numbered in the establishment. The master knew, or would soon, that she was the source of unrest upon which the staff had reacted, that she had "leaked" the rumour that their situations were in peril, though she had no proof that it was so. Moreover, he was annoyed at her reporting on the missing items—why hadn't he been annoyed at Miss Forsythe as she'd hoped would happen? She had gone to such lengths to make sure it appeared as if that lady was to blame for the thefts. Why didn't he seem to care?

She wasn't going to leave just yet. She'd wait for her next wages and then take all her things, most especially all the things she had squirreled away in a secret place in Molly's room. There were more things than what had been reported. Mrs. Hamilton had actually been stocking up her "savings" since she joined the staff, for if she didn't look out for her future, who would? She had no assurance of a pension of any sort—it was not guaranteed in her contract. So it only made sense that she had been padding her effects since entering the household. Lots of servants did the same thing, she knew. Her own mother, unfortunately, had not. And she had ended up at Draper's.

Her plan now was to slowly collect everything she'd lifted from the house and make a run for it, if need be. With that thought in mind, she went down the hall to the scullery maid's room. As the least important member of the staff, Molly had the smallest room. It was at the very end of the hall and had an outside wall, which meant the room was harder to keep warm. But Mrs. Hamilton had found a loose brick near the rafters during a routine inspection of the servants' quarters, and when she pulled it out, there was quite a large recess behind it. Perfect for stashing her articles!

As of this day, a little silver candlestick was there. So too was a lady's pistol she'd taken from the armoury, a small pile of guineas, taken with great trouble and mostly one at a time so as not to be noticed, and an assortment of other small but valuable items: a silver spoon, two elegant ivory snuff boxes, a necklace that had been Mrs. Mornay's (the most daring of her thefts!), a teacup and saucer, a watch fob, and other small objects that she had pilfered in the nine months she had been employed in the house.

The prospect of having a future mistress had only hastened the otherwise painfully slow acquisition of valuables, which she intended to sell for her future upkeep.

When she reached the room, she found that Molly was there already, on her knees beside her bed. *My word, but the child prayed!*

"What are you doing here so early?" she asked.

Molly looked up, startled. "Me work's all done!"

"Go down to the kitchen and fetch me some tea leaves."

"Tea leaves! Mr. Frederick keeps the tea, mum. Under lock and key."

"I know that, you stupid girl! Now go and tell him I've run out and must borrow a little. I'll buy some back for the house when I've had my wages."

"Yes, mum," she said and scampered to her feet and curtseyed quickly. Then she hurried from the room to do as she was bade.

Mrs. Hamilton watched her go and then went and found the loose brick. She pulled it quietly from its place, reached her hand in, and pulled out the silver candlestick. She'd pawn this now, before she found herself on the street! She looked it over briefly, admiring its shine, and then tucked it into her apron and replaced the brick with her free hand.

Satisfied, she went back to her chamber. Molly soon appeared with the tea and then left.

The coach was bulleting onward toward the East End, but Mr. Mornay was determined to read something from the little leather Bible the watchman had loaned him. He flipped through the pages, turning to the Psalms. He'd discovered that its pages were oozing with comfort for times of distress—times like this.

He felt exceedingly on edge, almost unable to contain himself. His passion to find Ariana was powerful—frighteningly so. But there was another side to that coin, a side he didn't want to think about. How terrible his heartache would be if something were to happen to her! The thought of her danger was almost too terrible to tolerate. Why had he brought the soldiers with him today when he might have left them with Ariana? Why hadn't he realized that something could occur even his own house? Why? Why?

It all came down to that reprobate Wingate! What should he do with the man? He looked down and saw that he had opened to Psalm 149, and he began reading. He wasn't on his knees, but he read the words as though it was the prayer of his heart:

> For the Lord taketh pleasure in his people:
> he will beautify the meek with salvation.
> Let the saints be joyful in glory:
> let them sing aloud upon their beds.
> Let the high praises of God be in their mouth
> and a two-edged sword in their hand;
> To execute vengeance upon the heathen,
> and punishment upon the peoples;
> to bind their kings with chains,
> and their nobles with fetters of iron,
> to execute upon them the judgment written:
> this honour have all his saints.
> Praise ye the Lord.

He stopped and went over two of the lines that had jumped off the page at him. "To bind their kings with chains, their nobles with fetters of iron"! He felt an unbelievable relief. God Himself had a "judgment written" against Wingate! This gave him great expectation that their mission would indeed succeed. With excitement, which would have been completely out of character for him only weeks earlier, Mr. Mornay, the Paragon, read the excerpt to his companions. The nodding of their heads and the spark of hope that jumped into their eyes—just as it had Mornay's—filled the air of the carriage with an entirely different spirit than the gloomy outlook it had contained before.

It was, thought Mr. Mornay, *nothing short of a miracle.* His terrible fear had turned almost to joy. He was that certain of success—just from reading a book! *The Bible truly is the most amazing thing.*

Back in her room, Molly got into bed but recalled that she hadn't finished praying. She climbed back out and fell to her knees. But something was wrong. There was a scratchy dust beneath her knees. It hadn't been there before. It was brick dust. She looked around wonderingly, saw the bricks below the rafters, and began touching a few. Bless her, one was loose! She pulled on it tentatively, and suddenly it came out easily. She took her small candle and tried to peek in the hollow that was revealed but could not make out the items. She shrank from the idea of putting her hand in without knowing what awaited.

Her first instinct was to run to Mrs. Hamilton's room to get the lady, which she started to do. As she got near the woman's door, however, something slowed her steps.

It didn't seem right that there was brick dust on her floor after Mrs. Hamilton had sent her from the room. With a sudden look of realization, she stopped in her tracks and backed quietly away from the housekeeper's door. Was Mr. Frederick in his chamber? A light from beneath his doorway showed that he was. Looking back toward the housekeeper's room, she knocked lightly on the butler's door. To his "come in," she opened it and found him sitting before the fire with a newspaper open on his lap.

"Look," he said, referring to an item in the news. "The master's wedding announcement! It's here in the paper, directly following those lies about an elopement! The right hand doesn't know what the left hand is doing!"

"Oh, heavens!" she said, duly impressed, coming around to gape at the spot, though Molly couldn't read to save her life.

Mr. Frederick seemed very kind all of a sudden. "Can you read?" he asked gently.

"No, sir."

He looked at her appraisingly. "Well, no matter. What did you want, Molly?"

"Sir!" The little waif said, her eyes large and anxious. "Can you come to me room? I 'av to show you somthin'."

He looked at her very thoughtfully. "What sort of something?"

"Please, sir! I think Mrs. 'amilton 'as been in me room, sir!"

He shook his head. "Molly, I see nothing wrong in that. If Mrs. Hamilton has been to your room, she must have had a reason."

"Aye, sir! A secret 'un." Her eyes pleaded with him, and she took the further bold step of pulling his hand and moving toward the door. Mr. Frederick's heart softened, and he allowed her to persuade him.

Minutes later she had told him what had happened, which of course he remembered, as he was the one to unlock the tea cabinet. Annoying that was too. Mrs. Hamilton couldn't possibly purchase the fine quality of tea the Paragon used. It was bought from the highest channels of imports and used by the Regent too. But he could hardly leave her with none, so he'd unlocked the cabinet and spared a little.

Now in Molly's room, she showed him the brick. He held up his candle and stuck it toward the hollow, and his eyes widened. He pulled forth the necklace, then the pistol—which he recognized. He exhanged looks with Molly, whose wide eyes were opened fully in dismay. A few other items followed, all valuable. The pile of guineas in a cloth tied with a small string raised his eyebrows exceedingly. When he was certain there was nothing else, he wrapped everything that would fit into a handkerchief and put other things into his pockets. He leaned down in front of the little maid.

"Thank you, Molly. The master shall hear of this and of your part in it." He stood up then, with a little worried frown on his face. "The thing is, how do we catch Mrs. Hamilton? She may simply deny all knowledge of this. In fact," he looked down at Molly, "she may blame you."

"Oh, not *me*, sir! I would *never*, sir!"

"No, I don't believe you would," he said. "Don't you worry, Molly. We'll get to the bottom of this!" He paused. "To think that Mrs. Hamilton cast suspicion upon our future mistress for these items! God forgive me for ever listening to that woman!"

Mornay's carriage came to a stop, and Holliwell jumped down from atop the board. He went to its owner. "Sir, the easiest and best way to get information around here is to pay for it." This he said with a knowing look.

"Of course," Mornay murmured. He dug into his waistcoat pocket and pulled out some guineas and crowns and started handing them round. "Use what you must, gentlemen, and run to the street and fire a shot in the air if you find the ladies or the man we seek! Time is of the essence, for every minute the women are in his power puts them at risk and, needless to say, must be horrifying for them."

"Sir!" Again it was Holliwell. "If I find my brother first, may I reason with him to give up the ladies? If he puts up no fight, I will not turn him in."

"You gave me your word earlier, Holliwell, that you would help me put an end to this business. If your brother is not taken into custody, I will have no assurance that this will end tonight. I'm afraid that's out of the question."

"May I at least give him the assurance that he will be sent to America a free man if he cooperates with us and returns the ladies unharmed? If he's transported, it will be a life of labor. The man is a marquess, after all, Mr. Mornay."

He remembered the words, "to execute upon them the judgment written," and knew in his heart it was not going to happen. Wingate would put up a fight to the end and suffer the consequences, his judgment at the hands of English justice. Therefore it made no difference what he said to Holliwell. The young man would feel better if he thought his scheme might work. It was, after all, his brother whose life was at stake.

"Make it India, sir, and I will allow that." He looked at the law officers, one of whom was frowning severely.

"If I come upon him first, depend upon it, I'll haul him off to Newgate and recommend him for the hulks, sir! 'E's of the nobility, but his crime tonight is despicable!"

Mornay nodded. "Agreed." In a bracing tone, he gave the rally, "Let us get this thing done!" The men scattered, having agreed to take different houses, different shadowy corners of the area, and started scouring them for sight or sign of Wingate or his prisoners.

Ariana and Miss Herley had been separated shortly after their captors had forced them into a crowded room in a run-down building. The entrance was only accessed from a narrow, garbage-strewn alley. The "door" wasn't a real doorway, but seemed to have been fashioned from a hole in the wall. Neither lady wanted to enter it, but both were feeling the cold metal of a gun barrel stuck in their sides and had no choice.

Inside the place was busy with the lower-classes at play. They heard raucous laughter from the dimly lit corridors. Ariana tried not to worry how they could ever be found in such a place but kept her spirits up by praying that angels would follow their every move and lead Mr. Mornay to them somehow.

To the girls' horror, Miss Herley was marched off with the other ruffian. She looked back at Ariana sorrowfully, with tears streaming down her face. Wingate took Ariana up a flight of stairs and then another and then yet one more to the top storey of the house.

"I must say, you are very calm. I have seen ladies go into hysterics. How is it you do not fear me?" Wingate asked.

She felt a stab of fear at his words, in fact, but kept it, as best she could, from her tone. They entered a dark room. She could see nothing, but she replied, "I gather you are desperate and after money. That does not make me fear you." She paused, heard him shut and lock the door, and then while he lit a small candle, she said, "It makes me pity you, sir."

He was startled for a moment and then angry. He turned on her, still holding the candle, and she could see that awful glint in his eyes. He put the light down and came over to her, a nasty look on his face. He took her by both arms—at that moment Ariana was indeed afraid.

"How dare you pity me! I am not desperate! I am fulfilling a wish I have long had—that of revenging myself on Mr. Mornay." He stared at her for a moment, and she looked away. "Be you careful, Miss Forsythe, or I shall exact another form of revenge that would be treachery, indeed. He'd have to kill me for it, I dare say."

She gasped and began silently praying. He released her arms, which were beginning to hurt where he'd held them, and she quickly moved away from him.

A sharp knock on the door made his head turn swiftly. "Be silent or I'll make you sorry for it!" he hissed instantly. He went over to her and pulled her so that she was against the wall, out of sight from the doorway. He took his pistol from his waistcoat and cocked it as quietly as he could.

"Who is it?" he called.

"Your friend, sir. Harold Chesley."

Ariana's heart gave a leap! If Mr. Chesley saw her, surely he would help her!

"What the devil do you want?" His tone changed to irritability.

"To share a pint with you, m'lord! I believe I have reason to congratulate you!"

Wingate seemed to think about this a moment. Ariana, meanwhile, was desperately trying to decide if she should hazard a scream. It might be her only chance! But what if Wingate got angry enough to carry out his prior threat? She was frightened and didn't know what to do.

Suddenly he whispered in her ear. "If you make a sound, Miss Forsythe, I will take you and make you mine. Do you understand me?" When she made no reply, he shook her. "Do you understand me?"

"Yes."

He moved to the door. "What are you talking about?" His tone was guarded.

"Oh, come, sir! We share a certain...shall I say, disregard? For the same man. You have taken steps to express your poor opinion of him. I can only applaud that."

Wingate's features lightened. Ariana's heart seemed to stop. What had she just heard? My word! Mr. Chesley was a devil, after all! Wingate took a look back at her, then unlocked the door, and peeked out just a little.

"Did you bring that pint?"

"I thought you'd join me downstairs."

"Not tonight. And tell no one you've seen me, by the by. Upon your life."

Chesley was surprised but cried, "Done. Not a word! I will go and procure something to your taste...and then return to you."

"Very well. But remember not a word!"

Chesley took the steps with satisfaction. Soon he would know what's what.

He had seen Wingate in the dim light entering the house with a lady and couldn't help thinking of the recent episode when he'd had to save Lavinia from his grasp. He'd heard the man went into a rage at losing her. Though Miss Herley was not a love interest, she was one of the few ladies Mr. Chesley called a real friend. What if Wingate had taken her again? He had to know. Unfortunately for Miss Herley, Chesley had looked up only in time to see Wingate and just one lady. He didn't know that another lady had also been taken upstairs.

Thus he'd followed the man surreptitiously and then concocted the scheme to get him to open the door. He should have known Wingate wouldn't let him in empty-handed. Now he'd have to hurry and get back up there and find out who the woman was. Antoine was in prison. Dash it! But if it was Miss Herley, he was sure to find help at White's or Boodle's. He might even stumble upon the rare constable. Imagine it, he, Chesley, asking help of a constable! He hoped it wouldn't come to that.

Ariana began to recite the ninety-first Psalm in a low voice. Lord Wingate was sitting on the floor, leaning against the wall with his head back. The candle was near him. He said, "Take a seat," and nodded at the single shabby chair in the room. The only other piece of furniture she could see was a bed! She shuddered and took the chair.

With a sigh, he got up and approached her, and then, using a large handkerchief from the pocket of his waistcoat, tied her hands tightly behind her back, making her sit up until he'd finished.

This was disturbing, but she knew Mr. Mornay would do everything in his power to find her. She knew too that God was watching, that He would somehow keep her safe. This reminded her to keep on reciting the psalm, one of the portions of Scripture she had memorized successfully.

"He that dwelleth in the secret place of the most high shall abide under the shadow of the Almighty."

Wingate looked at her.

"I will say of the Lord, He is my refuge and my fortress; My God; in Him will I trust."

"What—what are you saying?"

"The ninety-first Psalm." Then looking away from him, she continued. "Surely he shall deliver thee from the snare of the fowler, and from the noisome pestilence. He shall cover thee with his feathers, and under His wings shalt thou trust."

"Cannot you keep quiet?"

She ignored him, focusing on the psalm, being careful to say it correctly. "His truth shall be thy shield and buckler. Thou shalt not be afraid for the terror by night, nor the arrow that flieth by day; nor the pestilence that walketh in darkness; nor the destruction that wasteth at noonday."

"Miss Forsythe! I can easily bind your mouth, so do not force me!"

"Why do you not go to collect your money? You shan't get a thing from Mr. Mornay by remaining here!"

"I'll go when I'm good and ready," he returned. He took up a new post by a window, keeping carefully from sight behind ragged drapery.

"A thousand shall fall at thy side, and ten thousand at thy right hand; but it shall not come nigh thee."

He jumped toward her in anger. "I've given you fair warning! It's yourself alone to blame." He hurriedly began to remove his neckcloth, moving closer to her.

"Lord Wingate!" she pronounced icily. "I am speaking only to myself and in a low voice. I suggest that if the words of Scripture are injurious to your hearing, it is because you are not right with God. You need a change in your religion, and rather than silencing me, you ought to give heed to the welfare of your soul!"

He stopped but continued to stare at her closely. She hoped that she might have given him good cause to consider his ways. But then he came closer still, unwinding the cloth about his neck, and then he stopped again, studying her features. "You are a prime article, aren't you? Let us hope Mornay fully values you." He went back to his perch at the window. Although he had to keep his head out of sight, he kept an eye on the street below. After a few minutes, while Ariana continued her psalm to herself, he suddenly came to attention.

"It's Antoine! Devil take it! How did he get out of Newgate?"

Ariana's heart took a leap. If Holliwell was free, it stood to reason that Mr. Mornay would be with him—or not far behind!

Wingate turned suspicious eyes to her. "He's looking for you, no doubt. He could never have escaped from prison on his own, so it means Mornay must have effected his release. In exchange for his help. Blast brotherly affection! Dash it! I'll kill him, if it comes to it!"

She said nothing but thought, *Kill his own brother! Let it not come to that, O Lord!*

Her thoughts must have been evident on her face because he saw her expression and added, "Antoine is here to do *me* in, I assure you!"

"His object is surely to secure Miss Herley from danger, my lord. You might consider abandoning the place while you can and leave us to be discovered."

"If it weren't for Antoine," he hissed through gritted teeth, "your discovery would have taken Mornay days or even weeks! No regular swell would have found me in this flea trap so quickly! Dash it! He's interfered with me once too often! And I might say the same for your betrothed!" He fell silent for a moment, while he furtively peeked out the window again. He saw the prince's men and let loose an awful string of oaths. "My brother has indeed ruined the business! And I'll hold him to account for it, dash it!" He turned to her with a new thought. "Does Mornay carry a decent amount of blunt on 'im?"

"I have no idea, sir! It was never a part of our conversation."

He came at her, and she looked away frightened, but he turned her head to face him and said, "Do not trifle with me, Miss Forsythe. I remind you that you are entirely within my power."

"Not so, sir." Her steadiness of voice and look of conviction startled him.

"Eh? How is that?"

"I am always within God's power. Whatever you do to me or think you can, I assure you, you will answer to Him for it."

He looked sufficiently daunted at the thought, but then a look of sheer impatience replaced his better sense. "No more of your fustian, if you please, Miss Forsythe. You know the man. Does he carry a good amount of money on him or not?"

"I would think he does, but I've never seen inside his pockets, sir!" He was thinking again, and she added, "If it is money you want in exchange for me, I warrant he will give you whatever you ask, if he can."

"If?" He studied her again, this time taking in her finely chiseled nose and mouth, the large pretty eyes, the shining hair.

"If I don't get money, he will not get you. In fact if he tries to cross me, I'll smuggle you to America with me."

She heard him out bravely and might have collapsed into tears at such a nasty threat, but somehow Ariana had an assurance that no such thing would happen. "A thousand shall fall at thy side, and ten thousand at thy right hand, but it shall not come nigh thee...he shall deliver thee from the snare of the fowler."

The Almighty was her refuge. Angels were her ministers. And God had given her Mr. Mornay, who was too strong and resourceful a person to ever allow this scurrilous man's evil plans to take place.

Wingate took his handkerchief and forced it into her mouth saying, "I am afraid I must ensure your silence. Not very gentlemanly of me, is it?" Her muffled protests only seemed to amuse him. He took her reticule, searched it, and found more handkerchiefs—he smiled at finding three, for Ariana still carried one of her own in addition to two of Mr. Mornay's—and proceeded to tie her to the piece of furniture. "Never seen inside his pockets, eh? But you carry his handkerchiefs. How sentimental. I am going to see what's what. Pray that your betrothed has properly valued you, or I will come for you and keep you."

He blew out the candle and left the room, leaving her completely in darkness. After a minute or two she could see a very faint light from the window, but the moon was evidently not full, for it was an unsatisfactory source of relief from the thick blackness that now surrounded her.

With his absence, worries assailed her. *What if Mr. Mornay fails to outwit Lord Wingate? Will Lord Wingate abuse me? Will he be able to steal me away, even out of the country?* At this thought, her eyes did fill with tears. *That would mean separation from Mr. Mornay!* Even as she thought it, however, she felt a check within her heart. *I need* not *dwell on such a possibility. It isn't going to happen. How can I be sure? How? How?*

Trust. The word floated to her mind.

It had bubbled up from an invisible place of blessed assurance. She returned her thoughts to Psalm ninety-one and began once again reciting it in her mind, since her mouth was bound. *He that dwelleth in the secret place of the most High shall abide under the shadow of the Almighty.* With a start, she realized that Wingate had intended on this horrid dark room as being his secret place for her, when in reality she was in *God's* "secret place," under His wings. Her heart lifted immeasurably.

"Keep your shadow over me, Lord!" she prayed. *"Thank you for your protection! Lead Mr. Mornay to find me and Lavinia! Keep her from panic too, I pray, dear Lord!"*

Amazing. She really felt a great relief. No it was more—it was joy, a wonderful heart-satisfying joy. *No one can take me from God. No one.*

Twenty-eight

Just as Lord Wingate left the window from where he had spotted his brother on the street below, Mornay exited a seedy building from across the road. He and Holliwell hailed each other.

"Anything?" Mornay asked.

"Nothing."

Mr. Mornay looked at the typical flash house before them. "Is this place a likelihood?"

"Likely as twenty others! We have to check."

"By all means. Let's begin."

As they had done on their previous attempts to find the errant noble, they entered the premises separately, as though they were strangers. As Antoine entered the building, he was noticed immediately by Mr. Chesley who was holding two bottles in his hands and about to climb the stairs. Seeing Holliwell, his face lit up.

"I say, Antoine! Excellent! Well done! You're free!"

The young noble went up to his friend saying, "Mr. Mornay arranged it."

Mr. Chesley's features dropped then turned to amazement. "Upon my soul! That's dashed peculiar! How do you account for it?"

"Another time, I'll tell you all," Holliwell said, eyeing the bottles in his friend's hands. "Where are you going with those?"

Chesley had not yet seen Mornay, who instinctively stood back in the shadows listening. Before Chesley could answer, the sound of footsteps on the stairs above were heard, and someone coughed. He looked up a bit fearfully, and Holliwell was instantly of the opinion that he was about to see his brother. Just at that moment, Chesley saw Mr. Mornay, however, and there was something in the man's face he did not like.

"You brought him with you? Antoine!"

Truth was Mr. Mornay was exceedingly incensed. He'd been in hunting mode all day, trying to find Wingate and so far failing. But he could smell his prey, as it were. He knew they had to be close, in a relative sense. Holliwell had narrowed their searching down to a couple of streets of buildings, and this was one of them. Mr. Mornay had seen enough of the rented rooms in these places to last him a lifetime—the skin trade was more active than he'd thought! But they had to keep checking. When rooms could be had for mere shillings, Wingate might have rented one from any number of houses, particularly the flash houses most popular as criminal hang-outs like this one.

When Mornay's eyes alighted on Chesley, his features were set in a formidable mode. Mr. Chesley, moreover, was not innocent. He had not abducted anyone, of course, but he had been in favour of Wingate's revenge on Mornay. He detested the Paragon. When their eyes met, all the guilt in Mr. Chesley's thoughts was full on his face. Mr. Mornay's eyes narrowed as though he was about to move in on his kill.

To Mr. Chesley there was only one thing to do. He pushed the two bottles into Holliwell's hands and took off as fast as he could go. He should have known that if you run from a hunting animal, particularly a lion, and more particularly a lion that has been deprived of its prey for a very long time, it will dart after you with every fiber of its being. This is precisely what Mornay did.

Chesley bounded into the crowded roomful of culls, coves, and demireps, running blindly in a dead fright. He cared nothing for what havoc he created or who he blundered into or over. Mornay never let the young man leave his sight. The way he had taken off only strengthened his resolve to catch him at all costs, and so, brandishing his pistol, he got an instantly clearer path before him than Chesley had. The chase took a roundabout direction, and then Chesley gained the hall and the front door. Huzzah!

He felt much more confident now that he had more room, but wouldn't you know it, he could hear the heavy footsteps of Mornay's black boots behind him. They passed people, most of whom instantly took up the cause of the one being chased without knowing a thing about it. They fought like cats and dogs among themselves but would unite against the law in a second. Obstacles were pushed in Mornay's path. Then the night watchman saw the action, and he joined Mornay, so that two men now chased the young man.

A woman of leering countenance and ill-bred appearance jumped in front of the watchman and foiled his progress completely—as he had to move her aside and then get her arms off of him. She cackled wickedly when he finally got away, but now he was decidedly behind.

Mornay passed them without breaking stride. He'd seen his prey, no more than a dark figure at this distance, veering into an alley off the street. When he reached the alley, it was quiet and dead dark. He checked his grip on his pistol, held it carefully, ready to shoot, and walked into...darkness.

Back at the flash house, Holliwell put the bottles down quietly on the steps. He was astonished that his friend Chesley had run from Mr. Mornay. His recent help in getting Lavinia to safety had left no doubt in Antoine's mind that the man was a friend to be valued. But what on earth was between him and Mornay that had made him run like a scared rabbit?

He had no time to think about it. The sound of footsteps above were getting closer, and he suspected them to be his brother's. Thing was they might have belonged to a hundred different men, a thousand nameless underlings of London, but something in Holliwell's senses made him suspect it could be Julian. He waited, one hand on his weapon.

When his brother appeared, he was really not surprised. He had a feeling of inevitability, that this moment had long been coming. Now it had arrived, and there was nothing to prevent it. He felt sad for Julian despite everything.

Wingate spoke first. "So, Antoine, turned on your brother, now, did you?"

"Is that your greeting? Are you not surprised to see me?"

"My surprise is that you are willing to do me in."

"You've got Miss Herley, Julian! Miss Forsythe! Dash it, you're determined to nip the heels of old Grim as if you can avoid his fingers forever! You'll find, sir, that the noose is not a respecter of persons!" Holliwell shook his head, his face filled with distaste. "Are you actually eager to end your life?"

"I am eager to supplement it for once with enough blunt to stop merely ekeing out a living!"

Holliwell tried to keep his temper in check. "There are men all over the East End at this very moment seeking you out! Soldiers from the Regent!"

Wingate had thought as much himself, from his glimpse of the colours at the window, but his face blanched, nevertheless. "From the Regent? My, but I am making waves, eh?" He paused. "It's Mornay's doing."

"It is! Just as my freedom is!" He looked gravely at his brother. "He's a reasonable man, Julian. He said I might bring you to your bearings and yet spare you the gibbet."

"Bring me to my bearings?" He had slowly come down the stairs so that the brothers finally faced each other on the same level ground. "What does that mean, Antoine? That I come out from my dark corner holding out my hands for cuffs?"

"Give us the women! It is that simple."

"And then I may go as free as a bird? Is that it?"

"Not exactly. You'll still have to leave the country. But you'll be free, Julian! You'll have a chance at a new life!"

"Not on *your* life, little brother! I haven't got a chance in a million—I'd be as poor as a pauper!"

"I'll help you!" He sounded desperate. His brother should have been the one to sound desperate, but instead he seemed too buffle-headed to understand his own peril.

Wingate grimaced in contempt. "You'll help me? That's ripe! With what?"

"I will have the means," he said with difficulty, emphasizing each word, "to offer you help."

Their eyes met.

"That's a clanker! You think me a fool?"

"I'm telling you the truth! Miss Herley will have a stipend." He could not, for anything, tell his brother that he would be living off of Mr. Mornay.

"Ha! Miss Herley? If there is a Miss Herley!"

Antoine's face froze. "Tell me you didn't mean that!"

Julian said nothing, only looked away. Antoine was suddenly beside himself, and he pulled his pistol from his waistcoat and pointed it at his brother.

"Take me to her. Now!"

"But where is she?" Wingate asked, feigning ignorance.

"Take me to her. I won't go after you. You can do as you please!"

"I want a sum of money from Mornay. If he can produce it, I'll turn over the ladies."

"The game's up, Julian! They are here or nearby. We shall find them, with your help or not."

"Are you familiar with all the secret rooms on this street then?"

Antoine's eyes narrowed. It was well-known among criminals that certain houses contained secret doors that led to anything from small cubicles to entire rooms, which were used to "fence" stolen goods until they were sold. Some of these rooms were so craftily hidden that only the mistress or master of the house knew of their existence. If his brother had used such rooms for the women, it could indeed take a long time to find them—if they could be found.

"If you put us to that, the lords will hang you."

"It's Hobson's choice, sir. That or nothing. If they prefer to hang me right now and let the morts starve to death, that is *their* choice." He looked away, as if thinking of it. "Or die of thirst, more like."

"You blackguard!" Lord Holliwell had put his pistol away, but he balled up his fist as though he might use it instead on his brother.

Julian ignored his threat. "Tell Mornay what I want, and I'll meet you back here in, say, two hours."

"You haven't said what you want!"

"I'll settle for twenty thousand pounds. Ten for each of 'em."

"Why not ask for the crown jewels? He is just as likely to be able to come up with them as twenty thousand pounds in two hours!"

"He'll manage." Wingate snickered and disappeared back up the stairs.

Mr. Mornay had slowed to a cautious walk before entering the dark alley. It was strewn with filth and waste, garbage and darting rodents. He cocked his pistol, kept it close, and then stopped moving to listen. He heard a sound ahead.

"Chesley, there's no way out of here except by me." This was a guess, of course, but he hoped it was true.

No answer.

"If I have to search you out, I'll come with my pistol ready to shoot."

Again there was no answer. The stench of the place was unbearable, and nothing other than the gravity of the present situation would have made Mr. Mornay endure it for another second.

"Mr. Chesley, I'll offer you one more chance. You're not wanted for murder, so what have you to fear? I need to talk to you, that's all."

A faint sound came from the end of the alley, and Mr. Mornay inched forward. He had to go slowly for the darkness was that thick. "Come, I know you're there. The longer you wait, the more of my time you waste!"At first he heard only the sounds of other voices; angry shouting from far away, raucous laughter closer by, then a woman's voice in St. Giles' Greek so thick it was unintelligible. He took another step forward but heard, "I'm coming! Don't shoot me!"

As he approached, Mornay waited. He could hear, more than see him, but he pocketed his pistol and prepared himself to face the man. And the moment Chesley was close enough, Mornay grabbed him and quickly felt to see if he had a weapon. Then, taking him by the collar, he pushed him forward and said, "Keep going!"

Once they cleared the alley, a dim street lamp offered sight of each other.

Chesley looked relieved. "Thought I was apt to swoon like a woman from that stink!" He took his handkerchief, wiped his face and mouth, and blew his nose heartily.

"Why the devil did you run from me?"

"You looked devilish angry! Couldn't think! Didn't know! I just ran!"

"What are you doing in this neighbourhood?"

"Oh, come! We can't all afford Boodle's for our supper, and there's plenty friendliness of the petticoat sort in these parts! You can understand that, surely!"

Mr. Mornay was staring into Chesley's eyes as he spoke, and he was not convinced.

"You saw her. You saw Miss Forsythe, didn't you?"

"What? No, I haven't seen her! She wouldn't be around here!"

"I don't believe you!" He pulled Chesley up by the lapels of his coat. The watchman joined them at that moment and stood back watching. Chesley saw him and choked out, "Help me, sir! Get this man's hands off of me! I ain't done nothing!"

He was ignored.

"Tell me, Mr. Chesley, where did you see her?" Mornay was beginning to speak through gritted teeth. Chesley tried to kick him away, but Mornay pulled a pistol back out and stuck it against his side.

"Sir—" the watchman said. "He does look a gentleman. I say, is that necessary?"

"I only, ever, do what is necessary," Mornay replied, with the feeling that he had said such before. "I shouldn't like to kill you, Chesley. I know your parents. So tell me where you saw her, or I'll have to inform your family of the tragic death you suffered in the East End, where you were found cavorting with drunkards. Doesn't your father wish you to enter the church? It will probably break his heart, poor soul."

"Put me down," he gasped, "and I'll tell you!"

He was put down and more gently than he deserved. His face had grown exceedingly reddened, and he was sweating profusely. He looked up with an evil eye at his tormentor and hissed, "I shall tell you what I know not because I fear you! I don't think you'd have the nerve to kill me! Not when you know I haven't done anything!"

Mornay took a breath, forcing himself to be patient. "Go on."

Chesley took a deep breath, gathering his wits. "I didn't see Miss Forsythe. I saw Wingate. He had a lady with him, but I couldn't tell who she was."

"Only one lady?"

Chesley caught the note of surprise. "Only one."

"Where and when?" he demanded.

"The house we were just in."

"Do you have an idea where she might be in the house?"

Chesley was silent.

"Do not trifle with me, Mr. Chesley!"

"I don't know for certain!"

"Show us." Mornay motioned with his pistol for the young man to lead the way.

Ariana was sitting in the dark since Wingate left her. She didn't mind the darkness, in and of itself. It was the sound of little rodent feet that bothered her, and she had tried to scream out twice when the sounds came too close, only to find that her heavily muffled tones, which was all she could make with the cloth filling her mouth, did little to deter the beasts.

She had continued praying, not out of hopelessness, but due to her discomfort and fear of the rodents. So far they hadn't actually touched her, even though they'd come close.

With alarm—mingled with hope—she heard sounds from outside the door and then a key turning in the lock. And then her heart sank. It had to be Wingate. He had the key.

He came in saying, "I left you in the dark, did I? Beastly of me." He sounded out of breath, which encouraged her. He brought a candle in with him, and suddenly all the shadows—and the mice, for that's all they were—fled.

Her eyes were filled with accusations. He studied her and said, "It shan't be long now. Mornay knows what I want. If he is willing to pay, you'll be safe—and in his arms, I have no doubt—in two hours, more or less." She couldn't help but feel relief, though something told her Mr. Mornay would never pay for her release not because he didn't value her or couldn't afford it, but because he would much rather find her and nab Wingate. She didn't know if it was male pride or a sense of justice, but she would be shocked if he met Lord Wingate's demands.

Wingate checked the knots on her hands and those keeping her tied to the chair. She made sounds sufficiently with her mouth, letting him know she wished to speak.

"You need to speak." He paused. "Very well, I shall give you the opportunity, but—" And here he paused again and looked her point blank in the eye. "If you scream or call for help, I'll do my worst with you. Do you understand?"

She nodded.

When he untied her, he waited to hear what she would say, staying close by.

"You mustn't leave me in the dark like that again. Those horrid mice! It was too unkind."

He seemed amused. He scratched his head and then looked at her wryly. "If I leave you with a light, it could cause a fire, and then you'd end up dead. That wouldn't be good for either one of us, now, would it?"

She didn't want to admit that he was right, so she said nothing. "May I have a drink? My throat aches."

"Now there I can help you," he answered, as if pleased to be of service. He had removed a coat and now went and dug into a pocket, pulling out a flask. He opened it and held it up to her lips saying, "I'll have to give it to you. Here." She had no choice but to allow him to feed her the drink, but as soon as it hit her throat, she began to cough and splutter. He took a sip himself, watching her.

"Don't care for brandy, then?"

She didn't answer but shook her head. It was far too strong for her liking, and it felt hot on her throat.

The soldiers were back at Mornay's coach, looking around, not having turned up anything of the two women they were searching for or of Wingate.

"There! Isn't that Mornay?" said one.

"He's got someone," said the other. In tandem they came hurrying toward the threesome, ready to take Chesley into custody.

"This isn't your man, gentlemen," said Mornay, when they reached them. "But do come along, as we may be running into him shortly."

Holliwell came out of the house at that moment. He'd spent the last few minutes going around the first floor rooms, but all he'd found was various couples, most of whom cursed at him heartily until he'd shut the door on them. There was no sign of either lady on that storey.

He hoped that Julian hadn't been serious about the two women being in secret rooms. He knew Mornay would have houses torn down sooner than give up looking. He had to admit it was a good idea, on his brother's part, from a criminal's point of view. But he still hoped it wasn't true.

He joined the men in front of the house and gave his report.

"Your brother is in this house?" Mornay was already checking his weapon.

Holliwell turned to Chesley. "What made you run like a rabbit? Knowing my brother isn't a crime, you know!"

Chesley merely glowered at him. "Lost my head, that's all."

Holliwell added, "What room was Julian using for himself? Do you know?"

"Top storey, top o' the stairs. I was going to see if—" And here all the men turned as one to enter the house. Mr. Chesley's last words were muttered mostly to himself, though Mornay grabbed him by the coat lapel and dragged him along. "If he had Miss Herley."

The men started up the wooden stairs, which creaked very much. Try as they might to keep the noise down, anyone listening for sounds would have heard them. Mornay said, "One of you must stay downstairs—Antoine it will have to be you."

"Why?" He was indignant.

"Because you know the ladies. You will recognize them, and you know anyone who might try to smuggle them out while we search upstairs."

"Very well." But he wasn't happy about it.

As they neared the upper storey, the soldiers turned to Mornay. "We should go first. Remain on the stairwell until you see one of us, or if he comes out."

"No." Mornay spoke. "The safety of the ladies is our paramount aim here. I have a better idea."

Lavinia was straining her ears to listen to the sounds from the hall. There were people on the steps, of that she was sure. But what kind of people? Would they help her? Or would it be worse for her, tied up as she was, to draw in the wrong sort of people while she was in such a helpless condition? The man who had brought her to the room had fallen asleep, right on the floor and near the door. He was not too far from a candle that was burning low. She almost wished it would burn him.

Wingate sat down tiredly against the wall, as he'd done earlier. He soon sat up with a start, however, listening intently.

"Not a word! Not a sound! Or I'll make you sorry for it!" After listening with his ear close to the door for a moment, he stood back and bolted it.

Moments later a knock sounded. First one, then another. Wingate said nothing and kept his eyes fixed on her with a warning glare in them. Then they both heard, "Wingate! Open the door, man! It's me. Chesley! I've brought you a bottle of sherry!"

He flew to the door but did not open it. "I don't want it. Where the deuce have you been? And don't you know better than to find a man when he doesn't want to be found?"

"I've got news from your brother! It's about Mornay! Open the door, sir!" Wingate was thinking. Ariana was horrified. It sounded again as if Mr. Chesley was in league with Lord Wingate. And had something happened to Mr. Mornay? Her heart froze in her throat, and she listened intently. Chesley banged again.

"Be silent, you fool!" Wingate hissed.

"You're the fool if you don't let me in!" he returned, just as forcefully. "Do you want your dashed money or don't ya?"

At this Lord Wingate unbolted the door, then turned the key in the lock. The door flew open, and two soldiers in uniform with weapons drawn, immediately accosted the man, who attempted to fire at them but was foiled. Mr. Mornay was right behind the soldiers, and his eyes searched the room, spotted Ariana, and he rushed to her as though no force on earth could stop him.

"My dearest!" she cried, her eyes suddenly welling up with tears. He kissed her face, her cheeks, all the while undoing the knots on her hands. Meanwhile the officer of the law was undoing the ropes that kept her fastened to the chair. When her hands were free, she wrapped them around Mr. Mornay's neck and cried. She was so happy and exhausted, but she couldn't let him go. Thankfully he did not require it of her. He was too busy lifting her in his arms and holding her up against him tightly. With closed eyes, he just held her, feeling much of the awful tension he'd been experiencing slowly drain away. He was so, so sorry that she had been forced to endure such brutality.

The soldiers had Wingate's hands in cuffs, and each one took an arm to lead him down the stairs. The man was in a fury, cursing at Chesley and promising to be revenged on him, Mornay, and on his brother. He was trying to put up a good fight to get free of the soldiers, though it was hopeless. "The other lady isn't here, sir."

"She was brought with me into this house, but another man walked off with her on the storey beneath this one!" exclaimed Ariana.

"We'll get her," Mornay said. He put her feet down on the floor, gently loosened her hands from around his neck, and then put his arm about her to help her down the steps—and to keep her near.

Wingate was hauled down the steps, cursing and complaining all the way, while the others stopped to search the next lower floor. Mr. Mornay wanted to go with the other men to find Lavinia, but he couldn't leave Ariana's side, and he would never leave her alone.

In minutes the sound of a scuffle came from a room not too far down the corridor and then a loud report! In the next minute Antoine came running up the steps, all aflutter with concern. "Well, have you found her?" he asked, not even stopping to hear the answer. He continued down the corridor, listening and looking, and found the room with the commotion.

Not a minute later, he came back out the door triumphantly, holding a smiling Miss Herley in his arms. "Oh, thank God!" Ariana said, throwing her arms back around the neck of her beloved.

He instantly picked her up, nodded at Holliwell to go first, and followed him down the stairs. The soldiers held Wingate back, though he grew violent when he saw first his brother with his lady and then Mornay with his.

Ariana stared at the man as they approached him, and he actually grew quiet when he saw her watching him. "Stop!" she cried, when they could have passed him. Mr. Mornay was puzzled, but he did as she asked. Ariana's gaze was level with Lord Wingate's, since she was in the arms of her beloved. The prisoner's expression was surly, but she said, "May God have mercy upon you and upon your soul!"

There was a flicker of something in the steely glint of his eyes at her words—surprise perhaps. But he said nothing, and then they were out of the house and heading toward the coach.

Twenty-nine

By the time Mr. Mornay's carriage entered Mayfair, it was nigh three o'clock in the morning, and every occupant in the carriage was more than ready for "Bedfordshire." The night had been exhausting. Despite the fact that evening entertainments and house parties often lasted until the early morning hours, Mr. Mornay felt as if he had been awake for days.

"Lavinia, will you stay at Hanover Square with me now?" Ariana asked.

"We told my parents I would be with you. They have likely not had word about my abduction at all, and if it's not too impertinent, I should like it to stay that way. So, yes, I'll accompany you. They are bound to feel Lord Holliwell had a hand in it, if I tell them!" She turned to Mr. Mornay. "You, sir, will write to my parents? Of your new opinion of his lordship?"

He nodded. One more thing he had to do. Bother.

"Thank you, sir!"

Holliwell echoed the thought.

It was strange to realize that the threat from Lord Wingate was truly in the past, and that now Ariana was safe at Hanover Square. His instinctive response to the day's events—indeed, to the events of the past three days—was to keep Ariana with him. However, the facts had changed. Her family was expected the following day. Wingate was in custody. And with dawn, it would mean only three days until the wedding!

Lavinia interrupted his thoughts, asking Holliwell, "Where will you stay, my lord?" The young man looked helplessly to Mornay.

"Where are your possessions?" Mr. Mornay asked.

"What little I have, sir, is in the apartment I took you to earlier." There was a pause. "I ought to have stayed in the East End, I suppose."

"I will offer you a guest bedchamber for the night. Tomorrow we'll go to Miss Herley's family, and I'll speak for you."

"Thank you, sir!"

"Yes, thank you, sir!" Lavinia repeated.

Ariana squeezed his hand and quipped, "Yes, thank you, sir!" with a little grin.

~

When Haines saw the coach arrive, he sent a sleepy footman to summon the mistress immediately—as she had ordered. She was prodigiously indignant that Mornay had ignored her wish to speak to him earlier. So indisposed as she was, what with worry over Ariana and Miss Herley, it was unpardonable. Thus, her eyes popped open instantly. She was resting on the sofa, where she had been unable to sleep. Mr. Pellham was resting likewise in a wing chair.

She hurried out to the hall, while Mr. Pellham scurried to follow. Ah! The lady caught Ariana and Mornay saying good night at the door. His head was just coming up from planting a sincere kiss on her cheek. "Oh, thank God! Ariana! Upon my soul! Oh, Miss Herley, thank God! Thank God! You are both returned! Oh, look, Mr. Pellham! The gels are safe!"

"Yes, yes!" he said happily. He went and shook Mr. Mornay's hand.

"Mr. Mornay! Do not leave yet, sir!" Mrs. Bentley's strident tone, at this hour of the morning, made him look up with a pained expression. Mrs. Bentley gave her niece a heartfelt embrace—it seemed so natural a thing for her to do. Ariana accepted it gladly, thinking how wonderful to find her aunt becoming such an affectionate old soul. Mrs. Bentley had indeed grown to love her, she was certain, and she returned the sentiment.

Mrs. Bentley even took and kissed Miss Herley, and there were tears in the eyes of each of the females. She then turned to the Paragon. "Sir! I require an explanation of what has occurred tonight! I am thinking that you were right indeed. Ariana must stay at your house. Nothing is safe anymore. Nothing!" Mrs. Bentley had suffered an awful night, reflecting on all her vulnerability—her carriage wasn't safe, her own house wasn't safe. It was horrid, vexatious, and—devilishly unfair!

Mr. Mornay frowned. In a strong tone he replied, "Mrs. Bentley, your niece is safe. Miss Herley is safe. Lord Wingate is in custody. The threat is gone. I repeat, the threat is gone."

She blinked, trying to digest the good news. "My heavens! Is it true?" She looked around. "This is wonderful indeed!" She turned to her faithful companion. "Did you hear, Mr. Pellham? The danger is over!"

"Yes, yes, my dear." To the Paragon, he said, "And you must be the hero, sir, who saved the day for the ladies."

"I had much help," he said, though Ariana's shining eyes revealed that she shared Mr. Pellham's opinion. Mornay added, "We are all tired and in need of our beds. This is your explanation, Mrs. Bentley. Now let us all get some rest." He gave Ariana another soft kiss on the hand and said, "Good night." With a bow to the whole company, he left with Lord Antoine, who had just finished kissing Lavinia's hand.

Mrs. Bentley almost wanted to object. But she too was tired. Exhausted, in fact.

"Haines, quickly! Miss Herley and Mr. Pellham are both in need of beds. See that they are settled comfortably in guest rooms."

Finally she felt she could rest. Ariana was safe! Returned and beneath her own roof! Her brother would not find her lacking as a chaperone when he arrived the next day! And the wedding so near—my goodness! The wedding! Only three days away!

The butler at Grosvenor Square had a problem. Her name was Mrs. Hamilton. He knew his situation, and that of all the staff, was in peril, but somehow the thought of the housekeeper being a thief of the master's goods made that problem pale in comparison. His pending dismissal hadn't been confirmed by the master, for one thing, while Mrs. Hamilton's duplicity was undeniable. It bothered him mightily.

When Mr. Mornay returned with Lord Antoine, the loyal Mr. Frederick tiredly received their personal effects—hat, coats, and gloves. He awoke a maid to take the guest to his chamber, gave the young lord a hand-held candle sconce for light, and led the way for Mr. Mornay himself. Of course he was greatly relieved that his employer had returned safely, elated also at the news of Miss Forsythe being returned unharmed, but still the matter of Mrs. Hamilton lay heavy upon him.

The thing was, other than the circumstantial evidence that Molly had discovered, they had no actual proof the lady was guilty. Oh, they all believed her to be guilty. They felt it to be true, but they wanted *proof.* And Mr.

Frederick did not want to trouble the master with unproven theories, particularly on this night when his endurance had already been severely tried by the danger to his lady.

At the door to his bedchamber, Mr. Mornay took the light from Freddie and said, "Tomorrow gather the staff after my breakfast. I'll address the servants regarding the future plans for me and my wife."

"Yes, sir." He kept his countenance bland, but Freddie's pulse had quickened. Would this be the fateful announcement of their ruined hopes? Was his situation, after so long a period, to be ended with so little ceremony, no preparation, no asking of his future plans or concerns? He retired wearily and with small hopes of the morrow.

The next morning, Mrs. Hamilton could not believe it. Not a single item was there in the wall, in the secret crevice, as it ought to have been. All the small things she had napped—gone! Her eyes fell on the little bed, empty now, and blazed with anger. *That little upstart!* She rushed from the room, heading to the kitchen. *What I won't do to that girl! Taking my things!* Well, her *borrowed* things, for that was how she now viewed them. *Molly must be dismissed instantly!*

Belowstairs Mrs. Hamilton found the girl on her hands and knees, scrubbing the stone floor of the kitchen. She stopped in front of her, hands on her hips. Cook and another maid, Letty, looked at her wonderingly.

"Can I help ye, Mrs. 'amilton?" Cook asked affably.

"No! It is this chit I want!"

Molly looked up startled and then sat on her knees waiting. "Me, mum?"

Mrs. Hamilton grasped one of Molly's ears sharply between her fingers. "Come this way, my pet! You have something to answer for, and I warrant it had better be a good answer!"

Molly let out a cry of, "Oh, owww! I ain't done nothin' mum!"

Cook and Lettie exchanged curious looks, wondering what the girl had done.

Mr. Mornay scowled as he looked up from where he sat in the morning room. He had just finished off an enormous breakfast. His appetite had been ferocious when he awoke, understandably so, given the events of the recent hours.

The maid's cries reached him, however, and he slammed down his coffee cup rather too hard, causing a spill on the tablecloth. He wanted to ignore it, wanted to go on enjoying his coffee, and wanted, most of all, *silence.* How much did a man have to pay to have a little peace and quiet in his own household? *Servants! As much trouble as they are help.*

Lord Antoine, sitting across from him, noted the irritation. "Shall I see what it is?"

"No. I will." He got up reluctantly and followed the sound to the dining room since the workmen hadn't arrived yet. Mrs. Hamilton had dragged the girl from the kitchen to the dining room, seeing it as a quiet spot to grill the maid. She was heartily doing so over in the far corner, when he entered. She failed to notice her employer's presence.

"I will ask you one more time," she said between gritted teeth. "What have you done with the things in your room? You stole them, didn't ye!"

"I ain't stole nothin'!" cried Molly, covering her ears with her hands since Mrs. Hamilton had already given them a good, sound boxing.

"What is this about?" Mr. Mornay had his hands on his hips and a scowl on his face.

Mrs. Hamilton came to attention, astonished. She was speechless for a second.

"Sir! The missing items from the house! I saw them, sir, in Molly's room!" And she turned and glared at the girl.

"She put them there, sir!" cried Molly, gulping back tears. "Ask Mr. Frederick, sir!"

"Mr. Frederick?" Mrs. Hamilton was surprised.

"Ay. 'E knows about it." Molly wiped her nose with her apron.

In another minute or two, the butler arrived, and when he saw the occupants of the room, his face took on a knowing look. "Ah. So it comes out, does it?"

"Freddie—you knew about this?" Mr. Mornay asked.

"Sir—I must speak with you privately." To Molly he said, "Go to the kitchen and get back to work." To Mrs. Hamilton he said, "I shall settle this, Mrs. Hamilton. Leave the girl to me."

Mrs. Hamilton was in a fright, but what could she do? What could she say? She eyed the butler cautiously and left the room without another word.

Could it be that Freddie had found the things and believed Molly was guilty too? Tears of gratitude flooded her eyes! She was out of the money she might have got for selling the trinkets, but at least she wasn't on her way to Newgate!

Mr. Mornay pulled out a chair from the table and sat down. He was tired. The butler came over to him. "You see, sir, it happened like this…"

Mr. Mornay sighed. *Bother.*

As his butler gave him the story, the Paragon's eyes roamed the dining room walls and ceiling and—wait! Things had changed. He'd been vaguely aware, of course, of the ongoing work in his house, but his preoccupation with Ariana and Wingate had all but taken over his mind.

"Freddie, hold for a moment, won't you?" The issue of Mrs. Hamilton was annoying to the extreme, and frankly he wanted nothing to do with it. He got up and stood before the new plasterwork taking it in.

Freddie went over and examined the work also. He'd done so before, and it had looked to his eye perfectly pleasing. But his master was the Paragon, and here he was noticing it for the first time! What would he say?

Mornay circled the room, keeping that look of appraisal, his eyes curious, his head nodding from time to time. But Freddie couldn't read him. What was he thinking?

"Show me all the new work," he said. And so the butler took his master through the rooms that Miss Forsythe had seen fit to augment with new painted roundels, bas-relief work, and sculptures. Almost imperceptibly, finishing touches had miraculously been put in place. Paintings had been completed. Suddenly all the mess and upheaval came together in a masterly fashion, and the thorough cleanup had left the house looking newly finished.

The head of Mary Magdalene brought a strange little smile. At the sight of the mother of God, he commented, "She'll have us taken for papists!" But he wasn't frowning.

When he saw the bedchambers, he really had to stop, put his hands on his hips, and just look around and shake his head. But again he was smiling.

Freddie could stand it no longer. "Well, sir?"

Mornay looked over at him, almost as though he'd forgot the man's presence. "Amazing," he said. "Did Miss Forsythe conceive of it all?"

"According to Mrs. Hamilton, sir, yes, she did." Mrs. Hamilton had shared much more than that, including her opinion of the "appalling cheek" of some people and how the "future" mistress didn't know her place, but Freddie didn't bother to elaborate.

"Does it meet your approval, sir?"

The Paragon turned and greatly surprised his long-time servant by flashing that remarkably handsome, full smile. "I'm so proud of her, I hardly know what to say!" He looked back over the room. There was a greater softness in effect, a hinting at femininity but not so much that his masculine sensibilities were offended.

The bed, in particular, looked very inviting. Yes, it met entirely with his approval.

Mr. Frederick hated to ruin the moment, but he had to ask, "And Mrs. Hamilton, sir? Shall I wait for further proof of her part in the thefts?"

"I think what you have is sufficient. She wouldn't have known about the things in Molly's room if she hadn't put them there herself. That's enough to dismiss her, if that's your concern." He paused. "I'll need a new housekeeper quickly, and one who won't mind going back and forth from Aspindon to here."

"Shall you wish to prosecute Mrs. Hamilton?"

Mornay paused. "Anything of great value gone?"

"Quite a few small trinkets. I saw those ruffians stuffing their pockets, though; so it might be sticky knowing who took what. But we did recover many items in the wall including a silver candlestick and portrait if the king. And a necklace that belonged to your mother."

Mr. Mornay hesitated.

"We won't prosecute." When the servant still waited, he said, "Is there anything else?"

Freddie frowned. "Sir, Mrs. Hamilton was of the opinion that we were all to face dismissal…following your wedding." It sounded foolish now to his own ears, but he had to voice the thought.

Mornay seemed somewhat amused at the thought. "On what account would I do that?"

"She thought it was the wish of your…Miss Forsythe, sir."

"Mr. Frederick!" His amusement now turned to annoyance. "Miss Forsythe's wish? Surely you know her better than to think—" He stopped. In a different tone, he asked sharply, "Is this what caused the difficulty between you and her? She mentioned a troubling incident or two, and I've been so busy I'm afraid it slipped my mind."

"I regret to say that this was the difficulty, sir. I am terribly sorry." There was a pause while Mornay considered whether to give a further combing. Freddie spoke first. "I will offer my resignation, sir, if that will satisfy—"

"Don't be absurd! You're not going anywhere, Freddie."

The butler could have done a jig. "Thank you, sir!"

"See that the staff is given the correct information and in the future please check all rumours and speculations with me before acting upon them."

"Yes, sir!"

Mr. Mornay needed to get to the ground floor office to see his man of business on important matters, but he had gone down to breakfast without a cravat. He rarely appeared even in his own home without properly dressing, but he'd forgot about Holliwell's being there, and he was so hungry that he had no patience to get the knot right beforehand. Freddie had notified him that the man was in the office awaiting his pleasure, and so he was trying to get the neckcloth done speedily. Without success.

Holliwell poked his head in the door and yelled, "Mr. Mornay? Are you here, sir?"

Mornay took a few steps out of the dressing room. "In here. Come in."

Holliwell tried not to gawk as he entered the chamber, but he was clearly distracted. He and his brother had been in low tide for so long, he'd forgotten the feel of being surrounded by finery.

"Would it be possible, sir, to call upon the Herleys?"

Before Mr. Mornay could answer, Freddie came back. Fotch, who had not been aware that Mr. Mornay had returned to his dressing room and, therefore, was in need of his ministrations, darted around the men and began to fuss over the neckcloth.

"A note from your tailor, sir," said Freddie. "The coat sleeves have been redone and are ready for a fitting, and he begs to remind you that you wanted the coat before the wedding, sir."

"As though I'd forget. Tell them I'll come by. If it was cut *correctly* this time, I'll pay on the spot."

"Yes, sir. Also, a messenger from Rundell's, sir. The jewellery you ordered is ready for your inspection and approval, sir."

"Have them bring it here, and I will inspect it on the premises. If I'm satisfied, I'll pay for it directly. That ought to quiet their qualms."

"No, no, Fotch! Don't go getting fancy on me, I want the same knot I usually wear!"

"The note, sir, begs to remind you that the jewellery was to be a surprise for your future wife, to be picked up at Rundell's by yourself. Shall I still ask them to bring it here, sir?"

"Yes. I cannot go running all over town!"

"Very good, sir."

A footman came hurrying up and handed Freddie another note. "A note from Carlton House, sir. The Regent requests your presence on Thursday."

This made Mr. Mornay turn around and look at the butler exasperated. "And does he say what this is about?"

"No, sir." Freddie walked away with a smile.

Holliwell was still standing by, a little awestruck. "Carlton House? You really are friends with the prince, then?"

"'Tis no secret," he answered, while letting Fotch take over for him.

Holliwell swallowed. "Does that mean, sir, that you won't have a chance to speak to the Herleys on my behalf? I understand that your wedding is soon, sir—"

"I was going to write to them actually. Will that satisfy you?"

"If the result is my wedding to Miss Herley, it will."

Mornay smiled. "Rest easy. What you need to do today, sir, is to get a special license so you'll be ready!"

This perked up the young man. "Indeed! I nearly forgot! I would have done it following my stop at Mrs. Bentley's the other day, but they threw me into Newgate instead."

"Yes, well, go and do it now."

"Thank you, sir."

Mornay watched the young man turn to go and said, "Holliwell."

"Sir?"

"Return here afterward. I'll have the papers drawn up today for Miss Herley's stipend, including the conditions we spoke about."

"Yes, sir. Thank you once again, sir!" He turned to go again.

"Which reminds me," Mornay said loudly.

Holliwell stopped. He turned around but said nothing. "We have some business together. Part of the conditions, if you recall."

Holliwell nodded but remained silent.

"You must wait for me to see my man of business. Then we'll take care of it."

"May I get the license first, sir?"

"No."

Holliwell swallowed, bowed stiffly, and left the room. Mr. Mornay stood watching him leave with a thoughtful but not unhappy expression.

Two hours later, Mr. Mornay shook hands with a man who then proceeded to take up a pile of papers and put them into a neat stack.

"We only require the young lord's signature now, sir, and the contract will take effect immediately."

"I'll have him sign them today."

"Very good, sir. But could he do so now, while I'm here as a witness? This sort of thing requires a witness, you see, sir," he added, pointing to a spot on the bottom of the top paper where the witness must sign. A leather portfolio was opened, awaiting the finished business, its little leather straps at the ready to be tied securely. The solicitor handed Mr. Mornay a few envelopes saying, "These are your copies, sir."

"Much obliged, Meyers."

"My pleasure, Mr. Mornay. And allow me to offer you, on behalf of the firm, the very best congratulations upon your wedding and our hopes for only the happiest and brightest future for you and Mrs. Mornay."

"Thank you, sir."

Lord Antoine was pacing in the library, trying to interest himself in a book but with no success. He sat down and ran his fingers through his hair. This blasted waiting! Would the man never be done? He stared out the window, watching without seeing the people passing on the street.

Frederick entered the room and then escorted the young man to the ground floor office, where his lordship instantly signed the paper. He stopped only to give the papers the most cursory reading. Afterward he was congratulated by the solicitor on a most excellent arrangement and then was left alone in the room with his benefactor.

"Have a seat," Mr. Mornay said, while he sat himself behind the desk. The men eyed each other for a moment.

"Do you recall what our business is?"

Holliwell looked down, as if he was embarrassed. "I think so."

"Yes?"

"To pray?" He lifted his head when he spoke.

"Yes." Mr. Mornay took a breath, watching the young man. "We need to talk first, I think."

"Yes? That's fine."

Mr. Mornay chose his first words. "Tell me, sir, what do you believe about religion?"

Thirty

Mornay bowed politely to the Prince Regent.

"Ah, here you are, then. I know your wedding's tomorrow, and I won't keep you." The Regent motioned for him to take a seat. They were sitting on a picturesque rustic bench in the beautiful gardens behind Carlton House, which the prince had recently commissioned one of his favourite architects, Nash, to transfigure. His Royal Highness spent the next minutes describing the new wonders that were to come, and Mornay nodded politely, though he would rather be spared the narrative. Prinny was always ordering costly changes to things that were perfectly pleasing and agreeable to begin with.

"So you played the hero and rescued your lady and one other, I understand."

"With the help of other men, thank God, yes."

"And Wingate is in custody. Dashed cove! There's no unworthier blood in England than his line, I daresay, and I hope I may have the pleasure of retiring the titles associated with it one day."

"Don't be overhasty. There's a second son, you know."

"He's a cove too, from what I understand. Probably won't live to see his majority, I shouldn't wonder."

A smile flicked across Mornay's countenance and was gone. "I wouldn't count on it, Your Royal Highness."

"Well! The critical thing is that the ladies are safe! And I might say I had a hand in their rescue, mightn't I? You took two of my special guards with you for the feat."

"Say whatever you like," he returned amiably, "but regarding Wingate, you mustn't let the lords excuse him for this. I will be satisfied only with a permanent solution, sir."

"If you're asking me to hang him, I'll tell you right now I want nothing to do with the business. The papers would have a heyday with it."

"The papers will love it—the people will love it—they all feel there's no justice when peers are concerned. They will applaud you for it."

"Perhaps, but the lords won't. They are not happy to hang one of their own, as you well know. It means they're all vulnerable."

"All who *abduct women*, yes! They've nothing to fear so long as they're law-abiding!"

"Law-abiding?" The Regent laughed. "What is law-abiding under one king is treason under the next, Mornay. You know that."

"A hundred years ago but not today."

The Regent was silent. "I'll speak a few words to whomever I can," he conceded, "but wouldn't it be more effective if you yourself were in the House?"

"Even if I had a desire to sit in Commons—which I don't—you know full well it would do nothing to help my cause in this."

"I was thinking of the lords actually."

Mornay just looked at his friend. What on earth was he talking about?

"If you're talking about that baronetcy again, you know that wouldn't give me a seat—"

"No, I've thought better of it. I'm thinking of a barony."

Mr. Mornay gave a large sigh, to which the prince said, "Good heavens! You'd think I'd just promised to hang you!" He took a sip of wine, given him by a liveried footman. Mr. Mornay declined the same. "Most men would consider this quite good news!"

"My wedding is tomorrow. I think I have quite enough to think about right now."

"If you were pleased, sir, you should be happy to think about this one thing more." He was fairly irked that his surprise had not elicited more enthusiasm. "Dash it, you've got your bride, and your enemy is in prison. Why are you glum?"

Mr. Mornay took a breath. "Not glum. Out of patience. The past ten days have brought one calamity after another. Time has stretched to the point of breaking for me. If the wedding wasn't tomorrow, depend upon it, I *would* elope!"

The prince laughed delightedly. "Mornay, I begin to understand you. What's more, you may finally begin to understand *me*! I've felt the lack of your approbation when I engage in an affair, but if I wasn't heartsick for the lady, I wouldn't do it. I have no marriage, as you know. What is a man to do?"

To himself Mornay thought, *There are things a man can do, such as get on with one's wife,* but he chose a humorous tack. With mock seriousness he said, "Tell the princess to take a bath!"

The Regent gave a bitter laugh. "If only it were that simple, eh? But we shan't go there, shall we?" When his friend said nothing, he continued. "Now at last you see what it feels like—you are pining for love, sir! But you, at least, are marrying the woman you love, who deserves you. I was not, alas, so blessed."

Phillip motioned to the footman. Then taking up a glass, he looked at the Regent. "To my bride."

Prinny smiled and was pleased. Finally Mornay was being friendly. "To your bride." They both took good swigs.

The prince held up his glass again. "To your wedding."

"By all means." Another shared swallow. It was Mornay's turn. "To your future reign."

"Most definitely! To my future reign! Good show." Another swig. "To England!"

"To England!"

The glasses were refilled. More jovial toasts ensued.

And then Mornay stood up. "Sir, I beg your leave. I am expected at Hanover Square."

"Of course! You'll be quite the family man now, I expect! Only don't forget my offer, Mornay. I am depending upon you to take a seat in the House of Lords for me."

"Is that your aim? I should think you would have spoken to me about whether I have the least inclination of taking one, sir!"

"All I ask, Phillip, is for your decided vote. I cannot say how many times things would have swung my way had I one more dashed vote! I'll come to your wedding, if you like!"

"Who needs you there?"

The Regent cocked an eyebrow. "It would raise a breeze for you."

"The last thing I want."

"Since when has a dust bothered you? The papers love you."

"Thank you, but leave me a quiet wedding."

"Quiet? I hardly think so. Not with my daughter attending, and she is planning on it, you know."

"What? What on earth?" And then he realized at once that it must have had to do with Ariana. He'd find out when he saw her later.

The Regent said, "Yes, go, Phillip. I can see there is no reasoning with you now. You've no mind for anything but Miss Forsythe. The man who never loved a woman? Love appears to have forced your hand. It does have a way of trumping all else!"

Ariana was nodding and smiling with great satisfaction. To have her family around her once more! Alberta, who was Mrs. Norledge now, and her new husband, John. Beatrice, whom Mrs. Bentley had sent for this morning from the O'Brien's, and Lucy with Mama and Papa—it was wonderful to have them all here. If only they could have more time together! But she could not regret that her wedding was tomorrow. Ariana and Mr. Mornay would have time in the future to spend with her family, but right now what they needed and wanted more than anything was to be with one another. *Where is he?*

Mr. Timmons, the rector from her hometown of Chesterton, had also come to Mayfair with the family. It was he, perhaps more than anyone, who had spent hours expounding the text of various books on religion with Mr. Mornay. He had gone through the book of Romans with the man, almost verse by verse, and then had the honour and distinction of leading him in the "sinner's prayer." At the moment he was pretending to spar with Mr. Forsythe, who was doing an admirable job of "fighting" back.

Lucy was all energy and darting across the room in between the men or hanging onto Ariana's gown, which was rather irksome as it caused terrible wrinkles. All in all, she was having as much fun as any six-year-old could hope to. Beatrice was regaling her mama with a day by day account, or so it seemed, of her time at the O'Brien's. And Mrs. Bentley was sitting on the sofa next to Mr. Pellham, more quiet and unobtrusive than usual, engaging in small talk with the Norledges. The new couple was carefully sitting some distance apart from each other, as if afraid to reveal their new-found intimacy. By contrast Miss Herley and Lord Antoine were sitting only inches apart, with eyes only for each other. Ariana wished for Phillip's closeness at this moment. He was the only one missing from this perfect gathering.

Holliwell had told her of Mr. Mornay's call to Carlton House—again. *Will the Regent always be stealing him from me? And how long does the prince require his presence anyway? Where is he?* Supper was ended, and that had been in itself a great disappointment. She had so wanted him to be with her—she was so proud of him and delighted by his company. Her aunt had wished to send a man to the square to see what was what, but Ariana had forbade it. She would not nag him. *But if one more person asks me where he is as though I ought to know his every move—*

She wanted to tell him how her family was unanimous in thinking that she was much changed. She was older somehow, her mama said, with a happy sadness that only a mother could understand. Her papa saw it too. Ariana suspected it was due to the fact that she was a woman in love and that she had survived two episodes of horrendous handling by the likes of Lord Wingate. That would age anyone. That topic—of her recent trials—might have ruined the mood of the gathering, but she shared an exciting surprise at table: that Princess Charlotte herself had sent word that she would like to attend the wedding! Of course Ariana had accepted the honour!

Mrs. Forsythe, upon hearing of it, had tears in her eyes. The princess! At her own child's wedding! Mr. Timmons was as impressed as anyone, but he was at least as concerned over the absence of the Paragon as Ariana. He had written Phillip, sharing his wish to come for the wedding. It would do his heart good, he said, to see Phillip again, not to mention besting him with an epée—he couldn't resist taking the poke. Mr. Mornay was delighted and issued an invitation for the man to stay at Grosvenor Square this night.

Unknown to Phillip, Mr. Timmons was hoping to spend enough time with the man to assess his growth and understanding of his religion, now that he had made a step of true repentance. It felt like a long time since Mr. Mornay had fallen to his knees on the lawn at Mr. Timmons's house and recited the prayer with him. The man was not a member of his parish, but he was a member of the family of God and had opened his heart to religion following Timmons's tutelage. He had a personal interest in him, besides an enormous liking and respect. His was the only other face except Ariana's to frown this evening, and he wondered if Mornay had fallen into some mischief.

On the night before a man's wedding, these things were known to happen. Particularly when said man had friends who were not the marrying sort.

~

When Mr. Mornay left Carlton House, a good hour after his arrival, he ran smack into a coterie of the prince's friends, all of whom had been about to descend on Carlton House to buzz about the prince as they were wont to do. At the sight of Mornay, they halted.

"Look! 'Tis the man himself! Mornay, we've just been talkin' about you."

He folded his arms and gave a lazy, "Yes?"

"Doesn't he cut a dash tonight? Where're you headed, eh?" The men were grouping around him. "Come, come, do tell. You're all the go, ain't ya?"

He shrugged. "Saw Prinny straight from the tailor's. Just a new coat, gentlemen."

"'Tis for his wedding, I warrant. That's tommora, ain't it?"

Without answering he took his watch from his fob and held it so he could read it.

"Wait a minute, Mornay! We heard about Wingate taking the angel and all. Tell us about it, won't ya?"

When he didn't answer immediately, the Duke of Grafton stepped forward. He smiled and shook Phillip's hand. "Congratulations, old man! So tomorrow's the big day, is it?"

He smiled. "It is, Your Grace."

"You have our sympathies," he said, but he was smiling. His face grew more sober and he said, "I did hear about Miss Forsythe's unfortunate, ah, tête-à-tête with Wingate!" He sighed. "That man has been a terror for too long!"

"I agree entirely."

"I'm glad it has all worked out well, got her back unharmed, and all that."

"Thank you. I'd like to see Wingate hanging from a gibbet for his part in it, though."

"I don't doubt it!" He cocked an eye at Mornay. "Hey, come along and we'll talk more about it, eh? What can be done about that reprobate 'markee'? Transportation, at least, I don't doubt." He moved to take Phillip's arm.

"Prime, we've got him!" someone snickered from behind them.

"Shut it, you dandy-prat!"

Mr. Mornay stopped. How idiotic was he? The men were evidently doing their best to sneak him into going along with them for a night's entertainment. The night before his wedding. He had worked, it seemed, for a long time to reach this night. It felt, in fact, as though he had been waiting all his life for this! He wasn't going to ruin it by wasting it among these empty garrets!

Lord Grafton was back before him. "Did I hear correctly that you picked the brother—Holliwell, ain't it—from Newgate? What's the story there, eh? We thought the brothers were birds of a feather."

"You're trying to distract me, Grafton. It won't do."

"No, no, no. I'm in earnest, sir. I need your answer on this."

Mornay flicked a miniscule speck off his coat and said, "Without Holliwell, I would not have found Miss Forsythe so speedily. And he is a changed man. Reformed, if you like."

Someone else interjected with an oath. "Not another reformed man! I remember when Wilberforce was a regular chap, and look at him now. All he talks of is abolition—or even worse!"

The others laughed.

"Never become that sort of bore, Mornay!"

"Goodness, how could I live with myself?"

Only Grafton caught the sardonic note and an appreciative sparkle lit his eyes.

Mornay started to move on, but one said, "Come, gentlemen, he's entering the parson's mousetrap tomorrow! We can't abandon 'im to matrimony without a fight."

"No, by Jove! Look here, Mornay. You're about ta change, see? Planning a honeymoon, aren't ya? Then it'll be to Middlesex with you and the angel, and we won't get to see ya before the season ends! It's no good. You've got to come along—we just want ya for a little bit."

"Let's take 'im to Boodle's! First a good supper and then a rubber of cards and—"

Mr. Mornay shook himself free. "Not this time. Go see Prinny for your supper, if you like, but I have an engagement."

At that moment, Alvanley came out of Carlton House.

"Mornay! I've got a message for you."

"From?"

"From the angel. Says she understands completely, you're to feel free to spend one last night with your friends."

He almost grinned. They were trying so hard. "Alas, I am not available, gentlemen." His voice was firm.

Brummell popped out of the circle. "Dash it, sir. Devilish unfriendly of you. Do us the honour of a supper at the very least. Your sainted bride will have you all for herself soon enough. Aren't afraid of a woman's wrath, are ya?"

The men laughed at the thought.

Mornay frowned at him and folded his arms. "We've shared many a supper in the past. And we shall again—"

"No, sir, it must be tonight! 'Tis the eve of your wedding! We must be allowed to celebrate it with you."

Mr. Mornay looked around at the group. There were roughly fifteen men, all looking at him hopefully. He'd spent many a night with most of them. They'd spoken of politics, of Prinny, of England, of hunting, shooting, and shows of pugilism. Horses. Dogs. Agriculture. Napoleon. They were friends, even if more than a few were buffle-headed pigeons at times.

"Very well," he started to say, when their immediate outburst of "Huzzas!" forced him to silence. Holding up a hand, he shouted, "For a supper only, gentlemen! Then I must insist upon being off." A fresh cheer went up, and they started to move in on him, pushing him along toward someone's gleaming coach. Mr. Mornay had to suppress a frown and refused to contemplate the damage they were doing to his new coat.

"Married men in our society do not cease to associate with their friends because they are married. Nor do they give up their club memberships! I will not disappear into the netherworld, I promise you!"

"Not the netherworld. Just under the cat's foot, is all, and we must have you now, while you're still your own man!"

"Under the cat's foot!" Worcester snorted a laugh.

"A mighty pretty cat, I'd say," said another.

"Shut your bone-boxes!" shouted one man.

Mornay protested mildly but allowed himself to be carried, for it was useless to protest, to a carriage, where they finally hoisted him in with a jolly, "Heave Ho!"

Numerous men scrambled in after him. Alvanley jumped in and said, "Excellent! Well done, fellows! Let's to Boodle's! I'm all for getting foxed tonight! Mornay is to be wed, and we shall celebrate. The prince says we may expect him to join us!"

"Huzzah!"

"What did Prinny say?" one asked, as the coach wheels began to move.

"He's occupied for the next hour or two, but he wants us to keep 'Mr. Hickenbotham' here at Boodle's until he arrives. He says he has only the fullest sympathies for a man about to tie the knot and must endeavour to commiserate in style."

"That isn't what he said to me," Phillip responded.

"Well, he could hardly say it to your face, now could he?" To the other men, he shouted, "He'll help pay for the supper, gents!" Another round of huzzahs filled the air. Mr. Mornay glanced out of the coach and saw they were still on Pall Mall.

"So, Mornay, glad you aren't being a marplot!"

"I must send a note to Hanover Square, however."

"Sure, sure, we'll send a boy from Boodle's. Your other half will understand."

While they rounded the corner to St. Jame's, Phillip remembered the last time he'd been press-ganged by his friends into carousing with them. The last thing he needed was a repeat of that night. Besides, he would rather have been at Mrs. Bentley's right now than with these men. By Jove, he would! All right. He'd share a supper with them—and then extract himself and make it to Hanover Square. This was not going to be like the last episode. This time it was going to end his way.

Thirty-one

When Ariana's eyes popped open, the sun was just peeking over the horizon—as much of a horizon as could be seen over neighboring rooftops, that is. But it was enough to cause her sleepy eyes to flitter awake, and she knew at once that she could never return to sleep. It was her wedding day!

Her stomach was all aflutter. She rushed to the looking glass. Was her complexion good today? Whew, it was! She rushed to the wardrobe just to gaze at the new gown of white satin, silk, and opulent lace. The gown had a train of lace, and her gloves had a tiny lace edging at the elbows and along the seams to the wrists. Even her petticoat and chemise had lace trim, and she was excited at the thought of donning the garments. How seldom it excited her these days to wear a new gown, but this one was different! She could hardly contain herself, in fact. She happily drew the satin shoes from their resting place in the closet, just to be able to look at them and assure herself that the day had truly arrived.

In a flutter of joy, she tugged on the bellpull. Oh, if all women felt this happy upon their wedding day, then every woman must be married! She gave another yank to the cord. Evidently the servants weren't up yet, as no one answered the summons for minutes. By then she was already prancing down the hall and knocking on everyone's doors.

"Come, wake up! It's my wedding day!"

She made a quick circuit of the bedchambers and then was doubling back again, when her aunt came to her doorway and peered out at her, blinking back sleep. "It's your wedding day, yes, but I fail to see why that should give you the right to plunge the whole house into misery!"

"Misery? Oh, my *dear* Aunt!" She rushed to give the old lady an effusive kiss on the cheek, much to Mrs. Bentley's annoyance. Mrs. Bentley wasn't prepared for familiarity before breakfast. But Ariana was oblivious. "No one must be miserable today! I want the whole world to be as happy as I am! And you, of all people, must be ecstatically happy!"

"I am happy. Very happy for you, my gel." And then she started. "Oh, my! I'd almost forgot! It's *my* wedding day too!"

Ariana laughed. "Precisely!" And with that, she went whirling back down the hallway, her light cotton robe fluttering like a gossamer wing behind her.

Mrs. Bentley returned to her bed. *Oh, bother*. She supposed she ought to get up. Her guests would need to be seen to, her menu checked on—the servants could *so* throw a monkey in the pot, if she didn't watch them! Reluctantly she sat up and found her prayer book. Time for the morning's reading.

Mr. Timmons had gone to Grosvenor Square near ten thirty the previous evening, after giving up hopes of Mornay's joining him at Mrs. Bentley's house. Timmons had, after all, been invited, and he much desired to lay eyes on his friend, no matter if he had to wait up most of the night to do it.

Freddie installed the guest in the best parlour, as the rector would not countenance retiring for the night until Mr. Mornay returned home. He felt more than ever that he needed to see the man, needed to reassure himself that Mornay's new faith was taking root in his life. He'd rest easier for having some little proof that the man marrying the daughter of his excellent friends, the Forsythes, was indeed changed from his former ways.

Miss Forsythe had been concerned, he knew, when her betrothed failed to appear. It helped when a note, written in his hand, arrived and explained that he'd been enjoined to stay for supper at Boodle's and that even the prince expected him to stay. Though she tried not to show disappointment, Mr. Timmons was a good enough student of humanity to see that she hid it only with effort.

She told her family that the Regent required Mr. Mornay's presence, which impressed all of them mightily except for Mr. Timmons. He found himself hoping it was not a sign of a future pattern for the marriage. He was glad to know, then, that he'd be seeing Mr. Mornay later. He was glad to know now more than ever. The clock upon the mantel had slowly moved to eleven o'clock, then midnight. He had dozed off, and now it was nearly two in the morning. Rather late for a man to be out on the eve of his wedding. He shook himself awake. He would wait to see Mr. Mornay if it took all night.

Princess Charlotte was eager to attend this wedding. Someday, if her father was right, Mr. Mornay might be one of her own advisers. She wanted to groom him for the part as much as her father did. Who knew? He might perhaps aspire to Prime Minister someday. He had twice the presence of most men and as much acumen, it seemed to her, as Perceval or Jenkinson.

Finally and perhaps this was most important of all, the princess actually liked Miss Forsythe in a way that she seldom liked people. She sensed a true spirit in the girl, the sort of soul she could trust. Most everyone wanted favours for return of friendship—it was an inevitable fact of being royal—but Mornay's betrothed seemed the sort that would love one for oneself. The princess wanted to nurture their acquaintance, therefore, and had prepared a miniature portrait of herself, a copy of the original by Cosway, the noted miniaturist. It was not a costly gift but personal enough to convey her best intention. Yes, today was her way of cementing what she hoped would be a long and lasting alliance with the soon-to-be Mr. and Mrs. Mornay.

When Mr. Timmons awoke on the wedding day, he blinked a few times and then came fully alert and sat up quickly. He had fallen asleep again, dash it! Bad luck! He had missed Mr. Mornay at his return. He collected himself and went looking for a servant—he never thought to reach for the bellpull. Seeing no one about, he descended to the ground floor and continued his search. Wait. He heard someone. He went toward the sounds.

The ladies in the kitchen were busily at work when they looked up and saw a disheveled and bewildered-looking man staring in at them.

"Bless me!" cried Cook, with a hand to her heart. "An' who might you be?"

"I am Mr.—Mr. Timmons. A rector. I'm looking for Mr. Mornay."

"In the kitchens, sir?" One of the maids let out a giggle.

"Which—which room is his? Could you be so kind—"

"Wake the master? Oh, *no,* sir! I beg you, return to your chamber or the morning room. Breakfast will be done in a jiffy. Mr. Mornay is to be wed today, as you know, sir."

"Yes." He grew thoughtful a moment. "Do you know what time he got in last night?"

"Oh, bless me, sir! I'm not the butler or his val-lay!"

"Thank you." He bowed slightly, bringing more giggles, and made his way back to the main hall. There he saw the butler just coming on duty, straightening his waistcoat.

"Good morning, sir!" Frederick said crisply.

"Mr. Frederick—" Mr. Timmons was greatly relieved. "I'm afraid I fell asleep in the parlour. Do you happen to know when Mr. Mornay got home last night?"

"I thought it best not to disturb you, sir."

"I thank you, though I wish you had. What time did you say he got in?"

The butler regarded him a moment. "I must have been asleep by then, sir. I am not required to wait up for him, you know, though of course I like to. I'm afraid that last night I was very tired and—"

"Are you telling me that you didn't see your master last night?"

"That's right, sir."

"Are you not concerned for him? Are you not worried that he is not home and this, his wedding day?"

The butler shook his head. "Not at all, sir! Mr. Mornay is well aware of his wedding today, I assure you. He will be ready on time."

"When he has been out all night?" He looked squarely at the butler. "I need to know if the man is here. Would you check his chamber, please? If he is in any shape to rise, please ask him to do so and tell him that I am waiting for him in the ah…"

"The morning room, sir?"

"Yes. Very good. The morning room."

"Very good, sir."

As Freddie walked to the staircase, Mr. Timmons called out, "Excuse me, old chap, but which way is the morning room?"

Thirty-two

Mr. Frederick waited until Mr. Timmons was out of sight. With a furtive look back, he hurried toward the staircase. Of course he didn't believe for a second that his master was not at home. Preposterous suggestion! But it wouldn't hurt to take a peek at him either. He headed for the master's bedchamber.

Ariana was trying to contain her excitement. She had taken only tea at breakfast, as her fluttering stomach would allow naught else. She thought she might burst from all the happiness she felt inside. It was too wonderful. Her wedding day, after an *age,* had finally arrived! The idea of how long she'd been betrothed to Mr. Mornay seemed absurdly long.

Harrietta moved more slowly than usual, doing her preparations. "What is it, Harrietta?"

She seemed rather cast down, in stark contrast to Ariana's joy.

"It's jus' that I'll miss ye when you're married, Miss."

"Miss me? But aren't you coming with me?"

Harrietta looked startled. "The mistress 'asn't said a word to me about it."

"Oh, dear. I am sure I spoke to her of it. I suppose we each thought the other would tell you. You are to come with me, Harrietta, until we both decide if we suit."

"Oh, bless me, Miss Forsythe, do we suit? I'd be 'appy to stay with you forever!"

Ariana remembered that Harrietta had not been a lady's maid before her arrival, but Mrs. Bentley had promoted her with the help of some quick training in hair dressing and the proper handling of expensive fabrics. Harrietta's old duties were much more laborious, not to mention that the position of lady's maid gave her precedence over all other female servants, save Mrs. Ruskin, the housekeeper. Ariana's coming had lifted her from a life of drudgery, and she had no wish to return to it.

"Well, then," Ariana replied with a little smile. "As I assuredly *need* you, then 'tis settled." She was silent for a moment, while Harrietta expertly used her fingers to twist and turn the little curls about Ariana's face to hang *just so.*

"Oh, thank you, miss! I must write to my sister and tell her the good news!"

"Afterward pack your things directly," Ariana said. "You must come along with the other servants we will be bringing when we leave following the ceremony."

"Yes, miss! Thank'ee miss!" There were tears in her eyes.

When Freddie arrived at the master's bedchamber, he found a sleeping Fotch inside, on a wing chair. So far, so good. But the bed, when he pulled aside the curtain enough to peek, was empty! The bed hadn't been slept in.

"Mr. Fotch! Where is the master?"

"Hum? What? Where is he?"

"Wake up, sir! Where is Mr. Mornay!"

Fotch came to, sat up, looked at the bed, and scratched his head. "I never saw him! Is he not in the house?"

"Oh, dear." Frederick's face creased into a frown. "There is a Mr. Timmons here. A rector! He's looking for Mr. Mornay!" His eyes widened with a terrible thought. "Could this be the man who will perform the ceremony?"

"Not Mr. Hodgson? He presides at St. George's!"

"This may be Miss Forsythe's man!"

Fotch frowned and thought quickly. "It must be him, right and tight! What'll we do?"

"Well, he seems awfully suspicious for some reason. And now the master is gone! I say, it does have an appearance of ill-boding! Mr. Mornay would certainly not miss his own wedding! He's never been pigeon-headed in his life! What do you make of it?"

Fotch looked pensive. He quickly went to the wardrobe and had a look about, but he shook his head. "His church clothes are here." He looked at Freddie. "I don't like it, Mr. Frederick."

"Nor do I, Mr. Fotch." The two men stood there helplessly for a few minutes.

"We'd best do something about *him.*" Fotch said, referring to the rector.

"Indubitably. If he thinks the master hasn't been here, he may run back to Hanover Square and give the wrong impression." Their eyes met. "He may *cancel* the wedding!" It was an admission attended with all due respect, and the men hung their heads in sorrow.

"That mustn't happen!"

"The master would not intentionally miss his wedding."

"Never!"

"He's been too happy about it. Have you noted the change in him?"

"That I have!" Fotch remembered the way he'd seen his master with Miss Forsythe on more than one occasion—the softness of his manner toward her, the loosening up of his own bearing. Something was evidently amiss today, but whatever it was, he knew—he just *knew*—the master was not at fault.

Mr. Frederick took a breath. "Stay here in case *our rector* comes."

"Perhaps the master's at Hanover Square!" the other said. "Send and ask!"

"But how can we? If he is not there, it will give away that we, who should know precisely where he is, do not know! No, sir, that won't answer." They were both still frowning. "I'll go see to that rector. And then perhaps I'll make some inquiries of Mr. Mornay's acquaintances. They may know something of this."

"I dread to think you are right, Mr. Frederick, but you may be."

"Indeed."

They parted, and Fotch sat down, bewildered and at a loss.

Mr. Frederick suddenly appeared again at the doorway and stuck his head into the room. "Whatever you do, do not allow Mr. Timmons to know that Mr. Mornay is not at home! If he tries to enter this room, you cannot allow it!"

"Right. Send John up here, eh?" John was one of the larger footmen on staff.

"Right. Let's to it!" Mr. Frederick answered, even as he made his way from the room.

Mr. Timmons was enjoying his breakfast and the attention of servants, who had no one else to help save himself. He still felt a nagging concern about Mr. Mornay and hoped that there would be enough time for them to talk before the man had to rush off to his wedding. He looked at his watch. Eleven o'clock. A sense of real concern assailed him, and he frowned. Wait—he would pray. Troubling thoughts were always best when offered up as prayer. He bowed his head right there and then at the table and prayed. *Let there be time for a talk with Mornay. Let me see that the man has indeed made a clean break from his former besetting sins. Oh, if the man has a real religion, let it be evident today!*

Mr. Frederick entered the room and bowed slightly. "Mr. Mornay is still abed, sir. He begs your patience, asking that you excuse him as he rarely takes breakfast. He will be happy to meet with you afterward."

Mr. Timmons felt better at once. "Ah, splendid! Splendid, my good man! Thank you."

Ariana turned slowly, letting all her family admire the satin and silk gown with its matching veil of white lace. It was a fairly simple but elegant design, draping beautifully on the tall girl as Mrs. Bentley's excellent modiste had intended. Her bouquet had arrived and was also elegant. At home, girls used country wildflowers for their poseys, but here she had received the benefit of Mrs. Bentley's largesse as usual. The bouquet was made up of deliciously scented petals of tightly curled roses and fresh greens. It was lovely and soft and Ariana was enchanted.

Now Mrs. Bentley appeared in the parlour and all of the subsequent "oohs" and "aahs" that must accompany a bride's entrance, even an older bride, were made and smilingly accepted. Mrs. Bentley did indeed look lovely.

Ariana's aunt wore a veiled headdress over her face, a light covering of cobweb lace, and a gown of shot silk and satin that sparkled wherever light fell upon it. The gown's colour was a light blue-grey, and it reflected the jewels in her necklace and bracelets as though they were fashioned to accompany just that gown.

She and Ariana exchanged a smiling embrace. Ariana almost gave way to tears while it lasted. How had this crochety old woman become so dear to her heart? She was nearly as happy on account of Mrs. Bentley's wedding as she was for her own. Who would ever have dreamed that she and her aunt would both be tying the knot on the same day?

The Forsythes were dressed and ready. Little Lucy followed Ariana everywhere, wanting to carry the train that Ariana had securely fastened by a button on the side of her dress, which existed for just that purpose. Lucy's childish intuition told her she would soon be missing this sister yet again. Mrs. Bentley's fine coach was at the curb, ready to take them to the church. There would be no walking there today.

Already a small crowd had gathered near St. George's for the Paragon's wedding. Generally town weddings did not draw a large number of people, but not only did many hope to glimpse the man on his wedding day, they wanted to see his famously pretty bride as well. Others received word (as these things are bound to happen) that the princess might appear and were there to see her. In all, it was with extreme difficulty that the footmen who had been sent ahead were able to keep the church from overcrowding, and when the princess did arrive, of course there was a great fuss.

Her Royal Highness was equal to a fuss, being vastly acquainted with them. She walked to the front of the church, flanked by two of her ladies and one gentleman, and took a seat at the head. Her smiling countenance had already repaid the audience for their trouble of coming—and the principal beings hadn't even arrived yet. The mood was more jocular than for most weddings.

Mr. Pellham arrived. He made his way to stand before the altar smiling amiably, greeting acquaintances with a regal nod and looking cozy and dignified in his stiff dark trousers and tailcoat, as he carried his golden-handled cane. His face shone with happiness. The princess inquired about the little smiling man. She was informed, by a church dignitary, of the double wedding and nodded. She then asked for an introduction and gave Mr. Pellham a personal congratulation upon his marriage, which he would never forget. In a minute he began to regale Her Royal Highness with the sort of tales which had already made him a favourite among the *ton*. He had the rare gift of being funny without coarseness; interesting without tediousness. Now and then the princess's merry laugh rang out, and it added to the jollity in the air.

When Ariana and her aunt arrived, Ariana's father handed her down.

As soon as she stepped from the carriage, a cheer went up on the street. Amazing! People were everywhere, all craning their heads and necks to get a peek at her! She spied a man quickly sketching her appearance and another hastily jotting notes about her arrival, the crowd, the church—for the papers, to be sure.

She had still not grown accustomed to being of interest to the general population and felt strangely humbled by it. Her aunt came out next, and another cheer went up. Mrs. Bentley was elated at the attention and smiled all around and waved her bouquet. Afterward, the rest of the family disembarked and made their way into the church. Inside the excitement grew and then dropped to a hush as everyone craned to see the bride they had been waiting for.

Ariana saw Mr. Pellham at the head of the aisle and looked for Mr. Mornay—she did not see him. People were waving and gesturing at her from the pews, but she kept her eyes ahead. *Where is my beloved?* She saw the vicar, standing with a dour expression. *Something is wrong.* Mr. Mornay was not in front, like Mr. Pellham, smiling at her as the older gentleman was smiling at her aunt. Ariana tried not to look for him too obviously; she must act as though she hadn't a concern in the world.

Behind her, however, her father whispered, "Where is he?" And there was no question of whom he referred to.

"He'll be here!" she replied, in an equally fervent whisper.

She began to make her way down the aisle, with her aunt beside her. As she reached the front, she acknowledged the princess, who smiled gently at her. She curtseyed gratefully and smiled bravely. But inside she felt her first inkling that something might be gravely wrong. *Where is my beloved? Where?*

Mr. Frederick, about an hour and a half earlier, found Mrs. Hamilton near the kitchens. The housekeeper had taken a day off yesterday and had sold the little lady's pistol from the armoury. She was feeling guilty—a thing she hadn't expected.

Mr. Frederick had not had a chance to dismiss her yet. He dreaded doing it and wouldn't even think of dealing with it now. There was enough to do, given the mysterious disappearance of the master. He looked at her now, and suddenly he thought it might have been a good thing she was around to be of assistance.

"I have something you must do," he said. To her curious look, he added, "And not a word to the other servants about it!"

She nodded.

~

Mr. Timmons had eaten breakfast, washed and changed in his room, looked about the house for his host, and then retreated into the library for twenty minutes of reading and prayer. He was now back to the public rooms and wanted to know where Mr. Mornay was. He found himself feeling that something was afoot. *Does Mr. Mornay wish to avoid our meeting? Is he intentionally stalling?*

Mrs. Hamilton appeared. "Mr. Mornay has requested to see you now, sir."

"Oh, excellent!" He was vastly relieved to find that his fears were false. He followed her down the hall with a lighter heart, looking forward to the meeting and thinking of what he wished to say to the man. *Perhaps a few words on the blessedness of the estate of matrimony? The duty of husbands and wives?*

Mrs. Hamilton stopped at the door to a room he hadn't seen yet. He readied himself for another dose of grandeur. Mornay was certainly a solid oak, he'd grant him that.

"What room is this?" he asked lightly, as her hand went to the doorknob. It seemed a bit out of the way, now that he thought on it.

"An office, sir. The house has two of them."

"Ah." He was curious as to why he was being received there, but he had no concerns about it. Mrs. Hamilton turned the doorknob. She had unlocked it herself only minutes earlier. When she had opened the door enough to stick her head in, she said, "Here is Mr. Timmons, sir," and then motioned for the rector to enter before her.

When he did, she pulled the door shut swiftly and stuck a key in the lock and turned it with a click of finality. Already there was a protest from within. A banging on the door.

"I say! Open this door! What is this? Is this some kind of trick? I am a guest of your master's!" It was no good, however. Mr. Timmons, locked in the armoury with all manner of weaponry, was stuck. He was a patient man. But this was above all. This treatment! What bothered him even more than his imprisonment, however, was what it signified.

Mr. Mornay was up to devilish tricks. He was a blackguard! Why else bother to lock up a rector—his guest!—if not to conceal some deep infamy? Why else?

Mr. Frederick met Mrs. Hamilton in the hall, and his face revealed his anxiety.

"He's in there, sir, and yowling like a tom cat," she said distastefully.

"Very good, Mrs. Hamilton."

She looked at him expectantly. She was still rather nervous about the goings-on with Molly and whether she had been found out or not, but being asked to lock a man of the cloth in a small inner room with no outlet was so unusual, it pushed her fears to the back of her mind.

"Might I ask, Mr. Frederick, why you want that cleric locked in the armoury?"

"Not now, Mrs. Hamilton. You may ask later. Right now we need to discover the whereabouts of the master!"

"His whereabouts? Today's his wedding! He must be here!"

He gave her an agonized look. "We cannot find him!"

"Good gracious!" Mrs. Hamilton felt a rush of concern. My goodness, but she cared. She had seen, it was no use denyin' it, that Mr. Mornay had been happier than she'd ever known him to be of late. It was on account of Miss Forsythe. And yet all she had been thinking of was herself! All she had worried about was her own situation! She turned her eyes to the butler's.

"I'll check all the bedchambers!"

"I'll send word to Mr. Brummell and Lord Alvanley. Perhaps Lord Grafton."

She looked at him once more. "Well, let's be quick about it, sir!" She turned and headed for the stairway.

One hour before the wedding, Mr. Mornay awoke. He blinked a few times, trying to get his bearings. A dull pain…in his arm. No, a scorching pain. Something was amiss. He couldn't place it at first. Something was not familiar. He sat up abruptly to find that he'd been asleep in a guest bedroom of his own house! What on earth! He rubbed his eyes a moment, and then it hit him. *By Jove!* The wedding! He scrambled to get up, winced at the pain in his arm, and then his head, and thought, *"Oh, Lord! If I've missed it—Oh, God, no, don't let me miss it!*

~

After he'd been press-ganged into Boodle's, Mornay used the club's amenities to send Ariana a note. It was a lame sounding note, even to his own ears, but he had decided that he would satisfy his friends by sharing a dinner, his "last supper" as Scropes Davies called it. He fully expected time to extract himself afterward and make an appearance at Hanover Square. He hadn't forgotten that he was to entertain Mr. Timmons either.

The prince had indeed joined them, creating a stir at the club. The supper had far exceeded the usual spread, which was excellent to begin with. Mr. Mornay ate sparingly, as he felt an unusual restlessness—no doubt on account of the wedding. Cards were shortly produced, and no one even bothered to remove to the first floor card room. Ask the prince to move? It wasn't going to happen.

Phillip had a hand dealt in front of him while he was speaking to Prinny, and then numerous gentlemen appeared ready to keep him from even rising from his seat.

"Come, come, Mornay, we'll see you home in plenty of time for your beauty rest."

"Don't leave me, Phillip—I'm here on your account," the prince added, and in such a tone that Mr. Mornay knew His Royal Highness wasn't *asking*. It was a command! "I haven't played a game against you in an age," he added, taking up his hand.

Sometime later no one noticed when an uninvited guest came in, walked up behind Mornay, and then, without the least ceremony, quickly read out his hand, card by card. He might just as well have declared his alliance with France. His action in that room and among those men was akin to treason. There were immediate cries of indignation, and Mornay slapped down the cards and pushed out his chair, coming to his feet like lightning. Already a few men were holding Mr. Harold Chesley by the arms. When Mornay saw who it was, his eyes narrowed, and he made a little nasty grimace. He didn't consider the puppy worth the trouble, but his back was up. Mr. Chesley's infraction was grave indeed.

He stared at Mornay stupidly.

"Let him go, gentleman," Mr. Mornay said. He wouldn't hit a man who couldn't fight back properly. Disgustedly they released him, but just then Chesley gave way to drunken laughter saying, "I gotcha! I gotcha this time, Mornay!"

Phillip had already drawn back his fist for the punch, but he withdrew abruptly in disgust. "He's hocused!"

"He is. Get him out of here," someone murmured. The Regent was looking on with an angry scowl, and he whispered something to one of his men.

At that moment, Mr. Mornay realized he might have been given an exit pass by Mr. Chesley. His hand had been read out loud, and he should now be free to abandon it.

"Sorry, Mornay, but there's no rules to say we don't finish the hand."

"There's no rule for it because it isn't done!" he countered. "There's no rule to say women aren't allowed here either, but they don't come, do they?"

"Bad luck," someone else said, but they were smiling at each other knowingly.

"Give it up, gentlemen," Mornay said, as he stood up and straightened his coat. "And wish me a happy wedding!" He smiled fully while they finally accepted the inevitable, shook his hand, wished him luck, and made some jokes.

Meanwhile Chesley had been roughly escorted from the room and was given the boot, literally, in the hall. Someone pushed him in the direction of the staircase. "Go on, then, you lout! Stop interrupting gentlemen, or the prince will have you thrown into Newgate!"

Back in the room, Mornay was inching toward the door, still accepting good-natured slaps on the back and friendly wishes. He was a little tense, but he supposed it wouldn't cease until he arrived at Hanover Square.

Just before he reached the doorway, his back to the hall, Harold Chesley had reached it from the other side. He recognized his enemy even from behind. He knew what he had to do.

His leering countenance took on a more sober look, though he was not by any means sober. He pulled a small gun which was already cocked from his coat pocket. It was a miracle—if it could be called such—that the pistol hadn't gone off when he was booted from the room and sprawled along the corridor earlier.

He aimed it waveringly at his target.

"He's got a gun!" someone cried. "Mornay!" And then the report went off. There was a puff of smoke, and the acrid smell of powder, and Mr. Mornay clasped his left arm with his uninjured hand. Blood began showing between his fingers and dripped along the sleeve of his very fine, brand new coat.

When fifteen minutes had passed and Mr. Mornay had not appeared at the church, Mr. O'Brien could stand it no longer. He made his way to Mr. Forsythe, who was also having difficulty not giving in to angry speculation.

"Sir," he said, when he came upon the man. Mrs. Forsythe made room so that he could sit beside her husband. "Do you know the reason he isn't here?" They both knew who "he" was.

"No. None."

"Sir, may I remind you that my offer to your daughter still stands?"

"Eh? That's rather precipitous, young man."

"Your daughter, sir, should not be made to suffer the humiliation that will be upon her shortly, if he does not show!"

"No. Well, I'm not giving up on him yet." He added pointedly, "Thank you for your *concern*."

"Sir—I love your daughter. My offer stands."

Mr. Forsythe was frowning. "Will she have you, do you think?"

O'Brien's face lightened. Her father was considering the possibility!

"Charles!" Mrs. Forsythe was scandalized that her husband would even consider the offer. "She is in love with Mr. Mornay! How can this man possibly help?"

"I know that," Mr. O'Brien said. His face took on an appearance of noble acceptance. "I will have her knowing that. I will have her for my wife, gladly and willingly."

The parents' eyes met. Mrs. Forsythe shook her head. But Mr. Forsythe took a look at Ariana standing there, alone and on the brink of tears. People were whispering and pointing, and even the princess looked distressed. The vicar was clearing his throat.

"We will commence," he said aloud, "with the ceremony for the joining in marriage of Mr. Randolph Pellham and Mrs. Agatha Bentley."

Ariana swallowed, her eyes filling with tears. Mr. O'Brien saw her face, and his feet began to move of their own accord toward the centre aisle of the church. He must save his beloved girl from disgrace! But Mr. Forsythe's arm shot out and pulled him back to the pew.

"Julia," he said to his wife. "Go to your daughter, and tell her of this man's offer."

When she reached the bride, people started murmuring. Could it be the Paragon was not to be wed? Who was this woman joining Miss Forsythe?

~

When Ariana saw her mama, it was more difficult than ever to contain her distress. Mothers were chiefly there as shoulders to cry upon, were they not? And how very much she wanted to cry just now.

"Oh, my dear!"

"Mama!"

"What do you make of this, my dear?"

"Something has happened to Mr. Mornay! Oh, Mama! I just know it! He would be here, you must know. He would never miss our wedding voluntarily!"

"Can you be certain, my dear?"

"I am, Mama! I am utterly certain!" This dialogue was spoken in hushed tones, for the wedding of Mrs. Bentley and Mr. Pellham was being spoken at the same time.

Mrs. Forsythe took a deep breath. "My dear—Mr. O'Brien wishes you to know that he is—that he will be...happy to stand in Mr. Mornay's place." She looked nervously at her daughter.

Ariana's head turned sharply, and she searched her mama's countenance. "You cannot mean—"

"Yes, he is happy to marry you, if you will have him." Her own features were set in a disagreeable frown at the thought, for Mrs. Forsythe was greatly fond of Mr. Mornay.

"Mr. O'Brien is out of line!" Ariana countered firmly.

Mrs. Forsythe's features relaxed somewhat. But she had to tell all. "He says he loves you, dearest!"

Ariana's mouth set into a little pink line. "He is very bold! Far too much so! I will never have him, Mama!"

"He only wishes to spare you the humiliation—"

"He wishes me to betray the man I love!" The vicar stopped mid sentence, as Ariana had forgot to keep her voice low. There was a terrible look on the cleric's face, and she mumbled, "I beg your pardon, sir. Do continue." There were an awful few seconds of continuing silence, but then Mr. Hodges sniffed, cleared his brow, and resumed his office.

~

"Get a doctor! Your handkerchiefs, gentlemen! Hand them over!" This from the duke. "Get him out of that coat. Quickly! We've got to stop the bleeding!"

The Regent was instantly in a rage, and Chesley was shortly in handcuffs and on his way to Newgate. But first he had been relieved of his weapon and been given a good pummeling from some of the members. "You muddle-headed idiot!" Alvanley cried.

"Take care of him, sirs, and then deliver what's left of him to Newgate!" the prince had added.

Chesley was now bleeding from a broken lip and a gash on his face. "He tried to kill me," he was coughing out. "Mornay—he tried to shoot me last night!"

"You're a blasted fool!" Mornay countered. "If I'd wanted to shoot you, I would have." The others looked curious, so he added, "He knew Wingate's whereabouts but wasn't forthcoming with his information."

"That makes him twice as guilty—you filthy turncoat!" said one man, kicking him in the shins.

"That's enough," Mornay said. They had taken his coat off of him, removed his cravat and then his waistcoat. Rather than force his arms up to remove his fine linen shirt, which had buttons ending midway down the chest, they simply tore it in half. The garment was ruined from the bullet, in any case, so the Paragon made no objection. The wound was visible only for the merest second while various handkerchiefs were applied with force to stop the bleeding. Meanwhile someone had located a physician downstairs in the dining room, and he now rushed in, carrying a small leather bag.

"Make way, gentlemen," cried Grafton. The doctor came and looked at the arm. He moved and prodded a little, much to Mr. Mornay's discomfort, who winced at each touch.

"Give the man some laudanum, for pity's sake!" Alvanley cried.

"I shall in a moment," replied the physician. He stood up and looked around. "No major arteries severed. Providence has smiled upon your friend." He paused for cheering all around. "I'll just remove the bullet, and if we can keep him from an infection, I daresay Mr. Mornay will be as good as new soon enough." The men cheered again, and toasting began. When a constable arrived for the prisoner, there was more cheering and toasting.

Scropes and another man took on the service of barring entry to the room by anyone except the law or medical men.

The doctor made to give his patient laudanum, but he refused. "I need a clear head, thank you."

"He's getting married tomorrow, sir! I say double the dose for him!"

The doctor looked concerned. "Are you really being wed tomorrow?" At the nod from his patient, he added, "I daresay you will need to rest a great deal to recover properly. I must advise you to put off the ceremony if that is possible." A loud cheer followed this advice, but Mr. Mornay was shaking his head.

"I'd sooner *die*!"

Oddly this brought an abrupt silence. For the first time, Mornay's friends realized he was in love. He wasn't just getting married to beget an heir as many men did. Mornay—in *love*!

The very thing he had feared to reveal—that he was terribly and deeply in love—surfaced now unwittingly. Suddenly the atmosphere in the room changed.

"Scropes, this is all your fault," someone said.

"What! Not at all!"

"It is! That deuced game was your idea!"

"We should never have waylaid him. Let's face it, gentlemen."

"I said we hadn't ought to!" shouted another.

Alvanley's face lit up with a thought. "I say, can you fix his arm up all pretty? We'll see him home. It's not too late for him to catch his beauty rest, and he'll be patched up enough for the wedding."

~

Mr. Pellham took Mrs. Bentley's hand. They were facing each other, and Mrs. Bentley wore a wobbly smile and had watery eyes. She knew Mornay had not appeared yet, and she should have been up in the boughs over it but was not. She couldn't be, for she simply had no room in her heart at the moment. She was too busy cementing her relationship to Randolph Pellham. She was being married!

"I now pronounce you man and wife. You may kiss the bride." The two heads bent together momentarily, and a loud murmur of approval resulted in the church. When they turned around to face the onlookers, people began to clap. The princess stood up clapping, and so of course everyone else followed suit. Ariana was clapping, but her mouth was compressed in a hard line as she tried to control her distress. Tears built up and blurred everything, and she hastily wiped at her eyes, but it was no use. She could no longer control it. Mr. Mornay had changed his mind or some such thing!

My lord! My lord! Why hast thou forsaken me? It was perhaps an overly dramatic bit of Scripture to fall upon, and yet she felt forsaken, indeed.

Thirty-three

The pain of poking around for the bullet convinced Mr. Mornay that he would have to accept the laudanum. Or drink himself under the table. He took a dose of the physic. It did nothing to relieve the pain, though he did feel somewhat less tense. When the doctor was prodding inside the wound to actually remove the solid intruder, Mornay's other arm, his right, suddenly shot out and stopped him, grasping the man tightly.

"*Sir!* Have a care!" he said through gritted teeth.

The man paused, swallowed, looked around at the other men, and said, "He's getting another dose. If he doesn't have it, he'll kill me before I've finished."

Mornay took it too, which spoke eloquently in itself of how much the procedure hurt.

Nevertheless, with that and a bracing glass of port that he was heartily enjoined to accept—by his friends, not the doctor—he was taken home rather less in his own power than he had hoped to be.

It was going on four o'clock in the morning, and the servants, even the usually fortitudinal footmen, were asleep! The house was quiet! Alvanley joked that they should descend upon the butler en masse and give the man a fright he'd not soon forget for his lassitude. But Mornay muttered, "To bed, genelmen, to bed." He was acting foxed, to be sure. Must have been the drug.

They found the bedchamber—what they took to be his bedchamber, at any rate—and got the man into bed. Grafton was still along and said, "Hey, ought we not to leave the servants a note about what has befallen their master, do you think?"

"He hasn't lost his tongue, Your Grace!"

"Right. Well, draw the curtains. Let's leave him to rest."

When they were assembled outside, Lord Alvanley said, "Which one o' us is going to make sure he doesn't sleep past his wedding, eh?"

"Don't be a gull, the man's got servants! Surely they'll take care o' that!"

Grafton nodded. "Right."

It all flooded back to Mornay while he dragged himself from the room and went toward his own chamber. He'd been shot by that pigeon-head Chesley, after which his friends had no doubt had to bring him home and—best and worst of all—his wedding was today, but he'd slept late! When he strode painfully into the room, Fotch's eyes opened as wide as saucers, and he jumped to his feet.

"Sir!"

"Why the deuce didn't you wake me? Don't you know what day this is?" He strode into the room before Fotch could change his expression from amazement to relief, but it was short-lived. Mr. Mornay was a sorry sight. The Paragon, wounded like a soldier, was wearing half a shredded shirt, no cravat, no coat, and no waistcoat. The clothing he did have on was garishly blood-stained. If Fotch had not been a man of a stout heart, he might well have grown faint at the horror of it.

"Sir! Your arm! If I might be allowed to say how sorry I am!" He followed his master into the adjoining dressing room.

"Thank you. How much time do I have?" Mr. Mornay sat down and held out one muscular leg. His buff leather pantaloons were ruined by drops of dried dark blood, and his boots would need a good cleaning. Fotch immediately got before him and began to remove the boot.

"The wedding begins in fifty-four minutes, sir." When he'd taken the boots off, he darted to the bellpull and gave it far more jerks than necessary to call for help—desperate times, desperate measures! Soon the sound of hastening footsteps was heard approaching.

Frederick appeared first. When he saw his master, he sighed with relief and wiped his brow with a handkerchief. And then he saw the bandaged wound on his arm. His eyes bulged. He turned to a maid. "Send for the family doctor on the double!"

"No need for that," his master said.

Frederick said to a footman, "Get a bath up here at once!"

"There's not enough hot water for a bath, sir!" said the maid.

"I want it brought now! To the devil with hot water!" This was a severe oath to leave the lips of the butler, and both servants turned abruptly to do his bidding. "And do send for the doctor," he called after them.

"Freddie, are you my butler or my mother? I said no doctor!"

Fotch also wanted very much to have the doctor take a look at the injury—the bandaging was brown from dried blood, and Mr. Mornay's colour was pale. "Did you just get in, sir?" He was still trying to figure out what had happened.

"No. I was in the guest bedchamber."

"You!" Freddie and Fotch exchanged surprised looks. "My word, there all along!"

"Yes, and not my guest apparently. He never showed, eh?"

"Mr. Timmons, sir?"

"Yes, Mr. Timmons!"

Freddie cleared his throat. The master looked at him in amazement. "Well?"

"He is here actually, sir. He fell asleep apparently, waiting for you to come in."

"But not in the guest bedroom, or I should have had company. So where was he?"

"In the parlour."

Mornay gave a breath of a laugh. "So our guest slept in the parlour, and I slept in the chamber that should have been his." He closed his eyes tiredly. "Fotch, you know I must hurry!" Fotch *was* proceeding slowly, being gentle and careful instead of aiming for speed, as he usually did.

"I won't have time for a bath," he said.

Fotch, clearly scandalized, exclaimed, "But sir! Your wedding!"

Two footmen carried in a tub, followed by other servants with buckets of water. Fotch felt the water in one and then eyed the footman with surprise, who said, "Mr. Frederick told us to hurry. We hurried."

When the servants had gone, Fotch said, "Come on then. We've got a wedding to get you to."

Mr. Mornay was one handed and needed an arm to steady him as he got into the tub. No sooner did his foot and leg hit the water than he cried, "Aah! This water is freezing!" He began to pull his leg out again, but Fotch and Freddie stopped him.

The valet said, "Ah, sir, we didn't have time for a hot bath, did we?"

"Don't patronize me, Fotch! I'll have your situation!"

"Yes, sir," he said, hiding his smile. He and the butler gently pushed their master into the unwelcoming water.

Ariana faced the newlyweds to her right, hoping that her face showed only happiness for them, not distress. She smiled at her aunt, trying valiantly to hide her own turmoil, but Mrs. Bentley was aware of Mr. Mornay's absence, and her eyes grew wide when she saw that he had still not appeared.

Mr. O'Brien was there suddenly, and Ariana turned to him in alarm, ready to give him a set-down. He moved past her, however, and went up to the vicar.

Ariana's aunt whispered into Mr. Pellham's ear, and they waited there in front of the church instead of proceeding down the aisle. She moved toward Ariana, as though she merely wanted an embrace from her relation, when in fact she wanted to know if there might be an explanation that her niece knew of.

There was no way the coat was going to fit over the injured arm. Fotch and Freddie's attempts to make it do so resulted in involuntary exclamations from its owner—which at any other time of his life would have been laced with various epithets and oaths controlled now only on account of his newfound sense of religion. The bandaging was simply too bulky for the perfectly fitted sleeve.

"Sir, you can be married without a coat."

"Don't be absurd! Is that blasted doctor coming or isn't he?"

A sound at the door at that very moment reached their ears, and Freddie went to investigate. Mr. Wickford had arrived. When he entered the dressing room, Mornay said, "I need a new dressing, and it must be undetectable so that I may wear my coat today."

The man blinked saying, "What happened to the arm, sir?"

While Fotch speedily undid the snowy shirt and removed it, Mr. Mornay explained that he'd been shot at Boodle's by a man too deep in his cups. Fotch and Freddie swallowed nervously and exchanged glances once more. At Boodle's? One of the most exclusive men's clubs in town! And shot? My word! Thank God no worse harm had come to the master!

The doctor took out his equipment and asked for clean cloths, which were speedily supplied. The servants' attention was drawn to the wound, which Mr. Mornay himself could not fully see since Chesley had shot him from behind. He was well aware of the man's progress, however, and shot out remarks accordingly: "I don't need you poking in the wound! The bullet was removed by a man at the club! Have a care, Wickford! I cannot be bleeding at my wedding!"

"Your wedding, sir?"

"Yes, for which I am late this very minute. I need the smallest wrapping possible so I can wear my coat. And hastily done, if you please!"

"Sir, it must be sufficiently covered and with enough pressure to keep the bleeding stopped."

"My coat sleeve will supply it. I assure you, my tailor is incomparable at fitting sleeves." A good tailor did indeed fit a man's coat to the width and length of his arms for a snug fit. He did not make allowances for the odd chance that his client might suffer a bullet. It would supply some pressure.

The doctor, however, did not look happy. He eyed the servants for support, but they only shook their heads. He had best appease their master.

In a short time, the Paragon was looking much improved. He was clean and freshly shaved. He wore a beautiful snowy-white shirt, a cravat, and a fine waistcoat worthy of the Regent. His coat was successfully coaxed over the wound but not without discomfort. The greater bulge of the bandaging faced the back, which thankfully Mornay could not well see. Fotch assured him of its being undetectable—with his fingers crossed behind his back.

Dark fitted breeches, white stockings, shoes, and a new black hat completed the outfit.

"Freddie, where is Timmons? I've forgot all about him! We must be off. See that he's ready."

Freddie's face balked. He too had forgot all about him. "Sir, there's something about Mr. Timmons you'll need to know."

~

Mr. Forsythe had resorted to prayer. He knew his future son-in-law too well to conceive that he would purposely jilt his bride. In fact the more he thought on it, the more convinced he was that there must be a reason to account for his absence. So he prayed for victory against the obstacle, whatever it was. Even Mr. Timmons had not appeared, which further strengthened his conviction. Something was amiss. Mornay *did* want to marry his daughter, he had no doubt. Prayer was necessary. He shared his conviction with his wife, pointing out Timmons's absence, and she passed on the prayer concern to the Norledges. As a group the Forsythes fell to silent prayer.

Meanwhile the rector was speaking to Ariana. Did she know something of the delay of her betrothed? Did she believe the man would show? The new Mrs. Pellham stood nearby, glaring at O'Brien, who roundly ignored her. He had seized the chance to speak to Mr. Hodgson, telling him of his resolve and desire to wed Miss Forsythe, if the young woman could be convinced to have him.

"You had him *locked in the armoury*?"

Freddie explained their reasons. They hadn't thought he was home. They didn't want the rector to know he wasn't home, thinking he might cancel the wedding. Mr. Mornay ended up chuckling to himself, but he hurried down the steps and called impatiently for the butler to keep up and open the blasted door.

He heard Timmons banging and shouting before he reached the portal.

"Hold on, Timmons. I'll have you out directly!"

"You, sir, are a blackguard and a...knave!"

Mornay grimaced at Freddie, who was fumbling to open the door as fast as he could.

When Mr. Timmons appeared, his eyes blazing with righteous indignation, Mornay said, "I'm sorry, old fellow. It was a misunderstanding."

"I think I understand well enough, sir!"

Mornay looked at the butler. "Tell him, Freddie."

Timmons looked to the abashed servant, heard the account of the bewilderment of the staff, their desire only to protect their master, and the reasons for his imprisonment.

He was a good-natured fellow, and soon the three of them were first chuckling, then rolling with laughter. Mr. Timmons took his handkerchief and wiped his face, while Mr. Mornay came to with a start and said, "This is madness! Ariana!"

And he was off.

Freddie was enormously grateful to Fotch from that day forward, for the valet had thought to ensure the coach was ready and waiting at the curb when the men rushed out of the house.

"To St. George's!" the butler cried. "On the double!" He and Fotch exchanged satisfied glances for a split second. With a start, they hurried to jump on the back of the equipage—the surprised footmen made space for them. Just as the wheels started rolling, they had scurried aboard. They could not miss this event.

~

Mr. Hodgson, the rector at St. George's, listened patiently to Mr. O'Brien's objections but then settled the matter easily. He said, "Sir, even if the lady was eager to have you, there is no license. It is out of the question."

This had the immediate effect of deflating Peter O'Brien's last hopes for Miss Ariana Forsythe. With a care to maintain his dignity, he turned and made his way to the side aisle and exited the church. He had been willing to witness the ceremony on the grounds that his friendship with the family required it. His willingness was now exhausted.

Mr. Hodgson turned to Miss Forsythe. They could only be expected to wait so long for a missing groom. The princess herself was being forced to wait. Mr. Forsythe, with a keen eye, hurried to join the meeting. He had an opinion, and it must be shared.

"Before you dismiss this congregation," he said, "I must tell you, the man is surely coming."

"Do you know that for a *fact,* sir?"

Ariana's father consulted his deepest convictions on the matter. He had been praying fervently. He felt exceedingly sure of Mornay's intentions. He felt fortified in this belief from prayer.

The effectual fervent prayer of a righteous man availeth much. The verse came strongly to mind, and he felt it as a prompting of the Holy Spirit. He looked the rector in the eyes.

"I know it for a fact, sir."

Ariana gave a relieved gasp, her eyes brimming with gratitude—through tears. She did not know how her father had received the information, nor did she question it. She was simply profoundly grateful.

~

Outside the church Mr. Mornay's coach, though it could not reach the curb, stopped in the street. The door burst open, and he jumped down from the equipage without waiting for a man to let down the steps. He was followed quickly by Mr. Timmons. Ignoring the cheering, jeering crowd, the two men hurried into the church.

As soon as he was noticed, a great buzz began and spread quickly so that all the church was soon astir. People were on their feet. This was the moment they were waiting for! The Paragon had arrived! Beatrice and Lucy jumped up and down in their excitement, and Beatrice, watching wide-eyed, began to whisper a fierce chant of, "Huzzah! Huzzah! Huzzah!" to herself.

The rector had to motion for silence, which took a few minutes to accomplish. Mr. Timmons went right to the head of the church with his friend and found the bride and her papa waiting there with such looks! Gratitude! Relief! Joy! He spoke a few words to the rector. The rector shook his head, looking with interest at the man who he just learned had been shot the previous night. And then the rector shook Mr. Timmons's hand and thanked him.

He cleared his throat, and a deep hush fell upon the audience.

Mr. Mornay stood beside his bride, and using only his good left arm, entwined hers inside it. He met her eyes. His look was so full and intent and yet sorry, all at once, that Ariana was instantly reassured. Tears lingered on her face, but now they were happy ones. He reclaimed his hand to pull out a starched white handkerchief and gently removed the drops from her cheeks.

Together they turned to face Mr. Hodgson, waiting now with an indulgent look on his face and a prayer book in hand. He cleared his throat.

"Dearly beloved..."

Epilogue

By the time the carriage pulled into the winding drive at Aspindon, the setting sun was just visible, peeking through the trees that lined the path. When the road opened to reveal the stately manor, Ariana craned her neck to get her first look at the estate in months.

"Come back here," Mr. Mornay murmured. He had been planting little kisses on her neck and on to her shoulder.

She giggled but replied, "The first and last time I was here, I had been thoroughly versed in why I should avoid the frightful Mr. Mornay at all costs. And now look at us! Can you conceive of it? That we are the same two people?"

"We are assuredly *not* the same."

She waited for him to explain.

"For my part, I pray I may never revert to being the frightful Mr. Mornay, and for your part, you are no longer Miss Forsythe. We are both of us thoroughly changed."

"You must call me Mrs. Mornay now."

"I will call you 'Ariana,' for it is a beautiful name for my beautiful wife."

"My parents use their names with each other. But I can promise you that Mr. and Mrs. Pellham shall always be 'Mr. Pellham,' and 'Mrs. P' to one another!"

"That is their prerogative." He wanted to pull her back against him, but they were coming up to the house, the door opened, and the servants were already filing out to greet them. He took his hand from about her waist reluctantly, straightened her gown, and replaced her mantle. She allowed him to fuss over her for a moment, and then she smoothed down his coat with her hands.

"Is your arm hurting much?"

"I am too happy to give it any heed."

"Nevertheless," she said with resolution, "I am happy I insisted upon Mr. Wickford following us here tomorrow. I will not begin my marriage, sir, by putting your health at risk!"

"You are no threat to my health. Quite the contrary."

The couple stepped out of the coach and was met by the servants, all grouped in a semicircle now. They greeted the pair with smiles and sincere joy at their master's happiness, clapping effusively. Mrs. Hamilton was at the end of the semicircle, having confessed all to Freddie. After vowing her eternal faithfulness and gratitude to Mr. Mornay, she was to be kept on, under the butler's approval. Further, she herself was to train Molly to read and promote her within the household so that her position of scullery maid would be a thing of the past.

"Here," Phillip said, smiling proudly while he faced the staff, "is your mistress—Mrs. Mornay." Fotch and Freddie scurried to get in line, as did the footmen who had also come on the coach.

After the congratulations and best wishes were received, Cook announced, "Supper is waiting, sir."

"Are you hungry?" the groom asked his bride, as they moved toward the door.

"I can rarely eat but little when I am aflutter, and I assure you, being married has caused quite a stir." She patted her stomach. "Here."

Mornay eyed the servants reluctantly. He knew there would be talk—albeit harmless—if they were to forgo the meal in favor of exploring the *bedchamber*. While he was thinking thus, she added, "If there is soup, I think I can manage a little of that."

Freddie hurried to receive his new mistress's mantle, but his master's impatience was barely disguised to his affectionate eyes. He would be sure to see that the servants moved smartly.

The dining room was splendid—the house was elegantly sumptuous, even to Ariana's tenured eyes. But as the darkness settled and the rooms grew cosier by candlelight, she had eyes only for her splendid groom. Her *husband*.

Her place was set at the far end of the table from his, and she looked imploringly at him.

"Freddie—Mrs. Mornay will sit at my right." Their eyes remained upon each other.

"Very good, sir."

The meal was fashioned to be formal, with many courses, but he was watching her carefully, and as soon as she began to refuse further servings, he looked at his footman and said, "That will be all, Charles. Clear everything."

Phillip then leaned his head toward her. "Is there anything else you would like?"

Ariana's heart fluttered. All she wanted was him. She shook her head.

He stood up and took her hand in his left to help her from the chair.

More servants came in, already busily clearing the remnants from the meal.

Ariana blushed lightly.

"Take this," he said, giving her a candle sconce. He wanted his one good arm free to put around her waist, which he did with a great deal of pleasure.

Ariana looked quickly at him, still embarrassed. "Your servants will talk," she chided, trying to move out of his reach, but he tightened his hold about her.

"Nonsense. We are man and wife now." But he cleared his throat. "Speaking of talk," he said, looking at her wryly, "there are rumours abounding that you will soon bankrupt me."

This stopped her in her tracks. "What?"

"My servants tell me that every charity in London has discovered my direction and sends letters or messengers daily. Freddie sent ahead a full sack of 'em for me to go through."

Ariana's face coloured, and she averted her gaze. "Certainly I do wish to support particular charities, but of course they are subject to your consent or approval!"

"Is that so?" he asked.

"Of course!"

Freddie caught up to the couple, who were by now moving up the grand staircase.

"Well, Mr. Frederick? Is everything tight? Anything I need to know right away?"

Frederick grew thoughtful a moment and said, "Only that there is a great deal of correspondence for you, but none, I believe, that cannot await your pleasure."

"Correspondence?" He acted as though he was surprised. "What sort?"

He gave a knowing look to his wife, who blushed afresh and listened with a look of concern.

"I believe they are entirely from charitable organizations, sir."

"At this, Ariana immediately turned her head away, rather mortified. Mr. Mornay stifled a smile.

"Charitable organizations, you say?" he asked the butler, keeping his eyes steadily on his new wife, who was valiantly trying to behave as though she was blithely unaware of the exchange. She looked about at the huge stairwell, the casements, the portraits on the walls.

"Yes, sir. An extraordinary number of them, I might add, sir."

"Astounding! How can they ever have found me out? And what would you say the cost is in postage alone, Freddie, to receive all these letters?"

"I hesitate to guess, sir. Four shillings apiece, at least, and there've been well nigh a dozen or more a day. I brought them to your attention for precisely that reason, sir."

"And I appreciate that you did, Mr. Frederick." He eyed his young bride, who was staring at a portrait on the wall with eyes filled with alarm. She held the candle weakly in one hand, not even bothering to hold it up to the artwork. He wondered if she was actually seeing the picture at all.

"For the time being, Freddie, you will refuse any further letters if they should happen to find us here in Middlesex, unless they are of a personal nature."

"Very good, sir. And if they are addressed to Mrs. Mornay, sir?"

Phillip looked at Ariana, whose head came up with a start. She was still blushing, much to her distress, but she said quickly, "You must treat my mail no differently than your master's."

Mr. Mornay was still smiling to himself when she added, with a troubled countenance, "Unless it is from the London Orphan Society." And to her husband she said, "We promised to support them, you recall!"

"Unless it is from the London Orphan Society," he repeated with a smirk to Freddie.

"And I must receive mail from the Lying-in Asylum!"

"The Lying-in Asylum," Phillip repeated, with a nod at his butler, who was himself smiling.

They both waited, feeling sure that more was to come, and Ariana did not disappoint them.

"I nearly forgot," she breathed, turning to peek nervously at her husband.

"I did give my word to a nice woman from the Institution for Decayed Housekeepers—"

This made Mr. Mornay stop on the stairwell. "The *what*?"

"The Institution for Decayed Housekeepers," she repeated, her voice growing lower. She could hardly stand to meet his eyes. *Why did I agree to support that place? It doesn't feed orphans, or help the homeless! What was I thinking?*

He turned to the butler. "Leave them all on my desk. Goodnight, Freddie."

"Very good, sir. Goodnight, Mr. and *Mrs.* Mornay."

"Goodnight, Freddie. Thank you," Ariana said, watching him turn back down the steps. She met the eyes of her beloved.

"I *am* sorry. I suppose I did get carried away."

"I suppose you did," he agreed, but he was smiling.

They moved on in silence, reaching the second floor. He moved her toward a corridor that branched off to the left. Ariana felt more of the nervous fluttering inside. At least he wasn't angry about the onslaught of charities, and she knew he had not exaggerated, as she herself had received countless solicitations. She tried to break the silence, for it reminded her that she was anxious. "To think you are so familiar with this place and have walked here a thousand times, when it is all completely new to me! I want to know every inch of it because then I shall feel that I know you better!"

"You're about to know me much better," he replied.

"Will you take me back to the tree?" she asked brightly. "Where you first rescued me? What a fright you gave me that day showing up there. The last person I wanted to see!"

He continued to move her along, listening to all her comments with a little smile. Finally he stopped before a door, opened it, and put his arm around her waist, gently ushering her into the room. He locked the door behind them, turned, and beheld his bride.

The End

Discussion Questions for *The House in Grosvenor Square*

1. What was the most pleasant surprise for you in *The House in Grosvenor Square*?
2. Which character would you say is your favorite, and why?
3. Does a character need to be somewhat heroic to qualify as a favorite for you? Why or why not?
4. Many of the characters are given opportunities to act heroically in this story. Which character is most heroic? Talk about what makes him or her most heroic.
5. How are the qualities of the most heroic character godly? Name a character quality from this person that you would like to have more of in yourself.
6. Ariana Forsythe says she would have had a much worse time during her abductions if not for her faith. How did her faith help her to cope with the dangerous situations? If you were in her place, would you have fared as well? Why or why not?
7. Can you envision yourself relying on God in a dire situation and having good results? Why or why not?
8. Mrs. Bentley turns to the prayer book (*The Book of Common Prayer*) for comfort after her niece has been abducted. She asks Mr. Pellham to pray with her and then feels better afterward. Do you feel better after praying for something that's been bothering you? Explain to someone else what it is about praying that makes you feel better (God's faithfulness, your trust in Him, your experience in the past, and so forth).
9. Lord Antoine repents of his foolish past even before he entertains the idea of coming to faith in Christ. Can living right be its own reward? How so?
10. Is being good sufficient cause for a person to go to heaven when they die? Why or why not?

A Short Glossary for *The House in Grosvenor Square*

A

abbess: (slang) A bawd; the mistress of a brothel.

ague: (rhymes with "achoo"; pronounced "ah-gyoo") Originally, malaria and the chills that went with it. Later, any respiratory infection such as a cold, fever, or chills.

***annus mirabilis*:** A miraculous year; a year of miraculous events; a singularly satisfying year.

apoplexy: A stroke; a cerebral hemorrhage.

assembly, assemblies: Large gatherings held in the evening for the gentry or the aristocracy, usually including a ball and a supper. Almack's in London was the ultimate assembly in the early part of the nineteenth century. A number of high-standing society hostesses had autocratic power of attendance as they alone could issue the highly prized vouchers (tickets)—or not—as they chose. Competition to get in was fierce. The Duke of Wellington was once famously turned away for being late.

ball: A large dance requiring full dress. Refreshments were available, and sometimes a supper. Public balls required tickets; private ones, an invitation.

banns: The banns of marriage were a public announcement in a parish church that two people intended to get married. They had to be read three consecutive weeks in a row and in the home church of both parties. After each reading (and this was their purpose), the audience was asked to give knowledge of any legal impediment to the marriage. If there was none, after three weeks the couple was legally able to marry within the next three months in a church. To bypass the banns, a couple could try to get a marriage license instead. Without banns or a license, the marriage would be illegal.

beadle: A parish constable.

beak: (slang) A magistrate.

bishop: A mixture of wine and water into which is put a roasted orange.

"blocked at both ends": Finished; ended.

blunt: (slang) Cash; ready money.

bon ton: (pronounced "bawn-tawn") Fashionable society.

bone box: (slang) Mouth.

brown study, in a: Said of one in a reverie or deep in thought; absent.

buck of the first head, a: One who surpasses his companions in vice or debauchery.

canezou: A certain style of spencer for a woman.

cant: (slang) The characteristic or secret language of a group.

Carlton House: Given to the Prince of Wales by George III upon reaching his majority, Carlton House was in a state of disrepair (for a royal, at any rate). The house consequently underwent enormous alterations and changes and was the London palace for the Regent. He spent a great deal of time there but eventually came to favour the palace at Brighton—an even larger extravagance. The Brighton "Pavilion" is today a museum, but Carlton House, unfortunately, no longer exists.

cat's foot, under: To be under the dominion of a wife; hen-pecked.

cat's paw, a: To be made a cat's paw is to be made a tool for the purposes of another; to be used for another's gain.

Charley (noun): A word used for a local night watchman or law officer on duty.

chamber: A private room in a house, such as a bedroom, as opposed to the parlour or dining room.

chaperone: The servant, mother, or married female relative or family friend who supervised eligible young girls in public.

chemise: A woman's long undergarment, which served as a slip beneath her gown. Also a nightdress. (Previously the chemise was called a "shift.")

chit: An infant or baby; used to describe a young girl derisively.

clubs: The great refuge of the middle and upperclassman in eighteenth and nineteenth century London. Originating as coffeehouses in the seventeenth century, clubs became more exclusive, acquiring prime real estate on Pall Mall and St. James Street. Membership was often by invitation only. Among the more prominent were Boodle's, White's, and Brooke's. Crockford's began to dominate in the very late Regency.

corset: A precursor of the modern bra, usually meant to constrict the waist to a fashionable measurement as well as support the high bust required for a Regency gown. It consisted of two parts and often was reinforced with whalebone that hooked together in front and laced in the back. The garment was commonly referred to as "the stays."

Corinthian: (slang) Term for a male frequenter of brothels; or brazen, impudent young men.

countess: The wife of an earl in England. When shires were changed to counties, an earl retained the Norman title of earl; his wife, however, became a countess.

comb, combing: To give a combing is to scold; give a set-down.

cove: A man, most often a rogue.

cravat: (pronounced as kruh-vaht, with the accent on the second syllable) A loose cloth that was tied around the neck in a bow. Throughout the Regency, a fashion-conscious gentleman might labour much over this one detail of his appearance, hoping to achieve a number of different, much-coveted effects.

cull: A man who is the victim of a cove.

curricle: A two-wheeled carriage that was popular in the early 1800s. It was pulled by two horses and deemed rather sporty by the younger set.

curtsey: The acceptable mode of greeting or showing respect by a female. By mid-century the curtsey was less in evidence except for social inferiors like maids to their betters or by any woman presented at court.

demireps: Impures; women of questionable morals.

dowager: The name given to a widow of rank. For example, if you were a duchess and your husband died and your oldest son was married, his wife would become the duchess, and you would be dowager duchess.

doxie: She beggar; a lady of questionable morals; an impure.

drawing room: A formal parlour used in polite society to receive visitors who came to pay calls during the afternoon.

ewe (a white ewe): A beautiful woman.

eye (that's my eye): An expression of derision or irony, as "sure!" or "right!" used facetiously.

first floor: The second floor in the United States. The English called the street-level floor the "ground floor." Entertaining was never done on the ground floor.

flash house: A house that harbours thieves; a certain style of which was common in criminal "nurseries" in London in the early nineteenth century.

flummery: In actuality flummery was oatmeal and water boiled to a jelly; in speech it meant compliments "neither of which is over-nourishing"; that is to say flattery.

footman: A liveried male servant beneath the butler but above the boy or page. He had many duties ranging from errands to lamp trimming to waiting table or accompanying the lady of the house to carry packages when she shopped or to deliver calling cards when making calls.

footpad: A thief on foot; a mugger.

fortnight: Two weeks.

gaming: Gambling. Nothing to do with game in the sense of hunting or innocent playing of games.

glim: A candle or dark lantern used in housebreaking.

gospel shop: (slang) a church.

groom: The servant who looked after the horses.

Grosvenor Square (pronounced "grove-nuh"): Located in Mayfair and considered the most fashionable square in London. Mr. Mornay's town house is in the square.

gudgeon: One easily imposed on; easily taken in a trick.

hack: A hack was a general purpose riding horse, but the term might also refer to a "hackney coach," which was a coach-for-hire like a taxicab today.

hocused: Drunk.

"holy ground": Facetious term for flash house territory or criminal nurseries. Also brothels.

housekeeper: The top ranking female servant in a household, and the one who held the keys. She usually hired or fired the housemaids, oversaw their work, and supervised the kitchens, including the ordering of food. A housekeeper, married or not, was always "Mrs." someone or other.

jarvis: A hackney coachman; a stand-in.

ken (colloquialism): Know (for example, "How do you ken?").

lady's maid: The servant who cared for her mistress's wardrobe and grooming. A French lady's maid was preferred, and she was particularly valued if she could do hair in all the fashionable styles. A lady's maid was an upper servant and could not be fired by the housekeeper. She might also be better educated than the lower servants.

lorgnette: Used by ladies, a pair of eyeglasses (or a monocle) held to the eyes with a long handle or worn on a chain around the neck. The monocle used by a man was called a "quizzing glass."

link boy: A boy or man who would lead people to their desired destinations on dark nights, for money, by use of a bright torch.

laudanum: A mixture of opium in a solution of alcohol, it was used for pain relief and as an anesthetic.

livery: A distinctive uniform worn by the male servants in a household. No two liveries, ideally, were exactly alike. Knowing the colour of the livery of someone could enable you to spot their carriage in a crowd. The uniform itself was an old-fashioned style, including such things as a frock coat, knee breeches, powdered wigs, and a waistcoat.

Mayfair: The most fashionable residential area of London, located in the West End and only about a half mile square in size.

mews, the: Any lane or open area where a group of stables was situated. The townhouses of the rich often had a mews behind them or close by, where they kept their horses and equipages when not in use.

monastery (slang): A brothel.

mort: A woman, a wench;

a gentry mort: a gentlewoman;

a bleached mort: a blond-haired woman.

MP: Member of Parliament.

muslin: One of the finest cottons, muslin was semitransparent and very popular for gowns (beneath which a chemise would be worn).

nap: To steal furtively.

Nimrod: The earliest recorded hunter

in the Bible, Nimrod was described as a "mighty hunter before the Lord."

O

old grim: Death.

on-dit (French): Literally, "It is said." In the Regency it was slang for a bit of gossip.

P

Pall Mall: A fancy street in the West End of London, notable for housing some of the most fashionable men's clubs. Carlton House faced Pall Mall.

pantaloons: Tight-fitting pants that were worn, beginning in the early 1800s, and which pushed breeches out of fashion except for formal occasions. They had a stirrup at the bottom to keep them in place.

parlour: The formal or best room in a modest home. Grand houses often had more than one.

peer: A nobleman, that is, a titled gentleman with the rank of either duke, marquis (pronounced mar-kwiss), viscount (pronounced vy-count), or baron. The titles were hereditary, and the owners were entitled to a seat in the House of Lords.

pelisse: An outdoor garment for women, reaching to the ankle or mid-calf and often hooded.

pet (slang): A temper tantrum; a passion.

pianoforte: The piano. Genteel young women were practically required to learn the instrument.

pin money: A colloquialism for a woman's spending money. The allowance agreed upon in her marriage settlement to be used on small household or personal (vanity) items.

prime article: A handsome girl.

R

Regent: A person who reigns on behalf of a monarch who is incapable of filling the requirements of the crown. When George III's relapse of porphyria rendered him incapable of meeting his duties, his son, the Prince of Wales, became the Prince Regent. The actual regency lasted from 1811 to 1820.

reticule: A fabric bag, gathered at the top and held by a ribbon or strap; a lady's purse. Reticules became necessary when the thin muslin dresses of the day made it impossible to carry any personal effects in a pocket without it seeming bulky or unsightly. The earliest reticules (apparently called "ridicules," as it seemed ridiculous to carry one's valuables outside of one's clothing) were, in effect, outside pockets.

rubber: In games like whist, a rubber was a set of three or more games. To win a rubber, one had to win two out of three or three out of five games.

S

season: The London social season in which the fashionable elite descended upon the city in droves. It coincided, not unnaturally, with the sitting of Parliament, though the height of the season was only March through June.

smelling salts (smelling bottle): A small vial filled with a compound that usually contained ammonia and used in case of fainting.

spencer: For women, a short jacket that reached only to the high empire waist. For men, an overcoat without tails, also on the short side.

squire: Nineteenth century term of courtesy (like "esquire") for a member of the landed gentry.

St. Gile's Greek: Low class speech, specifically that from the parish of St. Gile's, which is so thick in its accent that it's unintelligible. For example, "I don't know, it's St. Gile's Greek to me!"

St. Gile's Parish: The parish belonging to St. Gile's in London, known for its large criminal population and poverty.

T

tag, rag, and bobtail: An expression meaning an assemblage of low people.

***ton*, the** (pronounced "tawn"): High society; the elite; the "in" crowd; Those of rank, with royalty at the top. To be "good ton" meant acceptance with the upper crust and opened most any door in fashionable society. Occasionally, those without fortune or pedigree could enter the *ton* if they were an original. For instance, they might have something either sensational or highly attractive about their person or reputation; or could amuse or entertain the rich to a high degree.

transportation: Banishment from England to particularly unsavoury penal colonies where hard labour could be expected. Botany Bay was one such place. Transportation was a dreaded sentence but better than hanging.

V

valet: The "gentleman's gentleman." The male equivalent of a lady's maid, his job was to keep the wardrobe in good repair and order, help dress his master, stand behind him at dinner if required, and accompany him on his travels.

W

wainscoting: Wainscot was a fancy, imported oak. The term "wainscoting" came to mean any wooden panels that lined generally the top or bottom half of the walls in a room.

waistcoat: Vest.

For more information about the Regency period,
see the author's website at:

http://www.LinoreRoseBurkard.com

To learn more about books by Harvest House Publishers
or to read sample chapters, log on to our website:

www.harvesthousepublishers.com

About the Author

Linore Rose Burkard lives with her husband and five children in a town full of antique stores and gift shops in southwestern Ohio. She homeschooled her children for ten years. Raised in New York, she graduated magna cum laude from the City University of New York with a Bachelor of Arts in English literature.

Ms. Burkard began writing her books about Ariana Forsythe because she could not find an Inspirational Regency Romance on the bookshelves of any store. "There were Christian books that approached the genre," she says, "but they fell short of being a genuine Regency. I finally gave up looking and wrote what I myself was looking for." She also enjoys writing articles, reading, parenting, family movie nights, swimming, and gardening.

Linore enjoys hearing from her readers.
She can be reached at admin@LinoreRoseBurkard.com.
Be sure to visit her on the web at http://www.LinoreRoseBurkard.com.
Sign up for her free mailing list and receive news
and announcements about her latest writing projects or books.
If you aren't online but would like to contact Linore, please write to her at

Linore Rose Burkard
c/o Harvest House Publishers
990 Owen Loop North
Eugene, OR 97402